Zoheleth

David, the warrior king, is old and weary. Who will rule the nation of Israel on his death? Conspiracy, intrigue and deceit poison the royal household.

The king's son Absalom—handsome, generous, vain, ensnared by his own lusts—becomes a pawn in the struggle for power. Only Zoheleth, his servant turned confidant, stays loyal through the turmoil.

This is Zoheleth's story: a story of power that is abused, of people who are corrupted, and the triumph of the soul that hungers after goodness.

J. FRANCIS HUDSON won widespread acclaim for *Rabshakeh*, the first episode in this great saga of ancient Israel. *Zoheleth* follows in the same vein: meticulous and scholarly research into the ancient world informs a gripping story which is accurate in its setting and full of powerful insights into the human soul.

ZOHELETH

J. Francis Hudson

A LION BOOK

With deep gratitude to Keith and to Mandy, for giving so generously of their time, wisdom and optimism; to James for all his advice and encouragement; to so many of my family and friends for their unstinting support, and in particular to Mum and to John; and to Lois, for her enduring enthusiasm and sharp editorial insight.

Copyright © 1994 J. Francis Hudson

The author asserts the moral right to be identified as the author of this work

Published by
Lion Publishing plc
Sandy Lane West, Oxford, England
ISBN 0 7459 3498 6
Albatross Books Pty Ltd
PO Box 320, Sutherland, NSW 2232, Australia
ISBN 0 7324 1450 4

First edition 1994
This edition 1997

A catalogue record for this book is available from the British Library

Printed and bound in Great Britain by Cox & Wyman Ltd, Reading

IN MEMORY OF ABSALOM
because the candle which burns too brightly
is all too quickly gone.

DAVID'S KINGDOM AND ITS NEIGHBOURS

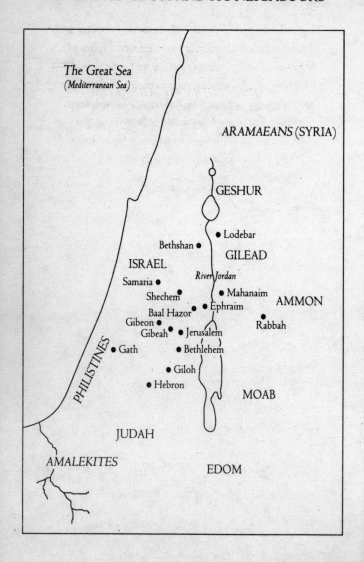

NATHAN'S PROPHECY AGAINST DAVID

This is the word of Adonai... From your own flesh and
blood I shall cause calamity to come upon you, and
the sword will not depart from your house. Before
your very eyes I shall take your women and give them
to one who is close to you, and he will lie with them
in broad daylight. You sinned in secret, but this
abomination I shall bring to pass under the open sky,
and in the sight of all Israel.

(2 Samuel 12:10–12)

DRAMATIS PERSONAE

ZOHELETH	The narrator.
AMNON	Eldest son of the king, and of one of his wives, Ahinoam.
JONADAB	Nephew of the king; cousin of Amnon.
DAVID	The king—Israel's second, who came to the throne after the death of the first king, Saul.
ABSALOM	The king's second son; half-brother of Amnon.
JOAB	Son of David's sister Zeruiah. Commander of David's army.
ABISHAI	Another son of Zeruiah. Commander of 'The Thirty', David's crack warriors.
ZIBA	Slave of Zoheleth's ex-guardian, Machir.
JEHOSHAPHAT	Royal recorder and herald.
BATHSHEBA	Widow of Uriah, one of the Thirty. Now the youngest and newest wife of the king.
SHIMEI	Companion of Absalom; a member of Saul's clan.
SHEBA	Another companion of Absalom; also a Saulide.
URIAH	Late husband of Bathsheba; born a Hittite but later took Israelite nationality and became one of the Thirty.
MAACAH	Mother of Absalom; daughter of Talmai, king of Geshur in Syria. David's favourite wife.
TAMAR	Daughter of Maacah and David; sister of Absalom.
MIRIAM	Tamar's handmaid.
ELIADA	Infant son of Maacah and David.
ELIPHELET	Another infant son of Maacah and David.
ADONIJAH	Third eldest son of David.
SHEPHATIAH	Fourth son of David.
ITHREAM	Fifth son of David. (David's first five sons were born when he ruled from Hebron; the rest were born in Jerusalem.)
AHITHOPHEL	David's chief adviser; grandfather of Bathsheba.
HUSHAI	Ahithophel's assistant.
NATHAN	Prophet of Adonai.
ISHBOSHETH	Last surviving son of Saul; had been David's rival for the throne until he was murdered by David's supporters.
ABNER	Cousin of Saul and commander of his army; murdered by Joab.
MICHAL	David's first wife; daughter of Saul. She was barren.

ABIGAIL	David's second wife. Her only child Chileab died in infancy.
MERIB	Zoheleth's estranged father.
MEPHIBOSHETH	Grandson of Saul, and son of Jonathan.
SOLOMON	Son of David and Bathsheba.
SERAIAH	Court secretary.
AMASA	High-ranking officer in David's army. A nephew of David.
ZADOK	One of David's chief priests.
ABIATHAR	Colleague of Zadok.
JEDIDIAH	A young son of David.
NAOMI	One of David's concubines.
RUTH	Also David's concubine.
BARZILLAI	Rich benefactor of David.
ITTAI	Philistine-born mercenary general in David's army.

GODS, PEOPLES AND PLACES

ADONAI	'The Lord'—used with reference to the Israelite God, since his name was regarded as too holy to be spoken.
AKHAIA	Greece.
AMMONITES	People of Ammon, living to the east of Israel. Their chief city was Rabbah.
ASHERAH	Hebrew name for Astarte.
ASTARTE	Goddess of the Syrians.
ATARGATIS	Akhaian name for Astarte. Also the name of Absalom's hound.
BAAL	God of various pagan nations of the Middle East, including Syria; in fact there were many Baals, for each city had its own.
GIBEONITES	A certain group of pre-Israelite inhabitants of Israelite territory; a treaty had been made with them and they were supposed to be exempt from destruction by the Israelites.
JEBUSITES	Pre-Israelite inhabitants of Jerusalem (Jebus).
NEPHILIM	Race of giants reputed to have lived in the Middle East in very early times. (Goliath was allegedly descended from them.)
SHEOL	Hebrew equivalent of Hades, the place of the dead.
ZION	Jerusalem.

1

For once I was sound asleep, and not even dreaming. Then I felt a knee in my back and a hand across my mouth.

Since I seldom spent two consecutive nights in any one place, I couldn't at first remember where I was. But by the time I'd got back my bearings and worked out that I was curled under my cloak in the cook-house courtyard, my limbs were already thrashing and kicking. Defending myself against regular beatings had been second nature to me since before I could walk.

There were two hooded figures moving above me. It was too dark to see them properly, but I could trace where their shapes blotted out the stars. More bewildered than frightened, I was dragged to my feet, then the hand on my mouth shifted just enough for me to sink my teeth into its flesh. There came a muffled cry, followed by a string of expletives.

'Thundering Baal and Asherah, you little rat!' snarled a voice I didn't recognize. 'You'll pay for that. I'll make you regret it if I have to break all the bones in your scrawny little body—'

'Come on!' rasped the other. 'We're wasting time.' He jerked me forward. 'Get moving, you.'

But the one I'd bitten was fumbling in the folds of his clothing; I glimpsed gold around his waist. From behind this showy belt he drew out a coarse piece of cloth, which he rammed between my jaws until I was gagging.

'What are you doing now, you stupid fool? The lad's dumb as a snake. Where d'you think he gets his nickname? He's not going to make trouble for us that way.'

'Who cares if he has no tongue? He's got teeth right enough.'

And thus, my mouth stuffed with rag, and one arm wrenched behind me, I found myself being propelled briskly inside the palace. Then I was hurried through a maze of passageways so oppressively silent I could hear my own heart pounding like something wild trapped in my chest. Torches glimmered feebly from brackets; I was lost almost at once.

11

Twisting and turning until I gave up counting corners, at length we were plunging down a steep stone staircase. The palace was terraced, for it occupied the top and one side of the citadel, and had more storeys at the back than at the front; but surely not this many? The air grew dank and foul with the stench of time. Disorientated as I was, I wasn't too witless to grasp what the smell had to imply. The King's residence was scarcely older than I was; we must be way underground, presumably in cellars of the ancient and long-gone Jebusite fortress.

When we reached the bottom of the stairs I contrived somehow to tear myself free. It was only with difficulty, and I'll warrant some cuts and bruises, that they succeeded in getting me back under control.

'Are you sure this is such a good idea?' whined the bitten one. 'He's like a confounded mad dog. And what if he's too big to fit through the hole?'

'Oh, it's no good getting cold feet now. You'd nothing but admiration for the scheme when I came up with it. And may I remind you, my lord Amnon: you're the one who needs the silver.'

'Watch what you're saying! Do you want the whole world to know who we are? We'll have a national scandal on our hands.'

'I told you, the creature's dumb! Probably deaf too. Get a grip on yourself, man. You're the King's firstborn son; you're entitled to have whatever you want. The scandal is that you should need to stoop to this kind of base trick to lay claim to it.'

With the two of them continuing to argue more or less under their breath, we pressed on into the bowels of the hillside. The passage began to dip downwards and there was water running at its edges. But there were still torches flickering against the walls, and now and again I was convinced I could hear voices or footsteps that weren't ours.

'Are you sure we're still going the right way?' whispered the one called Amnon. I'd heard the name before often enough, but never met its owner. He was one of the King's sons—the eldest.

'Positive, my intrepid Prince. If we turned right here we'd get to the main door of the treasury. That's where the guards are posted. But if we go left we'll hit the passage with the ventilation shaft. Our little serpent will have no trouble getting through and handing stuff out to us. We can always pass a torch in if he can't see. Getting him out again could pose rather more of a problem, mind you.'

12

The lefthand passageway was scarcely wide enough for one man to walk through. They made me go first; Amnon was behind me, with his hand around my neck, and he tightened it when I tried to remove my gag. His companion groped high on the right wall until he found what he was looking for.

'This is it, Amnon. Lift the kid up, let him feel where to go.' Meanwhile he began to explain to me what I must do. He said the same things five times, with his face right up to mine; like everyone else he seemed to think I was simple because, like everyone else, he thought I was dumb.

All at once Amnon's diffidence gave way to rash excitement. 'Heaven be praised, Jonadab, I can hardly believe it! All Father's loot, and I'm going to get my hands on it! It's a dream come true.'

'Calm down, won't you? We can't take too much out at once. Just enough to buy a night of your chosen lady's favours. You can always come back for more.'

'Oh, I'll be going back to *her* for more, don't you worry. Wait till Absalom finds out that I've been with the high priestess of Asherah! That'll stop him boasting about his conquests.' Now there was an unmistakable edge of malice to his enthusiasm.

'Amnon, we're wasting time again. Put the lad on your shoulders.'

'But Jonadab, suppose Absalom doesn't believe me? I can hardly visit her openly, Father would kill me! Going with a woman, and a pagan one at that, in the goddess's temple . . .'

The said Jonadab snorted in exasperation. 'He hasn't killed *Absalom* for what *he* gets up to, has he? By all the gods, you're eighteen years old, and the last time you touched anything female it was giving you milk. It's pathetic.' With that he yanked me viciously back towards him, all but crushing me between Amnon and the wall, then hoisted me into the air. My flailing arms found the entrance almost straight away; Jonadab thrust me forward with my belly on the sill, and that's when I got frightened.

No light came from inside the room. I didn't know how far down the floor was. I might never get out alive. I'd always prided myself on being hard, but small dark places made me go frantic; too many dreadful things had happened to me in them. I could neither scream nor kick; my gullet had turned to fur, and someone had hold of my legs. In the silence of my mind I was saying: please don't let them push me, please just help me get free . . .

Almost at once there were heavy footsteps coming our way. Then there were voices calling through the darkness. Jonadab's mordant bravado evaporated. In an unsteady hiss he demanded, 'Who the hell is that?'

'General Joab,' wailed Amnon. 'It couldn't be anyone worse. And it sounds like his brother Abishai's with him. I told you this wouldn't work. I always said we'd be caught.'

'Don't you dare start blaming me! Come on, we'll make a run for it.'

'What? And leave *him* here, to land us right in the drink?'

'How many times do I have to tell you? He's—'

'But are you *sure* he is? What proof have you got?'

'All right then. I'll give him something to make *certain* he stays quiet, if you'll feel better.' Jonadab dealt me a stinging swipe across the backs of my legs, growling, 'Breathe a word, and there will be plenty more where that came from.'

Then a great metal belt smacked down across the backs of my legs, and Amnon said, 'That's for what you did to my hand.'

They must have been seen as they issued from the passageway, for the approaching footsteps broke into a run. Then they divided; one set gave chase into the distance, whilst others were coming up close behind me. I was unable to move either backwards or forwards, and the sill dug into my midriff. I could feel blood trickling into the creases behind my knees. At the entrance to the passage a chain clinked, and a clipped voice said, 'Wait there, you two. Don't try anything.'

Someone was coming up the passageway: someone big enough to be having trouble squeezing through. Suddenly panic-stricken, I kicked out violently. There was a grunt of mingled pain and surprise, and I was pulled out by the ankles, landing in a dislocated heap on the ground. I was lugged bodily along the damp, gritty floor like a sack of grain, and thrown against the wall of the main thoroughfare. At last I managed to spit the chewed rag from my mouth.

Squinting up through a tangle of fringe, I saw a great bear of a man, in full military regalia, glowering down at me as though at some kind of vermin. Beside him cowered two bound prisoners, but they weren't Amnon and Jonadab. Both were semi-naked, their hair and beards bloodied, their chests a blotched patchwork of bruises and welts. As I stared at them, a fourth man came up, panting for breath.

14

'It's no use, Joab. They got clean away. They must know these rat-holes like the palms of their hands.'

'Well, it's certainly all happening tonight.' Joab gave me an experimental kick in the ribs; my whole body hurt, but no tear fell. I was well used to offhand cruelty. 'Tell us what your game was, then. We haven't got all week.'

I could still feel Amnon's gold belt across my legs, so I bit my lip. Joab repeated his question, and the kick in the ribs, then asked my name, and whether I was slave or free. When I still didn't speak he bent down and forced my mouth open.

'So you do have a tongue in your head after all.'

It was clear he took my silence for insolence, but I'd never told anyone my name in my life. Ziba, the slave of my ex-guardian, had made sure of that. His words kept running through my head . . . *No one must ever know who you are; they must never be allowed to find out what you are. Do you understand? Do I make myself clear?* And I'd nodded, and swallowed. I didn't understand, but Ziba scared the life out of me.

Joab turned to his colleague.

'Do you know this boy, Abishai? Have you ever seen him around the palace before?'

Abishai tugged on his beard and pursed his lips grimly. He was tall, like his brother, but not so broad. They both had the same small, ice-bitten eyes. 'He hangs around the servants' quarters, mostly the kitchens. I've had cause to make enquiries on more than one occasion. He doesn't seem to belong to anyone or have any duties. I reckon he must live on the scraps that the cooks throw out.'

'Probably some concubine's slave-gotten bastard,' said Joab, and dragged me at last onto my feet. 'I'm sure His Majesty would be interested in talking to you, you little worm. It's not every day that someone comes this close to rifling the royal coffers. And you could tell us who was with you.'

'His Majesty won't thank us if we take the rascal there now,' Abishai pointed out. 'We're barely into the third watch.'

Joab shrugged a reluctant agreement. 'Fair enough. We'll come back for him in the morning. A spell down here might do something to improve his attitude.'

The brothers steered us all a short way down the corridor. Then the two shackled wretches were flung into separate cells, and I got a third; but I managed to bite Joab's hand before the door shut.

The blackness was tangible; so was the silence. My legs were sticky with blood and still smarting where the belt had been. Panic rose in my throat and I found myself repeating, without any sound: please keep me safe, don't let the devils take my wits in here.

After that I felt calmer; I think I even slept.

Joab shook me awake. He marched me off without a word, back through the torchlit maze, up the steep stone staircase into the light of early morning. The spring heat hit us like a great wave breaking. Subdued by awe as much as by fear, I stumbled along beside the dour general past guardposts and gateways, through quadrangles, corridors and echoing halls. Everything seemed to be larger than life, as though built for giants: the yards and the rooms were so vast, the ceilings so high, the walls so thick. But as we neared the royal apartments themselves, thick defensive masonry gave way to airy colonnades; there were gardens and pools and lion-mouthed fountains. Like the cellars, this part of the palace belonged to a world I'd never set foot in, and had never expected to.

Presently we came to a place where bronze-breasted guardsmen with spears were lining the walls, and we fetched up at the curtained entrance to the throneroom itself.

Jehoshaphat the royal recorder and herald came out to us. I'd seen him a few times before, making public proclamations from the palace roof, but could never have imagined that a man of his importance would ever see me. Joab explained his business, including what I'd done, but was told it would have to wait; His Majesty the King was with the lady Bathsheba.

Joab made no attempt to mask his disapproval. He growled, 'Is the audience to last long?'

'I don't know, General.'

Joab turned to me. 'Stand there, with your face against the wall and your hands above your head. Don't move.' I complied, and again he addressed Jehoshaphat. 'I have some other matters to attend to. Expect me back shortly. Don't let this urchin out of your sight. He's savage, and bites like a camel.'

So I stood there without moving, until my arms hurt even more than my legs. I did contemplate bolting, but felt too battered and hungry to try. Then suddenly there was laughter echoing along the hallway, and barely broken voices, slurred at the edges.

'Pass me that wineskin, Shimei. Here—you've had nearly all of it! I shall be needing some extra courage inside me if I'm going to get back on that horse again.'

'Absalom, you wildcat, you're insane! Trying to ride a horse like it's no different from a mule. They're not meant for that.'

'If horses were designed just to pull carriages, Sheba, the great god Adonai would have made them with yokes ready fitted. I'll master it, don't you worry. If the northern barbarians can do it, and even the Egyptians, then I can. I'll do it if it kills me.'

'You won't be bothered if it kills you, will you? But what if it just maims you, and ruins your beauty? Rebekah won't love you then.'

'Oh, I don't care about Rebekah any more. She's so staid and serious. Her little sister Hannah, though ... now *there's* someone worth impressing.'

More laughter. Then: 'Poor Rebekah. Another broken heart to add to your string, Absalom. Maybe you could bequeath her to Amnon. He's as green as a cucumber.'

'Aye, green in every sense ...' Then their banter died away as the guards challenged them, and Absalom said, 'I want to see my father.'

'I regret that the King has given specific orders to the effect that he is not to be disturbed,' said Jehoshaphat, rather stiffly.

'Well, I'm the King's son, and I order you to disturb him!' Absalom retorted. Somewhere behind him—I could still see nothing but the wall—his companions Shimei and Sheba giggled drunkenly. But Absalom wasn't joking.

'I'm sorry, my lord. He is—in conference with the lady Bathsheba. And when it is ended, General Joab has the next appointment.'

There was a brittle silence. Absalom gave a forced laugh. 'In conference, eh. That's a new word for it.' This time he was the only one laughing. After another strained interval he muttered, 'And what about this boy? What's he doing here?'

Reluctantly Jehoshaphat expounded the whole situation. Meanwhile the Prince's two inebriated sidekicks sniggered and tried to persuade him to leave: why get mixed up in someone else's troubles? Quite enough seemed to come their way already.

But my upraised arms had lifted my tunic, baring the marks on my thighs, and Absalom guessed at once whose belt had made them. He knelt down, and I felt his hands on my shoulders. I winced, as I always did when anyone touched me; yet he was unexpectedly gentle so I didn't pull away. He turned me round to face him.

I'd never met Absalom before, but I would have known him anywhere. I had seen him just once, not many months earlier, and from a long way off. It was the day Israel celebrated her triumph over the Ammonites, and all Jerusalem was on holiday, fringing the streets or crowding the rooftops. Mingling with the palace servants and their children, I'd found a good place to watch from, because for a change no one could be bothered to scold me. Everywhere men were chanting and women singing, that we had once been slaves in Egypt, now God had made us masters of our own empire. The King himself led a procession through the city, riding in a captured enemy chariot, and wearing an enormous crown. A few folk around me were arguing about whether it had belonged to the Ammonite tyrant or to his god. But most people weren't even looking at their monarch.

Absalom was standing in the chariot with him, in a bright bronze breastplate and studded leather kilt. Gold gleamed at his neck and at his wrists; and he wore rings in his ears as well as on his fingers. His hair, blue-black as midnight and curled into ringlets, was dusted with gold like stars, and it was as long and thick as the tails of the horses he was driving. I had assumed, because of his place of honour, that he was the King's eldest son, but from snippets of conversation I overheard, I learned that I was wrong.

Today the blue-black hair hung loose to his shoulders whilst the kerchief he might have used to cover it was looped around his neck like a scarf. He was clad in a plain tunic and wore no jewellery. He must have been about sixteen, for his skin was still smooth and his eyes were lined with kohl, and cool as a leopard's. Yet somewhere behind them sparked a glimmer of kindness—at least, that's what I should call it now. At the time I had no word for it, because no one had ever looked at me like that before.

Absalom asked my name, but I could no more tell him than I'd been able to tell Joab. All I could think about was Ziba's face, and Ziba's fist, and Ziba's words. Even so, the young Prince could tell it wasn't insolence that stifled me. While Shimei and Sheba were still grumbling in the background, he took off his scarf, and wetting it from their wineskin, he began carefully cleaning my wounds. It gave him an excuse to keep talking.

'This is Amnon's doing, I'm sure of it. The two characters who ran off last night must have been him and Jonadab.' He glanced up at

18

my face for some sign of confirmation, but I didn't dare give any. 'I'd be prepared to bet you didn't plan the robbery all by yourself, did you?' I shook my head slightly. 'It's outrageous. Amnon throws his weight about, and a little slave boy winds up facing the King.' Then, seeing something flicker in my eyes, he prompted, 'You're— not a slave?'

Without a sound, my lips said: no.

'Then who *are* you?' Absalom put down the scarf and the wine-skin, and took hold of both my hands. Terror welled inside me. I'd learnt from being a baby how to survive without anyone's sympathy. Now, for some unaccountable reason, I passionately wanted to trust Absalom, to tell him everything. But if I did decide to risk it, what could I say? It was so, so long since I'd spoken to anyone.

And I didn't even know what name to give. The kitchen staff at the palace had coined my latest nickname: Zoheleth, the serpent. But before coming to the city I'd mostly been known as Mamzer, the mongrel. That was what Ziba had called me. I'd also answered to Parhosh, the flea; or even Abattiah, the pumpkin. I must have had a real name when I was circumcised as a baby, but I didn't know it. Then again, Ziba didn't know I was called Zoheleth, so what harm could it do . . . ?

'Zoheleth?' repeated Absalom, when I'd mouthed the syllables at him. He laughed a little, genuinely this time, and shook his head. Then Jehoshaphat bent down and whispered urgently in his ear.

Joab was on his way back; I recognized the heavy steps. Absalom straightened up, deeming it wise to make himself scarce. 'I'll come back later,' he said to Jehoshaphat. 'I still want to see my father. And I want to know how *this* business turns out.'

Just at that second the great throneroom curtain was swept aside. A pale, slight young woman stepped out, all in white and heavily veiled. Other than her eyes, precious little of her was visible; but they were the darkest and the largest and the most mysterious eyes I'd ever seen. Momentarily they caught Absalom's. Bathsheba looked away quickly, but not quickly enough.

Then Absalom and his friends were gone, and Joab and I were solemnly admitted to the royal presence.

I could never have imagined a room so long or so lavish. The walls were panelled in cedar and hung with carpets. On an exalted dais stood a great sculpted throne, flanked by white stone lions, but it was empty.

The man—who had to be the King—was standing by a small high window, with his back to us. His broad shoulders were hunched and his greying head bowed. He wore no crown, no purple cloak, not even a chain of office. This spectacle offended all my childish assumptions and I was so shocked that I forgot to be frightened.

Jehoshaphat coughed deliberately and announced, 'My lord: Joab, son of Zeruiah, Commander of Your Majesty's armed forces.' Then he withdrew. But the melancholy man only sighed.

'Make obeisance to the King, lad,' Joab barked, and when I did nothing but stare at him blankly he shouted, 'Bow!' Then he pushed my head down with such brute force that I finished up in a full prostration. I didn't dare look up.

I'd counted my heartbeats as far as twenty-five when Joab ventured, in the mildest voice I'd yet heard him use, 'My lord—the enquiries into the Uriah affair were concluded late last night.'

'The Uriah affair?' At last the King looked up. There was an edge of terror to his voice. Then I decided that a king would never be terrified, so he must therefore be angry. I wished I were invisible. In fact, I might as well have been.

'The case of insubordination among Uriah's detachment at Rabbah,' said Joab, more mildly still—almost pleasantly.

'Oh—yes. I'm sorry. The mutiny.'

'I should hardly call it that, my lord. We made sure that it was sat upon long before matters could get seriously out of hand. But we have at last finished interrogating all those involved, and isolated the two ringleaders who incited the rest to disregard orders.'

The King sighed again audibly. 'Good, Joab. That's good.—Who were they?'

'The brothers Jeziel and Pelet.'

'Adonai have mercy! Two of my longest serving soldiers. They've been with me longer than I've been king . . . ever since Saul's time.' Joab made no comment; the King murmured, 'What have you done with them?'

'They have been flogged, and shut up in solitary.'

'Flogged? How many strokes?'

'Forty apiece, my lord. The maximum.'

'Was that strictly necessary? Those are freeborn Israelites.'

'My lord.' I heard Joab's heels click to attention.

'No, I mean it, Joab. That wasn't a rhetorical question. Did you *have* to treat them so harshly?'

Joab paused before responding. Then reverting to his crisp military voice he said, 'Yes. If it's an army you want, and not a shoddy rabble of undisciplined peasants like Saul had. If you want my opinion, what they got was too good for them. Those who *did* obey orders are dead.'

'Jeziel and Pelet.' The King weighed the names wistfully. 'I should never have credited it. They have both waded into much worse situations in their time. Jeziel was one of the first up the shaft when we took Jerusalem from the Jebusites. Why should they pull a stunt like this now?'

'I'm sure I don't know, my lord,' lied Joab, unconvincingly.

'Joab, you've had years of experience in leading men into battle. And in interrogating would-be mutineers. You must have formed some impression of their motives.'

For a long while Joab said nothing. When he did reply, he'd dropped all the military crispness once again.

'With respect, my lord . . . the orders were insane, and they knew it. Sending a single detachment right up under the walls of a besieged city—nine times out of ten it's suicidal. I don't think many officers other than Uriah would have accepted an assignment like that in the first place, or expected their boys to go through with it. Uriah was a professional, David. He asked no questions. He will be a tremendous loss.'

The King sucked in a long, juddering breath. Then he said, very quietly, 'You don't think he knew.'

'Knew, my lord?'

'Knew I wanted you to . . .'

'I'm sure I couldn't say, my lord. Like I told you, he always followed instructions without question.'

Still more quietly, the King pressed him harder. 'You don't think anyone else was suspicious?'

Joab muttered something noncommittal, so that at length the King was left with no choice but to change the subject. He asked, 'And what of the boy you've brought here with you? What part did he have to play in all this?'

My heart started doing cartwheels. I'd begun to hope they'd forgotten all about me. Joab cleared his throat and explained, 'He's here on a different count altogether. Abishai and I caught him red-handed last night, in the act of breaking into the treasury.'

'Last night?'

'He's been locked up too, till this morning, my lord. In one of the guardrooms. I thought it might scare some sense into him.'

'You mean he's been left in the dungeons overnight on his own? Joab, he can't be any more than eight! God give me strength! On your feet, little jackdaw.'

He didn't exactly sound cross, or even surprised. Slowly—for I still ached all over—I stood up. I was trying ineffectually to brush the dust and creases from my ragged tunic, when the King raised my chin with his hand, and I found myself gazing up into his face.

Then I watched it turn pale. He took three shaky steps backwards, and sat down heavily on the edge of the dais. He whispered, 'Joab, who is this?'

Joab looked as baffled as I felt. He shrugged his massive shoulders. 'We couldn't find out his name, my lord. Insolent mite wouldn't say a word. Would you like us to—try harder?'

The King was staring, as though he couldn't wrest his eyes from me. He beckoned me closer, asked my name and my age, but as usual I couldn't find words to reply. And I no more knew my age than I knew my real name, though I did have an inkling it was rather more than eight. The King began mumbling, more to himself than to me, 'You're so like him. I can't believe it. It's impossible . . .'

I hadn't the faintest idea what he meant. The whole sequence of events was fast becoming too much for me. But when the King said he was tired, and asked Joab to take me away and deal with me himself, I must have looked so appalled that he changed his mind. He bade Joab wait outside instead while he spoke with me alone. No doubt he'd come to the conclusion it was Joab's formidable presence that was tying my tongue.

Joab began to protest, stressing how dangerous and ungovernable I was, calling him 'David' again rather than 'my lord', or even 'Your Majesty'. But in the end the King snapped at him, and Joab gave way. That startled me.

When he'd gone, the King put his hands on my shoulders just as his son had done. No doubt I winced again. With him seated on the dais, our eyes came level. His looked weary, but he'd been handsome once, a long time ago.

I told him I was Zoheleth, because I felt sorry for him. He had to read it from my lips, since no sound would come out. But I'd already told Absalom, so this time it was easier. For there hadn't been any thunderbolts and the sky hadn't fallen on my head.

After that he didn't seem to know what to say to me. He gave no sign of remembering why I'd been brought to him. Presently he simply sent me away, and I found myself standing in the hallway outside.

I might have guessed that Amnon and Jonadab would be lying in wait for me.

They dragged me out of earshot and started to harass me, demanding to know if I'd let my tongue wag and leaked their names to anyone who mattered. They hadn't quite got around to beating me when Absalom returned.

He was on his own now, apparently sober, and fearfully angry. He said, 'Leave the boy in peace, you two. You've done him enough damage already.'

'Keep your nose out of other people's business—*Syrian*.'

It was Jonadab who spoke, and who stood to take him on; they faced each other with whitened fists, while Amnon held me up against the wall. But it was the King's eldest son, and his own half-brother, whom Absalom wanted for his confrontation.

'Those were your chain marks on his legs, Amnon. You put him up to robbing the treasury.'

'Am I the only person in the palace with a belt?' Amnon retaliated, but he didn't meet Absalom's gaze.

'Why don't you just admit it? We all know what happened.'

'Are you calling me a liar? We'll see Father about that.' He let go of me, and squared up close beside Jonadab. Absalom betrayed no hint of anxiety. I thought, *this* is what a king ought to look like. No way was I going to run off now.

But then Jonadab growled, 'Let's not waste any more time on him, Amnon. He isn't worth arguing with. And it's no use talking to your father; this pampered witch's-brat gets everything his own way. He won't get the throne, though. We'll make sure of that.'

They swaggered off arm in arm, leaving my champion and me eyeing one another warily across the hall.

He said, 'We'd best find your parents. They will be going out of their minds worrying about you.'

I shrugged my shoulders.

'Come along now. Where do you live? Which part of the palace? The harem? The stables?'

23

I looked wretchedly at my feet. Again Absalom knelt down beside me, and I could smell the sweet scent of jasmine in his hair. He kept asking so patiently where my home was, that finally I burst into tears for the first time in months. Home was nowhere in the palace; nowhere in Jerusalem. And it certainly wasn't back at Lodebar with my old guardian and Ziba.

So Absalom dried my eyes and took me to his mother.

2

The entrance to the women's quarters was some way from the throneroom though on the same floor. A fat eunuch guarded it, but waved us on without a word; clearly Absalom was a frequent visitor. I marvelled that this should be allowed, but it seemed that the young Prince was used to getting his own way.

We passed through shady cloisters and courtyards, where women and girls sat sewing or spinning, or chatting as they played with the toddlers who tumbled in the sunshine and grubbed about in the flower beds. Here and there little wooden animals and building bricks lay scattered across the pavements, whilst a group of boys fought over a toy sword. I'd never owned a toy of any kind in my life. Meanwhile most of the girls followed Absalom with their eyes; a few he acknowledged. He grinned as I lagged behind, goggling, and he pointed out the rooms where the King's concubines lived, and those of his wives.

Maacah's apartment was finer than all the rest, and segregated from them. She shared it with her daughter Tamar—Absalom's sister—two infant sons, and three young servant girls, one of whom was Tamar's. But if thirty women and their children had lived there, they wouldn't have been crowded. We walked in unannounced; Absalom was enjoying the prospect of surprising them.

All seven were together, in a spacious room which gave onto a private courtyard from which the fragrance of flowers drifted in on the breeze. There were flowers inside too, in gold and silver vases. There were golden bowls and goblets, set on low marble-topped tables. There were screens made of ivory, exquisitely carved. There were couches draped with opulent fabrics and scattered with cushions, and on one of these couches Maacah was reclining, her two maids dressing her precisely curled hair. Her ample body was swathed in a deep blue gown, all but her face and hands and feet, and her long nails were tinted poppy red. Her face too was painted, and to me in my naïvety she might have been an incarnate goddess.

The two small boys were playing contentedly around her ankles; on a stool beside her perched Tamar, her head bowed over the garment she was stitching, and on the floor close by, her own attendant was sitting cross-legged, holding skeins of thread in her lap. This girl, who looked very little older than me, was the first to see us come in; her eyes lighted on Absalom and her cheeks flushed scarlet. Absalom raised a finger to his lips, so she said nothing.

'Tamar, you will be the most beautiful bride this poverty-stricken apology for a nation has ever seen,' Maacah announced with shameless self-satisfaction as her daughter held up the dress for her to admire. 'We must be sure to make the offerings to Astarte for your fertility soon. The day is coming so quickly.'

Tamar laughed softly and shook back her hair. It was thick and unbraided, unveiled, and as blue-black as Absalom's. She couldn't have been much above fourteen. 'We shall leave that in the hands of Adonai, along with everything else,' she said evenly, then saw Absalom and winked.

Unexpectedly Maacah gave a sharp cry of pain. She thrust both maids aside simultaneously and gathered her glossy curls into her neck. Their colour she had passed on to each of her children, and hers showed no more hint of grey than theirs did.

'Seventeen years I've lived in this miserable backwater,' she exclaimed. 'And still I can't find anyone to perform a simple task efficiently. I'm surrounded by savages, no one civilized has been to visit me for weeks...' and then, 'Absalom, darling! How wonderful to see you! Where on earth have you been? It's so cruel of you to rob me of your company for days on end.'

She stretched out both arms, with as much authority as affection, and Absalom dutifully went to embrace her, leaving me lurking awkwardly in the doorway. He submitted to a prolonged shower of kisses, all but smothered in the goddess's generous bosom. She stroked his face and smoothed out his hair, demanding to know why he hadn't bothered curling it; and where had he dug up this coarse shapeless tunic, and where were the earrings she'd had made for his birthday? Meanwhile her two little boys tried to crawl in between them, evidently resenting sharing her attention.

'Eliada! Eliphelet! Don't be so selfish,' she scolded, more or less indulgently. But Absalom drew them both onto his knee, so Maacah gave each of her sons a warm kiss on the brow, saying, 'I don't know! I have the four most beautiful children on earth, and I have to bring them up in a wilderness.' But she was smiling as she spoke; so were Absalom and Tamar. Maacah offered Absalom some of her new scented oil to try; he dabbed a little on his wrists to please her, and asked whether she'd made any mandrake love potion today.

'Love potion?' His mother failed utterly to sound offended. 'As if I—or you—could ever need such a thing.'

Absalom laughed and blew his sister's servant a kiss. The girl turned redder than ever, and the other two maids went back to doing Maacah's hair, deciding that her latest outburst of anger at their shortcomings was over.

'You still haven't told us where you've been all this time,' their mistress remarked conversationally to her firstborn, taking the babies from him and settling them in her lap, where they promptly fell asleep.

'Nowhere much. In my rooms mostly.'

'Drinking, I'll warrant.' Maacah affected disapproval. 'And with whom, may I ask?'

'Friends.'

'Which friends?'

Absalom fidgeted a little, twisting a coil of his hair around one finger. 'Shimei and Sheba.'

'Ye gods, not those two worthless characters again.' Maacah rolled her eyes to heaven. 'They're nothing but blood-sucking sycophants. Shimei's a bad temper on legs, and Sheba's as bloated and lazy as a gorged bullfrog. They only fawn over you because they like to be thought of as cronies of the King's favourite son. It won't do them any good, you know. David has no time for flatterers.'

'They aren't worthless!' Absalom protested. 'They were my comrades in arms on my first campaign.'

'Your only campaign, you mean,' said Tamar mischievously.

Absalom pulled a face at her, then continued unabashed. 'And it doesn't mean anything to *them* that my father's the King. They both belong to the clan Saul came from. Shimei's quite a close relation of his, if you must know, and so's Sheba, on his mother's side.'

Maacah looked singularly unimpressed. 'It's high time you found yourself some decent friends. Why not spend more time with your cousins? Lots of David's brothers have sons here in Jerusalem.'

'Sons like Jonadab, you mean.'

Maacah ignored the contempt in his tone. 'Yes,' she said, 'Like Jonadab. His father Shammah is such a gentleman.'

'Jonadab isn't.' Absalom swung round, tossing his hair over his shoulders, and began to look for me. I'd retreated almost out of sight around the corner, where I stood playing with the door curtain, squeezing it and chewing it and rubbing it on my face; the material was so soft and shiny, and cool against my chafed skin. Having had no experience of women at all for as long as I could remember, I was more inclined to be in awe of Maacah with her painted face and extravagant demeanour than I had been of Joab, or Amnon and Jonadab.

Then Absalom smiled at me and beckoned. I shuffled forward, though I felt more abashed than ever with so many people looking at me, and the temptation to run was suddenly all but overwhelming. Absalom showed his mother the marks on my legs, and told her my story, in so far as he knew it.

'But Absalom, he's filthy!' she expostulated, turning up her nose and pushing me further away; perhaps she feared her little ones might catch something from me. As soon as she touched me, I recoiled like a lizard, causing her to flinch in turn.

'I forgot to tell you his nickname.' Absalom grinned apologetically. 'I don't think he's ever been tamed. And he's an orphan, so it seems. Doesn't belong anywhere. He isn't a slave—there's no mark or ring on him. But it was Amnon and Jonadab who landed him in trouble and did this to him, I'm sure of it. I just wish I could prove it.'

Maacah made a clucking sound in her throat. 'Amnon's mother Ahinoam is such a little mouse. She has no control over him at all. Never did have.'

'It isn't fair.' Absalom pouted. 'He gets away with everything. And one day he'll be king. Woe betide Israel then.'

Tamar leaned forward and poked Absalom in the chest. '*He* gets away with everything? Not half as much as you do. What about the time you sneaked into the wine cellars, just after the new wing of the palace was finished? You got your three little half-brothers drunk as Amalekites—and don't you pretend you can't remember. Joab found you all dancing naked on the roof. You were only twelve; but Adonijah wasn't even ten, Shephatiah and Ithream even less. And *they* ended up bearing the brunt of Father's fury. Not you. It's you he loves best, and you know it.'

'Well, and so he should do,' Maacah rejoined. 'Absalom has bluer blood than any of David's other sons. He could wake up and find himself heir to *two* thrones one of these days. There's only my sister's son with prior claim in Geshur. Besides, he'd make a far better king than Amnon. David knows that as well as I do.'

Absalom lay back luxuriously among the cushions, stretching like a pharaoh's cat. 'Anyhow, it served those sapheads right for doing what I told them. They've no initiative, any of them. Especially Adonijah. He's still clinging to his mother's apron strings. He'll never make a decision for himself until the day it dawns on him that he must choose between sucking up to her, and creeping to me.'

Tamar let out a peal of laughter, but Maacah reproved her. 'It's perfectly true. All David's sons live in your brother's shadow, even those who were born back at Hebron, never mind the brood spawned here who'll never count for anything.'

Just then one of the slave girls tugged on Maacah's hair a second time. She rounded on the pair of them, cursing their clumsiness, screaming that they'd already had their last chance; they would be back in the market square by tomorrow morning. In her semi-hysteria she sent the comb flying, and it skidded across the floor to land at my feet. Used to retrieving dropped utensils for the cooks in the kitchens—I'd often be thrown titbits in return—I picked it up and ventured back towards her. Silently I held it out for her to take.

'At least there's one person here who can remember what manners are,' she muttered, by way of rather grudging thanks. Then she condescended to look at me more closely, and said, 'You know, I don't believe this boy is wild at all, Absalom. And he's quite pretty too, underneath all the dirt. Perhaps I'll have him cleaned up and keep him here as my page.'

Absalom's eyes widened. He didn't know whether to be shocked or amused. 'Not even you can get away with that, Mother. A male attendant in the harem? You'll be the scandal of the court.'

'So?' Maacah smiled sweetly. 'He's not much older than half the concubines' sons, and they still live here.'

'Besides, I don't think he can speak.'

'So much the better. He won't go gossiping my business all over the palace. In any case, darling, why all these protests? Do you want to keep the little beauty to enhance your own entourage? If Shimei and Sheba are the best it can boast of at present, perhaps it could do with some enhancing.'

Absalom looked daggers at her.

'Well, don't worry,' she concluded cheerfully. 'I shall break him in and get him thoroughly civilized, then when his beard starts to grow and he loses those rosy cheeks, you can train him up to be your charioteer.'

'I drive my own chariots, Mother.'

'Well, your armour bearer then. Have it your own way.' Maacah waved one elegant, red-tipped hand dismissively. 'That's settled. I shall inform David.'

'And if he disapproves?'

'I can't see that being a problem. If the favourite son can have his whims indulged, so can the favourite wife. I've never been frightened of him.'

'Quite true, my Syrian enchantress. It is I who am frightened of you.'

I don't know how long the King had been standing there listening in on the conversation. He entered from the courtyard; I realized it must link directly with his own private apartment. He bent to kiss Maacah and Tamar in turn, afterwards Absalom and the babies.

Then he caught sight of me, and started. I backed away behind my curtain, fearing he'd come to interrogate me some more. But he just blinked once or twice, looking suddenly tired again; the glimmer of humour which had lightened his voice and his features just now was already gone. He flung himself on a couch and closed his eyes.

Maacah laid the sleeping children gently in the cushions and went to kneel beside him, massaging his chest with practised hands. 'What is it, my dearest? Are you having to work too hard again?'

'It's been a busy morning. People to see, problems to solve, disputes to sort out. All the usual headaches.'

'Well, you can forget them for a while, now you're here. Stay and have something to eat.' She walked her fingers languorously down his body. 'Spend the siesta with me.'

'I wish I could.' He took hold of her hands and placed them back up on his chest. 'There never seems to be time for siestas these days. I have an appointment to keep at noon.'

'With Ahithophel, no doubt. Sometimes I wonder why you don't marry him as well, you spend so much time with him. I wouldn't trust him half a spearlength. Shifty eyes. Send a message to say you can't go.'

'It's not only Ahithophel who's involved, my love. Hushai his assistant will be there too, and the prophet Nathan is on his way in from the desert and coming up to the palace specially.'

'A veritable council session! It must be something serious.'

'It is.' David sighed, a huge, leaden sigh that came from somewhere a long way inside him.

'Come now, you can tell me. You never used to keep these heavy things to yourself. Let me share the weight with you.'

For a time he didn't reply. I thought he might have fallen asleep. He looked very close to it. Then in a distant, weary voice he said, 'Nathan has predicted a three-year famine because of what Saul did to the Gibeonites.'

Maacah was frankly nonplussed. 'And what *did* Saul do to the Gibeonites?'

'He tried to wipe them out. They're idolaters after all, descendants of Canaanites who were living here in Israel when Moses led our people back from Egypt. But they made a deal with Joshua and were supposed to be spared. Saul butchered hundreds of them. Now apparently it's Adonai's will that the surviving Gibeonites themselves decide what's to be done to punish Saul's house. What can I do? They could demand—anything.' Just then he opened his eyes and sat up, staring around him, blinking again and frowning. I shrank away further, though I wasn't sure why.

Maacah tossed her hair back haughtily; I could see where Absalom had learnt the gesture. 'Why let the jabberings of some rabid desert holy man get to you? There's no evidence of famine here. Last year's harvest was perfectly normal, and this year's corn is growing well, so they say. Nathan is no more to be feared than my father's twittering diviners back in Syria. Has he ever been proved right yet?'

David put his head in his hands.

For the first time, Maacah appeared genuinely anxious.

'Whatever is the matter? Nothing ever used to worry you so badly.' She put her arms around his shoulders, but he didn't relax. So she stood up again, exchanging taut glances with Absalom and Tamar, and poured wine into one of the golden goblets. At first the King wouldn't take it, but when she coaxed him, he drained it in one gulp. It seemed to do him good; he changed the subject and made an attempt to chat for a while. He even agreed to a game of senet with Absalom. But he lost abominably, and his depression returned. He had some more wine, then left.

No one wanted to talk after he'd gone. Or rather, they all wanted to talk, but none of them wanted to begin. Eventually Tamar murmured, 'Poor Father.'

'He never used to be like this,' Maacah lamented. 'It can't just be that prediction of Nathan's. It's months now since he's been himself. He used to be so carefree, reckless, exuberant... like Absalom.'

'Except that Father had a better sense of humour,' added Tamar, with a wry little smile. Absalom scowled at her, but she tickled him under the chin and he had to smile back. Their teasing did nothing to relieve the tension.

'We used to be so much in love,' Maacah was saying forlornly. 'I was the only woman who could match him in strength of will, and he adored me for it. I know they say he only married me for politics, to get my father as an ally against Ishbosheth when the two of them were rivals for the throne. But it was love at first sight, for both of us.' Maacah hugged Tamar impulsively. 'And of all his wives, only I have given him a daughter.'

Absalom reminded her that she'd borne David more sons than any other wife had, too, but Maacah didn't hear him; she was floating somewhere in her dreams of the past. 'He was the only man I'd ever thought worth bedding. I would have done anything for him. I *did* do anything for him. I even let him make me swear in front of Nathan that I would renounce the gods of my fathers. And the goddesses. Even the lady Astarte.'

'You didn't mean it, though,' Absalom baited her, but she didn't rise to it.

Tamar said, 'He's been worse since Bathsheba's baby died. It may be that he's still pining.'

'That was months ago.' Maacah turned back to her own two, the younger of whom had woken up and started crying. She put him to her breast and he quietened again. 'He ought to be over it by now. He's had other sons die in infancy—remember Chileab. And Bathsheba is such a recent addition to the harem. She can't mean that much to him; not yet. He only married her because her first husband had been killed in action, and was one of the Thirty, his corps of crack warriors. Besides, he seemed to take the child's death so well at first.'

Tamar shook her head ruefully. 'You really think so?'

'Well, he started eating again, after fasting the whole time the wretched creature was ill, didn't he? He combed his hair, and agreed to let himself be seen in public, after mooning about here like a ghost for weeks. He even composed all those hymns about God's love and

32

mercy, and had the choirs learn them for the funeral.'

Absalom poured himself some wine and sat sipping it petulantly. 'He never takes me hunting any more, *and* he hasn't been to see my new chariot. We always used to exercise together, and do weapons training, and everything. Now Jehoshaphat won't even let me see him. Today is the first time I've laid eyes on him in two weeks.'

Maacah said, 'He was always so good with you when you were little. Remember when you were five, you shinned up that palm tree to reach the dates, and got stuck? He climbed right up there and got you down himself. You always did have more courage than sense, though. Both of you.'

'Things have never been the same since we left Hebron,' sighed Tamar. 'I loved it there. The palace was so small and homely; and we always seemed to be outdoors anyway. We all got on together much better, too, I'm sure. Even Amnon was fun to be with in those days. Don't frown like that, Absalom. He used to make dolls out of corn stalks for me, and I used to make him cakes and sweets.'

'No, that *is* going too far, Tamar.' Maacah covered her breast and put the infant over her shoulder. 'Hebron was even more primitive than this place. Some day I shall take you all to visit your grandfather in Geshur. Then you'll appreciate what a *real* palace is like. It wasn't coming to Jerusalem that ruined everything. Nothing seemed to go wrong till he declared war on the Ammonites.'

'Father should have led that campaign himself, instead of leaving Joab and Abishai to do all the dirty work,' said Absalom. 'It can't have done him any good lazing around here with all the women and children. It sapped his spirit.'

'If Father *had* gone into battle himself, he might no longer be with us at all,' Tamar pointed out delicately. 'If the enemy had got wind of it that our king was in the field, their toughest warriors would have made a beeline for him.'

'He survived the final assault on the Ammonite capital well enough,' Absalom countered. 'At least Joab had the sense to realize the importance of Father being there when they were ready to take Rabbah itself. Strange, it never ceases to amaze me whenever Joab shows he has a brain as well as brawn—'

'Sometimes I'm tempted to say the same about you,' Tamar interrupted him, grinning, but this time her big brother succeeded in ignoring her.

'Maybe Joab understands Father better than any of us do,'

Absalom continued thoughtfully. 'They've been together so long.'

Maacah grimaced. 'David wouldn't agree with you. He has little love for Joab, if truth be told. Oh, I know he doesn't show it; but Joab and Abishai don't exactly make a positive contribution to the culture and sophistication of the court.'

Tamar pulled on her needle with such a surge of venom that it came unthreaded. 'They're nothing but a pair of thugs. I can't think why Father keeps them on.'

'Thugs perhaps, but competent thugs.' Maacah bent over and rethreaded Tamar's needle without thinking, as though her daughter were still a small child. 'And they would be lost without David to serve. They were both born out of wedlock, you know, they and their stupid brother Asahel who got himself killed in the war with Ishbosheth. All three of them had different fathers, so they say. With a stigma like that attached to them, it's no wonder they got used to standing up for one another and defying all comers. Their mother Zeruiah was David's sister as surely as she was a strumpet— what else could he have done but take her boys under his wing?'

Absalom sniggered. 'Yes, but look what happened to Abner. Saul's cousin, wasn't he? And chief of Saul's armed forces before he was chief of Ishbosheth's. Yet he still finished up with Joab's knife in his guts when Father tried to promote him over Joab's head. Joab is a thug; if I were king I'd have done away with him long before now. I wouldn't be able to sleep at nights with him around.'

Just then I sensed movement behind me. Tamar's girl noticed it too, for she got up gracefully, still holding the skeins of thread, and came over to where I crouched behind my curtain. I retreated still further; she glanced at me briefly but looked away at once. Then she stepped outside and brought in another visitor.

It was a middle-aged matron with uncovered, uncoiffed hair; her drab ill-fitting garb at least went some way towards disguising the fact that she was plump in all the wrong places. Although she was smiling, her face was of the sort which looks uncomfortable wearing such an expression. It was utterly unadorned, and there was intelligence in the high forehead and away behind the eyes. Yet the eyes were sad, and pale as if life had bled them of their colour. I was hopelessly backward for my age in some ways, but I was well placed to see when someone had suffered; and this woman had, though perhaps long ago.

'Abigail!' Maacah spread her arms wide as she'd done for Absalom, and the visitor embraced her, kissing both her cheeks. Her name wasn't unknown to me; she was David's second wife, whom he'd married before he was king, and many years before being introduced to Maacah. 'So many lovely surprises in one day,' Maacah was saying, and she sounded sincere enough. Clearly she no longer regarded her sister-wife as a threat, if indeed she ever had done. 'My luck must be changing. Come, sit down! Make yourself at home.' And she had her much maligned attendants bring wine and cakes and pickled olives.

Meanwhile Abigail fussed fondly over Tamar and her wedding dress, told Absalom he'd grown, and dandled the babies with manifest envy on her wide lap. They wriggled and squalled and one of them pulled her loose hair surprisingly hard in his tiny fist, but Maacah didn't intervene—she spoiled all her children equally.

Instead, she had me dragged out of hiding and admired in my turn, and it was agreed by everyone that I would steal the show at the wedding, once I was cleaned up. Absalom was at pains to point out yet again who was to blame for the state I was in, and went on at length about how his father ought to punish the offender severely. And so conversation turned once more upon the mystifying changes which had of late come over the King.

Abigail allowed herself a brief wallow in nostalgia. 'I'll never forget the first time I saw him. He was on the run from Saul, with nothing to live on but the proceeds of the protection racket he was masterminding from his base in the desert.' She smiled again as Tamar's eyebrows went up. 'He came to our house in person because my husband refused to pay what his henchmen were demanding. He was armed to the teeth, except that in place of a helmet he'd a checkered scarf twisted in his hair like a bedouin. I was smitten.' She looked away towards the window, and no one cared to interrupt her reverie apart from Eliada and Eliphelet who were now pulling one another's hair and squalling more loudly than ever. Then Abigail shook her head as if cross with herself, and cleared her throat. She said, 'Actually, Maacah, it's partly concerning David that I came here to talk to you. Have you seen much of his new wife Bathsheba?'

Maacah shrugged, and all at once didn't seem quite so accommodating. She took the babies back from her guest and focussed her attention on nuzzling and nibbling them, waiting for Abigail to continue without making any comment of her own. Abigail complied.

'It's just that I'm worried about her, you see. I came across her this morning for the first time since she lost the baby. She was on her way back from David's apartment, I think, and she looked so frail. I went to try and speak to her, but she backed off as though she feared I might bite her. She seems—well, *disturbed*, Maacah. Overwrought even. I can't understand why David brought her here so soon after her husband's death. And then for him to get her with child so quickly too . . . I feel it's insensitive of him to expect so much of her, especially when she's so young.'

Maacah shrugged again. But when she looked up, she saw that her guest seemed almost tearful. Tutting resignedly she gave the babies to Tamar's servant girl, and took Abigail's broad, unmanicured hands in her own slim and pampered ones.

Tamar asked, 'Isn't Bathsheba Ahithophel's granddaughter? Perhaps he's the only kinsman she has; and he spends far more time in his chambers in the palace than at Giloh where he comes from. She probably had nowhere else to go.'

'She'd had a husband,' her mother said drily. 'Had he no brothers? One of *them* should have married her.'

Abigail now looked ready to cry at any moment. 'Her husband was a Hittite, Maacah. He had no kinsfolk in Israel whatsoever. Tamar is right; Ahithophel is the only family the poor girl has in the city.'

Maacah made the clucking sound in her throat again. 'Confound Ahithophel! Since he became chief adviser he thinks he rules the world. He'll have wanted Bathsheba wedded to the King to increase his *own* reputation; just so he can say that he's joined in blood with the house of David. After all, he could have kept the girl in his own apartment with her maidservants if she'd nowhere else to go. David needn't have married her.'

Absalom, who'd been content to take a back seat while the women talked, pushed himself upright now and said with a flagrant leer, 'Bathsheba *is* beautiful, you know.' He drew two explicit curves in the air with his fingers. Maacah snapped, 'Absalom!' but she was half amused.

Abigail remarked pensively, 'She *is* very young to be a widow, I suppose. Perhaps that's what David was thinking—that she wouldn't be so distressed if she had another husband, and a baby too. Perhaps he thought she needed love in her life, and a child to be responsible for. If only the poor little thing had lived.'

Maacah squeezed her hands. 'You're like Tamar, Abigail. Too often prepared to think the best of people.' Then Maacah looked again at the tears welling in the other woman's eyes, and drew her close. 'I'm sorry. Your own first husband can't have been buried many weeks when David married you. It must have been dreadful.'

Abigail sniffed and pulled away a little, wiping her nose on the back of one hand. 'No, Maacah; that's not why I'm crying. You don't understand. It wasn't the same at all.' Tamar passed her a handkerchief and she used it gratefully. 'Nabal was a stubborn fool and a drunkard. He even beat me sometimes when he'd had too much. He wasn't in the least like Uriah.'

'Uriah?'

'The Hittite, Bathsheba's late husband, God rest his soul. He was such a good man. He even accepted our religion, and kept the Law faithfully, to the very end. I never once saw an idol in his house; and his ancestors had bowed to them for centuries.'

At last Maacah deduced the cause of Abigail's tears. She asked softly, 'You knew him well?'

'Yes. Long before they were married. He was a friend of my cousin's; they served together in the army. Uriah was so honest, so straightforward. You always knew exactly where you stood with him.' Then she gave up the struggle with her emotions and the tears poured down her cheeks unchecked. 'They say he died a hero, leading that daring assault on the walls of Rabbah. He was awarded posthumous honours and an expensive military funeral. But what use are speeches and medals to a shade in Sheol? What comfort are they to his family far away in a foreign land? I just can't bear it when I see the house all shut up and silent. There was always laughter there, especially when Uriah was younger, when he used to invite all his friends from the barracks home for Shabbat, before he had a wife's wishes to consider . . . And I see that house every time I look out of my window, Maacah! It haunts me. I can even see it from here.'

She stood up unexpectedly, and went to the little lattice window high in the wall which was furthest from the courtyard. Maacah followed her, so Abigail pointed to the house in question. Then she said, 'Oh, I shouldn't be grieving for myself. It's Bathsheba I ought to be weeping for. And I do, I really do. I just feel for her so much, and losing a baby too, like I lost Chileab, so young . . .'

Tamar glanced at Absalom, and put down her sewing. She joined the two older women by the window, winding one arm around her mother and the other round Abigail. Absalom squirmed on his couch, embarrassed and out of place.

'Poor Abigail,' Tamar whispered. 'And poor Bathsheba. She's hardly any older than Amnon, Father says. I should go and visit her. I feel so guilty now, that I haven't been earlier. I've been so excited about my own wedding. How appallingly selfish.'

Abigail's voice came muffled through the cloud of Tamar's hair. 'She won't let anyone near her. I've tried, Tamar, believe me, I know. I tried to go and see her in her rooms just after the baby died, but they told me she was ill and not receiving anyone. They say she was ill throughout her pregnancy too. Maybe that's why the poor mite was born so early, and got so sick itself.'

Even from my distance I saw Maacah stiffen. She repeated, 'Early? What do you mean, early?'

Abigail was flustered. She twisted her hands together and muttered, 'The baby came something like a month early. Perhaps even more. You must have worked that out. It was a miracle that it lived more than an hour.'

It took Maacah a long while to reply. Then she said, 'I saw Bathsheba's baby, my dear. David sent for me to treat it when all his prayers had failed, because he knows that I have skills, much as he may deplore them. And that child was not born early.'

'What are you saying?' Abigail asked sharply.

'I don't know,' Maacah murmured. 'I really don't know.'

Of course, had the child's father been anyone other than David, King of Israel, composer of a hundred psalms, man after God's own heart, the answer would surely have been obvious to everyone.

3

True to her word, Maacah sold her two maids and took me on in their place. I was given a plain wooden bed in a room no bigger than a cupboard, but it was more than I'd ever had in my life. I was given duties too; not that they were especially onerous. They amounted to fetching and carrying, dressing Maacah's hair—with which she was tolerably pleased, once she'd trained me—and looking pretty, which I suppose I was. I had plenty of heavy black hair, and fine features: signs of noble breeding, Maacah said, but that was hardly likely.

Certainly, she found out very rapidly that I hadn't been nobly brought up. Aside from the fact that I never spoke, I also regularly wet my smart bed and soiled my fine new clothes. Sometimes I think Maacah regretted keeping me, but Tamar felt sorry for me, and would never have allowed her mother to get rid of me the way she'd got rid of a whole string of my predecessors.

It never seemed to occur to anyone to give *me* a choice about all this. But then, it never honestly occurred to me that I was entitled to one. My entire existence had consisted of a series of bewildering changes over which I'd had no control. It didn't occur to me to be grateful to Maacah and her family, either, not at first. They had saved me from a life of begging and thieving, as well as from Amnon's malice—but for how long? Milk curdles quickly in the sunshine, sweet things so easily turn sour; I'd learnt that lesson all too often. I'd also learnt not to let myself love. There had been servants in the kitchens whom I'd made the mistake of growing fond of. But they would fall out of favour and be replaced, and I would at once be forgotten. Or they would betray my trust and make trouble for me. It got me angry that I couldn't stop myself growing to love Maacah, and Tamar, and Absalom.

Now my fortunes were looking up, I did think that the bad dreams which had so long tormented me might stop. Perhaps I would even be able to sleep a whole night without waking in terror of the dark. But I was disappointed. Over and over again on my sodden mattress I relived the tortures I'd been subjected to in the years before my arrival in the city. Yet none of those around me suspected anything of this, and I couldn't tell them. For all they knew, I'd been born in the royal kitchens to some scullery maid, and somehow avoided being exposed. In fact I'd been at the palace only one winter.

I was born in Lodebar, way to the north and across the Jordan. I grew up there in the house of one Machir, a great man with great estates; he was a distant kinsman of my father. I suppose he was a kind man, too, for he provided for the pair of us without hope of reward. But we barely saw him.

My father Merib was crippled, in mind as well as body. He couldn't walk properly, and he barely knew who anyone was; even who *I* was. He never talked to me—well, nothing that made sense, anyway. He just used to mutter to himself, and dribble, and twitch, and hum tunelessly all the time. Also he had fits, so it frightened me to be on my own with him. Really, he was like a little child, but one who could never expect to grow up to be otherwise. He spent his days playing with sticks and stones and petals, and little ushabti figurines from Egypt which some trader had given him. He and I were assigned to the charge of one of Machir's servants—Ziba.

Ziba was cruel to both of us. He called my father The Idiot, and me Mamzer—mongrel, or bastard. If my father's humming got on his nerves, he would beat him until he stopped. He would beat me for anything, or nothing.

He would lock me in a cabinet, or chain me to a wall in the fierce heat of noon with no water, just for the fun of it. He knew very well that there was no one around I could complain to, even if I were capable of complaining.

That was how he took his pleasure by day. The nights were worse. I didn't understand what he was doing to me, but it made me feel dirty, and guilty, and worthless. And he said that if I ever tried to tell anyone, he would kill me.

Then one day we were brought to the palace. I knew it was about to happen, because I'd overheard Machir and Ziba discussing it. Ziba had been away for some days, and when he came back, something had changed. I stood outside the door, silent as dewfall, and listened.

Machir was saying that it was too dangerous to take us to Jerusalem. There must be some vile trickery afoot; what could the King possibly want with us? All these years we'd been hidden, our identities carefully concealed—now everything was going to be put at risk.

So I was reminded of the other secret Ziba daily threatened me to keep: I must never, ever, tell anyone who I was. Of course this made no sense to me. So far as I was concerned, I was nobody.

Next I heard Ziba insisting to Machir that he, Ziba, must go with us, that we were used to him and it would make us feel more secure. Who else had his experience in dealing with Merib's specialized needs?

This outrageous lie made my skin crawl. But the master was plainly too trusting to suspect an ulterior motive. He merely registered faint surprise, saying, 'I thought you'd be only too glad to absolve yourself of responsibility for them. You weren't exactly keen to take it on when Merib was first brought here.'

Ziba answered him, smoothly as water sliding from a blade, 'Over the years I have developed a certain fondness for both the unfortunate creatures, my lord.' I wanted to slit his throat.

So our things were packed for us, and off we went. My father snivelled the whole time our luggage was being assembled. Ziba tried to force him to leave his ushabtis behind, but he got so angry it was likely he'd go into a fit, so in the end they were taken. Still, I knew Ziba was up to no good. He kept telling my father how he must bow to the King when we got there, and call himself his humble servant, and a worthless dog. He was laying all this on so thickly that I decided maybe he wasn't going to take us to the palace at all, but butcher us on the road and dump our bodies in a pit. So throughout the journey I made all the trouble I knew how to, finally biting Ziba's arm as hard as I could when he tried to thump me for throwing the contents of one of the trunks all over the road.

That's why, when we got to Jerusalem, he didn't tell anyone that I was Merib's son. And judging from my father's miserable condition, I don't suppose it occurred to anyone at court that he could have begotten one. Ziba took him away, and abandoned me in the kitchens. I don't know if he hoped they'd feed me, or put me in the supper. But from being Mamzer the mongrel I became Zoheleth the serpent, slipping silently around in the shadows.

Such were the dreams that shook me awake. Fear would rush at me from the darkness, and all I could do was hug myself calm and say over and over in my head: please take this poison out of my memory; please, please just let me go back to sleep. Usually it would work, until the next time.

Although I was meant to be Maacah's servant, it was her daughter I came to spend most of my time with; and to love most, though for many weeks she wouldn't have suspected it. I wouldn't have admitted it even to myself. Since I wouldn't be touched and had no speech, all I could do was follow her from room to room to show I liked being with her.

It wasn't that my body lacked any of the parts needed for talking. It was mostly that I'd never had the opportunity, and had grown so used to my own silence that the sound of my voice would have scared me. And the keeping of so many secrets got me terrified that if I did try to speak, I would say the wrong thing. But I loved it when Tamar spoke to me. She shortened my name to 'Zohel' and it made me feel warm inside whenever she used it. In time Maacah and Absalom came to use it, and so did Miriam, Tamar's maidservant. I grew peculiarly fond of her too, though she said little more than I did. I enjoyed watching her smile, and move, and brush Tamar's hair, and play with Maacah's infant sons, and balance a huge pot or basket on her head whilst walking like a queen.

Very occasionally Miriam would take me with her when she went to the market, or even out of the city, when she visited her family. Like me, Miriam was freeborn, but she truly was of noble stock; her parents counted it a great honour for their daughter to be the personal attendant of the only princess of Israel.

Once on the way home we walked through a meadow ablaze with yellow flowers. Impulsively I picked an armful of them to take back to Tamar. I wrapped them tight in the folds of my cloak to keep them safe, and when I gave them to her they were all crushed and withered. I decided that this was why she seemed to be crying as she went out to put them in water.

I saw quite a lot of Absalom also. He would take me to the stables and show me his chariots, and encourage me to stroke his horses and feed them barley from my hand. Tamar said he was probably just glad to have found someone new to impress, but I was as sure that he had a soft spot for me as I was that he genuinely loved those animals.

It was true that they were magnificent. I was well used to seeing people with mules, either riding them or yoking them to pull carts. But horses were still something of a novelty in Israel in my youth—we would buy our mules from foreign traders rather than breeding them ourselves. And Absalom's steeds were so proud, so serenely majestic, with their glossy black coats and switching tails. He had half a dozen grooms to care for them, yet still did much of the work himself.

'They are much more fitting for a king to ride than mules are, don't you think?' he said to me as we brushed them down after exercise. I shrugged happily. 'Some day I'll convince my father. Some day I'll make him race me. When he has time.' A fleeting loneliness clouded his eyes.

He'd more or less mastered riding them. Once or twice he'd swung me up there in front of him, and taken me galloping, swifter than a desert wind, along the road out of Jerusalem. Tamar was angry afterwards, but I was ecstatic. With my hands twisted in the tumbling mane, and the air rushing at my face, and Absalom reaching around me to hold the reins, I felt myself in paradise. For the first time in my life I'd forgotten completely to shrink away from the nearness of another human being. Speed blew away our worries, and was addictive like unwatered wine. I think that at heart Absalom and I were as wild as each other.

Of course, straightforward horseriding didn't satisfy Absalom for long. Once the girls stopped squealing whenever they saw him do it, he had to break new ground. He would practise jumping walls or pits, or even stand on the horse's back instead of sitting. One day Shimei dared him to sit backways on, so he had to do that too. Clearly the horse wasn't quite as keen; it careered off out of control, heading straight for a gateway much too low for its rider to pass beneath. I shrieked 'Absalom!' and he leapt off in the nick of time.

Only when we got home, and Absalom related the tale to a disapproving Tamar, did any of us realize that the stunt had ended miraculously in more ways than one.

After that first word, everything began to change for me. It was as though I'd been in prison all my life, and was suddenly set free. To begin with the freedom tasted strange in my mouth, and yet delicious at the same time. Gradually I opened up, trying out new words and phrases, feeding voraciously on the praises of those around me.

While I was still learning to talk, Tamar began to teach me to read, and to write. Visitors told her she was wasting her time, I would never be clever enough for that. But as she rightly pointed out, the same was usually said about women. Maacah had only taught *her* so she could understand the brittle old scrolls of herb lore which had been passed down through the adepts of Talmai's house from time immemorial.

Soon enough I proved Tamar right: I wrote 'Zohel' from memory, and not long afterwards, the Ten Commandments.

But I didn't tell her anything about my background after all; nor did I tell Maacah or Absalom. I no longer wanted them to know I had a father. I didn't know what had become of him and was afraid to find out. I was even more afraid of being sent back to him. Whatever fate Ziba had designed for him, I couldn't imagine it being one I'd want to share.

One afternoon in late spring Tamar and I were sitting outside in our courtyard studying a short portion of the Torah. She'd had to explain to me that the Torah contains the holy writings of Moses, the greatest prophet who has ever lived. We were working on the passage which contains the Shema, the first prayer an Israelite should hear when he is born, and the last before he dies. As for me, I'd never heard it at all, so far as I knew. Maacah was with us, feeding the babies, and all was peaceful until Miriam brought Amnon and Jonadab through from the reception room. I panicked instantly, but they didn't even recognize me. Jonadab told Maacah that Amnon wanted some of her mandrake love potion.

Maacah went very cagey and said she knew nothing of such things. It could indeed have been a trap; there were many folk besides David who frowned upon such heathen practices and might be out to stir up trouble. Jonadab assured her that the request was genuine, and that they had gold to offer if she would like it. But all the time they were arguing, I was watching Amnon.

He was hanging at his friend's elbow, yet he wasn't following the conversation. He was looking at Tamar out of the corners of his eyes. She didn't notice; she was still poring over our scroll, with her softly curled hair spilling over her shoulders like a fall of blue-black water. But I noticed well enough. The expression on Amnon's face reminded me of Ziba's, when he came in the night. It made my blood turn to ice, especially when shortly the two youths left without pressing the point about the potion any further. I doubted that it was what they'd come for in the first place.

But I kept my thoughts to myself. I still had no words for something the like of that.

Tamar taught me other skills besides my letters. She taught me to bake the little cakes she'd once baked for Amnon. She put honey in them, and made them to look like fat rounded hearts, explaining that soon she would be making them for her new husband. She could see that this bothered me, though. For all my nine or ten years, I knew nothing of what marriage meant, but something told me it would take her from me.

'You mustn't be sad, Zohel,' she said, hugging me spontaneously. It no longer made me flinch. 'The day I marry will be the happiest day of my life. Father has found such a good man for me. I've already met him. He's kind and considerate, and really quite handsome. He's a great warrior too, one of the Thirty.' Noting that I wasn't growing any more cheerful, she added, 'I shall come to see you whenever I can. Every day if he'll let me. But soon I'll be having my own children. I won't be able to go visiting for a while then.'

That made me still more miserable. I wandered out into the courtyard and stood alone, struggling to relearn all the old lessons I'd let myself forget.

Miriam was gathering flowers to put inside. As usual she didn't speak to me, just went on working quietly. I hung there absently, studying her grave face and graceful movements, until I felt Tamar's hands on my shoulders.

'You're growing up already yourself, Zohel,' said her mellifluous voice from behind me. 'But think twice before you set your sights on Miriam here. She's hopelessly in love with Absalom, more fool her.'

Miriam pretended not to hear, trying to hide her blushes in her hair.

'But then, they say *every* girl is in love with Absalom,' Tamar went on wickedly. 'Only Miriam is too chaste and shy to let him know it. That's why he just teases her and never pays her any proper attention. With so many doting damsels falling at his feet, why should he waste time on one playing hard to get? She'd make him happier than any of them, though.'

Miriam could take no more. She flung down her basket of flowers and turned away, silently and furiously chagrined.

Tamar laughed, but not unkindly. She could be as caustic as her mother or her brother when she wanted to be; but she would always stop when you were hurt. 'Forget him, Miriam. He's nothing but bad news. What about Zohel here? *He* has gorgeous black hair and dark eyes too.' Now I didn't know if she was serious or not. But then

45

she picked up Miriam's basket appeasingly and gave it back to her. 'I'm sorry. It's just that I hate to see love thrown away.'

They went back inside arm in arm, but I didn't go with them. I sat among the flowers, thinking: love could never be wasted on Absalom. He thrives on it, and drinks it in always, whatever its source.

But then, the rivers drink in water from the streams, and yet are never full; and I never saw water flow back the other way.

Singing was another skill which Tamar taught me. I dare say most children sing by nature, but I'd had little cause to. When Tamar sang, it made you think of grasses bowing to the breath of a soft wind, or the summer sun shining through tamarisk leaves. She'd inherited her father's gift for music, though she didn't play the harp or the flute. (David was reputed to be a master of both.) Together we sang sowing songs, and reaping songs, and hymns to Adonai.

Not that I'd had any idea at first of who this Adonai might be. I was as ignorant about religion as I was about most things; no one before had credited me with enough intelligence to comprehend it. So it was Tamar who had to explain to me that the word 'Adonai' means 'the Lord', and is used because the name of the one true God is too holy to be spoken.

Most often, though, we sang wedding songs; I think she wanted me to sing one at the feast on her own special day, for she assured me that I had a good voice.

One morning she was humming a low haunting melody, as we picked dew-misted herbs from her mother's garden.

'What's that?' I asked, enraptured.

'Henna,' she answered without troubling to look at me. 'She uses it for her nails, or to colour her hair, though Father objects to it.' Then she saw my face, and I watched hers light up, like the sky when the dawn breaks through rain. 'Oh, the song. It's lovely, isn't it? Father wrote it. It's called the Song of the Bow.'

'Does it have words then?'

'Of course.' And she sang them to me, poignant, painful words, about two great warriors called Saul and Jonathan, a father and son who had died together in battle on the slopes of Mount Gilboa.

'Who were they?' I whispered, when she came to the end.

'You really don't know?' She stared at me, disbelieving.

'I've heard their names since I came to the palace. Especially Saul's.'

'Saul was king of Israel before Father. The first king our people ever had.'

'What was he like?'

'Oh, I don't know.' Tamar flicked back her hair; she seemed to think we should get on with our work now. 'Brave, I suppose. He won many wars, and subdued many of our ancient enemies. And they say he was beautiful when he was young.'

'More than Absalom?'

She smiled. 'So I've heard. Though Father would disagree, no doubt.'

'Did he hate Saul?'

'Far from it. He was devastated when Saul and his son were killed. He's told me often; he calls it a tragedy. When Father was a boy he was a musician at Saul's court, and I think they were very close. Father used to sing and play the harp whenever Saul was depressed. His playing had the power to bind the demons that made Saul's life misery.' No doubt my mouth fell open at this, and I must have looked as though I were waiting to hear more. But she continued gathering henna. 'We're talking about things that happened before I was born, Zohel. You'll have to ask Father yourself if you want to know anything else about them.'

I giggled. The idea of my seeking an audience with the King seemed so ridiculous; then I realized that she didn't for a moment expect me to. All the same, she could see I wasn't satisfied.

'Saul and Jonathan were dead before he married Mother,' she told me finally, examining the contents of her basket and deciding we had enough. 'I should think that he and his first wife Michal are the only folk left in the palace who remember them. Michal is Saul's daughter. Perhaps you could ask her.'

We spoke no more about it, but I found myself still oddly intrigued by the song and its heroes. Perhaps it was just that the tune had been so plaintive somehow.

4

Spring hadn't yet turned to summer when the King sent for me. My heart went to my mouth, though it should have struck me at once that too much time had passed for it to be about the break-in.

Jehoshaphat ushered me directly into the throneroom. Today His Majesty was seated; not on the throne, but on a plush padded chair drawn up to a table, upon which was spread an assortment of tablets and scrolls covered in figures and diagrams. He wasn't really studying them. He glanced up at me at once, his abstracted frown revealing that something preyed on his mind. Too late I remembered I should have bowed, but he wasn't annoyed. In fact at the sight of me, the lines on his brow visibly relaxed.

'Come,' he beckoned. 'Sit down. Don't be shy.' He motioned me graciously to a couch close by his chair. This only made me more nervous still. Orders I'd learnt to cope with; polite invitations from persons of elevated authority—let alone the King himself—were something else. I perched on the edge of my seat, my fingers in my mouth like a three-year-old's. He drew them aside; his hand was firm and warm and roughened, a hand which had held a sword more often than a pen. He said, 'No doubt you weren't expecting to receive a summons quite like this. But since the first time you were brought here I haven't been able to get the image of your face out of my mind.'

I'd been nervous before. Now I was terrified. He was peering right into my eyes, and I couldn't identify the emotion behind his. He was still holding my hand, but I tore it from his grasp and sat rocking myself back and forth to calm myself down. I don't know what he must have thought of me; nor indeed whether he had any idea what I might be thinking about *him*.

'It's quite simple, Zoheleth,' he soothed me. 'You remind me of someone. Someone who was my friend, long ago. I have to ask you, and you must tell me: are you the son of Mephibosheth?'

I shook my head slowly. As of old, I didn't trust myself to speak.

'Are you telling me the truth? No one is going to hurt you.'

I finally managed to blurt at him that my father's name was Merib, but then my mouth dried out and my tongue turned to fur and I couldn't say anything else.

He put a hand to his forehead, where all the lines had suddenly crowded back. He began muttering that Maacah was right, he'd been working too hard. He hadn't been sleeping, and now his aching eyes were playing tricks on him; he was truly going the way Saul had.

I don't suppose he'd have let himself say any of this if he'd imagined me capable of comprehending it. But all at once a swell of pity rushed over me, and I tried to smile. At first I wished I hadn't; it seemed to disturb him even more. Then Jehoshaphat reappeared, and told him that Michal was requesting an audience.

'Michal?' he repeated distractedly. 'But it must be weeks, months even ... Very well, Jehoshaphat. Show her in.'

While the herald moved to obey, the King scraped the scrolls into a pile and deposited them on my couch. But he said nothing to me, and gave no indication as to whether I was to stay or go. This latest development had plainly driven all thought of me from his head. Too embarrassed to move, I huddled where I was, chewing a cushion.

A woman roughly Maacah's age came in. Her face was painted like Maacah's too, but whereas my mistress's make-up was never less than immaculate, Michal's looked as if neither she nor her maidservants ordinarily bothered with such things these days, and had somewhere lost the skill of them. She and the King stood face to face, stiff and awkward.

So I sat there gawking while they groped for words and traded platitudes, and said they wished they could see more of one another, which patently wasn't true. David in particular seemed to want the interview over, but Michal was wheedling, cajoling, stalling, steering the conversation gradually to what she'd come to say. Finally she got there; and told the King she'd come to ask permission to take over the care of Mephibosheth.

My attention had been wandering, but the name pulled me up sharp. Earlier that same day, it would have meant nothing to me. Now I'd heard it twice.

'He's my nephew after all,' she maintained, while the King grew increasingly suspicious. 'You think I don't care, don't you? You're just wondering what I'm up to. You think I only ever really cared about myself. I loved you once, David. And I loved Jonathan. His son is all I have left, having no son of my own.' Even I could see the reproach she harboured in her eyes.

Her husband said, 'We have servants to do this kind of work, Michal. You are the daughter and wife of kings.'

'And much good has it brought me! What matter who my father was and who my husband is, if I live the life of a hermit and see no one from one Shabbat to the next? Mephibosheth might have been king instead of you if things had gone as they were meant to. And I'm expected to sit back and see him treated like an object of charity.'

She didn't raise her voice, but her eyes spat fire. David regarded her intently for a while; perhaps he too thought about what might have been. Then he said, 'Just as you please. You have my permission.' He folded his arms, waiting for her to go, but she didn't move.

'There was something else too—my lord.'

'Something else?'

'Concerning your—new wife. The one they call Bathsheba.'

David growled, 'Yes? What about her?'

'There have been—stories, my lord. Rumours of—liaisons. I thought that you should be aware ... Nothing specific, you understand. It isn't my place to name names. It's not even my business to know, I can see that, and you'll grant I've never been one for gossip ... But for the sake of the love I once bore you, I couldn't bear to think of you being the last person to hear. I'd never want to see you made to look a fool, David.'

David didn't respond. He didn't even blink. But his silence and his stillness chilled my soul. A storm cloud massed around him, all but visible; and yet he seemed as much its victim as its creator. I wished with all my heart that I wasn't there; none of this should have been for my ears. All the same, I was unable to believe that Michal could have failed to take account of my presence. Only much later did I come to grasp that she didn't care about it. On the contrary, she'd *wanted* me to hear. Me, and as many other people as she could find an excuse to tell.

I felt horribly conspicuous huddled up on David's couch, and though to move would expose me further, I couldn't stay still any longer. Snakelike as my name, I slid noiselessly to the floor and crawled for cover behind the dais where the throne stood. David and Michal had fallen to arguing now, and both their voices were shrilling. I couldn't tell if the King was railing at Michal, at the absent Bathsheba, or at himself. But I was fairly sure that he would vent his wrath upon me once his wife had left, if he thought I'd been listening on purpose.

On the dais close by my shoulder, his harp lay wrapped in its mantle. I lifted the fabric aside, and pretended to be engrossed in studying the instrument which I'd already heard so much talk of. Then I made myself study it properly, to take my mind off the shouting. It was an exquisite thing, crafted lovingly from cypress wood. I was unable to resist stretching out my fingers and stroking it. The taut strings felt as thin and sharp against my skin as shards of glass.

So I jumped for my life when David turned on me like a she-wolf whose cubs are threatened, yelling, 'What do you think you're doing! Don't you dare touch that!' A moment later I was cowering in a corner, one thumb clamped between my teeth, my other hand tearing desperately at the roots of my hair.

It took him a considerable while to coax me out. Michal was gone and we were alone, but I was shaking from head to foot, and he was white with shock. He was shocked at what he'd just done to me—I know that, because he said so. But I think he was even more shocked at the thought of what must have made me the way I was. Neither encounter I'd had with the King so far boded well for the building of a friendship; yet both of us knew that the other was hurting, and in spite of everything, trust was growing.

'I'm sorry, Zoheleth,' he said, taking the harp in his arms. 'I didn't mean to do that. Here.' He held his priceless treasure out for me to handle, then thrust it to my breast and let me hold it for myself. At first I just stared incredulous at his expectant face, then I wrapped one arm around the frame and brushed my fingers across the strings: softly, reverently, entranced by the broken silver chords that shivered up and down like ghosts playing among pine trees.

Before I had time to grasp what he was doing, David was down on his knees right beside me. There he was on the floor: the King of Israel in his gold-bordered robe, kneeling with a damaged waif of a boy who until so recently had been no better than a beggar. But he seemed profoundly moved by the way I riffled the strings, my gentleness, my natural sensitivity, the delicacy of my touch, the whole way I handled this precious instrument which had glorified God Almighty, and charmed the troubled Saul.

So when David asked me if I'd like to learn to make real music, I knew it was nothing so sentimental as guilt or pity prompting his offer.

That's how, for a while, I came to spend as much time with His Majesty as I did with Maacah or her children. On the third occasion that he sent for me, Maacah demanded to know what was going on.

I said, 'He's started teaching me the harp. He says I've a gift and it shouldn't be wasted.'

She stood with her hands on her hips and looked sideways down her nose at me. 'So he can't spare the time to eat a crust of bread in my apartment, but somehow he can find enough to entertain you.'

'I shan't go any more if it displeases you, my lady.'

'No, no. You're a freeborn Israelite, not my slave. It's not you that I have a quarrel with.'

For several weeks I saw the King twice or three times between Sabbaths. Before the second one, he gave me a harp of my own. I couldn't believe that he meant me to keep it. I owned nothing in the world, not even my clothes. But he said I must practise between my lessons, and I'd already deduced that he was gaining as much from teaching me as I was from learning.

Despite what Maacah and Absalom said, David never appeared to be busy. Rather, he was broody and morose, and the only thing that occupied him seemed to be examining the scrolls with the numbers and drawings. Even these he always put away when I arrived. He explained that they were plans for a great temple to Adonai, and that one day he would build it, when the time was right.

There was no mistaking the fact that our sessions restored his spirit. He spent his days pestered by courtiers and captains, counsellors and clerics, the vast majority of whom were out more or less blatantly to feather their own nests. I never met any of them personally, except one; David always gave orders that we were not to be interrupted, and not even the likes of Joab dared disobey. Only Ahithophel apparently considered himself grand enough to ride roughshod over the King's express wishes, and Jehoshaphat was too in awe of him to interfere.

I'd barely had time to unfold my harp from its wrappings the first time he intruded on us. A dignified, elderly nobleman, fastidiously dressed, with precisely trimmed beard and meticulously symmetrical turban, he barely looked at me, yet at the same time succeeded in communicating his utter contempt for my presence.

Without requesting permission to speak, and with the merest hint of a bow, he informed the King that he'd been going through the accounts of the reparations paid by the Ammonites consequent upon our vanquishing of Rabbah, and that certain figures were found not to be in order. David made his displeasure plain enough, and suggested that surely this might wait until later. But Ahithophel persevered undaunted, and presented the relevant lists of calculations for David to inspect. David sighed heavily, and bade me come back again tomorrow.

In contrast to Ahithophel and his colleagues I was a breath of clear mountain air to the King. He could never in a thousand years have suspected me of bootlicking or intriguing.

'You're so innocent, Zohel,' he would beam at me, using my pet name and squeezing my shoulders. I would grin back at him, with no idea what he meant. I'd only heard the word 'innocent' when Ziba used it; he'd often said, 'Don't try to look innocent at me,' so I'd thought it meant 'good', and David certainly knew I wasn't that.

As my playing improved, he began to teach me the songs that they used in the Tabernacle. Of course I'd never been there, but Tamar had told me of the bands of virtuoso musicians and the glorious choirs who constantly strove to outdo one another in the praise of Adonai. I learned new words and melodies quickly, and once they were fixed in my mind I seldom forgot them. David said that my memory was exceptional, and as precious a gift as my musical ear.

But I always found it easy to recall the Tabernacle songs, because they gave me so much pleasure. Some of them were noisily exultant, others serene and contemplative, bathing your soul in light. It was these quiet ones that I liked best. I would close my eyes and play by touch and instinct when I practised; the beauty of the music would lift me out of myself, so that I was lost to my surroundings and basking in a warm dew of peace which settled upon me. I was amazed that music alone could possess such power and exercise so profound an effect upon my feelings, especially when I was used to keeping them locked away in secret inside me. And to think that it was my own inexperienced fingers coaxing the chords from the harpstrings, and my own thin, childish voice carrying the tune!

But something more wonderful than usual happened, the first time I lost myself in music like that in front of David.

I hadn't meant to let myself go. But the ebb and flow of the melody and the fervency of the words gave my soul wings, and my fingers played on of themselves while I felt to be floating out of my body on a bright cloud of joy. Even while it was happening, I started to see that it wasn't the music alone which was moving me. The piece I was playing was an ancient psalm composed in the time of the great prophet Moses, when the faith of Israel was fresh and raw, and holy men needed to be thoroughly immersed in the divine if they expected to acquire the charisma to make people follow them. These holy men had breathed the very breath of Adonai into their hymns, and woven into them spiritual power of mystic intensity. I wasn't merely performing; I was worshipping. In fact, presently I wasn't performing at all—at some point I had laid my harp aside, and the music I was hearing in my heart was from another world.

Then a shadow passed across my shimmering sunlight; my eyes came open, and there was the King with his hands upon my head, praying in some language from heaven and watching me with a joy equal to mine.

'Don't stop,' he whispered. 'Adonai is doing something miraculous inside you. Let him fill you. This is beautiful.' I allowed myself to drift off again, floating, gliding, windborn. It was utterly unlike me to relinquish control in front of anyone for any reason; normally I found it hard enough even to go to sleep with someone else in the room. But this was right, and I knew it. And I began to understand how David's music could have mollified Saul's demons. I passed through visions and tears and laughter; there was heat coursing through my body, a buoyant love bubbling up in my heart. When I came back to myself I was lying on the couch, and I'd never felt so free in all my life.

'You're very special, Zohel,' David said. 'Adonai has something unique in store for you.'

I searched his face for a clue as to his meaning. The joy was still there, but it was fading, and now there was a hazy regret mixed up with it, a faintly disoriented yearning, as for a dream lost and forgotten with the coming of morning. I asked, 'Something unique? How do you know?'

He didn't answer me directly. Instead he plied me with questions of his own, to which he already seemed to know what I would say in reply. Yes, there had always been heavy doses of danger and despair in my short existence; yes, when in trouble I had always prayed to someone, though I didn't know to whom, and I wouldn't have called it praying; yes, I'd always been able to sense atmospheres, and often to understand things about people which I'd never been told. And yes, I'd often found comfort somewhere deep within myself when I was lonely.

David said, 'You need never be lonely again, Zohel. You're a Shining One; one of the Few. Adonai has chosen you, and revealed himself to you, as surely as he did to Moses, who came down from Sinai so radiant that no one could look at him. Now you've given yourself over fully to him, now you know what power it is you're dealing with—there's no way your life can be the same any more.'

In my head I didn't understand, but my heart knew he was speaking truth.

'You'll be a different person,' he explained further. 'In fact I shall give you a new name, to show it. From now on between us you'll be Zohar, not Zohel. Zohar means Brightness. I can see it in your eyes. I tell you, Adonai has marked you out for a special task.'

Momentarily my head got the better of my heart. I said, 'But you could have done that for anyone. Put your hands on whoever's head you chose, or passed on the spirit of Adonai to *everyone* if you cared to.'

David shook his head. 'One day, they say, everyone will know Adonai for himself if he wants to, when the world is ready. But not yet. I could only release his spirit in you because I already saw it at work.'

'So who else in the palace knows God like this?' I enquired dubiously.

'Just us, and Nathan the prophet, who is here sometimes.'

'Is that all? Not even Tamar, or Absalom?'

'Tamar loves Adonai very much, that I know. But I'm not sure that Absalom even believes in him. Not single-mindedly anyway. Maacah made her promises about his upbringing, but he can see into his mother's heart as well as I can. He's always been closer to her than Tamar has.'

I lay back among the cushions, gazing at the high panelled ceiling, inwardly feeling for the first time in my life that perhaps I had a right to be accepted somewhere, to belong. I said, 'And only a few people have ever known Adonai? Just Moses and Joshua, and the judges and the prophets?'

David said quietly, 'Saul did.'

Saul! The name seemed to hang between us in the silence.

When the time came for me to leave, David told me to come next time with a harp accompaniment worked out for a song of my own choosing. He said, 'Choose carefully, Zohar. Try to find one that means something to you. You must never squander your gift on empty trifles that don't reach the soul.'

So I had Tamar teach me the Song of the Bow. It was beautiful, and I knew David had written it. Tamar copied the words onto a tablet for me, and I sang them with her until I had them by heart. I spent many days composing and perfecting the part for the harp, for I didn't want to go back to the King until I could perform the whole piece without faltering.

Meanwhile I was too engrossed even to notice that the bad dreams had stopped, I could last a night without waking, and my bed was no longer wet in the mornings.

On one occasion Absalom heard me practising, and taunted me for letting his father indoctrinate me with pious nonsense.

'You're like Michal, Absalom,' Tamar retorted, springing to my defence. 'They say that's why Father doesn't visit her any more. She even mocked him when he danced before the Ark of Adonai's presence.'

Absalom shrugged all this off, with a characteristic toss of his long hair; it simply didn't occur to me that he might be jealous.

Over the next few days, Absalom's attitude began to disturb me more and more. While I worked on my song, the seeds of doubt he'd tried to sow in my spirit took root; while the forefront of my mind was occupied with chord patterns and poetry, the back was filling up with questions. *Had* I been right to throw open the gates of my soul in front of another person? *Had* I exposed myself too rashly to forces I didn't understand? Surely it was important for me to remain in charge, to hold onto the reins of my life with all my strength lest like one of Absalom's horses it should go careering out of control . . . ?

When finally the song was ready, for the first time ever on my own initiative I asked Jehoshaphat for an appointment with the King.

But as soon as I went in, something warned me that my timing was wrong. David was alone, and he wasn't busy, but he appeared harassed and distant. I told him what I'd come for, and he made an effort to smile at me. I did think about saying I would come back later, but foolishly decided that maybe I had the power now to lift his spirit to heaven, however low it had sunk, just as David himself in his youth had done for Saul. Perhaps this was even the ministry to which Adonai was calling me. I suppose I'd forgotten that never before had I visited His Majesty when he hadn't given himself time to prepare fully to receive me.

I hadn't got much beyond the first line when he started weeping. At a loss for what to do, I ploughed on doggedly to the end while he sobbed like a little child, his war-weathered hands pressed against his eyelids.

Suddenly he reminded me of my pathetic snivelling father. All the bad memories came flooding back, and all the fears, and I thought: he's going mad. Without question the King of Israel is losing his sanity. He may well be the anointed ruler of the Chosen People of God, and he may well know Adonai like a father, but what use has any of that been to him, if he hasn't been kept from *this*? No wonder he sees less and less of my mistress, of Absalom and Tamar, and of Michal and Abigail too, as far as I can gather. He ought not to be seen by *anyone*; and certainly not by me. There has been enough sorrow in my life already. I don't want to stay in a place where there is more.

The moment I'd struck the last chord, I threw down my harp and fled. I think David called out to me not to go, but I'd made up my mind: I would spend as much time as I could with Absalom and his friends from this day on. They were always laughing, they never let cares or responsibilities weigh them down. There would be no more harp lessons, no more playing with the fire of Adonai. My fingers were already burned.

5

Just before the corn was due to be harvested, swarms of locusts swept in from the deserts. Almost the entire crop was devoured or poisoned; what could be salvaged was scarcely enough to feed one of the twelve tribes of the Israelite nation for a month. Arrangements were made to buy grain from Egypt; this was no particular problem because Israel was comfortably rich on the proceeds of her foreign wars. But the thing worried David—out of all proportion, or so it seemed then.

It drove him to visit Maacah for the first time in ages. I hid myself in my room, though from behind the half-drawn curtain I could see and hear well enough what went on. Tamar and Absalom were there too, squabbling good-naturedly as usual, until David came in.

He accepted wine straight away, and said that to expiate Saul's crime, the Gibeonites had demanded blood for blood.

'And whose blood exactly do they want?' queried Absalom.

'They haven't made that clear. Not yet. They say they must consult their gods. Presumably they'll want one or more of Saul's descendants—but I only know of Michal and Mephibosheth. How can I hand over members of my own household to idolaters?'

'Father, you can't,' said Tamar. 'They must be protected.'

But David demurred, draining his wine to the dregs. 'Nathan says I must. Only blood *can* atone for blood. Otherwise the locusts will come next year too, and the year after. Who can say how many lives will be lost then? Even Ahithophel thinks it would be—"expedient" to accede to the Gibeonites' demands. The King must show himself willing to sacrifice his own personal concerns for the good of his people.'

Maacah said, 'There must be other carriers of Saul's seed you can hand over instead. All kings have their women. Jerusalem must be crawling with his bastards and their progeny.'

'Saul wasn't that kind of king,' David chided her, and he sounded more burdened than ever.

'But the Gibeonites aren't to know that,' said Absalom, with a sideways smile. 'Make a few—enquiries. Dredge up a few characters of dubious ancestry who you wouldn't mind being rid of.'

'I should think your cronies Shimei and Sheba might be the ideal candidates,' Maacah returned wryly. 'You're always boasting about their connections with the house of Saul.'

David ground his teeth. 'It's not the Gibeonites we have to satisfy.'

Maacah poured more wine all round. 'Personally I can't see why you're objecting so strongly to being rid of Michal and Mephibosheth. Michal has done nothing but find reasons to despise you for years, and Mephibosheth is just a drain on your resources. You'd be more secure without them in any case. When my father took the throne of Geshur he wiped out the whole of the deposed royal household within a month. It's only prudent.'

Tamar exclaimed, 'Mother! What a dreadful thing to say. As if those two poor creatures could ever pose any threat to Father.'

'The only impotent Saulide is a dead one,' Maacah said stiffly. 'Kings cannot afford to be mawkish.'

'No doubt Ahithophel would agree with you.' David was well into his second cup of wine by now. 'Not to mention Joab and Abishai. But it isn't Adonai's way. It shouldn't be necessary. Besides, I made a statement in front of all my counsellors that Mephibosheth would be allowed to live out the full course of his life in peace. And I gave my word to Saul, the last time I ever saw him, that I wouldn't let his line be cut off.'

Absalom prevaricated, 'Anyhow, this whole thing could be a coincidence. The locusts coming now, I mean, fitting in with Nathan's prophecy so neatly. Why not play for time, see what happens?'

'I wish you were right,' David murmured wanly; then fervently: 'Oh *God*, how I wish you were right.'

His unexpected vehemence shook everyone. Somehow I suspected that the famine couldn't be the real reason why Nathan's prophetic gift disturbed David so profoundly.

Trying to change the subject, Tamar asked, 'How is Bathsheba? Abigail says she still isn't well.'

Of course this only made things worse; Tamar was perplexed, but then she hadn't heard what I'd heard from Michal. David finished his second goblet and reached for the jug himself this time, but was more fuddled than he knew, and almost knocked it over. Maacah wisely put it out of his reach, whilst he muttered about how worried he was on Bathsheba's account. Tamar took him to mean that the girl's illness was worse than we'd thought. She announced, 'I *shall* go to visit her. I don't care what anyone says.'

David looked as though he might be sick at any moment, but I was sure it wasn't the wine. His mumbling was becoming increasingly incoherent, but he seemed to be saying that Bathsheba didn't want any contact with his other wives or their families; it put her under too much pressure.

'Yes, I can understand that,' Tamar acknowledged after a moment's reflection. 'Of course she's not used to the idea of sharing her husband. She wasn't brought up to the life of a royal harem. But someone must get through to her, for her own sanity. Perhaps I'll send Zohel to call on her, with some of my little cakes. There's no way she could feel threatened by him. He can tell her I'd like to come myself, and we'll just take things on from there.'

I could see that the mention of my name disturbed David, and I knew he was looking round for me, but I was safe enough for now because it seemed that he'd drunk enough to cloud his vision. Absalom, fond though he was of such pleasures himself, looked vaguely disgusted, and I found myself once again thinking him so much more regal than his father. The affection and respect I'd been nurturing for David over recent weeks, until the day I'd run away from him, seemed to have withered beyond revival.

The following day, Tamar and I baked a batch of her heart-shaped cakes, and I was sent with them to Bathsheba.

I started out with mingled apprehension and excitement; Absalom called after me, 'Tell my lady that *I'll* be glad to visit her too, if she's in need of cheering up!'

'Absalom!' scolded Maacah, in her half-indulgent outraged-parent voice, and Tamar was giggling. But right outside the door I ran into Amnon and Jonadab loitering, and almost dropped my basket. I'm not sure which of us was disconcerted the most. I froze.

'Is the princess Tamar at home?' Jonadab began, swallowing, and making a passable attempt at regaining his composure. This was more than could be said for Amnon, who looked pasty-faced and petrified. 'My lord would like to speak with her,' Jonadab added lamely, but this for some reason sent Amnon into a paroxysm of coughing.

'No,' I lied. 'No, she isn't here,' and I set off at a run down the passageway.

Bathsheba's rooms lay off the main courtyard of the women's quarters. Most of the other women kept their doors unlocked and unguarded, and they would be in and out of each other's chambers all the time, with each other's children squealing and squawking amongst their skirts. Bathsheba's door was firmly closed, with a formidable negro slave woman planted outside it. But the woman must have judged me pretty, or reckoned that her mistress would, and she let me in.

David's youngest wife was reclining listlessly on a couch, with attendants fanning her face and feet, others polishing her nails, mixing scents or bringing trays of cosmetics for her to appraise. And young she certainly was. Without her veil I could see she wasn't so much older than Absalom, and he was right about her beauty. The flimsy robe she was wearing left little of it to the imagination. She was slender, fine boned, silken haired, pale skinned and pouting. The listlessness aside, however, she gave no sign of being ill. Her cheeks had colour, her eyes were bright, and although she was made up heavily I doubted she would look much worse without it. By the way she sized me up and spat me out with one sweep of her thickened lashes, I would have guessed at once who her grandfather was.

Stricken mute as I'd ever been, all I could do was hold out the basket of cakes towards her. She waved one of her girls forward to examine it more closely, then demanded, 'Who has sent this? Whose slave are you?'

I wanted to deposit the present and run, but all at once couldn't bear to let Tamar down again. Somehow I managed to gibber, 'It's a gift from the Princess. She heard that you were ill.'

'The Syrian sorceress's whelp!' exclaimed Bathsheba, tipping back her head to laugh. This gesture was calculated to set all her servants laughing with her. 'Well, I *am* privileged. How touching. So you must be the poor little orphan, the creature David calls Zohar.'

At the back of my neck the hairs were bristling. It would have agitated me enough to hear the King speak that name now; but to hear it on *her* lips was like tasting poison. And it incensed me to think of David talking to someone like her about me. Apart from my private name, what else might he have told her?

'Now there's no need to be so bashful,' she said, bidding me come up closer, and even as she did so one of her attendants propelled me forward, until the cloying tide of Bathsheba's perfume engulfed me. 'Come, sit down here beside me and have one of these delightful little cakes yourself. By the look of you, your new owners can't be feeding you very well.'

Blinded by the red of my anger, I didn't realize why she was all of a sudden acting so generously; not until I was installed amongst her pillows, one of the cakes was inside me, and she said, 'Well, that's a relief at least. One can't be too careful in times like these. It was uncanny the way my poor sick child grew so much worse after the Syrian had been here.' But she still didn't eat a cake herself. She prized the basket from my hands, touching me lingeringly with her long-nailed fingers as she did so, and gave it to one of the servants. I resolved that I would deliver my message and get out.

I gabbled, 'Tamar would like to visit you, if you would allow her. She's worried you might be lonely.'

'How thoughtful,' Bathsheba drawled. 'But I think not. We want no acolytes of the goddess Asherah here... Oh, I do beg your pardon. *Astarte*, isn't that what they call her in Syrian Aramaic? Still, you may thank the gracious—Princess for her concern.'

Then trying, but failing, to inch away from her debilitating closeness, I blurted out, 'Absalom says he'd like to come too.'

I can't think why I was foolish enough to say that; except that by now I was so embarrassed and desperate to make my escape that I might have said anything, if I'd thought it likely to distract her attention from me. It worked.

'Absalom.' She savoured the syllables, turning them around her tongue as though they were some rich exotic sweetmeat. 'Now this is much more interesting. I suppose I might be persuaded to overlook the maternal ancestry of one so well spoken of by his father. Tell me: is he as charming as he is handsome?'

I replied, 'Absalom is very kind. He's concerned about you, like Tamar is.'

I knew that wasn't what she wanted to hear; I also knew that it wasn't strictly true. But it was suddenly all I was prepared to tell her. I felt to be running on quicksand.

'Well, you may inform him that his *kindness* has not gone unrecognized. He may hear from me in due course. Now, you had better be on your way before they start wondering whether I've eaten you.'

Barely convinced that she hadn't, I beat a thoroughly grateful retreat. The young widow of Uriah might be half Maacah's age, and weigh half as much, and have half her knowledge and experience, but I felt sure she was twice as dangerous.

Bathsheba perhaps didn't appreciate Tamar's cakes, but there were plenty of folk in Jerusalem who pretty soon would have done. According to official propaganda, ample supplies of corn had been imported, and this was supposed to be distributed to the people in return for nominal payment. But it was beginning to be evident that those without power or influence were being charged a rather less nominal sum than their more esteemed brethren. Those who had somehow incurred the displeasure of the administrators were apt to be turned away empty handed. On the city streets the first signs of hardship appeared: the skinny children with bloated bellies, and the able-bodied reduced to begging alongside the maimed and the blind. Out in the country, stocks of quality fodder for the livestock were running low, and precious cattle were having to be slaughtered. Behind the scenes the men muttered, whilst the women eked out their rations as best they could.

Meanwhile, we didn't see Absalom for weeks. Messages sent to his apartment elicited no response, and even Shimei and Sheba were unable, or else unwilling, to shed any light on his elusiveness. At length Maacah sent me, with a letter written on a sealed tablet, to pay him a visit in the middle of the night. She got me up out of bed to do it, shaking me impatiently as I tried to avoid having to rub the sleep from my eyes, and when I moaned out my resentment, she said it was an emergency.

He wasn't in.

Still only half awake, I reported my discovery to Maacah in some consternation. But she only said, 'As I thought,' from between gritted teeth, and let me go back to bed.

The following evening I was sent to wait outside his quarters in hiding, with instructions to follow him assiduously if he were to come out. I asked Maacah, 'Where's the tablet? Don't I have to take that?'

'No,' she answered. 'The tablet isn't important. But I want you to take this amulet in case you have to go out of the palace gates. Show it to the guards and they'll know you're on my business.'

Each of the King's five eldest sons—the ones born in Hebron—

had suites of rooms on the same storey as the harem, but at the opposite end of the palace complex. I'd been to Absalom's often, and knew the best place to conceal myself, where there was cover from the pillars of the colonnade which gave access to his hallway. It was a while since I'd had occasion to practise my skills of stealth and secrecy, but they were too well ingrained in me to be forgotten. I crouched in the shadows, my eyes pinned to Absalom's door. Darkness fell, and a slave came by kindling lamps, but he didn't see me.

Towards midnight Maacah's son emerged. He stood in a pool of yellow lamplight glancing this way and that along the colonnade. His hair was curled and gold-dusted, there were rings in his ears and patches of colour around his eyes, and I could smell his scent from five spearlengths away.

Unobserved I tailed him back to the harem. Bathsheba came out swathed in a welter of dark robes, with a heavy veil thrown around her head, but I would have known her anywhere. She slipped something into the hand of the fat eunuch, and then drew her veil back just far enough to kiss Absalom lightly on the lips.

They left the palace by an obscure side gate I hadn't known was there. It must hardly ever have been used, because there was only one sentry on duty, and he was asleep; I marvelled that our two separate sorties shouldn't have woken him. But I hadn't yet grasped how far the web of Bathsheba's influence spread, nor what crafts her underlings were adept in. I didn't need Maacah's amulet.

The streets were deserted, but there was a strong moon, and merciless shafts of blue-white light thrust among the jumble of mudbrick houses. Absalom and Bathsheba walked briskly but not furtively. Presumably it was only to be expected that the King's most eligible son should be seen abroad at night furthering his education, whatever the Law of Moses might have to say on the subject, and his discreetly camouflaged companion might have been a willing tutor from any one of the less reputable women's establishments in Jerusalem.

It was when they slunk into the house which Bathsheba had once shared with Uriah that I decided it wasn't safe to follow them any further. They used another small side entrance; the main one was barred up, and the lattice windows all had boards hammered over them. Even the door they went in by had had its hinges disabled and would only open a little way. Creepers had begun to finger their way across it, and these the couple were careful not to dislodge. Once inside, they could have lit a hundred torches and not been detected, but I don't suppose they felt the need for any.

Next day, Maacah sent for Shimei and Sheba and threatened to have them denounced to David as Saulide sympathizers if they didn't find Absalom immediately and deliver him to her.

I can't imagine why this should have worried them; David had for a long time been perfectly well aware of who his son's friends were related to, and thus of where their political sympathies would most probably lie—if they had enough intelligence to possess any. But he had never shown the slightest inclination to take action against them.

In truth I think Maacah herself frightened them more than her threats did; I could almost smell their sweat as they grovelled, and babbled their simpering promises to do their best on her behalf.

I couldn't help agreeing with Maacah that Absalom might have been a little more discriminating in his choice of friends. Shimei was small and scrawny, a vortex of nervous energy and volatile temper. His eyes were small in keeping with the rest of him, and febrile, and they never looked at any one thing for more than a few seconds. When he spoke to you, they never looked at you at all. He was so highly-strung that the enormous quantities of drink he consumed hadn't yet fattened him.

This was by no means the case with Sheba. He was overweight and over-oiled in every sense, with lank greasy hair and a shadow of adolescent beard; his breath smelt of wine and garlic, and he always appeared vaguely disorientated and dissatisfied, as if there would be much more to his personality if he could ever sober up enough to discover what it was.

But whatever hidden qualities these two likely lads might possess, they were no match for Maacah's. By noon Absalom was standing to attention before his mother, straight-backed and quivering with indignation, and for the first time there was no half-smothered indulgence in the anger she unleashed on him.

'Absalom, have you taken leave of the last mortal remains of your senses?' she demanded, springing from her couch and pacing up and down in front of him like a lioness strutting before her prey.

Absalom tossed back his hair in flagrant effrontery. His face was flushed and his eyes glittered. 'Mother, I am sixteen years old! Man enough to take up arms and watch wretched Ammonite worms squirm on the end of my spear; man enough to take life! Doesn't that make me man enough to take a woman if she wants me to?'

'A woman?' screamed Maacah. 'That's all you see her as: a woman? By all the gods in heaven, Absalom, she's your father's wife! And as far as he's concerned, it would break his heart to know you'd been with her even if she *was* just any woman! You know the Torah as well as anyone.'

'The Torah, now, is it? And since when has the Torah meant any more than a heap of hot camel dung to you? Oh yes, you'll quote chapter and verse when it suits you, but you'd use every scroll of it as fuel for your heathen sacrifices if you didn't think you'd be flogged in public for it.'

'How dare you speak to your mother like that! I can't believe I've bred anything so monstrous! How can I have deserved it? You're playing with fire, Absalom, and you'll be burnt to ashes! You're my son, for God's sake! Do you think I want to see you ruined?'

'I can't see what you're afraid of. Do you suppose he'll expose her as an adulteress and have her stoned? I doubt it. Somehow I don't think I'm her first. He must already know what she gets up to as soon as his back is turned. He's hardly likely to advertise the fact that she's cuckolded him.'

'Absalom!'

'Well he isn't, is he? And if he *did* have her disposed of, I don't suppose *you'd* mind for a moment.'

Momentarily rendered speechless, Maacah lashed Absalom across the face with the back of her hand. Stunned in more ways than one, he walked backwards into a chair and sat down, shamed and seething. Horrified now at what her fury had made her do to her precious child, and at the torrid red marks her fingers had left on his beardless cheek, Maacah lowered herself unsteadily onto her couch and stared at Absalom in dismay. I could see she thought him appallingly beautiful in his rebellion; and perhaps for the first time she truly did begin to see the man within the boy. When at last she spoke again, her anger had dissolved, her horror had been mastered, and a quiet determination had come in place of both.

'There is no need for me to be jealous of Bathsheba, Absalom. I'm the only woman David has ever loved, the only one who's ever been strong enough for him. She is nothing. Oh, a pretty face perhaps, and a supple young body, but no more. It's you I'm afraid for, you crazy fool, though you're too stubborn to see it.'

Absalom didn't reply straight away. He looked out of the window; he looked at the furniture and the vases of flowers; as Shimei might have done, he looked anywhere but at his mother's face. But in the end he just said, 'Perhaps you *are* the one wife he truly loves. But am I not his dearest son? He's not going to let *me* be put to death.'

Maacah fixed him with a gaze which was at the same time so exasperated and so woebegone that he was forced to meet her eyes. She said, 'That's the whole point, Absalom. He loves you so much, he'd be utterly devastated if he thought you were capable of deceiving him like this. He thinks the world of you.'

Absalom snorted. He might have considered himself old enough to make war and to make love, but he wasn't too old to sulk. With a petulant droop of the shoulders he muttered, 'It's months since we talked. I told you, I never see him. I've been deluding myself for far too long about my special status, and so have you. Oh, I was special to him once, I know. But he doesn't care a fig for me any more.'

A sick look passed across Maacah's face and made her suddenly seem older. For all at once I saw she knew that, in his heart of hearts, Absalom *wanted* David to find out about him and Bathsheba. Maacah whispered, 'But suppose David has no choice, Absalom? Suppose you leave him no option but to have you executed, whether he wants to or not?'

'I—don't know what you mean.'

'Oh, Absalom, do I have to spell it out to you? Suppose you get her with child? Are you going to try to pretend it's *his*, and attach a chain of cheap and cruel lies to your betrayal? Suppose he finds out the truth about *that* as well? He says she's so ill . . . perhaps he really *believes* she is; maybe he's not even sleeping with her! What happens then? Do you really think men like Nathan would let you live if you were known to have gotten a child on your own father's wife? That meddlesome prophet and his fanatical followers would have you torn limb from limb and the pieces thrown to the dogs.'

Absalom took a long, deep breath. He said, 'I don't think there's any danger of that, Mother.'

'Oh? And what makes you so sure?'

'Bathsheba is with child again already. By the King.'

6

It was noon, midsummer; the hottest time of day, and the hottest time of the year. Maacah and Tamar sat side by side on a bench in the shadiest corner of our secluded courtyard, heads bowed together, earnestly reviewing final arrangements for the wedding which was due to take place within the fortnight.

Miriam and I waited in attendance, though there was precious little left for us to do, and Abigail had taken Eliada and Eliphelet to market to choose their own gifts for the bride and groom. Miriam was weaving long chains of flowers and practising braiding them into her own hair, ready for the great day. Drowsy with heat and idleness, I was picking blossoms I thought looked pretty together and offering them to her, smiling and watching her unashamedly when she would let me get away with it.

Every so often, snatches of Maacah and Tamar's conversation would penetrate my reverie, such as when they began talking of the wedding night and wondering aloud how soon it would be before Tamar was with child. I had to bite back the jealousy; the thought of losing Tamar was once again pricking like a needle in my heart. Then I was ashamed of myself for being so selfish, when Tamar hinted at her fears for the future if for some reason she couldn't conceive. 'It would be awful to end up lonely and bitter like Michal,' she said sadly. 'Though they say she's been better lately for having Mephibosheth to take care of.'

'They say Mephibosheth has been better too,' Maacah added; then I heard a knocking from inside the house, and ran through to see who was at the door.

It was Jonadab, alone. I took a step backwards involuntarily, then recovered myself enough to lead him out to the courtyard. He bowed low before Maacah and Tamar, then explained with a tremor in his voice that he had brought bad news, and had a favour to ask of them.

'What is it? Whatever has happened?' Maacah made Jonadab sit down on the bench between her and her daughter.

'It's Amnon. He's been taken ill. His father has been to see him and he's very worried. That's why he sent me here. Amnon hasn't touched food for three days, and now he's too weak to get up.'

'Poor Amnon,' Maacah sympathized. It was not an altogether sincere reply, I felt. But she did ask, 'Well what can we do?'

'His Majesty tried to find out from Amnon if there was something he could get for him, to make him feel better... some delicacy perhaps, to restore his appetite. Amnon said the only thing he might be able to face eating was one of the honey cakes Tamar used to bake for him when he was a boy.'

Maacah raised her eyebrows. 'A strange craving indeed. Don't you think it would be more useful if I came and had a look at him? I might be able to prescribe something to cure him, never mind make him *feel* better. I seem to remember you were keen enough to take advantage of my skills the last time Amnon was in need of a little— medicinal assistance.'

'Please, my lady, don't make light of this.' Jonadab seized Maacah's hand so suddenly that she started. 'He's been delirious all morning,' he continued, turning to Tamar, and his voice was much steadier now. I began to be suspicious: could he really be enjoying the effect he was creating? 'He keeps rambling about his happy childhood, how you all used to be such close friends. Perhaps if you could just bake him a few of those cakes, or even just one, to comfort him and convince him everything could be as good as that again, it would bring him round. And if it didn't, well, at least he might die at peace.'

'Die?' Tamar caught his free hand in hers. 'Has it truly come to that?'

'I'm afraid so, my lady.' Jonadab let his head droop onto his chest.

Tamar, the colour draining from her face, said she would bake some cakes at once and have me bring them over to Amnon's rooms as soon as they were ready. But Jonadab shook his head, muttering into his clothing.

'No. No, he wants you to come and bake them in his kitchen, so he can smell them cooking. I mean—I think that's what he'd like, if he could say so.' Then before anyone could question him further, he got up abruptly, wiped his eyes and said, 'Please excuse me. I mustn't leave him alone any longer. If you could come very soon, Princess Tamar...' And he was gone.

We stared at one another, dismayed. Then Tamar said, 'Come,

Zohel. We must gather the ingredients together. You can help me carry them over.'

I mumbled, 'Tamar—I don't want to go. And I don't want *you* to go.'

'What? Of course I must go. Don't be so heartless, Zohel.'

She bustled inside and began piling up pots and jars, bowls of barley-flour and tubs of honey and dried fruit. I trailed after her, sucking my thumb dejectedly until she yanked it out of my mouth and told me not to be such a baby: what on earth had got into me all of a sudden? I very nearly sank my teeth into her fingers as she pulled mine away from them.

She bent down and took hold of me. 'Zohel, you haven't been like this for months. What's the matter?'

But even now that I had her full attention, I couldn't tell her. I averted my gaze. 'Nothing. I'm sorry. I'm all right.'

She hugged me briefly. 'That's better. I know you're sad because I'm getting married. Let's just enjoy our last few days together, shall we?'

I nodded miserably as she heaped a jumbled assortment of utensils into my outstretched arms.

Amnon's apartment was in darkness, and a convincing odour of stale sweat and vomit lingered on the stagnant air. Jonadab opened the door to us, cautioning us to keep our voices down: Amnon was sleeping. Tamar asked to see him, so we were taken through. He tossed in a tangle of clammy covers, with a damp cloth draped across his forehead. This he succeeded in flinging off onto the pillows as soon as we entered, and he began groaning and mumbling, repeating Tamar's name and demanding to be told where she was, then asking where he was himself. Jonadab knelt beside him and gently replaced the moist cloth. I wanted to scream.

Next Jonadab showed us into the kitchen, apologizing for the mess: the slaves had been sent away because of the danger of infection. We set to work, but Tamar kept dropping things. The sight of her half-brother manifestly racked with suffering seemed to have disturbed her profoundly.

Somehow we got the dough mixed and patted into the familiar rounded heart-shapes, and put into the tall clay oven. The sweet smell of honey and raisins mingled with the fetid stench of sickness, and turned my stomach. Tamar sat folding and unfolding her hands while we waited for the cakes to cook.

With both of us tense, fretful and tongue-tied, each for our own reasons, time dragged. I was sure the dough would be burnt and ruined when finally Tamar roused herself to take the lid off the oven and detach the cakes from the inside. We set them out on a warmed plate, and took them to Amnon's bedroom; he didn't even seem to notice us come in. Tamar made as if to put down the plate and go out again, leaving Jonadab to coax Amnon to eat. But as she retreated from the bed, Amnon's eyes flung open and he cried out, 'Tamar! Tamar, where are you?' and then, 'Who are all these people? So many people! Tamar, make these people go away! Get them away from me! I can't breathe.'

Tamar hovered, at a loss for what to do; then suddenly Jonadab leapt up and grasped my hand. 'We had better go, Zoheleth. He can get violent when he's like this, if he doesn't feel safe.' Gripping my fingers hard enough to hurt me, he steered me out of the room, then out of the apartment altogether.

I knew at once that I should have made more trouble earlier. I made some now, writhing and flailing until I managed to bite a chunk out of Jonadab's hand and draw a great deal of blood. While he yelped and turned the air blue with his cursing, I gave him the slip, melting into a darkened alcove and watching him blunder off down the passageway, bawling at me to come back if I knew what was good for me.

I did know what was good for me, and once I was sure Jonadab was out of the way, I ran back to Amnon's. If Jonadab knew what was good for *him*, I reasoned he would go and get his hand seen to before pressing his search for me; there were splashes of blood the length of the corridor.

The door was locked, from the inside. I flattened myself against it, then twisted round and put my ear to it. At first I could hear nothing. Then voices: Amnon's, quiet, malign, insistent but not really audible; Tamar's, husky with fear, and rising.

... No, Amnon, please. Don't touch me like that ... Amnon, by the mercy of Adonai, I beg you ... Amnon, this is Israel, Jerusalem, the Holy City of God, such things ought not even to be spoken of here ... I'll never be able to marry, never be able to raise my head in public; you'll be disgraced ... please, think of Father, think of what you'll put him through; it's not fair on him, he's already so depressed ... look, why don't you speak to him? I'm sure he'd let you marry me yourself if you can't ... I mean if you ... Amnon ... oh God ...

Then nothing.

Beside myself with dread, I began rattling and beating on the door, but to no avail. A hideous ravaged silence leached from the apartment; a thousand generations might have lived and died in it, a thousand eternities might have rolled past. Once upon a time, I would have been praying at a moment like this. But I'd cut myself off from Adonai when I'd run from David, and the words wouldn't come, even in my head.

Then there were thudding noises coming from inside the apartment. It sounded as though every piece of furniture in the place was being rammed against the walls. Finally the door heaved and shifted against me, and Amnon said hoarsely, 'Get out. I never want to see your face again, you Syrian whore.'

The door shook harder, but the lock was still across, and there was scuffling and whimpering behind it. Amnon repeated, 'Get out!' but more urgently this time; he kept on chanting the words like a spell, in between cursing Tamar and saying it was all her fault: she was a witch like her mother and had made him mad for her with the spices she'd put in the cakes. Meanwhile she sobbed and pleaded with him not to throw her out like this; it would be worse than what he'd done to her already. They were still arguing and struggling, both their voices rising hysterically, when I heard Jonadab returning, and retreated into my alcove.

He arrived just as Amnon got the door open. With the King's eldest son still shrieking that he'd been bewitched, calling on all the gods in heaven as witnesses, and ordering whoever might be within earshot to get the enchantress away from him, Jonadab picked up what remained of the Princess and dumped her in the corridor. The door banged shut, and was locked again.

She didn't move. Neither did I; I thought she was dead, and was terrified. There was a great gash on one of her temples, and the blood from it was running in her eyes. There was more blood on her clothes, and they were rumpled and torn, with her bare arms and legs poking out of them stiff and inert like a doll's, except that they were all cut and bruised. But then she started coughing; she was lying on her back, the sick was gurgling in her throat and choking her. So I crept out of hiding and got her head over my shoulder. After she'd thrown up all down my tunic, the tears came.

Of course I asked her what had happened. I asked her over and over as I sat with her on the floor helplessly trying to calm her, stroking back her matted hair and holding her head into my neck. But she wouldn't respond either to my words or to my touch, hanging limp as a drained wineskin. I don't think she even knew she was weeping; the tears flowed on, but when I raised her face to mine her eyes swam right through me.

That frightened me more than anything else did, though I knew what had happened well enough, and for reasons no child my age should have known it.

With her head in my lap I looked around wildly, desperate for someone to come, and equally desperate that no one should stumble upon the King's daughter like this. I half expected Amnon or Jonadab to come out and work me over; it must have dawned on them by now that I would know everything. Perhaps they would even kill me. But neither of them emerged; perhaps Amnon's distress had been in some part genuine?

In the end I accepted that I'd have to go for help, and leaving Tamar huddled against a wall I headed blindly for the nearest apartment I knew. She didn't cling to me or beg me to stay with her. She didn't even notice I was gone.

Absalom couldn't have heard me knocking at first. *I* could hear *him* all right, his boasting and his laughter amplified by wine, and his already inflated ego being bolstered by Shimei and Sheba's extravagant and drunken flattery. It was still only mid-afternoon, but the trio were clearly well on with their party; from what I could make out of their occasionally coherent conversation they seemed to be celebrating Absalom's victory over his young half-brother Adonijah in a chariot race that morning.

'Could you believe it when his mother turned up to take him home, the little wimp?' Sheba was crowing as I bashed a second time on the door. 'It was nearly as funny as when your whip caught Shimei on the nose.'

'That wasn't funny at all,' Shimei retorted, his slurred voice now edged with anger. He had a fiery temper at the best of times, and drink only made it worse. 'If anyone but Absalom had done that . . . and me a kinsman of King Saul, I'd have—'

'You'd have *what*?' drawled Absalom in mock aggression, 'O seventh cousin by marriage, seven times removed, to a petty chieftain thirty years dead? You and whose army would have dared lay a finger on a man who stands to inherit two thrones one day . . .'

Unable to tolerate any more, I lunged at the door, expecting it to be barred. It wasn't, and I went sprawling into the room, landing spread-eagled with my head under Shimei's chair. He forgot his quarrel at once and broke into raucous laughter as I battled to my feet and stood quaking with rage and frustration before Absalom.

Tamar's brother lolled full length on a couch, his hair splayed over the cushions like the rays of a great black sun. He scowled faintly up at me, as though with a vague awareness that he ought to be cross with me for some reason, if only he could be sure of who I was. I spluttered, 'Absalom, you have to come with me, now. Something's happened.'

'Something? What?' He flung one arm over his eyes to shut me out. 'Stop shouting, will you? You're giving me a headache.'

'Absalom, Tamar...' I said, then checked myself. Suddenly I couldn't bear to put her shame into words; not in front of Shimei and Sheba at any rate. But something of my agitation must have cut through to Absalom eventually, for although he was still moaning, he got up and staggered after me to the door, warning his two friends to stay put.

Clawing at the nearest doorpost for support, he hung there staring at his ruined sister, and I watched the daze gradually clear from his eyes. I tried to tell him what had happened, but I wasn't making much sense, I know, and he wasn't really listening. Nevertheless, by the time I'd finished babbling, he'd shed his drunkenness like an unwanted cloak. He dropped to his knees, took Tamar in his arms and asked her outright, 'Has Amnon lain with you?'

She couldn't speak, but I'm almost sure she nodded. Certainly Absalom was sure. He said, 'Why didn't you shout for help? I'd have heard you, and saved you! Why didn't you scream, so people would know he was forcing you?'

But Tamar said nothing, and the more he shook her and talked at her, the more she sobbed and withdrew into herself. He held her against him then, soothing her, urging her to say nothing of this to anyone else, but to stop crying and let him sort it out.

We almost had to carry her back to the harem. Thankfully the long summer siesta meant that the corridors were deserted, and we encountered no one.

Once Maacah had grasped what must have happened, she beat her breast and set up a wailing loud enough to raise the dead. It was left to Miriam to see to Tamar whilst Absalom and I sought to restrain her mother. Absalom pleaded with her to be quiet: did she want the entire palace to hear of her shame? Sure enough, at this moment Eliada and Eliphelet came running, and Miriam had to whisk them away before they saw Tamar and got frightened. Tamar herself wound up crouched whimpering in a corner while Maacah howled manically that her only daughter had been raped, and that all her son could do was tell her to be quiet.

'But she didn't scream!' Absalom said, seizing Maacah by the forearms. 'I never heard her scream, for God's sake! No one did. Who will believe it was rape? You know the Torah. She'll be stoned to death if this gets out.'

Maacah and I must have caught on to his meaning simultaneously. My innards turned to water, and Maacah left off her keening and stammered, 'Just look at her. She's bleeding all over. Who can say she didn't struggle?'

Absalom said, 'Amnon could have done all that afterwards, in a fit of guilt.'

'You don't think that! You can't think that!'

'Of course I don't. But there are men who will. And women.'

Maacah wrung her hands. 'We can inspect her. See if she is torn.'

I knew she wouldn't let them. Ever since Miriam had gone out, I'd been inching closer to Tamar, trying to coax her out of her corner. But now that she had the strength of two solid walls behind her, she wouldn't let me near; just sat rocking herself backwards and forwards the way I'd once been given to doing. I knew exactly, horribly, what she was feeling, and there was absolutely nothing I could do to help. Tears and blood scored her cheeks and ran in her hair, and the nearer I went the smaller she curled up, and the less her eyes would focus on my face.

Naturally Maacah and Absalom were convinced they would succeed where I who was not of their kin had failed, but they were wrong. They kept badgering her to let them look at her, and to tell them exactly what had happened, stressing that Amnon couldn't be punished unless there was proof of his crime, but they might as well have been total strangers for all the notice she took of them. When Maacah tried to peel away the stained remnants of Tamar's dress from between her legs, she earned a kick between her own.

I think that was when the enormity of the thing really hit her. All the howling and wailing had been unleashed from the stormy surface of her emotions; now there was anguish deep in the very well of her soul. Too quietly she said, 'It wasn't Tamar who did that. Tamar would never, never do such a thing. Amnon has killed her. Amnon has killed my daughter.'

A dreadful silence descended, into which Absalom whispered at last, 'Zohel, get my sword. I'm going to kill Amnon.'

'No. No!' Maacah rebuked him, with such vehemence that he listened to her. 'Do you think I want you condemned to death too? What good will it do me to lose two of my children rather than one? For once in your life stop to think, Absalom.'

He did, momentarily. I watched his eyes flicker between Tamar, hunched up insensible on the floor, and his mother, sitting erect now on a couch, her back straight as a spear, her face white as alabaster. Then he swung round, tossed the hair from his eyes with deliberate disdain, and said, 'Very well. I'm going to see my father.'

7

While we sat about waiting, Maacah tried twice more to get a closer look at Tamar. I could see that the blatant rejection she met with hurt like having a knife blade twisted round in her breast; again I thought: it is better to arm yourself against love altogether than to lay yourself open to such grievous wounds as this. Still, I went and stroked her hand and said, 'Leave Tamar be for a while. She's feeling too dirty to be touched. She'll come round soon.'

I don't know if I believed it, but Maacah was so taken aback at my unexpected display of maturity that she did as I suggested. She went off and busied herself boiling up some concoction of wine and spices, which she sipped at and it seemed to make her feel calmer. She offered some to me, but I refused it; I didn't fancy addling my wits when everyone around me was fast going to pieces. Perhaps I *was* growing up after all.

So I just sat cross-legged on the floor, keeping an eye on Tamar from a respectful distance, and listening forlornly to Maacah chanting prayers, though not to Adonai. I contemplated swallowing my pride and crawling back to him, and I did try half-heartedly to talk to him again in the way I'd once found so easy.

But no one had ever explained to me that there are powers in the world and in the heavenly places who are opposed to Adonai, and to whom I was a threat now in a way I'd never been back then when I was ignorant. And so I let them walk all over me, let them bind the whole thing up inside me with the contempt I felt for David, which the events of the day had done nothing to dispel. I blamed him now for being taken in by Amnon's so-called illness, and for sending Jonadab to fetch Tamar. I blamed him for allowing all the evil that pervaded his household. And I very much doubted he would give Absalom the sort of response he was hoping for.

In this at least, I was proved to be right. Absalom came back pale and shaking with spite, and blurted, 'He doesn't believe me! He thinks I'm lying, that I'm just jealous of Amnon and trying to get him into trouble.'

Maacah said, 'Tell David to come here. Tell him to look at Tamar.'

'I did.' Absalom shrugged helplessly. 'He won't.' His rage was quickly running to despair; he brushed a hand across his eyes, pretending to scratch his temples. 'He's done nothing for months but heap insults upon the house of Geshur. It's one thing after another. He doesn't care.'

So Absalom and his mother launched into a fresh rehearsal of their grievances against David, and it was hard to say which of them was worse. Each plunged in turn from anger, through anguish, to hopelessness, and each alternately sought to soothe or to goad the other. Unwilling to put up with the situation any longer, I said, 'I'll come with you, Absalom, and we'll go back to him. He'll believe *me*.'

Absalom laughed bitterly. He meant: why should a king listen to a puny orphan when he won't listen to his favourite son? But he would never have spoken like that to me. And I did begin to wish straight away that I hadn't made such a rash suggestion, when I'd seen nothing of David for so long, nor had I had any wish to. Yet I knew he *would* believe me, and that this was partly why.

His Majesty didn't know whether to be thrilled or stricken when he saw us. The joy that came alive in his eyes when they met mine put me to shame. Then he realized that Absalom was with me, and he knew why we'd come. I saw a cloud of despondency condense around his shoulders.

He was gentle with me, but didn't spare me close questioning. What exactly had I seen? What had I heard? Did I even know what the word 'rape' meant? Did I really think Amnon was strong enough to force Tamar and gag her at the same time? And how could I be sure of what had taken place, if she hadn't screamed?

'I just know,' I answered, and I looked him right in the eyes; he *had* to believe me. The cloud that hung about him grew blacker as I watched, and it came to me strangely that it had always been there, as long as I'd known him. I shrank back, and he shook his head sadly.

'Don't be frightened, Zohar. You must never be frightened of telling the truth.'

I said, 'I'm frightened of Amnon. He's always hated me. If he finds out that I've told on him he'll be mad.'

Before David got the chance to reassure me, Absalom rounded on him. 'So what are you going to do? Amnon must be punished. At once. He's brought disgrace to my family.'

'I will talk with him,' replied David, resignedly.

'Talk? Is that all? What use is that? The penalty for violating a girl promised in marriage is death, and you know it. And when she's the brute's own sister . . .!'

'Absalom, he's my son just as you are. He must be given the opportunity to speak for himself.'

'He isn't fit to be the son of a king! He never has been. You intend to give the throne of Israel to a rapist!'

'*I* intend to give the throne of Israel to no one, Absalom. It isn't mine to give. This isn't Egypt—or Syria. Adonai anoints whom he chooses. And let us not talk about Amnon in his absence. I've told you, he must speak for himself.'

'Then I insist on being told what he says. I'll come back tomorrow to find out.'

'Absalom, you have no right to insist on anything.'

For the space of ten ghastly heartbeats, father and son confronted one another: David harassed and doggedly dispassionate, Absalom on fire with indignation. Then I said, 'Come on, Absalom. We'd better go.'

He complied, but bawled over his shoulder as we left, 'I shall be here again first thing in the morning. And I'll be expecting some answers—Your Majesty.'

That night Absalom spent with us in the harem. I don't think Maacah trusted him out of her sight. But he didn't go to bed. He paced back and forth the whole time, every so often unsheathing his knife and running his fingers nervily along the blade. Tamar remained crouched in her corner; none of us could get her to bed, not even Miriam, who had taken the toddlers back to Abigail, and returned to tend to her mistress. Tamar gave no sign of recognizing her, and Miriam was so upset, she scarcely registered Absalom's presence.

I didn't sleep much either. I spread a pallet on the floor to be near to Tamar, and each time I awoke, there were her sightless eyes staring huge and wet in the darkness.

At first light Absalom stormed out without breakfast. I tried to get on with some chores, one of which required me to leave the apartment. Outside the door there was a group of women whispering. Everyone I passed stopped to look at me, and the very air was alive with rumour. I slunk back to Maacah shaken and subdued and didn't go out again that day.

I'd never seen Absalom so crushed as he was when he returned. He said his father had told him that Amnon had confessed, and repented; so now the whole thing was over. I need have nothing to fear from either Amnon or Jonadab, and the best any of us could do was forgive and forget. Absalom ordered me to fetch him some wine; he seemed intent on drinking himself senseless, perfunctorily draining one cup after another.

'How *can* we forgive and forget?' Maacah wailed. 'Can we send Tamar off to her wedding as though there's nothing wrong? What do we tell her husband when there's no blood on the bridal bed? And how long is she going to be—like that?'

'He keeps on saying she didn't scream,' mumbled Absalom. 'So she'd have to die too, the people would demand it. He'd have to put his own firstborn son and his only daughter to death on the same day. And that's to say nothing of the scandal it would cause, and the damage it would do to the reputation of the royal family if the facts became common knowledge. There's no punishment for an outrage like this except stoning; that isn't appropriate, Amnon has repented, so the wisest thing to do is hush it all up.' He banged his goblet on the table in frustration. 'And by heaven, he's right. There's no way he *can* legally punish Amnon without condemning Tamar. Certainly not if she won't tell her side of the story.'

Maacah said, 'He is king. He should be free to do whatever he pleases, never mind what people say.'

'This is Israel, Mother.' Absalom's voice was sour as vinegar. 'Not even the King can take liberties with the Torah.'

'David knows it was rape. Doesn't he, Zohel.'

'He knows,' hissed Absalom. 'He knows all right.' Angry again, he leapt to his feet, but all that wine on an empty stomach made him sway where he stood, and his eyes were everywhere. 'He reckons himself pious, calls himself a man of God, Adonai's anointed, sets himself up as some paragon of justice. What sort of justice is it to set an incestuous rapist on the throne? What sort of justice is it to keep us all guessing about Adonai's choice of heir so we don't know where we stand? Well, I *want* justice. I *demand* justice! If he won't give it, I'll get it for myself. I *will* kill Amnon. I don't care what happens to me.'

It was just as well he'd had so much to drink, because he hadn't gone two steps before he keeled over onto his couch and lay there, venting his pique upon the pillows. Maacah fetched him some of her spice-drugged wine and watched him pass into oblivion. He was unquestionably safer that way.

He slept all day; unsurprising, since he hadn't slept all night. In the end Tamar slept too, slumped against the wall; Maacah and I at last managed to carry her to bed. Miriam was sent for fresh water to get her mistress cleaned up, but at the door ran into the same gaggle of gossips I'd encountered; to such vultures scandal must have its own smell. From just inside the door I watched them crowding round her, jostling and hustling with their shoulders together so she couldn't slip away. I could hear them asking if the Princess was well, but the enquiries weren't friendly, and Miriam was as shaken as I had been.

Just after sunset, Absalom got up. I showed him Tamar asleep in bed; he nodded abruptly, and said, 'I'm going out.'

Maacah begged him, 'Absalom, leave your knife here. I don't want you doing something foolish . . .'

He unbuckled it from his belt and threw it down on the table. He knew as well as she did that he'd never get away with it.

'Where are you going then, if not after Amnon?'

'I don't know. Back to my own place,' he said, but he was lying. We all knew where he was going; if he couldn't wreak open vengeance on his brother, he would have his own kind of revenge upon his father. Mercifully, Maacah was still in no mood to care.

Two days passed, but Tamar was no better. The only times she spoke or moved were in her sleep; once she got up in a dream and awoke to find herself halfway to the kitchen. Absalom stayed away, dividing his time between his friends and Bathsheba, employing any means available to drown his sorrows.

On the third day, the women got in.

I don't know how; one moment there was the usual crowd outside the door—we'd almost grown used to them—but the next, the apartment was thronged with David's wives and concubines, and thrumming with their voices. 'Good day to you, Maacah. It's so long since we've seen you.' 'Where's the blushing bride? Only two days till the wedding.' 'We haven't seen the dress. How come you're being so secretive?'

We tried to make them leave, but they sailed past us brazen as a fleet of the Sea People, profaning our privacy, defiling everything with their greedy eyes and hands, finally spilling through into Tamar's bedroom squawking like ravens. 'Tamar, my dear, how pale you look!' 'Have you been ill? You poor darling.' 'Are you all ready for the happiest day of your life?' 'You must hurry up and get well. How dreadful if things had to be—*postponed*.'

At least they pierced Tamar's stupor; we had that to thank them for. She cowered away from them whining, as they rifled her storage chests and scattered her trousseau across the bed and the floor. One of them seized upon the dress which she'd spent so many days stitching, and thrust it up against her sallowing skin, cooing, 'How becoming! How utterly stunning! Isn't she the very picture of modest virginal purity?'

Tamar shrieked, and grasped the garment with both hands, pulling it over her head to hide her face. The women tried to drag it away, and in the ensuing struggle the fabric stretched and tore and the dress came in half.

'A sign!' cried the hag who had one half in her hands. 'The Princess does not wish this wedding to take place. It may be that she has found another man more to her taste. One closer to home, perhaps? One with whom she has more in common, having been gotten from the same regal loins?'

Brittle and helpless as a leaf in the wind, Maacah said to me, 'Zohel, go for Absalom. Before they tear *her* to pieces too.'

I found him in the stables alone, grooming his racing team and talking to them earnestly as he worked, brushing with fierce downward strokes that betrayed his inner turmoil. He was unarmed, but had his horsewhip, and came just with that; I think he feared we might already be too late. He burst into his mother's apartment flailing the whip around his head, then brought it crashing down on a table stacked with crockery. Gold and silver vessels clattered to the ground, potsherds flew to the four corners of the room, droplets of wine sprayed into the air. The invaders squealed and screeched and fell over one another in their haste to escape the madman's thong, which flicked and coiled snake-like above them.

That night we smuggled Tamar out of the harem and carried her to Absalom's chambers. She was still clutching the remains of the wedding dress; her fingers had frozen rigid around it and none of us could prize it from her.

Aside from this bizarre concentration of strength, the rest of her body was as weak as water; she had neither eaten nor drunk since her ordeal. She might be safe now from attack, but no one could save her from herself. Miriam went with her to see to her needs, under instruction to report to Maacah every day concerning her mistress's progress.

Since in theory I was Maacah's attendant, it fell to me to stay with her and attempt to cheer her, whilst a nurse was procured to look after her little sons lest they be neglected, and a hefty eunuch to discourage the vultures from making another attack. Twenty times a day Maacah would hug me against herself and say, 'Why doesn't David come to see us, Zohel? He must know how we feel. Is he scared to face me? He who was once scared of nothing, and slaughtered giants single-handed?' I had nothing to say. And the women still came to the door, watching and waiting, and driving Maacah slowly out of her senses.

As for me, I was keeping myself in control. I'd grown up amid crisis and abuse; sometimes in spite of everything they had remained easier for me to cope with than love.

Miriam came daily, and at first the news was encouraging. The move seemed to have done Tamar good. The night we took her to Absalom's, she'd slept right through until morning, and then got up, awake. She'd asked Miriam to bring a tub and hot water so she could bathe, and even drunk a little warmed wine, though she persisted in refusing to eat anything.

But then each day she began spending more and more time in her bath, pouring jug after jug of water over her head until her skin must have been wrinkled and raw. She wouldn't allow even Miriam to see her naked, but made her walk backwards into the room when she brought more pitchers from the well. Of course, Miriam had peeped when she could, and said Tamar was already thin now rather than slender, her skin was flaking and she had torn her hair. She was systematically tearing up the wedding dress too, into tiny little pieces which floated lily-wise on the bath water and heaped up on the floor like silken snowflakes.

'And Absalom?' asked Maacah. 'How is Absalom?'

Miriam hung her head. 'We hardly see him. And he's drinking far too much.'

The day of the wedding came and went. No word was sent to Tamar's fiancé, nor did word come from him. He must have heard the rumours, just like anyone else.

It was on the day itself that I first wondered whether I ought not to be bearing some part of the burden of guilt I'd been so eager to lay at David's door. After all, hadn't I been the one to wish that the wedding might never take place? Supposing Adonai had read my thoughts and taken them for a prayer?

No, I told myself, you're being a fool. You tried and tried to deter Tamar from visiting Amnon. You did as much as you could.

Yet that wasn't quite true, and there was no point in pretending that it was. I hadn't told Tamar *why* I was afraid for her. Perhaps if I had, it would have made all the difference?

Then I felt more guilty than ever, for the old guilt from my past in Lodebar became mixed up with the new, and I felt as wretched and worthless as I'd ever done. A child with a background like mine is all too ready to take the blame for anything.

I didn't speak to a soul all that day. I squatted in a corner of the courtyard sucking my thumb, willing myself to hate David, to leave all of the burden with him once more. I hated him and hated him until the whole of my insides were churned up with it. Indeed, there was so much hate in me that I couldn't stop hating myself, but whenever an arrow of guilt threatened to pierce my heart, I redirected it towards David, and by sundown I felt stronger.

Next morning Miriam came again as usual; and still Tamar hadn't taken food.

'I think she's decided to die,' Miriam sobbed. 'What has she got left to live for?'

'I must see her,' said Maacah. 'I can't let her do this.'

'Oh no, my lady, please. It would only distress you. Don't put yourself through any more pain.'

'Being a mother is a painful thing, Miriam. It must be borne.'

So we set off to go back with her, taking grapes and olives and sweetmeats we thought might prove tempting. Outside our door the women crowded us, despite the eunuch's attempts to keep them back, and I heard them whispering 'sorceress' and 'infidel' and 'whore-mother'. I cringed: Miriam must have had to face their malevolence every day.

Tamar was in a room by herself; Miriam called to her softly from the doorway, telling her that Maacah was here. Tamar refused to admit her. Maacah herself began pleading from a distance: 'Tamar, it's your mother. I'm not going to hurt you,' but Tamar just told her to go away. I don't know why Maacah didn't walk in regardless, except that I think she was afraid of what she might find.

We went back home defeated, but the following day Maacah was wanting to try again. The same failure was re-enacted, and the next day too. On the day of our fourth visit, I decided to bake some of Tamar's heart-shaped cakes and take them with us.

Maacah was less than supportive. 'What good is that going to do, Zoheleth?' She only used that name in full when she intended to belittle me. 'You'll only remind her of what happened. Don't make things any worse.'

I said, 'Things can't get any worse,' and set to with my baking. Perhaps what I was doing would provoke a bad response, but any response would be better than none. And maybe, just maybe, she would recognize the familiar smell and remember our happy times together, along with the pain.

Miriam also tried to dissuade me. 'It isn't helping, both of you coming here every day,' she hissed at me when Maacah wasn't listening. 'It upsets Tamar more. She can't bear to think that folk know what has become of her. And people will guess why you keep visiting, and the harassment will start all over again.'

I said, 'Don't tell Tamar I'm here, Miriam. I'll just go in, alone.'

'Zohel, no! She's bathing, I can't let you see her. She says not to let anyone; and as for a boy—'

'Then you'll have to stop me by force, and I bet I've had a lot more practice at fighting than you have. I'm not going to stand by and let her starve.'

Tamar sat in the tub with her back towards me, aimlessly scooping water from the bath with skeletal fingers and letting it run down again over her narrow shoulders. Her hair was shorn off in clumps to the scalp, and I could trace every rib and every bone in her spine. I wouldn't have known her.

She must have heard me behind her, but made no attempt to cover herself. I wondered if she could smell the cakes. Quietly I walked round to stand before her, and looked into the dull sunken eyes of a stranger, set in a hollow, grey face. The skin around her neck was already going slack, and her breasts seemed small and shrunken. She recognized me, but she didn't cry out or turn away. Bracing myself I thrust one of the cakes towards her; her fingers touched mine as she took it, and they were cold as snow, but perhaps it was just with the water.

Then she smiled, a weird, vacant smile, and ate the cake.

I wanted to shout for joy and fling my arms around her. But only for a moment. The blank smile had gelled on her face like a death-mask, and made me want to throw up. I gave her another cake, and she ate this one too, though I had no more idea of why, than I had of why I'd been moved to bake them in the first place. Still, it might mean that she wasn't going to die now, so we had longer to pray for a miracle.

I left the remaining cakes with Miriam, saying simply, 'She'll eat those. I'll bring more tomorrow.' Maacah embraced me, too grateful to be jealous.

Morning and evening Maacah and I took to praying together for our miracle. Curious prayer meetings they were too, with neither of us specifying who we prayed to: Maacah, because she didn't want to offend me; I, because I just didn't know any more; and my words, for all their vehemence, felt to return to me void.

Leaving the cakes with Miriam didn't work, however. We quickly learned that Tamar would eat them only if she took them from my hand. This puzzled everyone, but when I lay in bed alone in the darkness I allowed myself to believe I knew why. I had never told her about Ziba, but now that all the rest of her understanding had been taken from her, perhaps she understood this one thing for the first time. Perhaps she felt a new and bitter-sweet kindred with the strange little boy she had sought to draw out of his shell.

So every day I had to go to Absalom's chambers on my errand of mercy. Sometimes I went at first light, sometimes at noon, sometimes in the evening, and I stayed out for varying lengths of time, lest anyone should question my routine and learn that Tamar had been moved, and where to. I always had to pass the women, yet they took me for a slave going about my normal business.

One day I was sitting in Tamar's room singing softly to her as I often did, still hoping for a response, when I heard a commotion coming from the hallway. Absalom was shouting, with Sheba, Shimei and Miriam's voices all seeking to pacify him. Tamar began whining pathetically as was her habit now when she sensed harmony being shattered, so I got up to chide Absalom for letting his drunkenness upset his sister.

But when I poked my head through the curtains, I realized he wasn't drunk. He was too livid to be coherent, but I managed to glean that he'd had an encounter with Amnon.

Miriam was too much in awe of Absalom to be of any real use in calming him; Shimei and Sheba were winding him up as much as they were smoothing things out. So it was I who had to get him sitting down and composed enough to explain what had happened.

'I hadn't seen him since the—since he—since Tamar—I hadn't seen him all this time until today. Father said he'd repented; I thought he must have got him doing some kind of penance. But he's as good as boasting about it, Zohel! I mean it! Yes, of course I said something first. I wasn't going to walk past him and behave as though there were nothing amiss between us. But he said he couldn't see what all the fuss was about. He's the firstborn son of a king, he should be entitled to have what he wants. The kings of Egypt marry their own sisters and get sons on them, so what has he done that's so terrible? And he's so blasé, Zohel, so—unscathed, and so offensively *healthy* with it, while I come home day after day to find Tamar still like this ... She's being punished for his sin, while he walks free! Father must be going senile if he can't see it.'

I asked gently, 'Did you tell him?'

'Tell who? Tell him what?'

'Did you tell Amnon what's become of Tamar.'

'No.' Absalom slumped, all the fire gone out of him. 'I don't think I want him to find out. Why should I give him the pleasure of knowing how much power he has to wreck innocent people's lives? Because he *would* get pleasure from it. I know what he's like.'

I found myself clenching my fists; a futile gesture, but what else was there for me to do? Then out of the blue Miriam said, 'Why don't you go to Nathan?'

'Nathan?' repeated Absalom, taken aback. 'Nathan the prophet?' He frowned, and held the bridge of his nose with both hands. Then he said, 'Oh, no. I can't go to *him*. He hangs out in the wilderness somewhere with a pack of wild-eyed crazies. I'm not wasting my time wandering round frying my hide in the desert. What good could it do?'

'Nathan's here at the palace,' Miriam averred. 'I saw him this morning.' Then conscious of all the eyes trained upon her, and especially Absalom's, she coloured, and lowered her face. 'It might do a great deal of good. He's a man of God if ever there was one. He won't turn a blind eye to injustice. And he has the ear of the King.'

Absalom sat a while in sullen contemplation. Then he said, 'Come with me, Zohel. In case *he* doesn't believe me either.'

But I don't think that this was really why he took me. Rather, he reckoned that even at my tender age I had more experience of the ways of Adonai and of his servants than he would ever have, for all that he was the son of David the giant-slayer. He didn't appreciate the confusion that now reigned inside me.

Nathan was staying in a small guest room which I later learned only he ever used. It was bare of all decoration, and unfurnished except for a thin sleeping-pallet and two hard-backed chairs. But he welcomed us as graciously as a pharaoh might have received two visiting diplomats. A shock-headed boy, younger than me, and dressed in a coarse brown cloak, fetched us wine and olives, and we were installed upon the two chairs while the prophet sat contentedly on the floor. For some reason I was surprised to note that the lines on his face had been created by smiling more than by frowning, and his deep-set eyes were guileless and bright as a small child's. He was one of those men who make you feel you're the most valued person in all the world, just by greeting you; and they are few and far between. They always know Adonai.

Absalom launched into his tirade without waiting to be invited. He was patently nervous, and what he saw as righteous anger came across as something mean and spiteful somehow. Nevertheless, Nathan heard him out, studying his face intently the whole time, occasionally nodding. This seemed to throw Absalom still further; he concluded with some lame but sniping criticisms of David and hung his head, the blue-black curls falling in front of his face, and not by accident.

'You would do well to recall the fifth commandment, Prince Absalom,' remarked Nathan, when the diatribe was over.

Absalom said nothing.

'Your father is Adonai's chosen king. There may be good reasons why he cannot punish Amnon in the way you would wish. Do you know everything there is to know about both of them? Do you think a public scandal will do anything to help Tamar, or undo what has been done? Will it do anything for the stability and security of Israel? Or is it her heathen neighbours whom you want to see exulting? With respect—perhaps it is, son of Maacah.'

Absalom lost control. 'My lineage has nothing to do with this! Do you think Amnon is any less polluted with paganism than I am? He goes with prostitutes, Canaanite temple-women! He squanders gold from the royal treasuries on buying their favours!'

'Oh? And you have proof of this, do you?'

'Proof? Everyone knows it's true! I've heard a hundred people say so.'

'How do they know? How do *you* know?'

'I have proof he *tried*.' Absalom seized hold of my arms and dragged me off my chair, holding me rigid between himself and Nathan as though using me for a shield. 'I found his belt marks on a child's legs, a child he used for his own evil designs because he knew the defenceless creature couldn't speak! Well, he can speak now, thanks to Tamar and me. He'll tell you what Amnon is like.'

I opened my mouth, unsure where to start, but Nathan hushed me. 'Let me tell *you* something, my angry Prince. I once heard of a poor widower who had four beautiful but very careless daughters. They always seemed to be losing things—sometimes things that mattered to them very much. The eldest lost a gold coin from her dowry chain, the second a precious jewel from her loveliest cloakpin, the third a silver necklace which had been a wedding gift from her new husband. The youngest, who was, incidentally, the most beautiful, lost a plain copper ring, the only thing her dead mother had ever given her.'

Nathan paused, long enough for Absalom to start muttering that this whole conversation was leading nowhere; we hadn't come here to listen to irrelevant sob-stories.

'You may decide in due course whether it is irrelevant,' counselled Nathan. 'But I do agree it is a sob-story. The youngest daughter was sobbing so much, and howling so loudly about how someone had robbed her and ought to be punished, that her unfortunate sisters set about turning the house upside down to prove her wrong. They didn't find the ring, but they found all *their* missing treasures—in her secret cupboard.'

Absalom went white. 'What are you saying?'

'You're not the only one with over-keen ears, young man. You're hardly a sexual innocent yourself, are you?'

'I—don't know what you're talking about.'

'No? You really want it in words of one syllable? You consider yourself slighted because your brother stole what you regarded as sacred. Yet you have taken what was consecrated to your own father.'

Absalom was trembling from head to foot. 'How do you know?'

'I am the ears, eyes and mouth of Adonai, Absalom. It is my business to know everything.'

Absalom babbled on wretchedly, 'You don't understand. You've got it all wrong. I didn't take Bathsheba by force. *I* was the virgin, *she* took *me*!'—and when Nathan raised a sardonic eyebrow—'Oh, I know there's always been talk of me and other women. But that's all it was: talk! God knows, I spread enough of it myself—'

'None of that makes what you've done any less sinful.' Nathan got up from the floor and unexpectedly bestowed on Absalom his most ingenuous smile. 'I fear that this is the beginning of the fulfilment,' he said.

But Absalom was far too mortified now to ask what he meant.

The whole way back to his apartment, Absalom didn't open his mouth. I felt sorry for him; in my eyes, as well as in his own, his crime was *not* as shameful as Amnon's. Like most children, and not a few adults, I still regarded sinfulness as something to be judged according to degree, not as a condition of the spirit which leads to death no matter how wantonly or how discreetly we choose to express it.

We were on the point of crossing the threshold when Absalom changed his mind about going home. At first he tried to get rid of me; I'm sure he meant to go to Bathsheba. Then he changed his mind again and decided to visit his mother, and since I'd done my duty by Tamar for the day, I went back with him. I wasn't surprised he couldn't face seeing his unprincipled mistress, even for the sake of spiting Nathan. The flavour of their clandestine affair had suddenly turned sour.

But the inner turbulence which each of us was now experiencing soon paled into insignificance. For we arrived to find Maacah's chambers being pulled apart at the seams, and Maacah herself nowhere in sight. The eunuch too was noticeably absent, and a whole gang of slaves I'd never seen before was busy piling up our belongings and packing them into storage chests. The vases of flowers were gone, the furniture was stacked like a stallholder's wares in the middle of the floor, the rugs were rolled into bales and even the curtains and the wall-hangings had been unhooked and heaped up beside the door.

Absalom swore and accosted the nearest slave, demanding, 'What is all this about? What's going on here?'

The slave stared at him as though amazed he didn't know; then he turned suspicious, assuming that Absalom must be out to test him. 'The lady Bathsheba's things are to be moved in tomorrow morning, m'lord. All this stuff has to be out by then.'

'The lady Bathsheba? She's moving in here?'

'Yes, m'lord. Day after tomorrow. King's orders.'

'What? Why?'

All the slaves had stopped work now and were staring at Absalom. The foreman of the gang stepped forward. 'We understood that you and your mother had been informed and consulted, my lord. The lady Bathsheba has not been well since she came here, and now is also with child. Her quarters among the other women of the harem aren't quiet enough for her, so the King has arranged a straight exchange.'

Absalom growled, 'Where is my mother?'

'I believe she has gone to see the King, my lord.'

There was an acute hiatus, then I heard a rustle of garments from behind me, and the words: 'There is no one here worthy to be called king any more.'

Maacah's voice came from the doorway: dejected, defeated, yet even now tinged with incredulity. She walked forward slowly, saying, 'This isn't being done on David's orders. Nor even on Ahithophel's. And it has nothing to do with any illness. It is the lady Bathsheba's desire to be quartered next to her husband's chambers, in the suite reserved for his principal wife. *That* is what has been arranged.'

Clearly this was news to the slave-gang. The foreman set down the rug he was holding. Absalom breathed, 'You mean, Father knew nothing of it?'

'Not until I told him.'

'Wasn't he angry?'

'At first. He sent for her, while I was there, so she could explain herself. But she only had to look at him and he gave in. Your little harlot must have something, Absalom. He must be besotted with her. Or else it's her grandfather that he fears.'

'It's over,' muttered Absalom.

'What's over?'

'Bathsheba and me. This is the ultimate insult. I shall never see her again.'

Maacah put her face in her hands. 'I wish I could say the same thing. When I left, she followed me. She threatened me! She threatened to fill the palace with lies about me, saying I poisoned her baby, and tried to poison *her* with Tamar's cakes. She says I'm a witch, and so is Tamar, and that it was Tamar who wanted Amnon, not the other way around. She says if I make trouble about moving out she'll have David put Tamar to death.'

Absalom took his mother in his arms; she clawed at his hair with her nails, wailing that he was all she had left, her only hope, and begging him not to let her down. He whispered, 'It doesn't make sense. None of this makes sense.'

'Oh, yes it does,' wept Maacah. 'We've been as blind as moles all along, Absalom. It's ever since the Ammonite war that things have been wrong, as I've told you a hundred times. But now I know the reason. It's because men of Geshur fought on the side of David's enemies, it's because we're a proud people who won't lie down and pay him tribute, he can't forgive us. And she's fuelling his resentment every day. I should never have said I renounced the goddess. This is my punishment. Well, if David wants to see me as a heathen sorceress, I shall play the part for him.'

Pulling away from Absalom's embrace, she squared her shoulders and briefly appeared as majestic as she had on the day I was first introduced to her. Crossing the ransacked room in three sweeping strides, she pressed her hands against a section of the cedarwood panelling that lined the wall, and slid it aside. Behind in an alcove stood an idol wrapped in cloth, the size and shape of a woman. Maacah dragged the covering from it, revealing a brazen Aramaean Astarte—she who is known to us as Asherah—complete with curled hair, naked breasts and belly, and wearing a sun and crescent moon around her neck.

When we took up residence in Bathsheba's old apartment, Maacah set up the statue with an altar on the roof, where it would be flagrantly visible from half the palace. Let them all see it, she said: what do I care? . . . there is nothing left now for David to take from me; not without sparking off all-out war with Syria.

8

Two years went by, and two more harvests were destroyed by locusts. In addition there were freak frosts each winter, and hundreds of ancient olive trees died; some kind of blight attacked the vines, and they shrivelled on their stakes before the grapes had even formed. In the streets of the city, and out among the villages, ill-feeling against David began to be voiced openly. It would have been worse still for him if the folk had been told of Nathan's prophecy, and that the King already knew perfectly well what he must do in order to avert the evil which beset us.

For the royal treasuries no longer had the resources to import food and distribute it cheaply. Israel had fought no foreign wars since the crushing of the Ammonites, so no booty had accrued. In the market places, prices soared; the head of a sheep could fetch what two whole animals had sold for three years earlier. Haggard women, bone-thin and flat-chested, carried out the corpses of their children for burial. Sickness spread rife in the wake of malnutrition; shortages led to the disregard of Moses' laws, with people eating what was unclean, or had died of itself. The little food which the poor could get might be heaved up again or wasted in diarrhoea.

In the palace we never went without, but our fare was plainer than usual. And we weren't immune to disease.

Servants died of it, then one of the concubines; then while David was still seeking to avoid doing what he had to do, little Eliada and Eliphelet both fell ill the same day. Within the week they lay stiff and cold, with wispy candles burning by their heads, and their bodies shrouded in white, a cruel parody of the swaddling bands they'd so recently outgrown.

But Bathsheba's new baby prospered, or so they said. We never saw him; no one did. His name was Solomon, and it was widely believed that she kept him in secret, fearing the jealousy of the King's other sons. The rumour was well-founded, and so was the fear.

Had David not found himself witnessing the funeral of two of his own children, I doubt he would ever have made the critical decision. But finally the Gibeonite ambassadors were summoned to the palace once more. They announced that their gods had now been consulted, and that seven males in direct line from Saul must be surrendered to them and hanged outside the walls of Saul's capital. Apart from the so-called Mephibosheth of whom I'd heard talk, I didn't know any were left. I don't think anyone at the palace did, least of all David. But somehow Ahithophel's agents managed to dredge up seven wretches who they said were sons of Rizpah, Saul's concubine, and of Merab his daughter (Michal's sister). Perhaps for the first time in her life, Michal was glad she'd remained childless; and no doubt David was glad of that too. But if only he had faced up to the crisis sooner, the famine might have been forestalled, and Mephibosheth could still have been spared.

At the height of summer, when all the hillsides were parched barren and all Jerusalem stank of death and decay, I watched from the palace roof as the seven sacrificial victims were brought out in chains and handed over to the Gibeonites. David performed the dreadful transaction himself, but from the distance he could have been some sick old peasant. His cheeks were dark hollows and he was stooping, bowed, it seemed, by the weight of the black cloud I could still see draped over his shoulders. Nathan stood passively by, inscrutable, but when the task had been completed I saw king and seer exchange heavy glances. I was convinced there was some deeper, perhaps more personal, reason for David to wish that this prophet were a false one. However, any kind of seed planted from that day forth yielded a bumper harvest.

Of course, I wasn't the only person to observe Saul's descendants being led away to die. Just as they passed through the main gates of the palace, a disturbance broke out in the courtyard behind them, and Shimei came running in pursuit, yelling and cursing like a street-boy. Sheba followed hot on his tail, evidently attempting to restrain him, but without success. Shimei's vitriol was directed quite blatantly against David, the murderer of princes, shedder of royal blood, traitor to the memory of Saul— without whom he, the runt-son of Jesse, would still have been looking after sheep at Bethlehem.

Sheba was beside himself: did Shimei want to get *them* sacrificed also? But Shimei refused to be silenced, swearing that he would yet avenge these kinsmen he hadn't even known he possessed, and that he would see a member of Saul's house once again sit upon the throne of Israel. I think he only escaped with his pelt intact because he was taken to be drunk or mad.

Every day for those two years I went to visit Tamar and entice her to eat. After a while she let me give her sweets or fruit as well as those cakes, the very smell of which I'd come to loathe. But never in all that time did she say a single word to me. As soon as her hair grew, she hacked it off or tore it out in chunks. Whenever she wasn't in bed, she was in her bath, and she refused to put on any garment given to her, shredding each one into tiny pieces. I still chanted my prayers each day for a miracle, but the words were no more than ritual. The Tamar I had known was dead, and so was the love she'd kindled within me. Absalom and Maacah too had their own preoccupations, and neither was inclined to ply me with affection any more. Gradually I retreated back inside my shell, speaking less and less, and never singing. The bad dreams began to creep back, the nights grew longer and lonelier. The first time my mattress was wet in the morning I burst into tears; I was nearly old enough for my voice to be breaking.

Absalom might not have noticed that I was hurting, but I certainly saw that he was. There were other signs besides the inevitable drinking. He'd given up racing his horses and chariots, and the care of his once precious team was left to his grooms. He was womanizing indiscriminately now, if he hadn't been before; of the innumerable toddlers running around the harem, more than one was rumoured to be his. I don't imagine David even knew how many sons he himself was supposed to have any more, but with one exception only the ones born at Hebron seemed to count for anything, although some of those begotten in Jerusalem were approaching adolescence. The one exception was Bathsheba's.

The affair between her and Absalom came to an abrupt end the day we went to see Nathan, as Absalom had promised it would. I don't know if Bathsheba had intended that to happen when she deliberately humiliated his mother, but perhaps even she considered it a trifle unseemly for the King's principal wife to be carrying on with his son. Then again, maybe she was surprised that he should have taken his mother's part so readily—after all, Bathsheba knew nothing of Nathan's role in all this. But if she was disappointed at losing her beautiful young lover, she wasn't going to let him or anyone else suspect it. If she had made a formidable enemy, so had he.

As for Maacah herself, I grew increasingly disturbed by the way she was behaving, and my position as her attendant became more and more distasteful to me. She never grieved openly for her two little sons; indeed, she never spoke to me of them. She simply filled our cramped new quarters with idols and amulets, and spent hours up on the roof burning incense on Asherah's altar and pouring libations to the moon and stars. She would make me stand beside her, holding knives and phials and cups of blood, while she recited incantations and wove elaborate curses against David and Bathsheba. If she'd been single-minded in all this, I dread to think what might have happened. But a part of her still loved David desperately, and during hours when that part happened to prevail over the other she was far more likely to have given him mandrake potion than poison. Besides, she was allowed no access to David at all any more, to do him either harm or good; Bathsheba saw to that.

On several occasions when Absalom visited, Maacah tried to involve him in her outlandish rituals, but he was no more comfortable with these than he was with the worship of Adonai. He dismissed all fervent religion as hysterical and superstitious, observing only those formalities which he couldn't avoid, and keeping anything more spiritual at arm's length. It reminded him he was neither truly Syrian nor a pure-bred son of Israel. It made him profoundly unsure of who he was.

One night Maacah didn't go to bed at all. While I lay tossing and sweating I could hear her intoning prayers in Aramaic, and I knew she was preparing some drug at the same time. While it was still dark she got me up. She'd been on the roof and a desert wind had whisked her hair wild about her face; her eyes were avid and wandering. She pressed a little burnt-clay flask into my hand and said, 'At first light you must go and ask permission to see the King. If you go early enough *her* agents won't be about, and Jehoshaphat will let you in. You must tell His Majesty that you would like to be taught music again. He'll offer you wine, then go and tune his harp. While he's busy with that, you must pour this liquid into his drink. Can you do it?'

I stared into her ardent face, then at the tiny flask, and knew I could. My serpent stealth would enable me physically, and my contempt for David would take care of the rest. I got dressed and

96

slipped the flask into the folds of my cloak. But as I was on my way out, Maacah gripped my shoulders and snatched back what she'd entrusted to me, smashing the container into fragments on the floor where its contents soaked into the rug, mixed with her tears.

Since I'd had to rise early from my pit, I decided to get my daily visit to Absalom's over and done with before anyone else was around. I had some cakes left over from yesterday, and a handful of dried figs, so I put them in a basket and crept out.

When I arrived, Absalom was still asleep, sprawled fully clothed over the couch nearest the door. No doubt this was the furthest he'd managed to crawl after a typical evening's entertainment. Miriam's door was closed.

But Tamar wasn't in bed. Neither was she in the bath, or so it seemed at first, for I couldn't discern the familiar outline of her cropped head and bony back against the half-light. I went to the window and pushed open the shutter to let in the morning, and when I turned round I saw her. She was lying in the tub with her arms folded across her chest, her eyes wide open and her face underneath yesterday's cold water. Miriam found me a long while later, crouched rigid in a corner.

I don't remember what happened after that. Not the grief, not the keening, not the funeral; nothing. For weeks—months?—I must have lived like a caterpillar in a chrysalis. Some long-submerged level of my mind couldn't cope. I think I spent most of that hopeless, half-real time in bed, hugging the pillows.

But I was a little boy no longer, and in a while I came to myself and learned to carry on. I wasn't the person Tamar had wanted me to be any more, though. I still waited on her mother, and I was still civil to the people around me, for I didn't want to go back to begging in the kitchens. Yet I knew I'd been wiser in those days. I'd had it all worked out back then: let no one love you, love no one in return, and the world can't hurt you. Surely I must be able to live like that again?

So that was what I did. I watched, I listened, but I didn't get involved. I watched Maacah sink in a morass of despair, and I listened to Miriam, who was no less devastated, striving futilely to redeem her. Miriam came back to live with us, for she'd lost her own parents to the famine-plague, and there was nowhere else she wanted to go.

But it was Absalom who seemed the most intensely affected by the final episode of Tamar's tragedy. He changed overnight. He gave up the drinking and the womanizing. He took to spending most of his time with his mother, but they hardly talked. He grew withdrawn and broody, which was wholly unlike him; and calculating. He was planning something, but I didn't know what, and I'd given up communicating enough to find out.

'We should go back to Syria,' Maacah said one evening, after we'd eaten our meal in silence. 'There's nothing to keep us here any more. We've lost Tamar, and Eliada and Eliphelet. We've as good as lost David. Let's go home to Geshur, Absalom, where my father rules. I should be better off as a daughter there than as a widow here. And we could find a rich Aramaean princess for you to marry.'

'Geshur isn't *my* home,' growled Absalom. 'It's not where *my* father rules.' But I could see a dark flame burning behind his eyes, illumining the confusion.

Two days later he went to the King, and asked to be given an advance on his inheritance forthwith. He bought a large estate at Baal Hazor near the town of Ephraim, about a day's journey north-east of Jerusalem, and announced his intention to move there—alone.

He remained impervious to his mother's tearful reproaches. 'Absalom, my darling, how can you do this?' she pleaded with him. 'Can't you take me with you? I'll be so lonely—am I to lose the only child I have left?'

'You are the wife of the King, whether he likes it or not,' Absalom stated flatly. 'It wouldn't be right for you to leave Jerusalem; you'd be giving Bathsheba exactly what she wants, *and* you'd be a laughing-stock. Besides, the house has been neglected. A lot of work needs to be done on it before it would be a fit place for a noblewoman to live.'

'Won't you send for me when it's ready, then? At least I could come to stay for a while. I could help you choose the furnishings, and supervise the decoration—'

'Mother, when it's ready I shall throw a magnificent party. You can *all* come, you and Miriam and Zohel, and anyone who is anyone. Will that make you happy?'

'Happy?' Maacah laughed bitterly. 'It would take more than a party to make me happy now. And this hardly seems an appropriate time to be thinking of such things, Absalom. I can't for the life of me see why you have to go to Baal Hazor at all. You could employ someone to manage the estate while you stay here. Though the gods alone know why you bought it in the first place.'

Absalom kissed her lightly on the brow. He just said, 'You'll have to trust me.'

It was several weeks before we heard from him. I'd begun to think that perhaps we never would. Then he sent a servant with the invitations to his party.

Maacah read his message with mounting incredulity. The event was being planned to celebrate the completion of the summer sheep-shearing, and half Jerusalem was expected to be there, including the King himself and every one of his sons—even Amnon.

'I don't understand it,' Maacah said, when the slave had gone on his way. 'This will be the most extravagant party Israel has ever witnessed, and all in honour of a few sheep. He'll never rise above the debt it will put him into.'

'I should imagine that his sheep number rather more than a few,' ventured Miriam, quietly but sagely as always. 'More like a few thousand. He's no doubt making a healthy profit up there already and wants to show off his success.'

'But imagine what it will cost to lay on a banquet fit for the King, and then to entertain him and his entire entourage for as long as it takes them to recover from it! Why does Absalom have to be so ostentatious all the time? It will be the ruin of him.'

This in effect was the reply David sent back; with the result that Absalom swept into Jerusalem in person, in an attempt to make his father change his mind. From what he told us afterwards, he'd argued with David for half a morning but couldn't persuade him. The King had hedged and stalled, labouring the expense and the security risk, and the trouble Absalom would have to go to in order to accommodate all the royal bodyguard and see that protocol was observed. Absalom wound up convinced that David simply couldn't face the journey. For in the end he'd agreed to send his sons to represent him, and with that Absalom would have to be content.

And so he was, to a point.

'Bathsheba doesn't even want him to send my brothers,' he remarked with some relish, after flamboyantly declining the wine his mother offered him as lubrication for his journey back up north.

'You've seen her?' Maacah rasped.

'She was there seething all the time I was talking to him,' replied Absalom, 'Though I'd have got nowhere near him if she'd found out beforehand that I was in the city. She doesn't trust me an inch any more, I could see that. She wouldn't have let him come to Baal Hazor even if he'd wanted to, and she said he'd regret letting any other member of his household come up either.'

'And will he?' Maacah knit her brows, and Absalom squirmed a little.

'Mother, Tamar is gone. There's nothing we can do to bring her back. I haven't spoken to Amnon in two years. Don't you think it's time to put things right?'

'Who said anything about Amnon? I don't even want to talk about him.'

'For heaven's sake, Mother! I came home to encourage those I love most to come and help me celebrate, not to get into arguments with them! Why don't you just set your mind to deciding what you're going to wear?'

Maacah blurted, 'Your sister is dead! I can never forgive, and nor should you. How can I fill my head with frivolities? How can I contemplate eating and drinking and making merry at the same table as my daughter's murderer? I don't even want to *be* there! Miriam and Zohel may go, if they like. Abigail can take them.'

Absalom pressed her hands in his. '*I* want you to be there. I want you to witness the occasion and share in it. I want Amnon to witness it too. Afterwards you may feel better. The experience may bring healing.'

'Absalom, you're talking like some feeble-minded prophet, not a prince! I should never have allowed your father to pollute you with the half-baked teachings of Adonai. Healing, forgiveness, putting things right—'

'Mother, promise me you'll come. It's important to me. I love you. Make me happy.'

He was smiling, his kohl-smoky eyes were imploring; his mother shook her head but with fading conviction. Then when Absalom pouted coquettishly she kissed his jutting lip, and I knew she'd be going.

The forthcoming extravaganza quickly became the talk of Jerusalem. It seemed that everyone had sorely missed the King's handsomest son since he'd been away from the city; for he was more handsome than ever, despite the abuses to which he'd subjected his body throughout adolescence. Now he was eighteen and still not betrothed, so every girl in Israel wanted to be at his banquet.

Besides, as the land was still struggling to recover from the famine, there had been no treat such as this promised to be in as long as anyone cared to remember. No doubt many of the northern farmers would have to tighten their belts in order to furnish the luxuries Absalom required. But knowing him, and the effect his charms tended to have on folk he met, regardless of their station, they would probably contribute voluntarily.

It was a spectacular cavalcade that left Jerusalem for Baal Hazor. At its head rode David's sons: those born in Hebron—Amnon, Adonijah, Shephatiah and Ithream—and the four eldest of those born in the new palace. They wore their finest robes, and the bridles of their mules were festooned with flowers. Next came a score of David's wives and concubines with their children and servants, travelling in covered wagons to protect them from the elements and from the eyes of men. Maacah, Miriam and I were among them; Bathsheba and her cosseted son were conspicuous by their absence. Behind us followed a host of courtiers, noblemen, traders and officials, with their wives and grown-up children; Shimei and Sheba and a crowd of Absalom's old drinking companions; and anyone else who'd managed to wangle himself one of the coveted invitations. As the procession approached the town, dusk was falling, and the road leading to the Prince's estate was lined with slave girls waving torches.

The banquet had been laid out in a large open courtyard. It was already thronged with people: mostly local dignitaries and their families from Baal Hazor, for Absalom would certainly have won their favour by now. But there were also a dozen or so plainly dressed, dour-faced youths moving in attendance among them, all clad alike in coarse tunics, with bulky woollen cloaks clasped around their necks.

I hadn't yet seen Absalom himself among the revellers, so I was startled when he appeared at my shoulder and drew me to one side. Shaking off a succession of maidens, matrons and matchmakers trying to fawn over him, he led me indoors and sat me down in an unlit room smelling of fresh plaster, from which the noise of the crowds was barely audible. There was no one about, but he addressed me in a hoarse whisper.

'Zohel, listen to me carefully and don't ask questions. Afterwards you may have to get Mother, Miriam and yourself away from here quickly. It may not be wise for you to go back to the palace. Shimei has a kinsman who lives alone in a large house near the Tabernacle—you know the place I mean? He's got plenty of space to accommodate you, and will be well paid. Do you understand?'

I didn't. I stared at him blankly, then said, 'After what?'

'Zohel, I told you not to ask questions! Do you understand the instructions? That's all I want to know.'

'Well yes, but . . .'

'Good. I'm relying on you, little serpent.' He patted my cheeks, then was up and dragging me back to the party; he seemed as restive as a rock-badger. I wanted to ask him what was wrong, but found myself squashed in amongst the milling guests once more. No one took any notice of me; they were all too busy circulating, weighing up who it was best to be seen with. Absalom was just a bobbing black head in the distance.

Presently the time came to sit down for the feasting. Trestle tables ran the length of the courtyard, and the cloaked attendants were charged with apportioning places. Maacah was next to Absalom on his right, at the top table, and Miriam and I were surprised to be given seats there too; I'd expected to be standing up serving. To Absalom's left sat his brothers, Amnon first. Jonadab had to be content with a place further off, among the King's less immediate relatives.

Everything seemed to be going swimmingly. The food was rich and varied and exquisitely prepared, and the pleasure-starved diners devoured it voraciously. Wine flowed in abundance, and the smiling faces around our table rapidly went red in the torchlight. Adonijah, Shephatiah and Ithream, barely past boyhood, got shamelessly drunk—expertly aided by Shimei and Sheba. Absalom let everyone see the attendants bringing him goblet after goblet of wine, but I never saw him drain one of them.

In contrast, Amnon drained several, but slouched moody and morose beside his brother, not knowing how he should behave. A troupe of local girls playing pipes and drums and dancing up and down between the benches provoked a flagrant display of flirting from Absalom, which delighted all present except Amnon and Maacah; and Miriam. Absalom tried to detach one of the girls from the chain and get her to sit on Amnon's knee, revelling in the latter's embarrassment, but the joke was abruptly foiled when a brawl broke out further down the table. Someone must have insulted the memory of Saul, for Shimei was up on his feet with his fists clenched, railing, while Sheba vainly tried to intervene between him and the burly clan chieftain who was baiting him. Normally Absalom would have been amused. But now he despatched four of his attendants to break the fight up.

I think Amnon was already wishing he hadn't come. I wasn't sure why he had done, except that he was patently so uneasy with Absalom that maybe he couldn't stomach the tension between them any longer, and had his own reasons for wanting to mend their relationship. Absalom was certainly trying hard to engage him in conversation.

'Amnon, my dearest brother, why all these frowns and sour looks? You're going to spoil my party! Come, we used to be such good friends once upon a time, and we have so much in common. Now don't say you can't see what! We are both eligible young bachelors, princes no less, sons of the same pious and illustrious father. We both share the same desire to find favour in his eyes, and one day to—take over from him when he leaves off, so to speak. And we both have a way with the girls, don't we, Amnon? We both have our methods of getting them to do what we want them to.'

But Amnon only shrank away and looked round frantically for Jonadab. Two of Absalom's youths had got him well and truly distracted by an exotic beauty who was professing to read their fortunes in the lees of their wine. Two brainless-looking thugs who passed for Amnon's bodyguard were similarly occupied.

'After all, Amnon,' Absalom continued blithely, wrapping his arms around his brother's neck and breathing spice into his nostrils, 'The one thing that kept us apart is gone now, isn't it? What is there to prevent us from laying the past to rest? You're a rational and intelligent man, just as I am. We can't let history ruin our lives for ever, now can we? Life is too short to spend it in vain regret for what might have been, don't you agree? The time has come to act, Amnon, to exorcize old ghosts and look to the future.'

Amnon's wine-fuddled eyes bulged wider and wider, as Absalom's face loomed closer and closer to his own.

'You're looking so confused, my dearest. I thought I was making myself perfectly clear. Perhaps you'd like me to explain my meaning a little more bluntly.' Absalom paused, drew back slightly to look Amnon straight in the eyes. When he spoke again, he'd dropped the unctuous flattery, and his tone was barbed as a hunting-spear. 'Tamar is dead.' And when Amnon still sat there dumbstruck,

Absalom threw back his head and yelled to the kindling stars, 'My sister Tamar is dead!'

That must have been the signal. The dour-faced youths moved on Amnon in concert, drawing iron swords from the folds of their bulky cloaks. Absalom stood out of their way as they went in for the kill, his face still tilted to the sky, the blue-black hair streaming rampant as dark fire down his back. He was aloof, unarmed, unstained by the blood, exultant.

No doubt this was how he would have liked it to end: Amnon prostrate at his feet, the blighted royal ichor spread like a red carpet over which he would walk to claim his throne, accompanied by shouts of acclamation from his awestruck admirers. No one loved a spectacle more than Absalom did. No one but Absalom would have arranged for a murder to take place as the climax to a banquet rather than down some dark desolate alleyway. More to the point, no one had liked Amnon, everyone had heard the rumours, and now they had witnessed things being put right between the two brothers in the only way they could be, if justice were to be done and seen to be done.

But Absalom didn't quite get his way. At the last moment some of the hired killers, well drilled though they'd appeared to be, lost their nerve and fumbled. Amnon emerged from their circle crawling on all fours, howling, with blood pouring from half a dozen shallow and ill-aimed wounds, and a great flap of skin hanging from his neck where one of the youths had made a clumsy attempt to slit his throat.

Suddenly everyone was screaming, and scrabbling for cover; Amnon grasped the edge of the table to try to haul himself upright, and overturned it onto himself, sending cups and plates rolling among the panicking multitude so that many tripped and fell, bringing others crashing down with them.

The killers, terrified now of being rounded up and brought to trial, or of simply being cut down where they stood, shed their distinguishing cloaks and went to work with their swords, hacking at anyone who got in their way. Blood, wine and sauces ran together in the gutters, torn human flesh was trampled along with the daintily carved joints which had graced the feast. Amid the chaos Amnon crawled on, howling and dying, but no one was there to hold his hand. Jonadab had left already, anxious to save his own skin, and David's other sons were swiftly whisked away by their minders.

Absalom too, when he saw the way things were going, simply vanished. At first I couldn't fathom where he would run to, though I was sure he'd have thought of somewhere. It was only when I pulled myself together enough to shepherd his mother and Miriam to safety, that I saw the mingled horror and pride stamped on Maacah's features, and realized.

There was no other reason why Absalom should have bought a property so far to the north-east.

9

Absalom was gone; and it was as though the light had gone out of our lives. Yes, he was a lawbreaker who had brought about the death of his own half-brother, yet no one could deny that it was Amnon who had brought about Tamar's. And as Absalom had probably hoped, he was by no means alone in considering Amnon's crime the more heinous of the two. There were even some who regarded Absalom as the instrument of Adonai's righteous anger.

Certainly no one could dispute that Absalom had displayed courage: the courage which his father ought to have shown, and once would have done, in the days when he'd slain giants and massacred entire Philistine garrisons virtually unaided. Now David was seen as old and weak and vacillating, in contrast to his avenging son who was young, strong and virile. But the fledgling hero had flown.

Predictably, there were also those who saw Amnon's murder as nothing more than the savage handiwork of a jealous and greedy adolescent; or worse, as one step on a ruthless schemer's bloody quest for the crown.

Personally I doubt it. Oh, I know Absalom was hardly stupid enough to have overlooked the fact that he'd summarily disposed of his arch-rival—impetuous though he was, and perhaps not quite so intelligent as he liked to imagine. But securing the succession wasn't his prime motivation; I'm convinced of that. He was always one to follow his heart sooner than his head. And in his heart, the loss of his sister and the disgrace which her defilement had brought upon his close family had left some very ugly scars.

It was several months before we heard for definite where the fugitive Prince had holed up. No doubt he had trouble finding a reliable messenger who could get the news to us without it falling into vindictive hands along the way. But we were hardly surprised to learn that he was in Geshur.

Meanwhile, although the famine was over, Israel's fortunes still seemed to be sliding irrevocably downhill. Her enemies languished, thwarted and subdued, but something was eating away at her welfare from inside. The way I saw it, we had a rotten king at the core of our nation, and everything with which he had contact was manifestly decaying.

Nowhere was this more apparent than in the royal household itself. Only weeks after Absalom's departure Shephatiah, the fourth of David's sons, died of a wasting sickness. He'd been deteriorating all through those three barren summers, growing thinner and thinner like the poor wretches in the streets, although unlike them he'd had plenty to eat. When Jerusalem's granaries were full again he'd seemed to pick up, and at Absalom's party had been as merry as anyone. Perhaps it was the drink that set him back, or else the shock, because he was never the same after that. And before the olives were harvested, he was dead.

Ithream, the fifth son, survived him by less than three weeks. His broken body was found dumped outside the palace gates early one morning, already stiff and stinking. He was alleged to have been jumped by a gang of peasant farmers who had lost their sons in the famine. They blamed David and wanted to show him what grief felt like, though it was hard to see why they thought that this was necessary. Of the princes born in Hebron, only Absalom and Adonijah now remained.

As for the King himself, he hadn't been seen in public since receiving the news of Amnon's murder. It hadn't exactly been broken to him gently. Panic-stricken survivors with their garments in tatters had arrived hot-foot from Baal Hazor crying that Absalom had gone crazy and slaughtered every one of his half-brothers. Not until Jonadab appeared on the scene, dry-eyed and tight-lipped, did the real truth become established. An ocean of blood had been shed, but with the exception of Amnon's, none of it had been royal.

So while David mourned in private, Ahithophel and Hushai his assistant dealt with matters of international diplomacy, leaving Joab and Abishai to take charge of defence.

In the day-to-day enforcement of law and order, and in the administration of local justice, no one seemed to have any interest. The strong took advantage of the weak, the poor were exploited increasingly and the northern tribes resented what they saw as the relative prosperity and influence of those in the south. Gradually, various downtrodden minorities came to adopt the King's absent son as their champion. Thus a half-Syrian murderer living in exile paradoxically acquired a reputation as the staunch defender of all that was right, and the only hope for the future of Israel.

From time to time I got wind that David wanted to see me, but I heard nothing official so I didn't go. Not that anything official could reach me, for Maacah, Miriam and I were living, supposedly in secret, at the house of Shimei's kinsman. For over two years we believed that no one at court knew where we were. We never went outside, except to sit in our own courtyards, and spoke to no one except our host and his servants, who provided for our every need. I took our imprisonment in my stride, as I did most hardships. After all, I'd lived the same kind of life back at Machir's, even if I'd never known why. And at least here there was no Ziba.

I did see him once, though, quite unexpectedly. I was up on the roof, peeping over a parapet where no one would notice me, watching the comings and goings in the street below. It was Passover, and Jerusalem was thronged with pilgrims. Stalls lined every alleyway, pedlars tramped up and down hawking the goods piled on their shoulders, children shouted, dogs barked, and the whole city heaved like the inside of a wasps' nest. Then I heard a trumpet blaring above the tumult, and seven burly slaves came marching abreast down the road, elbowing aside all who got in their way, clearing a path for the great personage whom they served.

It was Ziba, being carried in a litter. The curtains were partially drawn, but not so far that people couldn't tell who was inside, and be impressed. He was fatter these days, and his podgy red fingers dripped with gaudy gems. The bile rose within me, as I laboured to understand how this obnoxious toad who'd once been a slave himself could have acquired such odious wealth and status. Might it have something to do with his fetching my father and me to the palace so very long ago? Then a strange melancholy got mixed up with the bile in me. I hadn't seen my father in five years.

Every night for three weeks after that, bad dreams awoke me. I was a half-starved little boy again, mute and defenceless, cringing in a corner as Ziba came to get me. I could feel his clammy hands about my body, hear his heavy breathing, see the demons dancing behind his eyes. I think that's when I first conceived the notion of one day taking my revenge upon him, as Absalom had done upon Amnon, for what he had done to me. I was in no position to do it yet, but the time would come, and I would be ready.

About two and a half years after Absalom left us, Ahithophel turned up in person on our doorstep. I don't know how he'd suddenly located us. Perhaps he'd known where we were all along and it had suited him—and Bathsheba—to leave us there; or perhaps Nathan had just now divined our whereabouts the way these prophets sometimes can. Be that as it may, I was instructed to appear before the King; at once. Ahithophel would accompany me to the palace.

I was confounded. We all were. Supposing David had deduced that I knew where Absalom was, and intended to torture me until I told him? Miriam expressed this fear aloud, and was beside herself. She was pining for Absalom hopelessly; as indeed was Maacah. But Ahithophel stood waiting, with his arms folded placidly across his silken sash, while we panicked and prevaricated, and in the end of course I had to go.

I wasn't taken to the throneroom. David lay in bed in his own private quarters, and was clearly in a bad way. His hair was thin and receding, his cheeks sunken, his lips bloodless and cracked. I thought he must be dying, and I reckon his courtiers thought so too. I stood awkwardly by the foot of his bed, staring at my own fidgeting fingers. I was alone with him, for Ahithophel had immediately bowed himself out.

'Zohar,' said David, though his eyes had been closed when I arrived and he still hadn't opened them. 'Come closer. Take my hand.'

Swallowing hard, I did so. His knuckles were bony, his palm cold. I tried not to shudder, as he smiled at me and raised his eyes at last. The irises had gone pale, making the red veins in the whites seem redder.

'I'm sorry I had to send you such a formal summons.' He pushed himself up a little on his pillows. 'I'd much rather have asked you as a friend. But I didn't think you'd come.'

There was nothing I could say.

'The fact is—I've missed you, Zohar. I would have sent for you long before now if I hadn't felt so low, and if you hadn't got so upset when you saw me weeping. But I've missed our lessons, and the talks we used to have.'

I tried to pull away, but he still had a grip like iron.

'Poor Zohar; so many bad memories to live with, I think,' he said to soothe me. It didn't work. 'But you used to be happy when you came here. We were good friends, weren't we? I have so few friends,

Zohar. It's strange, don't you agree? To have so many companions but so few friends. That's why I miss you so much. I miss everyone who ever meant anything to me. Saul and Jonathan. Tamar. Maacah's little boys. And Amnon, Shephatiah, Ithream... Five of my sons dead within three years, and my only daughter. And so much of it my own fault.' He looked as though he wanted to say more, then lost the thread of it; his eyes wandered past me, to the corner of the room where his harp lay wrapped in its mantle. He said, 'Play to me again, Zohar. It's been so long.'

My mouth went dry and my fingers were trembling. 'Your Majesty, I can't. I've forgotten how. My technique—'

'Never mind your technique. It was never your strong point. Play from your heart, your *spirit*, Zohar. That's what you always did best. You can't forget that.'

How could I tell him I'd rejected Adonai? Part of me thought he ought to know anyway. He let go of my hand, and I walked reluctantly over to where the harp lay, folding back the cover and lifting the heavy instrument in both arms. That was when I realized it wasn't his harp at all, but mine. Something squirmed, deep down inside of me, just like it did each time he called me Zohar.

Nervously I perched on the edge of the bed and spread my fingers across the harpstrings. The patterns of the chords came back to me, but I could play nothing but mechanical exercises I'd learnt as a raw beginner; and those slowly and hesitantly, peppered with mistakes.

He didn't seem to mind, or wouldn't show it. He relaxed and lay back, and started to say something. I stopped, but he bade me play on and pay him no heed. So I did, and realized he was trying to pray. It seemed to be a struggle, and presently he was no longer addressing Adonai, but me once more.

'You know, when I was your age I spent hours doing this for Saul. I never imagined everything could be turned on its head. To think that one day *I* would be the sad, sickened monarch, no longer able to serve the God he loves. I dreamed of building him a Temple, you know. I'd made all the plans; you saw them. It didn't seem right for me to be living in this fabulous palace while the Ark of Adonai was still in a tent. Now Nathan says I can't do it, I've fought too many wars. I must let the dream go, and some other man will dream it. What is there left for me to do, Zohar? Am I simply to go mad like Saul did? Is that the fate in store for every king of Israel?'

I couldn't play any more; my thoughts were in turmoil. I'd wilfully turned my back on Adonai, so why should it disturb me now that David himself seemed to be losing his grip on his God? I hung my head and hid behind my fringe.

'Zohar, I'm so sorry. But there's no one else I can talk to who'd have a hope of understanding. Nathan is the only man at court who knows Adonai, and not even he can begin to comprehend what I'm suffering. When Saul was sick, I was no older than you, but I understood.'

Momentarily our eyes met, and I think he did know, then, that I no longer had what he'd once had, when he'd been in my place with the man he'd supplanted. He pressed the palms of his hands against his eyelids. 'What have I done to you, Zohar? Not even you have been spared from the blight I've brought down on my own household. It's my fault Tamar was ruined, and then taken from us . . . I ought never to have trusted Amnon or Jonadab; yet Jonadab is my nephew, and Amnon was my son! Amnon's blood must be on my head too. Bathsheba warned me not to trust Absalom; for once I overrode her, and what good did it do me? Even Jonadab told me I should have known better! He said I could have guessed for two years what Absalom was planning, just from looking at his face. Was he right, Zohar? I'd barely even *seen* Absalom since Tamar's rape. I'd neglected him, I'd neglected *all* my sons. Now it's too late.'

He fell silent, his face turned into the pillows. I thought that he was weeping again. I muttered without conviction, 'Adonai is a God of forgiveness, my lord. Can't he forgive you for all this?'

'That's just it, Zohar. He *has* forgiven it—and worse. Much worse. I know he has, and Nathan assures me it's true. But I don't deserve it! I'm not *worth* forgiving, when I've done things so much more terrible than Saul ever did! I am much worse than Saul, yet Adonai rejected him as king, and cut off his dynasty before it even began! Whilst I'm still here, and Nathan says that one of my sons will inherit my throne come what may. I can still pray to my God and know he listens, I can even feel his peace when I worship, until I refuse to accept it any longer. I'm in hell, Zohar, because I'm *not* cut off like Saul was, yet I deserve to be! One sick secret is holding me to ransom . . . I don't think I can bear it any longer.'

Then while I sat there with the harp clasped to my breast in mute irresolution, he started rambling again about my face and how it haunted him, and how it brought back to him so much that was painful. I mumbled, 'I ought not to be here,' and got up to leave. But he begged me not to go, saying I was all he had left. In the end he broke down utterly and admitted he missed Absalom.

I said, 'But *Absalom* isn't dead. You could find out where he is and pardon him, and welcome him home.'

'After what he's done? No, Zohar. I would never be allowed to. Besides, what have I got to offer him any more, to compare with what he has at his grandfather's court? Oh yes, I know where he is. Ahithophel may be arrogant, but he serves me well. Poor Absalom . . . I so much wanted him to be king after me. He's comely and confident and the people have always loved him. But there's no chance of it now. Not after what he did to Amnon.'

'He'd never have got to be king if he *hadn't* done it. Amnon was the eldest son.'

'I'd told him before, Zohar. This isn't Egypt. Adonai chooses whom he chooses. It needn't even have been one of my sons, except that he's chosen to promise me it will be.'

'You could offer Absalom your love,' I suggested. 'That's the only thing he's ever really wanted.'

I was shocked by my own temerity as soon as I'd spoken, and the more so when I saw the renewed anguish on David's face. I whispered, 'Is that the secret? That you still love Absalom best, even after what he's done?'

'Oh, if only that were all it was.' He tipped back his head and closed his eyes; he was so pale and drawn, he looked almost as bad as when I'd first come in. 'I wish I could tell you. Truly I do. And one day I shall, if it's the last thing I do, because I have so many wishes that can *never* be fulfilled. I still wish I could give the throne to Absalom . . . but the future isn't in my hands. Adonai has made his choice, and today I have learnt what that choice is. That's why I had to talk to someone.'

My blood went to water. 'You know who is going to be king?'

'Yes, Zohar. I know.'

'Who? Who is it? Or is that a secret too? Adonijah?'

'No, not Adonijah. Solomon.'

Solomon! I said nothing, but my face must have been thunder.

'Zohar, she made me promise her! Bathsheba . . . I had no choice! Then Nathan confirmed it was the will of Adonai! Can you believe it? A boy not five years old whom no one ever sees—not even me! Suppose I die tomorrow? Are the tribes going to accept a child who can't even say the Shema yet? Who will be appointed as his regent? I don't even know if the lad is fit to be presented at court, let alone be its sovereign! He could be half-witted, deformed, leprous, anything! At the very least he'll be like *her*. Oh God, what a nightmare.' And when I did nothing but stare at him aghast he added, 'You thought I loved Bathsheba better than Maacah, or Absalom? My precious Zohar, if only you knew.'

Whatever the cord was that had held me to the bed and kept me listening until now, snapped like a bowstring made of glass. For the second time I fled from him without asking permission, thinking: he's right, he *does* deserve to be punished. It's his own fault that he's in this pit. Bathsheba rules him, and now her brat will rule Israel; she even has Nathan in her pay. And it's Nathan who ought to be David's confessor, not me. Let him keep the job, because I can't handle it.

But I wasn't going to get away with forsaking David this time round. Ahithophel came back for me the next week, and the next. He said that my visits still did the King good, though for my part I couldn't begin to see why they should do. I never spoke to him after the day he told me that Solomon was to be his heir. I played my harp, after a fashion, and let him talk at me, but I didn't even listen. I'd had plenty of practice at building walls around myself, and I put it to good use.

One good thing to come of my renewed acquaintance with David was that Maacah, Miriam and I no longer had to live like stowaways. Plainly no harm was going to come to us; but none of us were in any hurry to move back into the palace. The house of Shimei's kinsman had to be preferable to the old cramped quarters of Bathsheba, which would only serve to remind us of how far our fortunes had fallen.

Meanwhile it was clear to me that David's condition was getting worse, but the doctors could find nothing wrong with him. Ahithophel and Hushai, Joab and Abishai, and even Jehoshaphat, were deeply anxious—I might have found their concern for him touching if I hadn't realized it was actually themselves that they cared about. They feared for their own futures at court if he were to die on them. Ahithophel at least ought not to worry, though, I thought: he's about to see his own great-grandson inherit an empire.

One day some months later, when I was with David, a stooping

113

old crone was shown in by Jehoshaphat. I was startled, because lately no one outside of the King's immediate circle had been allowed to see him, and I had never laid eyes on this woman in my life. She was patently distraught; her loosened white hair was uncovered and dishevelled, her black robe torn in mourning. She grovelled on the ground at the foot of the royal bed and quavered, 'Help me, Your Majesty. You're my only hope.'

David didn't answer. I'd been playing to him, and he'd drifted into sleep; I had to touch his hand before he opened his eyes and grasped that we were no longer alone. He was too far gone to be embarrassed about his appearance, or even to be angry with Jehoshaphat for letting this miserable creature in. In times past, when he'd been himself and kept court in his throneroom, he must have seen a hundred suppliants like this one every day. Recently their plaintive cries had gone unheeded.

But now David had me prop him up on his pillows; he planted a watery gaze on the woman's prostrate body, blinking his eyes into focus, and asked what he could do for her.

She answered him without raising her head. 'Your Majesty, I'm a poor widow. I had two teenaged sons—wayward and headstrong, both of them, since my husband died; too much for me to control on my own. But I loved them, Your Majesty, I really did. Then one day last week they got into a quarrel out in the fields where there was no one to separate them, and the younger one killed the older.

'Now all my relatives have turned against me, and are demanding I hand over to them the one who survived, so they can put him to death for murdering his brother! If they do this . . . Your Majesty, I'll be left childless, with no one to take care of me. And my poor late husband will have no one to keep his name alive.'

I could see her plight had moved him, and it wasn't hard to guess why. David said softly, 'Get up off the floor. Let me look at you properly.'

The woman rose, with some difficulty, for she gave the impression of being more than seventy. She lifted her deeply lined face, but kept her eyes averted. Both of us took it for modesty.

'Go home,' said David with weary tenderness. 'Leave your burden with me. I'll take care of it, as soon as I'm better.'

But she didn't move. 'Your Majesty—something must be done at once. They may even have arrested him while I've been here.' She buried her face in her hands, her shoulders jerking, but there were no tears running between her fingers. 'I'm sorry,' she blurted. 'I shouldn't have said that. Whatever happens, my kinsfolk and I are to blame, I can't deny it. I ought to have been firmer with the boys. My relations ought not to be so heartless. It isn't your fault; you and the royal family are innocent.'

David said, 'Please, don't worry. If anyone threatens you, I shall deal with him personally. He'll never trouble you again.' Then the King closed his eyes; he hadn't conversed with a stranger at such length for months. Despite the sympathy which the old woman had evoked from him, the interview had already exhausted him utterly and he wanted it over. But she was apparently intent on making it last as long as possible.

'Your Majesty—please will you pray for me and my family now, to the Lord your God? You know Adonai. If I could go home believing that he too cared about me, that he could intervene so that the kinsman who is responsible for avenging my first son's death won't commit a greater crime by robbing me of my second...'

It was at this point that I decided she was being too much of a nuisance. I put my harp down on the bed and took hold of the woman by the shoulders, meaning to steer her out quietly. But she sprang forward out of my grasp with unnerving agility, and shamelessly seized the King's hand.

'Your Majesty, I need to ask you one last thing,' she said, and all the quaking had gone from her voice, and the stoop from her back. 'Why have you done such a wrong to God's people? Why do you deprive them of *their* only hope? We shall all of us die one day—we're like water spilt on the ground which can never be collected up again. Even God doesn't bring the dead back to life. But the King can at least find a way to bring a man back from exile.'

All of a sudden David's eyes flung open, so wide I could see the whites all round. I really thought his heart had stopped. I got hold of the woman round the waist this time, to drag her away from him; as she struggled to fend me off, I saw that most of the lines on her face were painted, and the flour from her hair fell like snow on my tunic. Somehow I got her to the door, but froze as David's cracked voice cried, 'Wait!' I turned to find him sitting on the edge of the bed, with its coverings still swaddled about his legs.

'Come here,' he ordered, with such unexpected authority that I loosed my hold on my prisoner, and she walked towards him unsteadily. In the back of my mind something was chiding me for writing David off, but I suppressed it; and that wasn't too hard to do, for as soon as she knelt before him, he looked as though he wished he'd let her go. It was plain terror that had jolted the wits back into him. Ashen-faced, he said, 'Woman, there are two things I must ask *you*. You have to tell me the truth.'

'Your Majesty.' I think by now she was as scared as he was.

'This story about your sons; that's all it is, isn't it? A story. None of it really happened.'

The woman looked at him sideways, wrung her hands; and admitted it.

'Someone put you up to this. I want to know who it was.'

But she kept quiet. David asked her a second time, and a third; still she knelt in cringing silence, darting a couple of furtive glances in my direction. Perhaps she was hoping I might have another go at expelling her. Then something must have fallen into place in David's harried mind, and he whispered, 'It was Joab. Am I right? Answer me!'

She nodded, and David crumpled like a punctured wineflask.

Guilt loosened the woman's tongue at that. She began babbling that she hadn't wanted to tell him; she'd done her level best to avoid it; Joab had warned her of the effect it would probably have if she spilled the beans. But he'd only played this tasteless trick out of concern for his King—his uncle—for he knew the pain David was suffering through being apart from his precious Absalom whilst at the same time being too stubborn to recall him. All the while I was looking daggers at her, willing her to leave while I got the King back in bed. I was afraid lest somehow *I* might get the blame for over-taxing him. Eventually she took the hint and crept out, but the moment she'd gone, David was begging me to have Jehoshaphat send for Joab.

I said, 'Please, my lord. Not now. Rest a little first.'

'Now, Zohar! Do as I tell you . . .' He broke off, heaving for breath, but by gestures convinced me that he wouldn't change his mind.

Confused, I scrambled to obey. All along I'd imagined that the King would have recalled Absalom already, if it hadn't been for opposition from those around him. Perhaps the opposition was all in his head; or perhaps it all stemmed from one root, the root which had also given birth to Solomon. But I couldn't imagine why David should have traced Joab's hand in what I'd witnessed. Artful deception didn't strike me as Joab's style at all, nor the use of a parable to get a man hung up in his own noose. This kind of stratagem was much more like Nathan, from what little I'd seen of him, though I was sure Nathan wouldn't be advocating Absalom's restitution. I was reminded that something else lay behind all this; there was some piece in the puzzle that I was missing.

By the time Joab arrived, David was a nervous wreck. I think he'd wanted to appear stern and formidable—he'd had me comb his hair and drape an uncreased gold-trimmed cloak around his shoulders. But he was shaking all over, and as soon as the general walked through the door, he demanded, 'How much do you know? What did Nathan tell you?'

Joab was clearly as bewildered as I was. It wasn't the kind of question he'd been expecting. He mumbled, 'I beg your pardon, my lord?'

'About the Uriah affair! What did he tell you?'

Joab played for time by standing to attention, then asking permission to stand at ease, all the while studying David's face for any clues as to how much he would have to give away. Finally David lost patience entirely, and yelled at him, 'I may be old and sick but I'm no fool, Joab. You know as well as I do that you'd never have dreamt up a scheme like that by yourself. He's been talking to you about the Uriah affair behind my back, hasn't he? Admit it, or you're relieved of your command from this instant.'

The Uriah affair . . . Vague memories were stirring in the recesses of my mind, clouded images, the haggard faces and lacerated backs of two frightened prisoners . . . Then Joab must have realized he was going to have to come clean, and decided to make the best of it. Squaring his shoulders he said crisply, 'Yes, my lord. But to be frank, I didn't leave him much choice.'

David gaped. 'What did you do to him?'

'Don't be alarmed, my lord. He is perfectly all right. There would be little point in trying to crack that one under torture. But if for some reason he were to fear for the safety of his daughter . . . I merely applied a little pressure, that's all.'

Now David groaned; he looked nauseous. Joab stared fixedly at the wall directly above the King's head, only the way he kept shifting his weight almost imperceptibly from one foot to the other betraying his unease. Then in a small voice David asked, 'Why? What made you want to interrogate him in the first place?'

Again this wasn't the question Joab was expecting. He began hedging once more, but David went on pressing him until at length he too lost his cool; a rare occurrence, and mercifully so.

'For God's sake, David, I was worried to hell about you! I had good cause to be, don't you think? Just look at you! You used to be the finest warrior and military commander in this whole rotting world, damn you! I've talked to Ahithophel and Hushai and Jehoshaphat, and a dozen other feeble-minded ministers in your accursed government; I've talked to physicians and priests and even bleeding astrologers and not one of the lousy creatures knows what's wrong with you! I just thought Nathan might, that's all.'

'And . . . you think he does?'

'No I don't, confound him! He says you've sinned, but he's convinced you're forgiven. He believes your "relationship with Adonai has been restored"—whatever the hell *that* means. So why are you like this now? By any god in heaven, David—what's the matter with you?'

The King covered his face with the royal cloak. His shoulders sagged, and he whispered, 'You still haven't said how much he told you.'

Joab had been poised to rail at him some more, but he must have seen then that it was doing no good. He snorted, stamped his feet back to attention, and answered, 'My lord—he told me everything.'

'Everything . . . ?'

I knew they'd both forgotten I was there; and I knew that even if David did want me to learn his secret, this wasn't the way. I fidgeted, and Joab at any rate became conscious of my presence. His mouth had been open ready to elaborate; now he began more cagily.

' . . . Well, how he'd known for some time about your—indiscretion, my lord, and how you'd tried to cover your tracks. And yes—he did tell me the trick he'd employed to make you confess it all to him.' He glanced at me again, and decided he'd already divulged enough. 'Like I said, my lord. Everything.'

'So you know why Uriah had to . . . you know why I told you to . . .'

'Yes, my lord.' And as David's tears began to stain the cloak he added, 'If it's any comfort, my lord—I've known for a long time.'

Plainly it wasn't any comfort. David wept uncontrollably, leaving Joab acutely embarrassed and struggling for words. He wasn't the sort to take David in his arms, and instead mumbled, 'Really, there's nothing to fear, my lord. I've known this for longer than Absalom has been in exile.' The mention of his beloved son's name made the King look up, so Joab seized on the subject with alacrity. 'David, please! Why don't you fetch him back? Only a handful of pious prigs still hold Amnon's death against him, and they are merely jealous. All the rest of Israel wants to see him brought home. And *you* do, that's obvious to everyone. Perhaps *he'll* be able to mend your health and your spirits. I hope to goodness he can, David, because it seems nothing else will.'

The King did attempt to respond, but it took me a while to get any sense from what he was saying. We finally managed to make out that he was granting Joab's request and sobbing, 'Yes, bring him back, oh God, how I miss him.' Joab smiled slightly, clicked his heels, and strode out.

10

As you might imagine, there was nothing subtle or solemn about the exile's homecoming. He rode into Jerusalem on the crest of an early summer heatwave, with all the pageant of some oriental potentate returning victorious from a thousand battles. (So far as I knew he still had only one under his belt.) You might certainly have been forgiven for supposing he'd been made king already.

Maacah, Miriam and I ran up onto the roof to catch our first glimpse of him. The teeming crowds thronging the streets were if anything more exuberant and more densely packed than those which had once gathered to welcome their new idol's father from his triumph over Ammon.

All that seemed a very long time ago. Now the name of David might as well have been forgotten, because all the shouting and screaming was for Absalom himself, though as yet few of those present could actually see him. Personally I could see nothing but swaying arms and ecstatic faces, and could hardly hear myself think. Sundry factions of the turbulent assembly chanted their fervent devotion to the pardoned Prince, and waved banners acclaiming him as the saviour of his people, and the champion of any one of a dozen causes. Most of these he'd probably never even heard of, but no one seemed to care.

A fresh surge of excitement sweeping through the multitude in our direction warned us that we were about to see him at last. Although I'd been looking forward to this moment for weeks, and had dreamed away countless sultry afternoons picturing how he would look after so long abroad, I was still shocked.

He rode bare-chested as well as bare-headed, at the forefront of a veritable army of muscle-bound bodyguards and castrated slave boys and laden pack animals, in a flimsy two-wheeled racing chariot flagrantly Syrian in style. He drove it himself, and pulling it were two spotlessly salt-white horses decked in all-gold trappings, their manes braided with scarlet ribbons. Absalom's own hair fell almost to his waist, and was twisted into a hundred beaded plaits. All down his back and down the backs of his legs hung an ankle-length cloak of Tyrian purple, but the matching pleated kilt barely covered his thighs. Though at least twenty-one years old now he was still beardless, and his face was shamelessly painted. He wore heavy golden armbands, anklets and earrings, a ceremonial ivory-sheathed dagger slung on a leather thong across one shoulder; and for the first time, at least in Jerusalem, a sun and crescent moon around his neck. I wasn't exactly sure what meaning these had for those who normally sported them, and still less for Absalom, but I knew that Nathan would have had him burn them, or cast them in the nearest river.

All this would have been enough, but at Absalom's left-hand side (Joab rode on his right) stood a huge camel-coloured dog, half as tall as he was. Israel's darling had come back a tawdry foreign posturer, a walking violation of all that was modest and decent and sanctioned by the laws of Moses; and no one turned a hair.

I'd assumed that the procession would head for the palace first, out of respect to David as king, as well as because Absalom was surely desperate to be reunited with him as father. Indeed, he was steering the chariot that way. Then I noticed a man dressed in the uniform of the palace guards forcing a passage through the crowd. He ran up beside Joab making urgent gesticulations until Joab leaned down, and the man whispered in his ear briefly before losing himself once more among the rabble. Joab was left frowning. Absalom however remained blissfully unaware of this exchange, elated as he was by the extravagance of his reception. Despite the boundless confidence he'd always had in his own charisma and popularity, I don't think he'd expected to come back to anything quite like this. Finally Joab had to jab him unceremoniously in the ribs to gain his attention and bring him back to earth. After a short but apparently rather heated conversation, Absalom changed his course. He looked vaguely disgruntled; but then I realized he was making for our house.

Simultaneously Maacah and Miriam reached the same conclusion, and together we ran back downstairs into the courtyard. Our host's slaves drew back the bolts and flung the gates open, and the procession entered. It was longer even than I'd thought; behind the pack animals came horse-drawn wagons and mule carts. It cost the brawny bodyguards considerable time and effort to keep the general public from surging inside in their wake, but eventually they managed to get the gates shut again. While his retinue formed up in ranks, impressing even Joab with their discipline, Absalom leapt from his chariot and into the arms of his mother.

Predictably, Maacah thought he looked wonderful. She showered him with kisses and told him he was as beautiful as Baal the god of her ancestors, and that she'd missed him like she'd have missed half her own soul. And all those strapping soldiers and gorgeous young eunuchs ... could they really all be his? Absalom laughed happily, and told her that his grandfather King Talmai had insisted on his bringing them with him, together with a large quantity of gold and silver, and treasures of superb Syrian craftsmanship. For he couldn't have his grandson, a prince of Geshur, travelling like a pauper, and at the mercy of any bandit or tent-dwelling raider who felt like taking advantage of him. 'Besides,' he added, 'The prettiest three eunuchs are for you, Mother. Zoheleth is far too old to serve you now; his voice has broken! I'll take him and train him as my armour bearer—remember our agreement? You may have these. With your father's compliments—and mine.'

He snapped his fingers, and three of the gelded boys came forward. They had impossibly pale skins, and hair like gold.

'They're Akhaians,' Absalom explained. 'They've a smattering of Aramaic but no Hebrew at all. So they're even less likely to gossip than he is.' Absalom winked at me saucily; he was his old self inside. 'And they've spent every waking hour of these past three years as apprentice hairdressers. They're the best, I promise you. And you'll still have the lovely Miriam to instruct them in the finer points of Israelite etiquette.'

Miriam flushed crimson; Absalom bowed to her flamboyantly and kissed her fingers. Then he turned his attention fully upon me, planting his hands on my shoulders and looking me in the face, nodding approval. My heart swelled; I couldn't help it. I was thinking: there are those in the crowd who would give their right arms to be in my place now. I *shall* serve Absalom, because for the first time in my life I can be somebody, not the worthless nobody which Ziba tried to make of me.

'Well, you've certainly grown up, little serpent,' Absalom enthused. 'You'll be as tall as I am before long. And almost as handsome.' He laughed again as I felt myself go redder than Miriam. 'Now then, if you're going to be my constant companion, you'd better be introduced to the latest woman in my life.'

122

He gave another snap of the fingers, and to my abject horror, the great camel-haired dog loped down from the chariot, where it had waited as obediently as any of the attendants. It resumed its place at Absalom's heel, nuzzling his hand and swinging its tail alarmingly from one side to the other. Instinctively I shrank a pace backwards.

'Come, come, Zoheleth,' Absalom upbraided me with obvious enjoyment. 'You two will be seeing a lot of each other. You must become good friends. She won't hurt you, look: she does precisely as I tell her.' He whispered something in Aramaic, and the beast sank onto its haunches; something else, and it lay flat on the ground. 'Only my enemies need fear her. And she's so beautiful—don't you think so? I can't imagine why you Hebrews take such a dim view of one of Adonai's noblest creatures. This little lady has ancestry classier than mine! She comes from a long line of the finest hunting hounds in the world, and can trace her forebears back over at least six generations. Every one of them served a king.'

So, we were 'you Hebrews' now. But aloud I just enquired dubiously, 'She has a name, then?'

'Most certainly.' He grinned. 'Atargatis. That's what our blond-haired friends here call the lady Astarte.' I baulked, shocked that no one in Geshur should have minded their goddess's name being given to a dog. These repulsive animals must indeed be held in high regard there. 'But she'll answer to Gatis,' Absalom informed me. 'Why don't you see for yourself? Call her to you.'

But I couldn't bring myself to do so. Like most people, I'd grown up believing the only place for dogs was in the street, where they could chew up carrion before it spread disease.

After that, we went inside the house away from the stifling afternoon heat. Having presented his mother with whole baskets full of perfumes, fabrics and jewels, Absalom sat with the dog across his ankles, quaffing wine and extolling the virtues of Geshur until I wondered why he'd bothered to come back. Shimei and Sheba turned up with a handful of hangers-on, and began teasing him mercilessly, just about the only way they knew to go about communicating the fact that they were pleased to see him. They wanted to know how many hearts he'd broken in Syria, to which he replied only one or two. Then he got his own back by inciting the dog to lick their arms and legs and faces, at which they got even more agitated and disgusted than I'd been. Absalom feigned disappointment that none of us would dare to stroke his beloved Gatis, or even feed her any of the sweetmeats which Miriam brought round. Really, he was in his element.

Presently he got round to suggesting that Joab should accompany him to the palace, or he might be considered to be behaving disrespectfully—hardly a good way to begin. Perhaps life at a sophisticated foreign court had taught him manners, or at least some diplomacy. Joab grew distinctly uneasy at this juncture, however, and started making all kinds of excuses. David hadn't been well lately, he said, and since he often took a nap in the afternoons it would be better to wait until the evening. 'But surely he'll feel better once he's seen me?' Absalom objected; no, said Joab, the excitement might well prove too much for him just at present. 'Well, you could go in alone first, and give him time to prepare himself.' But Joab wouldn't have it, declaring instead that it was time for a party, seeing as so many of Absalom's old friends were already here; it wouldn't be polite to walk out on them now.

Of course, this proposal was guaranteed to appeal to the likes of Shimei and Sheba, especially when Joab commandeered half a dozen of Absalom's own servants to fetch as much food and wine as they could carry, at Joab's expense. Absalom I think was as wary as I was, yet neither of us could fathom what the general was up to, and Absalom hadn't noticed the man from the palace approach his chariot.

When the provisions arrived, Maacah and Miriam retired to the women's quarters whilst the men got down to the serious business of the day. Joab set out with awesome singleness of purpose to get Absalom utterly inebriated as fast as possible. Not that this posed any real problem; only when his mind was fixed on some nobler objective or more exquisite pleasure—such as the planning of his brother's murder and savouring the throes of it—could Absalom ever resist alcohol. Joab was ably abetted in his design by Shimei and Sheba, Shimei as usual growing louder and more aggressive the drunker he got, and Sheba vainly striving to placate him. After a while they inevitably came to blows, and in the largely good-natured brawl which ensued among their cronies, Absalom was successfully distracted from any further thoughts of visiting the King.

Joab sipped at well-watered wine with an expression of grim satisfaction on his face, and the more outrageous Absalom's antics became, the more he seemed to approve, which I knew went totally against the grain. Having torn off his cloak and kilt, David's son proceeded to give a lascivious demonstration of some Syrian sacred dance, balanced precariously with one foot on a table and the other on the back of a couch, and wearing only his loincloth. When Sheba tipped the couch over backwards, to the manifest delight of the whole company, Absalom collapsed snoring in Joab's lap, and the latter knew that his latest mission was accomplished.

It wasn't long before most of the other revellers were in the same somnolent condition, myself included—after all, it wasn't often I found myself being plied with as much wine as I could drink, with nothing better to do than drink it. I remained conscious just long enough to realize that Joab was still stone-cold sober, before passing out curled up on the floor with Gatis—which shows how far gone I was.

A good while later I woke up with a pounding headache, to discover I was being rudely shaken and slapped by Joab. It was half dark, and I didn't grasp for some time that this wasn't dusk falling but dawn breaking. As soon as he saw my eyelids flutter open, Joab clapped a hand across my mouth and hissed, 'I have to see the King before sunrise. I'll be back as quickly as I can. You mustn't let Absalom out of your sight.'

'What?' I said inaudibly through Joab's fingers, struggling upright and holding my hands to my temples to deaden the pain. My eyes wouldn't focus, and neither would my brain.

'I received a message from the palace yesterday. Absalom is not to go there until I've seen the King, at sunrise this morning. I know no more than that. So just don't let him out of the house till I get back. Come on, lad. Pull yourself together.'

'But—how can I stop him if he wants to go?'

'I don't care how you stop him. But you shouldn't have any trouble for a while yet.' Joab cast a sideways glance at Absalom, still flat out on the couch where he'd dumped him, and before I could ask any more questions, Joab was gone.

I lay quiet until it got lighter, waiting for my head to feel more normal, and vowing never to have another drink in my life. One by one the guests were coming round, groaning, getting their belongings together, and crawling home. Absalom didn't stir, even when Gatis padded up to him and began licking his cheeks. I shuddered; had I really gone to sleep with that monster's paws all over me?

When it was fully light, everyone was awake except the Prince. Most people had left; slaves had appeared to clear up, and Maacah and Miriam both came and asked me if I'd had any breakfast. Still Absalom slept like a baby, and it came to me then that Joab had probably drugged his wine. Maacah grew anxious and made several attempts to rouse him; I let him be, preferring a quiet life.

It was almost noon when Joab returned, and it was clear from his face that all was far from well. Luckily for me, Absalom was still unconscious; Joab seemed a little surprised but passed no comment. Maacah said, 'We tried to wake him up. Shall we try again?' But Joab only grunted, meaning, there's little point; and he settled himself to wait. Gatis was starting to whine, and Maacah to talk of summoning a physician, when Absalom moaned and stretched and demanded something to eat, and to know what day it was.

Having devoured a plateful of barley cakes, he seemed much refreshed, and asked Joab if they might go to the palace now.

Joab cleared his throat.

'My lord Absalom, there is a problem. I'm afraid you're not to go to the palace at all.'

'What? Why not?'

'Your father His Majesty the King cannot bring himself to see you.'

Absalom was incredulous. 'But he gave permission for my recall, you told me so. Didn't he! Didn't he . . .?'

There was fear behind Absalom's eyes now. It was instantly clear to me that he suspected Joab of tricking him, and that his father had had nothing whatever to do with the general's mission to Geshur. Absalom was well aware that the son of Zeruiah had never liked him. Now he would have him convicted of Amnon's murder, and put to death after all.

Joab affirmed hurriedly, 'My lord, I swear that I mean you no harm. I understand this no more than you do. I swear it in Adonai's name.' And when Absalom looked no less distrustful, he added, 'I swear by my mother's life, Absalom.' Then knowing what Zeruiah meant to both Joab and Abishai, since they hadn't a father, the Prince had no choice but to believe him.

After that, the two of them sat facing one another without speaking. Then Absalom's eyes opened very wide, and he said, 'Bathsheba.'

Joab said nothing.

'This is her doing, isn't it? *She* doesn't want me to see him. She didn't know about my recall until now, and she's got it into her head

126

for some reason to prevent us from being reconciled.'

Joab only grunted again, but Absalom took it for an admission, and was presumably right.

'I thought so. She's the only person who can get him to go back on his word like this.' Absalom clenched his fists and beat them on his knees. Gatis, curled around his feet, growled in sympathy, and I marvelled that a mere beast could be so sensitive. She was somehow as besotted with Absalom as everyone else was, except for those who were jealous. 'But why?' Absalom demanded, more of himself than of Joab. 'Why should she want to keep us apart? She has everything she wants now. She's recognized as his principal wife, she has the most prestigious apartment, and unlimited access to his chambers, and no doubt to all his riches. Surely she has nothing left to fear from me. Or is Ahithophel behind her, wanting something for himself?'

That was when it struck me. No wonder Absalom had seen fit to enter Jerusalem with all the pomp of an anointed monarch. No wonder he'd decided it was worth coming back from Geshur. Adonai have mercy... I was the only one outside of the palace who knew the truth, and I would have to break it to him.

Absalom must have seen the colour drain from my face. He asked if I was all right; I said no, and that I had to speak with him alone. I think he fancied I was just attention-seeking. When I persisted he looked cross, but reluctantly bade Joab wait outside for a few moments, and ushered the slaves out after him. Maacah and Miriam had already left us, wanting Absalom and Joab to be free to talk men's matters.

Desperate to get it over with, I gabbled, 'Your father has promised the throne to her son, Solomon. She must be afraid he might change his mind about that, too, when he sees you.' Then I sat with my eyes screwed shut and my fingers in my ears, because I knew he would go wild, and I was right.

He began storming about the room like a wounded lion, pummelling the cushions and flinging what remained of yesterday's repast against the walls. Fearing he might use me when he'd run out of other more suitable projectiles, I didn't move until he'd worn himself out and slumped with his head on his arms on the table. Gatis whimpered, and poked her muzzle between his legs. He buried his face in her fur and wailed, 'He's gone mad, Zohel. I can't believe it. The boy can barely be weaned.'

'I know, my lord. But it's with Nathan's backing.'

Absalom choked bitterly. 'How can a holy man back that son of a whore!'

I shrugged, though he wasn't looking at me. I wished we could talk about the affair rationally, but it wasn't in Absalom's nature to be rational about a thing like this. Finally I could no longer endure looking at him bent double with his plaited hair all splayed over that detestable dog's fur, and I muttered, 'Prophets can see things from a long way off, Absalom. Maybe he could see that sun and moon around your neck.'

Of course, I should never have said that. I thought he was going to take my head off. Thankfully the sickening sound of flesh thudding against flesh, and against the walls, brought Joab running; not to mention the obscenities Absalom was yelling at me as he worked me over. It was hard to believe this was the man who'd once rescued me from a similar fate at the hands of another. But this time he didn't regard me as innocent.

Eventually the seasoned soldier managed to drag us apart. Absalom stood heaving and panting, more from exasperation than exertion I think. When he got his breath back, he rounded on Joab, but his anger sounded hollow now, and diluted with grief.

'So what does he expect me to do, then? Where does he expect me to go? Back to Geshur?'

'He has made a house available for you, my lord, here in Jerusalem. It's a very fine establishment, quite close to the palace. There are stables for your horses and chariots, and plenty of rooms to quarter your slaves, as well as some very elegant chambers for your own personal use. In fact'—Joab paused, uncertain how Absalom would react—'I am instructed to take you there now.'

Absalom too paused before responding. Then he asked unsteadily, 'Am I under arrest?'

'No, my lord. You are free to come and go as you please.'

'So long as I don't attempt to enter the palace.'

'That is correct, my lord. I think you understand the situation.'

11

Absalom's suspicions were confirmed when the house turned out to be Bathsheba's—where the pair of them had long ago kept their tryst. Some time and money had evidently been spent on it since then. It had been very recently decorated, in a sumptuous style which I soon realized had been calculated to appeal to Absalom's taste. The doors and shutters had been unbarred and painted, and no longer had creepers trailing over them. Joab showed us around at a brisk pace—it was quite obvious he was keen to get away.

I was easily impressed, and Gatis sniffed contentedly at each corner we turned, but Absalom did nothing but curse under his breath and keep chuntering that he should have stayed in Geshur, and that perhaps he would go back there after all.

Joab however made several valiant attempts to dissuade him from this course of action. At first I concluded that his royal paymasters had simply instructed him to be conciliatory in order to give Absalom less excuse for rocking the boat. Later, the truth came home to me: although Bathsheba and her hirelings didn't want Maacah's son in the palace, they had decided they *did* want him in Jerusalem. He'd be easier to keep under surveillance here than in Geshur, and would be much less likely to succeed in raising an army to fight Solomon for the throne, if such a notion should occur to him. Absalom's reappearance in Israel had come as no surprise at all to the mother of the invisible little Crown Prince, and she'd been preparing for it for weeks.

I realized in addition that Joab's own reasons for wanting Absalom recalled were probably somewhat similar, though his fears were no doubt for David himself (and hence for his own position as commander of David's armed forces) than for Solomon. I wondered if there might be any substance to them. After all, at that time I'd no idea what Absalom really *had* been up to in the lost years he'd spent with Talmai. But Joab, Ahithophel, and even Nathan had their spies. And our neighbours in the north would presumably be overjoyed to see a carrier of Aramaean blood installed upon Saul's throne—even if that blood was watered down with David's.

So when Joab had gone on his way, and the slaves and soldiers had been assigned quarters, I said to Absalom, 'Perhaps you *would* be better off back in Geshur.'

He pretended to be hurt. 'I thought you'd missed me. Are you trying to get rid of me again so soon?' Then he remembered how I came to have scratches on my face and black and blue blotches all down my legs, and momentarily he did look almost penitent. But when he apologized to me, it came out as: 'It must've been the after-effects of that wine—or whatever that scurvy son of Zeruiah laced it with.' So I was still left with a sour taste in my mouth from the way he'd chosen to deal with my insolence. As though she understood, Gatis padded over and began licking my bruises; I pushed her away instinctively but then Absalom embraced me with spontaneous delight. I was angry at myself for letting him.

'She isn't so friendly to just *anyone*,' he exclaimed, releasing me with an affable slap between the shoulder-blades. For the time being he seemed to have laid his annoyance at his circumstances to one side. 'You and I must be destined to achieve great things together, little serpent.' He waited for my own anger to subside, before continuing, 'But no; I shan't be going back.'

I regarded him quizzically, and he grinned, unexpectedly embarrassed, and prepared now to be deliberately transparent.

'Oh, I had a good time there, don't get me wrong, and it will do no one at the palace any harm to believe I'd walk out of here again tomorrow. My grandfather was kind to me, and Mother's right: his court does make ours look like some shepherds' assembly. But I'm no more likely to inherit his throne than this one; I have a canny older cousin there. And this is my home, Zohel. I've missed these hills, these streets, my friends; and my father.' He sniffed my scepticism and said hesitantly, 'Does that sound horribly sentimental to you?'

'No.' But I found it significant that it was David he'd missed, more than Maacah. I fell to wondering whether he could have found it within himself to forgive the King his contemptible leniency. Was he no longer ashamed to be his father's son?

'What's the matter, Zohel?' The harsh note of accusation in Absalom's voice interrupted my thoughts. 'You remind me of Nathan going off on one of his excursions into the seventh heaven... oh, I forgot: you got yourself mixed up in all that with my father, didn't you? "Dedicated your life to Adonai", as he calls it.'

I narrowed my eyes at him. 'I live for no one but myself, Absalom. I'm a free man.'

'And you won't let me forget it, is that it? Well, it's refreshing, I suppose. So many of the people I meet seem to want to die for me, or in my arms.' Gratified to have got one over on me again, he set about placating me. 'Don't worry, my tough little friend. You're free to go any time you like. You needn't be my squire if you don't choose to be. You're freer than I am, let's face it.'

'I don't know what you mean.'

'They wouldn't let me go back to Geshur if I *did* want to, would they?' So he'd realized it too. 'I'll wager they're having us watched even now.' He went to the nearest window; the shutter was open, like all the rest—to air the place off, Joab had claimed. 'You can see the palace pretty well from here. I wonder what the view's like from the roof.'

We went out into the courtyard and up the steps; Absalom took them two at a time and went to stand by the parapet. You could almost have thrown a stone at the royal residence from there—in fact, right into the King's private chambers or onto his private rooftop. As he gazed up at the palace he asked, 'Do you still see him?'

'Who?'

'The King.'

'Ah, *that*'s why you want me to serve you, isn't it? You have all these pretty slaves and burly bodyguards—I knew there had to be a reason why you wanted me as well. What if I *don't* see him?'

Absalom swung round to face me, leaning back against the wall. In places the stonework was flaky and crumbling; I found myself desperately hoping it was strong enough to bear his weight. He never worried about such things, and again I was angry at myself because I didn't want to care either. Scanning my face with his smouldering kohl-rimmed eyes, he said, 'Do we have to wind each other up like this? Can't we just be friends?'

He looked very vulnerable then; only for a moment, but long enough for me to reflect that this was the secret of his popularity, this was how he got everyone with whom he had any dealings to love him rather than merely to covet his looks. He would open himself up to you, make you believe he valued you, needed you—but only when he knew it was safe to do so. He seldom risked anything real by it. Still searching my face, he asked again whether we couldn't just be friends, and I replied, 'That's what your father always says.'

'What? Do you wind him up as well?'

'No.' I couldn't help laughing. 'He's always saying he wants me to be his friend. You're both alike, aren't you? You both need me because you know *I* don't need you, unlike all the creeps who compete for your favours because of who you are. You can't bear to think that someone exists who isn't passionately devoted to you or else passionately devoted to destroying you. Well *I'm* devoted to *nothing*. I don't need *anyone*.'

But he only nodded, smiling, acknowledging the outbreak of defiance that hardened my features; there was pity softening his own, which made me wilder than ever. I knew he was seeing me once again as the trapped, hurt child he'd brought home to his mother so long ago, and loving me for it. Yet I resented him fiercely for reawakening the memory, and would almost rather have him thumping me again.

However, he was still beautiful, and outrageous, and brazen in his contempt for Adonai, and all that meant I couldn't stop myself admiring him. I already knew in my heart that I *would* stay and serve him, if only because he would always be where the action was; that he would be right at the centre of it.

Besides, freeman or no, what alternatives did I have? I couldn't have served Maacah respectably for much longer. I wouldn't serve David. I could only have looked forward to a life of poverty and obscurity trying to eke out my own living somehow. With Absalom I should have status as well as excitement—and a roof over my head. He said, 'Well? You're still wriggling away from answering my question, little serpent.'

'What question?'

'Whether you still see the King.'

'Yes. I have no choice.'

'Does he trust you?'

'Yes, though I wish he didn't. He's obsessed with me for some reason, but I've never found out what it is.'

He said, 'Maybe *you* can get him to see me somehow.'

'Maybe.' But I didn't hold out much hope.

Nevertheless, Absalom made no further mention of returning to Syria. He spent the next two days getting all his belongings unpacked, including the gifts his grandfather had bestowed on him. It wasn't surprising he'd needed so many wagons and pack-animals to transport them. Along with precious metals and gemstones, there were couches and tables inlaid with ivory; and even a bed, fashioned by Egyptian craftsmen in their native style and leafed in pure gold. It had blue and red cloisonné flowers on the headrest, and feet carved to look like a lion's. There were countless alabaster jars and priceless Akhaian amphorae, filled with choice wines from the sun-drenched vineyards on the western shores of the Great Sea; chests of sumptuous silks and linens and jars of spices from legendary lands in the east; and a hundred little pots of perfume, half of which he set on one side to give to his mother.

'You could spare at least one for Miriam,' I suggested. 'You've got so many, and it would make her so happy.'

'So you do have a heart after all? But no; it might give her the wrong idea.'

'Then let me have one, and *I'll* give it to her.'

'Suit yourself,' said Absalom, and picked one out. Then he grinned wryly, knowing full well what I had in mind. 'But it won't change anything. Only the cheapest girls can be bought for so little.'

He was right, of course; only the cheapest girls can be bought at all.

Despite Absalom's expressed intention to train me as his armour bearer, I soon began to feel more like a butler. I wound up being responsible for keeping the slaves in order, whilst the Syrian soldiers continued to act as Absalom's bodyguard. Not that he ought to have required such a thing in the security of a walled city, but as he said, he couldn't be entirely sure about how far Bathsheba was prepared to go. So I vetted all arrivals at the house, as well as attending increasingly to Absalom's personal needs. I also became indirectly responsible for Maacah and Miriam again, for once some sort of routine had been established in our household, it made sense for them to join us.

They were given a suite of rooms to themselves, but with access to the same roof as we used, and here Maacah insisted on setting up her shrine to Asherah. Absalom didn't object, though it was in full view of David's apartment. Maacah was well aware of this; she wanted David to be constantly reminded of how far he'd caused her to fall.

Thankfully I wasn't expected to look after Gatis. Absalom did this himself. He bathed her, deloused her, shared his food with her, and even let her sleep on his bed. She was eager to accept any friend of Absalom's as a friend of hers, but although so far as I was concerned the feeling was definitely not reciprocal, she never gave up on me. After a while I came to doubt she was capable of treating anyone any differently, and I couldn't imagine she'd be much use on a hunt either. But when Joab walked in uninvited one day to 'check we had everything we needed', I soon found out otherwise. He didn't do it again for a long time.

Two weeks after Absalom came home, a stranger arrived at the house requesting an audience with the Prince. Absalom wasn't busy, so I let the fellow in. He was dressed coarsely, though not shabbily—he'd clearly made an effort. When asked his business, he launched into a lengthy tale of woe concerning his one item of livestock: a solitary and rather elderly cow.

Apparently the wretched animal had been let loose one night by a gang of drunken hoodlums, and gone wandering off. A wealthy neighbour had found her but kept her, claiming that she was his. The local judge had been bribed and so ruled in the rich man's favour; our visitor had appealed to the King, as was his right, but been told that His Majesty wasn't dealing with matters of this nature at present, and it would have to join the waiting-list. The case might come up in six months. In the meantime the poor man's family would have no milk.

Absalom was plainly at a loss to know how he should react. I could see he was annoyed that this peasant should have intruded on his privacy, yet at the same time he was flattered by further evidence that he'd been adopted as People's Champion. He issued orders for the man to be taken away and given food and drink and accommodation, while he decided what to do.

'I can't understand it, Zohel,' he said to me. 'Father would never have allowed this sort of thing to go on when I was a child. He heard all who appealed to him for justice, in person. Now it seems he can't even be bothered to assign the job to someone else.'

I said, 'Maybe he feels he'd be a hypocrite, interfering in other people's domestic squabbles and doling out justice to them when he won't see that it's done in his own household.'

Absalom's eyes widened. 'You're more bitter against him than I thought.'

'Well, aren't you? You were once. Don't you blame him any more for what happened to Tamar?'

I'd been dying to ask him that ever since the day we'd moved into the house; now I wished I hadn't. He went very quiet, then said, 'I don't know. I'm not sure I'll ever forgive him. But I can't stop thinking about when there was real love between us. Life was good in those days, Zohel. I just want it to be good again.'

The next day Absalom sent two of his brawny Syrians to accompany the peasant and fetch his rich oppressor back with them, along with two witnesses from the same village who could vouch for the cow's ownership. The matter was settled in less time than it takes to win a game of senet. Absalom had made another friend; and another enemy.

In terms of using me as a link with David, Absalom decided at first to wait for Ahithophel to summon me, for I told him that this happened once a fortnight at least. But three weeks passed and he didn't appear. Meanwhile we entertained a steady trickle of nondescript individuals who came seeking Absalom's intervention in a whole variety of petty legal disputes. He did what he could, and because many of their grievances were easily dealt with, the majority of his petitioners went home satisfied. None of them were men who counted for anything in their own right. But together they soon amounted to a sizeable company, and the word was spreading fast that the King's prodigal son had come back as an angel of mercy.

Absalom soon had no trouble filling his days; his evenings were taken up with answering our questions about life in Geshur. Maacah never tired of asking after her father and her sister, and her sister's son; once he'd admitted it, Absalom never tired of telling her how much he'd longed to come home, and how he'd suffered in those first few months when he hadn't dared send word to us.

Gradually it emerged that Talmai had lost no opportunities when it came to indoctrinating his young guest against everything Hebrew. He'd given vent daily to his rage at the scandalous way in which Absalom said Maacah and her offspring had been humiliated, and harped endlessly on the gross enormity of the tribute he was compelled every year to send to David. With Absalom ruling in the place of this upstart from Bethlehem, the whole intolerable situation could be rectified, Talmai had pointed out; also the true gods could be reinstated in Canaan, and relations between Syria and Israel could be warm as they'd never been before.

'He's right, of course,' said Maacah. 'And he'd have helped you bring it about, if you'd danced to his tune.'

'And if I'd been prepared to depose and probably murder the one who gave me life and the only happiness I've ever known,' came the cutting retort. 'Besides, do you really think the People of Adonai would accept as their ruler someone who'd ousted their anointed king, and done it with Syrian backing—even if that someone was me?'

But Maacah only rolled her eyes, and shook her head in exasperation. I thought: if Absalom *did* kill David, you'd be the first to condemn him. You don't really know what you want, any more than your son does; and you're growing old because of it.

All the same, I knew, from the frequency with which Absalom brought the subject up, that he'd been seriously tempted by what Talmai seemed to be advocating. To march into Jerusalem at the head of his own army, to put down the weak and weary old King and set the crown on his own head . . . of course the notion had its appeal. Yet I think he saw that he would end up as nothing more than Talmai's puppet, dependent upon him for the maintaining of his power just as surely as he would have been for the winning of it in the first place.

When the fourth week passed with no word from the palace, Absalom said, 'Zohel, this is more of Bathsheba's doing. She's either persuading or forcing him not to send for you; or she's intercepting any messages that *are* sent. You'll just have to go anyway.'

I protested, 'But she has eyes everywhere! She'll know why I've come.'

'We'll send you in disguise. You've no beard yet, and you're comely enough—we'll make up your face and dress you as a girl.'

'Don't be stupid. What girl would go on her own to see the King?'

'You could be the daughter of one of his concubines, wanting to see her mother on her birthday.'

'Yes, and pigs could fly, Absalom. They'd take me to the harem and I'd never get out.'

'Lucky you! I can think of worse fates. Some people simply have no idea how to enjoy themselves.—Oh well, never mind. We'll shave your head and get you kitted out Egyptian-fashion with all this stuff my grandfather sent, and you can be an ambassador from the Pharaoh.'

'I'd have to take half your Syrians with me as my escort to look convincing. Besides, I'm not having my head shaved.'

'Zohel, you're as vain as I am. Have *you* any better ideas?'

In the end we agreed that I should be a bedouin bard, since I could play the harp; Absalom swathed my head in an enormous checkered kerchief, found me a long woollen robe, and put some dried figs and dates in a little silver box for me to present to His Majesty as a souvenir of the desert.

I was sure it wouldn't work, and it didn't. It turned out that absolutely no one could get an audience with the King these days without being invited by him personally; he was too sick.

So we were back to waiting again. More weeks went past, and months; winter came and kept us all inside, and Maacah no longer even went up to her rooftop altar. When spring returned, she didn't go back to it, and then I *knew* she was giving up and growing old. So many years spent loving and hating David, and playing off Adonai and Asherah, had quenched her vitality, and the warring forces within her cancelled each other out in apathy.

But the same conflicts within Absalom were lashing him to fever pitch. Once he went to the palace openly, by himself, to see what would happen; predictably he was simply turned away. He tried a second time, with a detachment of his bodyguard, armed. He didn't intend to force an entry, merely to make a show of strength. But one of the guardsmen on the gate had known him as a boy; he took the Prince to one side and warned him to withdraw, because if reinforcements had to be summoned, the incident would be construed as an attempted coup. And no one needed reminding of the penalty for treason.

Well over a year after Absalom's return to Jerusalem, we resolved that *I* must go openly, as David's former pupil, wanting to see him on my own behalf. This was no more likely to achieve success than any of our previous ploys, but we could think of nothing better. The sentries on the outer gates let me through for old time's sake, though they knew that both they and I might get into trouble. I penetrated as far as Jehoshaphat, and it felt profoundly odd to be walking along those once familiar corridors after so long. Jehoshaphat said it was impossible for him to admit me without Bathsheba's say-so.

I gaped at him. That Bathsheba should now be checking on all the King's visitors I could well believe, but not that it should be frankly admitted by someone like Jehoshaphat to someone like me. Then he said, 'I can send to ask her permission, if you like.'

I was surprised he should think it worthwhile, considering who I was. But I decided I'd probably nothing to lose; I couldn't see even Bathsheba getting away with abusing Absalom's personal attendant when everyone knew that was who I was. So he despatched a slave, who returned in due course saying permission for my seeing the King had been refused, but I was welcome to see the Queen.

The Queen! I wondered if David knew she was using that title; but I had no time to ponder the question further, for I was immediately shown into her chambers.

She didn't appear for some while, however. I've no doubt she kept me waiting on purpose, so that I might have space to appreciate fully the changes she'd brought about in the apartment which had once been ours. It felt like a different place altogether, so different that it was hardly strange to be standing there on ceremony. There were no ivory screens or pots of flowers. Everything seemed to be floating on a sea of exotic saffron-tinted silk. Silken curtains pooled from ceiling to floor, masking the cedarwood panelling completely—if it was still there—and rippling gently where the warm autumn breeze from the courtyard caught them. Silken quilts draped the couches, and slave girls in silken gowns lounged about with nothing better to do than chat and pout and be alluring.

They all stopped chatting when they saw me, though. They stared at me, looking me up and down with their lovely, scornful eyes; I must have been as red as a desert sunset. I began to feel ugly, and coarse, and very small, despite the fact I really was nearly as tall as Absalom, and dressed in fine white linen, and I'd let my thick heavy hair grow almost to my shoulders. Then Bathsheba's low lilting voice said from somewhere very close to me, 'Zoheleth! How handsome you've turned out. I should hardly have known you.'

I glanced up, my heart racing; she'd entered silent as a dream and arranged herself on a couch not a spearlength from me. She was as slight and slender as ever; you would never have believed she'd borne two children. Of Solomon himself there was no sign; it crossed my mind that maybe he didn't exist at all.

With her elegantly manicured fingers she smoothed out the folds of saffron silk beside her, making me a place to sit down. Then she beckoned me forward in such a way that I felt it would be unwise to resist. It was doubtless still more unwise of me to acquiesce; as soon as I felt her warmth and saw the lustre of her skin, and sensed the gentle swelling of her breasts as she breathed, I knew I'd grown up since the last time I'd been close to her. I knew she found my confusion gratifying.

She said, 'I hear you are in service to Prince Absalom these days, for your sins. I also hear that he wishes to arrange an audience with his father. Do you think we should allow it?'

'I . . .'

What could she be expecting me to say? Was I included in the 'we', or was she using it after the royal manner? My voice trailed off helplessly, and I found myself staring frantically at the door. Still she made no reference to my awkwardness.

'You see,' she drawled on, idly smoothing the creases in my tunic now, as though I were part of the furniture, 'If you could convince me that the Prince merely wishes to—iron out some ruckles in his somewhat untidy personal relationships, I might be less apprehensive about permitting this meeting to go ahead. I do wish I didn't have such a suspicious mind, it's so tiresome on occasions. Do you think you *could* convince me?'

Her hand still rested on my leg; I glanced back at her hurriedly, and when I saw the way she was looking at me, my insides went to jelly. I croaked lamely, 'I wouldn't know where to start.' Then she drew back and studied me down the length of her nose, her eyes cold and disdainful and saying: no, I can believe you wouldn't; and I don't have the time to teach you.

'Well,' she purred after a prickly pause, 'I dare say he wouldn't mind trying to convince me himself. Tell me—is he as ravishing as ever, or has three years' riotous living in Syria blunted the edge of his beauty?'

Again there was nothing I could say. She smiled, but her eyes remained cold as before. 'I do apologize, Zoheleth. That was hardly a fair question. But they did tell me you weren't dumb any more; or was that just another of the lies they keep trying to feed me? Now don't look so hurt . . . I shall ask you something simple, and you may just tell me yes or no. Do you think Prince Absalom would like to come and see me?'

Of course, this had me more tongue-tied than ever. Absalom had vowed he was through with Bathsheba for good. Yet three years away certainly seemed to have modified his feelings towards his father; there was no means of knowing how he might respond to what his father's wife appeared to be offering once more. I shrugged miserably, with every fibre of my being wanting to say no, but too daunted. Eventually Bathsheba rose, and motioned me to do the same.

'Well, Zoheleth, if you do manage to find your voice, be so kind as

139

to inform your benefactor that if he wishes to visit the palace, he may ask for me,' she said; then swept away as swiftly as she'd come.

I returned to Absalom in a quandary. Should I relay Bathsheba's proposition to him, or not? If I didn't, I knew she would reach him with it somehow. Having decided for some reason best known to herself that she wanted to see him, she was bound to set about achieving this with unswerving determination. Then I would like as not get into trouble with both of them for withholding information.

Yet there was no doubt in my mind that he ought not to trust her. They'd been enemies more recently than they'd been lovers; Bathsheba wasn't one to let bygones be bygones. And the granddaughter of Ahithophel was no less adept at the arts of the politician than was the old counsellor himself. It was nothing so uncomplicated as lust which had led her to risk reopening her door to her own husband's son, of that I was sure. Nor was she in love with him; I was even surer of this. I doubted she'd ever loved anyone.

In the end I gave Absalom her message, though if I'd been pronouncing his death sentence I could hardly have sounded less cheerful. Now he faced a dilemma more perplexing than mine had been.

'What shall I do, Zohel?' he groaned, fretting and pacing, alternately excited and dismayed. 'How can I turn down a chance to get into the palace, after all this time? Maybe I *can* persuade her to let me see him.'

But at what cost? I thought, saying nothing; I didn't need to.

'Who's to say she wants *anything* from me? What if she simply finds me attractive?' he demanded, and he was perfectly serious.

'You said it was over,' I reminded him. 'Will it be so easy to swallow your pride?'

'I shall have to get used to doing that before I face my father.'

'*If* that ever happens. Oh Absalom, be careful! You don't know what game she's playing.'

'If I know Bathsheba, she's simply *on* the game, Zohel. She's young, beautiful, sensuous. Is it any wonder my father doesn't satisfy her? She's as starved as Potiphar's wife was, in the old story.'

'And look what happened to Joseph! What if she wants to discredit you entirely? Suppose she says you raped her? Her apartment is right next to the King's now, remember. And you can be sure *she* won't fail to scream.'

But the longer we argued, and the more causes I gave him for caution, the more eager he became to risk the encounter. I'd forgotten how reckless and stubborn he could be.

Nevertheless, he didn't go to her at once. It wasn't caution that delayed him; he just wanted to keep her guessing. Each evening he would go up onto the roof—to breathe the cool night air, so he told me—and see her watching him from the King's private chambers, or from *his* roof. He would curl his hair and redden his lips, and I would be in agony, incredulous and incensed that he could be such a fool, and certain that his vanity would be the undoing of him, sooner rather than later. Then I would scold myself for letting his fate bother me.

On the seventh night of this infuriating ritual, Bathsheba blew Absalom a kiss and beckoned him openly, so he knew it was safe to visit. On his way out he ruffled my hair and said, 'Wish me luck, Zohel. And stop worrying. If my father catches us red-handed, he'll *have* to speak to me.'

When he came back the next morning, there had been no screaming. He was exhausted and went straight to bed, saying he must be fresh again for tonight. No, he hadn't seen David yet, nor was he likely to, immediately. But Bathsheba was working on it, so he assured me, and undoubtedly would succeed in pulling the appropriate strings for him in time.

I made no secret of my dissatisfaction with this explanation. Who did he think was standing in her way? She must want to prolong their affair for a while before denouncing him, so there would be more evidence against him. But Absalom was well and truly drunk on desire, despite everything he'd once said about Bathsheba and her greed and how she'd slighted his family.

Four months into Absalom and Bathsheba's renewed liaison, it transpired that she'd already been pregnant by David before it began. She'd probably known all along; as Absalom had once pointed out, it was the surest way for her to see to it that she didn't conceive any bastards. But she was soon too big to have much interest in adultery. She was sick, too, not just in the mornings, and instead of this sickness passing off as the pregnancy progressed, it apparently grew worse. I'd begun to take reports of Bathsheba's illnesses with a year's wages in salt, but perhaps she was harried by poor health, especially when expecting, though she'd certainly learnt to use this to her advantage.

Despite Absalom's original pretext for getting involved, while his relationship with Bathsheba lasted he somehow forgot how urgently he'd wanted to see David. When it petered out, he remembered with a vengeance. He sent message after message to the palace, ever optimistic that Bathsheba might no longer be up to intercepting them. Her watchdogs had been well trained, however, and remained at their posts.

Something like a month before the baby was due, reports filtered through that Bathsheba had taken to her bed and was not likely to leave it until after the delivery.

'This is it, Zohel,' said Absalom. 'This has got to be it. If we can't outwit her now . . . Come, we must send for Joab. He carries enough clout to scare off Bathsheba's minions if she's not around in person to stop him. And he can get my father to listen when no one else can. He'll make him see how desperate I am.'

But Joab wouldn't come. We sent word to him twice and got no response. Clearly he'd had his fill of mediating between his equally exasperating uncle and cousin; at least he was under no illusions about his gifts as a diplomat.

Absalom had had more than he could handle. It was early summer, the grain was all but ready for harvesting, and he said to me, 'Take two of the boys and set fire to Joab's barley field. That'll fetch him.'

I was staggered. 'You can't mean it! Joab's the last person to take an insult like that lying down. He'll make you regret it one way or another, even if he has to die in the attempt.'

But I was wasting my breath; as all too often, Absalom was well beyond the reach of reason.

So the next moonless night I crept out of the house with two of the least feckless of our eunuchs, who like me carried burning torches hidden beneath upturned jars: a set of Absalom's priceless and utterly distinctive Akhaian amphorae. We bribed the guards on the city gates, smashed our jars and threw the sherds around Joab's boundary stones, and ran the length of his field like three shooting stars leaving flaming tails behind us. The crop was tinder dry and went up like a barbarian's funeral pyre; the sight of it got us high and we stood arm in arm, pointing and laughing like men possessed as the night turned to day across the dome of the sky. Then we raced each other back home, battering on doors as we passed yelling, 'Fire! Fire!' until the sleeping city came alive with shouting, and the roads rang with pounding feet.

It took Joab's servants and soldiers and half the male population of Jerusalem the rest of the night to douse the blaze and prevent it from spreading. At dawn Gatis' barking wakened me, and there was Joab, sooted and feral in his scorched, sodden clothing, clutching two chunks of Akhaian pottery in his hands and demanding to see Absalom.

Absalom was ready for him. He hadn't been to bed all night, though he didn't want Joab to think so, and emerged with his hair all dishevelled and a white silk cloak thrown around him to half-hide his nakedness. When Joab launched into an incoherent tirade liberally peppered with curses and spitting, he tossed his head and said calmly, 'Of course I admit responsibility. What would be the point of provoking you anonymously? You tell my father I demand to see *him*, or I start on your home and family.'

Joab would have gone for him physically then, had Absalom not let go Gatis' collar. She leapt forward slavering; Joab drew a knife, and the dog was called off. She crouched growling by her master's slippered feet, and Joab muttered, 'You don't know what you're asking. He may not even be prepared to forgive you any more. Suppose he can't help seeing that old dried blood on your hands?'

'Stop making excuses, Joab. You know as well as I do that he couldn't bring himself to have me killed. Not any longer, if he ever *did* have it in him. He's missed me more than he'll ever miss Amnon. Ask Zoheleth.'

'It's out of the question all the same. It's beyond my control.'

'Oh yes? So who *is* in control of such things these days? Bathsheba? She's at death's door, by all accounts; I fail to understand what you have to fear from her.'

'It's not myself I fear for, if you must know. It's what she'll do to your father that worries me.'

'From what I'm led to believe he's dying already, Joab. This appalling state of affairs is killing him! How can she do any more damage than she's already done? I've had it up to *here* with waiting!'—and he smacked the palm of one hand across his brow—'You do as I ask or I'll kill you.'

Joab had seldom before regarded Absalom personally with anything other than contempt. Now for the first time, I think he found himself respecting the indignant youth, just a little. But also for the first time, he was finding him worth hating. I saw that being born in his eyes as the two of them outstared one another, Absalom boiling over now, Joab silently seething. I was in no position to know whether the hot-headed young Prince any longer had an enemy in Bathsheba or not, but he'd certainly made himself another new one today.

'Very well.' Joab examined his dagger thoughtfully, then huffed once along the blade and wiped it with deliberate nonchalance on the arm of one of Talmai's couches, before replacing it in its scabbard. 'I'll make sure you get to see the King. But don't blame me for the consequences.'

Less than two weeks later, Bathsheba went into labour, and that very morning Ahithophel came at last to our house, not for me but for Absalom.

12

Absalom was gone all day. The atmosphere in our house was as thick and sour as rancid milk, and made me feel just as nauseous; I can't imagine my stomach could have churned any worse if he'd been called up for battle. I was annoyed with myself, as ever. I told myself that the outcome of this meeting had nothing to do with me in the slightest, that neither Absalom nor David meant any more to me than the King of Assyria, and that I was only connected with them by random circumstance. Whether or not they became reconciled was of no concern to me at all.

But I couldn't convince myself, and grew even crosser from trying. I snapped at the slaves, at Maacah, even at Miriam, and in the end locked myself in Absalom's room before I did any further damage. There I came upon Gatis, whining dejectedly, so I snapped at her too, but she only whined all the louder. It occurred to me that she'd never been apart from her master for so long since he'd brought her to Jerusalem; grudgingly I was forced to admit that the lumbering beast might indeed possess the capacity for something not unlike love. The realization made me ashamed.

So I stood by Absalom's window, Gatis with her paws up on the sill beside me, and together we watched the sun go down over the rooftops of the city. A slave brought me something to eat, but I wasn't hungry. Gatis sniffed at the plate, reminding me that she hadn't been fed since last night; this brought home to me like nothing else how much today must mean to Absalom. Then I reflected that I didn't even know what he normally fed her on. So I gave her most of what had been meant for me, and she didn't object.

When the last hint of pink had faded from the sky, I began to be anxious in a different way. Whatever the outcome of the meeting, surely Absalom would have come to tell us by now? He was an unpredictable and volatile individual, true, but generally only too eager to share his joys and his griefs with us, and especially with Maacah because she still took his part and treated him like a spoilt little boy when he needed it. But there was no sign of him, and Gatis' whining had run to growling, and a rhythmic thumping of her tail on the floor. I was horribly weary with worry and waiting, but couldn't bring myself to go to bed. I dozed on my feet, with my head on the sill where Gatis' paws had rested, wishing there were someone I wasn't too proud to pray to.

A change of tone in the dog's growling roused me. There was a fresh urgency in it, and the promise of a bark; she thrust herself up beside me to look out of the window again. Instinctively I looked out too, and fuzzily opaque against the twilight, a figure was crossing the courtyard below. It was a man, with a gait like Absalom's, but wearing a kerchief twisted loosely about his head, peasant-style, and some kind of ankle-length coat to match. If it was Absalom, he didn't want anyone to know it. And whoever it was, he didn't enter the house, but made for the stables.

By now Gatis was barking furiously, running up and down beneath the window and almost knocking me off balance. Somehow she knew it was Absalom right enough, and I was inclined to believe her. But what could he be doing? Swallowing my aversion, I stroked Gatis into silence, then looked outside again, and Absalom was on his way out of the gates, on horseback.

I don't know what made me decide to follow him, except that I was in no doubt but that something was very wrong. There was no point in my trying to pursue him on foot, so I went to the stables myself, there discovering it was a mule he'd taken and not a horse; the world and his wife would have recognized him otherwise. At least if he were on a mule, I might catch him—if I *did* take a horse. And I'd have to take Gatis, who according to her master was capable of sniffing out a bean in a mountain of garlic.

I could have chosen any one of Absalom's racers, for they were all there, and I'd ridden them all at one time or another; but never with much confidence, and never without him on hand to supervise. Now they were snorting and neighing as I moved among them, edgy at all this activity so late at night. In the end I took the smallest, a star-white mare not yet full-grown, but well used to being ridden. She was the only one I felt I could mount without falling, and the only one I thought likely to let me. Fumbling in the thickening darkness, I finally managed to loop a halter over her head and lead her out into the yard, without anyone questioning me. Dimly I wondered what Absalom had done to the groom who usually kept watch over his bevy of beauties after dark.

So I set out, my knees gripping the flanks of a beast I only half trusted, with a beast I half feared running beside me. As I'd hoped, Gatis seemed to understand the nature of our quest perfectly, and to know exactly where to go. We worked our way downhill from the citadel, along dark, fetid, criss-crossing backstreets, and out through the city gates to the north. Surely Absalom couldn't be intending to ride alone all the way back to Geshur? I shivered, though the night wasn't cold, and was thankful for the moon which rose full and wan above the hills starkly silhouetted on the horizon.

My four-legged companions seemed tireless, and we made faster progress than I'd anticipated; on occasions rather too fast for my liking. But my confidence increased the more ground we covered, as did my control over the horse. Yet I must have ridden as far as a man could walk in a day, without seeing any sign of Absalom.

Eventually we happened upon a small village—more like a cluster of hovels really, hastily cobbled together with mud-bricks and rubble. Presumably it had risen from the ashes after Philistine depredations in Saul's day, but it hadn't risen far enough to have any defensive walls or a proper market place. There was just an irregular clearing amongst the ramshackle cottages, and here Absalom's mule was tethered, with no trace of its rider.

I dismounted, only now noticing how my back ached and how tender my buttocks were. I needed to rest even if my companions didn't, and there was always the hope that whoever had offered accommodation to Absalom might do the same for me.

It was late now, though, and few people were about. I might have been approached sooner had I not had Gatis with me; I saw two old crones whispering in a doorway, who were probably ashamed to leave a stranger without shelter among their roofs, but they weren't for coming any nearer to a monster.

Presently Gatis herself began nuzzling at my fingers and pulling at my tunic gently with her teeth. She must have decided I'd rested long enough, and she *did* know where to go next.

I tethered the horse near Absalom's mule, and followed her. She led me to a cottage no different from any of the others: squat, low-roofed, having only one storey and a single shuttered window. Hesitantly I knocked on the door. A shabby middle-aged woman invited me in, but I had to leave Gatis outside.

I found myself in a cramped sooty room littered with sleeping children and several young goats. A couple of smoky oil lamps sputtered feebly in the corners, but most of the light came from a central hearthfire, and there was no chimney. It took me some while to get over coughing; having spent my days as a penniless parasite in rich men's houses, I'd never been in a place like this in my life, and was suddenly all the more committed to serving Absalom rather than trying to make ends meet on my own.

While I sat struggling for breath, the woman washed my feet from a cracked clay pitcher and brought me food, but there was nothing to indicate I'd got the right house. My hostess never enquired what I wanted or why I was travelling so late; it would have been grossly impolite. So in the end I had to ask outright if my master had been here, and I gave her a description of how he'd been dressed. But I didn't say his name, for she'd likely have died on the spot.

'Yes,' she said. 'He's here. But we have another room. He said he was very tired and wanted to be on his own.'

I said, 'I need to speak to him. It's important. He won't mind me waking him up.'

She jerked a grimy thumb over her shoulder, and I picked my way past the snoring infants and animals to a rough wooden door in the dingiest corner of the room. It took some getting open; I gave up trying once the gap was big enough for me to squeeze through.

Absalom crouched trembling among the reeking rushes that passed for a mattress, his face streaming with tears, and a knife at his wrist, from which blood ran like water between his fingers and over his legs and clothing.

'Absalom!' I lunged at him, striking the knife from his hand. He tried to fight me off, but was too weak, and his eyes were rolling; I think he'd taken something, it wasn't just the loss of blood. I yanked the kerchief from his head and wrapped it frantically around the flooding wound—a struggle enough in itself because his head was lolling and his long hair got everywhere. While I worked he kept mumbling, saying he knew who I was, and telling me to go away and leave him alone, but naturally I took no notice. I finished up with blood all over my own clothes too, but despite the mess he hadn't hurt himself as badly as he'd no doubt intended. Once I'd got the kerchief securely knotted, the bleeding slowed to an ooze through the cloth, then to nothing.

My relief came out in anger. 'What the hell were you thinking of, you fool? What in God's name got into you?'

He tried to say something but it made no sense, and his eyes kept turning backwards until I shook him and slapped his face. I heard movement outside the door; then the woman asking if things were all right. I bit my lip and said yes, and I could hear her clucking as she went away; I wouldn't care to speculate on what she must have thought of us. I was glad the mattress was only made of rushes, and not fabric—what he'd done would be easier to hide. Then I hissed, 'Absalom, whatever he said to you wasn't worth this!'

'It's all over,' he murmured, slightly more audibly. 'I've lost everything. It's all over.'

'What's all over? For God's sake what happened?'

'I don't want to talk about it, Zohel. Go away. Leave me in peace.'

'Peace? You don't know the meaning of the word! I shan't go away till you tell me what happened.'

'I shall never be king. My father will never speak to me again. There's nothing I can do except...' He started groping after the knife with shaking fingers, but I threw it against the wall.

'And what good do you think *that*'s going to do? Are you just going to give Bathsheba what she wants, and leave the throne vacant for her brat without even a fight?'

He didn't reply for a moment; he had his head against my shoulder and I thought he was going to be sick. I wondered if he'd taken poison, not simply something to deaden pain; he was Maacah's son after all. Then he drew back and managed to focus on my face; he croaked, 'Zohel? What are you suggesting?'

'I'm not suggesting anything, damn you! I'm just trying to stop you killing yourself!'

'Why? Why should you bother? No one cares about me, not really. My father doesn't, I know that much now. *You* don't. You're always telling me you don't need me.'

'Well I changed my mind! All right?'

He continued staring at me, though his eyelids were drooping, and there were fresh tears beneath them. Then he went green and was sick all over the blood-soaked rushes. I was reassured.

I got him lying down, and he seemed to go to sleep at once. So I began cleaning up, poking my head around the door to ask for some water on the pretext that my master was ill. The woman obliged but looked horrified, fearing I suppose that her hospitality had been rewarded with plague. I told her that what he had wasn't catching; though she'd have had worse than plague to worry about if the

149

King's son had been found dead with his wrist slashed on her premises. When I closed the door again, Absalom was already pouring out his soul. I'm not sure he knew any more who he was talking to, for he was curled up like a baby, his eyes were still shut, and there was sweat beading on his brow. But I sat and stroked his hair and made the right noises, and out it all came.

David had received him in the throneroom; the King had been decked out in full state regalia, and looked nowhere near as decrepit as folk had had Absalom believe. In fact he'd been little short of radiant, and the moment he saw his son he'd stepped down from the throne as nimbly as a youth, and taken him in his arms. They were both soon weeping; after all, it was nearly five years since they'd last spoken, and it seemed like a lifetime since they'd embraced. As they had kissed and laughed, it came out that Bathsheba had been telling David ever since Absalom's return from Geshur that he'd been *angry* at being recalled, that he'd rather have stayed with Talmai, and had no wish at all to set foot in his father's palace. Joab had had to fetch him to Jerusalem by force; that was why Absalom had fired his barley, in revenge. David had been distraught at her claims, but had then interviewed Joab in person. So now he knew better, and all would be well.

'But why did you believe her?' Absalom had asked. 'She lied to you, Father. She's lied to you a hundred times. How is it you don't learn?'

'I have known so much sadness these past ten years, my son. I too soon believe anything that casts me down further. It's what I have come to expect, somehow. Good things don't happen to me any more.'

'But they can, Father. They must! We can *make* them happen, from today. Isn't *this* good? Aren't you happy *now*?'

'I'm too happy for words. I can't believe you're here. Kiss me again, Absalom. Convince me I'm not dreaming.'

Then they'd wept some more, and kissed some more, and Absalom was weeping again from closed eyes as he painted the picture for me. Then the King had called for food and wine and they'd feasted together, and David had finally accepted in his heart what his eyes were telling him: that his beloved Absalom was home, and everything could once again be perfect. For ten lean years he'd suffered because of his sins; perhaps Adonai had decreed that enough was enough, the debt had been paid. Perhaps now there would follow ten fat years when all David's dreams could come true.

But if everything could be perfect, Absalom had said, if it were within David's power to realize his heart's desire, if all that was past could be forgotten and a clean start made... then surely he could make Absalom his heir after all? Bathsheba was a liar and ought to be exposed as such; and her worthless offspring should be discredited along with her.

'No, Absalom,' David had replied. 'I've given my word.'

'But you are king! Revoke it! Why should you feel obliged to deal honestly with someone like her?'

'Because it's not only her that I'm dealing with. It's Adonai.'

'Adonai? What has he to do with this?'

'How many times must I tell you, my son? The choosing of Israel's kings is Adonai's prerogative. He has chosen Solomon, for good or for ill.'

'But why should you even deal honestly with Adonai? Look how he's treated you! You've had ten years of misery at his hands. You said it yourself.'

'No. I've had ten years of misery at my *own* hands. Absalom... Absalom, please. Don't let's spoil this day. I've missed you so much. I do love you.'

'No, you don't, or you'd act on it. You'd promise me the throne. You're squandering your love on a harlot; you're utterly besotted with her. She isn't even half your age. It's disgusting!'

'Absalom... Please calm down. I know you feel you've been treated unfairly. I know I haven't been the father you needed. But I'm sorry, I truly am. I really do want us to begin afresh.'

'But only on your terms! You won't throw Bathsheba out of my mother's apartment, will you? You let her go round calling herself Queen, saying "Maacah is a Syrian sorceress, the people don't approve of her." Who cares what people think? Surely Adonai's anointed ought to be above such nonsense? But you wouldn't even have pardoned me if you hadn't thought the masses were clamouring for it. Your own house is a cauldron of injustice, and now its poison is pouring out all over Israel as a witness to your weakness! Go on, sign your precious people's death warrant, bequeath their empire to a mollycoddled minor who still sucks his thumb! I don't suppose the world will notice any difference. Israel has had no king since the vanquishing of the Ammonites!'

David had said again, in an unsteady whisper, 'I'm sorry, Absalom.' Then: 'There's so much you just don't know . . . no one knows. Perhaps the time has come to tell you, whatever the consequences . . . I so much wanted to make you understand, you of all people. I still do—'

'Then try me!' Absalom had retorted. Then he'd felt himself flush crimson with chagrin as the truth came home to him: his father had been on the very point of saying something that could have altered everything, until he'd been shouted down. Absalom had bitterly cursed his own petulance.

And instead of opening his wounded heart to his son, David had said quietly, 'Perhaps Bathsheba is right in any case, Absalom. You *are* too hot-headed to make a king. You claim you were so eager to see me, yet you'd barely dipped your bread in the bowl with me before you'd picked a quarrel. You were responsible for starting a fire which could have destroyed half Jerusalem's harvest. You made away with your own brother, and you show no repentance—'

But Absalom couldn't bear to hear reference to Amnon's murder. Despite himself, the fury had risen once more within him, and he'd spluttered, 'But he murdered Tamar! Tamar, who was innocent, and beautiful . . . he ruined her, and you did nothing!'

'And that gave you the right to take the law into your own hands? Vengeance is mine, says Adonai.'

'Then why didn't he take it? I *despise* Adonai!'

'Absalom!' On an impulse David had reached out and grasped his wretched son by the arms; but Absalom thought he meant to strike him, and recoiled involuntarily from the blow. As he did so, the sun and crescent moon had spilled from the safety of his cloak, and David had said, 'Get out.'

He'd crept away to his old rooms and wept for hours. Then he'd gone in search of Shimei and Sheba, wanting to drown his sorrows, but they hadn't been around. Unable to face his mother still sober, he'd wandered the city aimlessly until sunset, in clothes borrowed from a servant of Sheba's so no one would know him. He'd bought wine in the market and drunk alone, then conceived a crazy notion to ride out to his estate at Baal Hazor where there wouldn't be so many prying eyes and wagging tongues. But he'd missed the road and wound up here in this god-forsaken shanty, and resolved to put an end to his torment.

'You ought to have let me go through with it,' he upbraided me. 'Everyone would be better off with me out of the way. I'm a threat to Bathsheba and Solomon, and an embarrassment to my father. Oh, he'd grieve for me for a while, and blame himself, no doubt, but then he'd be over it. I've ruined everything.'

I said, 'Don't you start blaming yourself. It's not your fault everything went wrong.'

'Then whose is it? I'm the one who lost my temper.'

'I don't see it matters whose fault it was. What matters is that you're still alive. If David had promised you the throne, you might not have been. You'd have left Bathsheba no choice but to kill you.'

He hadn't thought of that. At long last he opened his eyes, and I smiled, for it was such a relief to see something in them which wasn't unalloyed despair. I whispered, 'It's like I said, Absalom. Why *should* you give them what they want? Your people need you.'

13

The following day Absalom let me coax him back home, so long as I agreed to tell no one what he'd tried to do. He didn't tell anyone else what had passed between himself and David, either, but it was hardly necessary. He drifted from room to room disconsolate, cloaked in distance, and barely spoke except to Shimei and Sheba who scarcely ever spoke of anything pertinent anyhow.

I knew he was mulling over what to do next, and I kept a close watch on him to make sure it was nothing stupid. I asked myself several times whether I really did care one way or the other, but couldn't come up with an answer. No one asked any questions about the heavy bronze wristband he was wearing, for he wore it occasionally anyway.

To this day I've no idea what he would have done, if Ahithophel hadn't turned up to see him the very next morning. He arrived on our doorstep and informed me that he wished to congratulate my master on effecting a reconciliation with his father.

I couldn't believe that this elderly statesman with all his experience at court hadn't ascertained otherwise. I still don't believe it. But he never betrayed himself for a moment, not even when Absalom stared at him in bewilderment, and said he was wrong.

'Wrong?' repeated Ahithophel, easing himself with dignity onto the couch I offered him, and accepting wine and a sprig of fresh grapes. 'But I escorted you to visit His Majesty myself. I saw him embrace you, before I left you both to your private celebrations.'

'There was nothing to celebrate,' Absalom muttered. 'There still isn't. Nothing has changed.'

'Well, I must confess I'd no idea. You don't know how sorry I am.'

Absalom retorted, 'I'd have thought you'd be only too pleased, sir. It's your granddaughter's fault that my father and I were estranged in the first place, as much as anyone's. And it's certainly her fault we were kept apart for so long.'

Ahithophel chuckled softly, his slight smile a subtle blend of gracious indulgence and repressed exasperation. He ran his eyes coolly over the faces of those present: Shimei and Sheba, Maacah and Miriam, as well as Absalom and myself. Then inclining his head towards Absalom with a look which said quite plainly, 'You've a lot to learn', he asked aloud, 'Are we among friends?'

Absalom shrugged, nonplussed. 'Of course.'

'Then let me tell you a secret. Between the seven of us here and these four walls, you understand.' He paused to watch for reactions, then said, still smiling, 'The lady Bathsheba and I don't always see eye to eye, you know.'

Absalom raised his eyebrows; the rest of us went on staring. So Ahithophel continued, 'Perhaps that makes you feel a little better about the way things seem to have gone between you and the King? It may be that the pair of you are too alike.' His smile broadened, but was utterly without mirth. 'I am quite sure that this is the case where my granddaughter and I are concerned. I regret she has inherited all my—least endearing qualities.'

He paused again. I fell to wondering where all this could be leading. I was fully persuaded that Ahithophel hadn't come to exchange pleasantries, still less to offer Absalom misplaced congratulation or emotional counselling. I was equally certain that he was unlikely to divulge secrets of any consequence in a room full of people he couldn't trust unreservedly. But for the time being he was clearly enjoying being the centre of attention as much as Absalom normally did. He finished the grapes at his leisure, arranging the pips with fastidious symmetry on the rim of his plate, washed and wiped his fingers, and took up where he'd left off.

'Her parents were hoping for a boy, so they said, when she was born, and I've very often reflected that it might have turned out better for all concerned if they'd been granted their prayer. Bathsheba would have made a fine politician. But a woman with her accomplishments is seldom anything but trouble.'

Absalom grinned; Ahithophel wasn't too cerebral to guess why. He chose not to comment, however, saying instead, 'My son and his wife made things hard for her during her childhood, you know, from what I saw of it. She was brought up to believe that only males get their own way, and that she would live a life of submission first to her father, then to her husband, then to her own sons. Once they'd got her married off to Uriah they lost interest in her entirely and lavished all their wealth and attention on her brothers.' Then he curled his lip wryly. 'But it didn't take her long to work out how a woman *can* gain control of those who wield power.'

Absalom said, 'I'll warrant she enjoys the means as much as the end.'

Ahithophel's wry smile hardened. 'Yes,' he said. 'I'm sure there are men who have cause to be glad she was born female, my handsome Prince, though personally I doubt sometimes whether His Majesty is one of them.'

Absalom's grin disappeared. He too had recognized the importance of trying to work out what Ahithophel was up to; and in particular, what this latest remark had meant. When Ahithophel leaned back and settled to his wine, showing no intention of elaborating, Absalom said peevishly, 'She's borne him a remarkable son.'

'She has borne him more remarkable sons than one, to give her her due,' Ahithophel announced calmly. 'She gave birth first thing this morning to another healthy boy. Two whole days in labour, and she herself hovering inches above Sheol, so I am informed, yet the baby has strong enough lungs already to wake half the palace. *So* unlike her firstborn, whom we must not be forgetting of course, rest his poor little soul. A sad and mystifying business altogether ...'

'The one they say arrived early?'

This interjection came from Maacah. She rarely opened her mouth in company these days; in fact she rarely displayed much interest in life at all. Now there was an intensity about her features I hadn't seen there in a long while.

Ahithophel replied, 'Quite so,' and an odd flicker of understanding seemed to spark between them, though a moment later I decided I'd imagined it. Maacah had never trusted Ahithophel, and had no more reason to do so now than previously. He added thoughtfully, 'We never did quite get to the bottom of all that, you know. Her sudden arrival at the palace; her instant pregnancy when to all intents and purposes she'd been barren with Uriah. I had nothing whatever to do with her coming to court; can you believe that? I know few people do, but it's true nevertheless. I wasn't at all sure I wanted her there even once she'd arrived.' He broke off and cleared his throat, as though he'd said more than he'd planned to, but I was sure he hadn't. He'd never said or done anything unintentional in his life. He glanced at Absalom suddenly and said, 'May we talk alone?'

Absalom baulked. 'If you really want to.'

'Let's say I would feel more comfortable.'

The others left, reluctantly; Absalom had me stay, saying I was his personal attendant and above reproach. I stifled a snigger; I knew he wanted me there because I was quicker than he was at picking up the point when people spoke in riddles. At least he realized it, though I never made him admit it aloud, and he never would have done so.

Still, even after relative privacy had been secured, for a while Ahithophel said nothing more confidential or more compromising than he had before. He hinted and alluded, and side-stepped anything Absalom asked, but all the time he was weighing him up, though I couldn't think why. He expressed a little more of his own mistrust of Bathsheba, and did concede that he was worried what would happen if the King should depart this life sooner rather than later.

'Do you think that's likely?' Absalom sounded more apprehensive than he'd meant to.

'I shouldn't have thought you'd be so concerned, if what you told me earlier is true.'

They sat in silence then, reading each other's eyes, though I still couldn't fathom what was going on; and Absalom was plainly more perplexed than I was. At length Ahithophel broke the tension.

'You see, Absalom, I have heard that you're as anxious as I am about what may happen if David dies with things as they are at present—and whether that is "likely" is hardly relevant. Since you asked, however, I think it extremely likely. He's very sick, though the finest doctors from Egypt and Babylon can't determine the cause; and thus can't prescribe an effective treatment. But even if he were in the best of health, accidents happen, Absalom. And the son he's named to succeed him is barely seven years old.'

'If he even exists. Have you ever seen him?'

'In person? Not for five years; she won't allow it. She fears me as much as she fears anyone, and hates the thought of my being able to recognize her precious progeny. She's having him brought up by one of the concubines in the harem so he can't be distinguished from the King's other sons or his women's bastards. But he exists all right.'

Absalom said suddenly, 'And is she right to fear you?'

Ahithophel chuckled softly again. He hadn't anticipated being faced with a question like this, but I think it pleased him. Perhaps he thought there was hope for Maacah's egotistical son after all.

'I'm not sure how I should answer that, my shrewd young friend. Let us just say I'm interested in—exploring alternatives for Israel's future. I should imagine that this might give the two of us something in common?'

'I—don't know what you mean,' said Absalom, and I think it was the truth. For myself, I was putting two and two together, but could hardly believe I was hearing this type of talk from Ahithophel.

'Come come, Absalom, you've lived a greater portion of your life at court than I have. You have ears in the palace where I have ears; and ears in the city where I don't. You know as well as I do what people are saying about David; and about you. Israel needs a strong king again, someone who can restore the nation's morale, unite factions and tribes, enlarge our empire and put some wealth back into the treasuries. A plant which doesn't grow soon withers, and it is the same with kingdoms.'

'Are you suggesting I—'

'Now let us avoid unseemly haste! Don't put words into my mouth. I am merely suggesting . . . that you begin to dress yourself modestly, leave your sun and moon pendant at home, and perhaps those earrings. And certainly your hound.'

'What?'

'You heard me. You want to know what I'm suggesting you should do. And that's it.'

'But no one cared what I looked like when I rode back into Jerusalem. They were just happy to see me!'

'True enough. But it all depends in what *capacity* you want them to see you.'

With Absalom still gaping at him, Ahithophel rose to his feet.

'Well, I regret I cannot sit here all day sampling the delights of your wine cellars, Prince Absalom. Now don't take your quarrel with your father too much to heart. Perhaps I shall visit again in a week or two, to satisfy myself that you aren't becoming unduly depressed.'

I showed him out; one of the others must have heard me close the door, for they came crowding back, demanding to know what the great man had said.

But Absalom all at once seemed more distant than ever. He replied hoarsely, 'I don't know.'

'You "don't know"?' Shimei mimicked him scornfully, his rabid little eyes screwed up; he was never one for subtlety, being about as brash as Ahithophel was refined. 'What did he come here for? He doesn't waste his time paying social calls, that slimy sneak. I've seen less oil in an olive press.'

'Come off it, Shimei,' Sheba sneered at him. 'It's perfectly obvious what he came for. He wants Absalom to get rid of David and Solomon the same way he got rid of Amnon, and seize power himself. It's written all over him—he didn't need to say anything. He's just not sure yet whether Absalom's got what it takes to go through with it. Am I not right, Absalom?'

Absalom was speechless. He gripped the edge of his couch until his knuckles were like knotted rope. Then he stormed out of the room, slamming the door so hard it flew open again behind him. Still worried what he might do, I set off to follow. But Shimei and Sheba shouldered up as if with one mind, and somehow contrived to block my way. With his face uncomfortably close to mine and his garlic breath making me retch, Sheba snarled, 'What *did* he say, Zoheleth.'

I gritted my teeth, determined to say nothing. Sheba took hold of my cloakpins, but though I was out of practice at handling this kind of abuse, lessons learned young die hard in a crisis, even when we've tried to forget them. In any case I knew I was unlikely to be beaten seriously in the presence of ladies, especially when one of them was Maacah. She might be less formidable than in her younger days, but Shimei and Sheba had long memories.

However, they still weren't prepared to let me out. I sat down warily, and Maacah said, touching my hand, 'Zohel, don't let Absalom trust him. There's little I wouldn't put past Ahithophel, and I mean that.'

I growled, 'I'm not sure what he *is* suggesting anyhow.'

'No, but suppose Sheba is right? What can Ahithophel's motives be? He'll use Absalom for his own ends without a second thought about the dangers he'll be exposing him to. Or what if he's just out to trap him? To set him up? What if he incites him to conspiracy and then presents David with a dossier of evidence against him? He could be working for Bathsheba in spite of what he says about her. He *wants* us all to believe he dislikes her. That's why he said what he did in front of us all.'

Then a voice from the doorway said, 'Or perhaps he knows Solomon's accession *will* be a disaster for Israel, and he doesn't wish to be associated with his nation's downfall.'

Absalom stood propped against the doorpost, looking fragile as a reed before the wind. His mother held out her arms to him, and he went to her obediently as he'd always done, and perhaps more gratefully. But over her shoulder I could see that his eyes were far away.

Ahithophel didn't return for almost a month. But in the meantime the stream of suppliants who came to the house in search of justice swelled to a river, and I was in no doubt as to who was diverting the flow towards us. Before long we were dealing with individuals who hadn't even bothered to appeal to the King first, but come directly to us; when we questioned them we were assured the belief was now widespread that Absalom was a more competent and compassionate judge than his father had ever been.

Our satisfied clients presumably constituted the principal source of this conviction, but Ahithophel's propaganda programme was scarcely less influential. He knew Absalom's weaknesses as well as his strengths, and how to exploit them to the full. Pampered by his mother and neglected by his father, the young Prince was a sucker for flattery.

Then, soon after olive harvest, Ahithophel paid his second visit. He still didn't come out with any specific proposals, though he allowed himself to make less ambiguous reference to the social and political unrest which he claimed was on the verge of erupting in many parts of the country and from the ranks of several of the most powerful groupings within the population.

'Take the northern tribes as an example,' he said. 'They've never wholeheartedly accepted David's authority. From the outset they saw him as a southerner, and were much more willing to follow Saul's surviving son Ishbosheth until he was so treacherously murdered. They were never convinced that David didn't issue the orders for that himself, and who can blame them? And don't forget: there are ten tribes who consider themselves northerners, and only two in the south.'

Absalom retorted miserably, 'That's slander, Ahithophel. My father had nothing to do with what happened to Ishbosheth, and you know it. I thought you were his friend.'

'Alas, there is little place for personal affection in the world of politics, my dear Prince. We are talking about the destiny of our nation, the fortunes of tens of thousands of people. Is it right for us to put all that at risk for the sake of the feelings of a few individuals?

Suppose the northern tribes were to reject your father's overlordship altogether, and set up a rival king of their own? Where would our army's allegiances lie? It stands to reason that ten out of every twelve soldiers are northerners.

'In fact I'm none too sure where the army's allegiances lie even now. It isn't just David whose popularity is on the wane. Joab and Abishai don't command as much respect as they used to. In the old days the men used to put up with their harsh style of leadership because they could see results. They were winning glorious victories and raking in booty.

'Why aren't we seeing that any more? Why aren't we pushing out the boundaries of our empire still further? Egypt is weak, as is Assyria, but you can be sure it won't always be so. Why aren't we taking advantage of their decadence now, before *they* take advantage of *us*? I'll tell you why, Absalom. It's because our troops have grown fat and lazy due to prolonged inaction. Even Joab can't get into his armour any more for the spare flesh around his waist.'

Yet more wretchedly Absalom murmured, 'It can't be as bad as you say, or the peoples we've conquered would have revolted by now. What about the Ammonites and the Moabites? They wouldn't still be wearing our yoke if they thought they could get away with throwing it off. To say nothing of Syria.'

Absalom virtually spat these last five words, and Ahithophel shifted uncomfortably in his seat. 'I take your point, Absalom, I take your point. There haven't been any serious revolts—to date. But it's only a matter of time, and once it has begun there will be little we can do to prevent things getting entirely out of hand. Besides, I can think of ways in which the Syrians in particular could be persuaded to accept our sovereignty less reluctantly...'

Absalom said, 'I'm tired, Ahithophel. I don't want to talk any more about this. It's making me depressed, and it was you who said you didn't want that.'

When Ahithophel had gone, I said, 'Perhaps he's in your grandfather's pay, Absalom. He must have contacts there—*someone* from the court tracked you down in Geshur.'

'But why won't he come clean and say exactly what he wants from me? I dread him coming here, Zohel.'

'I suppose Sheba was right for once. Ahithophel isn't sure about you yet. He needs time to find out what *you* really want before he risks laying himself open to charges of treason. And I suppose he's taking his time gauging how much support there would be for some kind of uprising, from the army and from the people.'

Absalom shook his head, unexpectedly flashing me one of his most disarming smiles. 'You impress me sometimes, you know, Zohel. You're getting to think like a politician yourself. Perhaps you can be my official adviser instead of my armour bearer. How do you do it?'

I shrugged. 'A childhood spent trying to come to terms with the motives of evil men, maybe.'

'You never told me about your childhood, Zohel.'

'There's nothing I'd want to tell.'

He felt the silent sting of my old defensiveness then, so asked instead, 'Do you think *Ahithophel* is evil?'

'I don't know. Your mother told me to warn you not to trust him.'

'She's warned me herself a hundred times. I've had enough of people warning me about what not to do. I just wish someone would come up with something I *should* do.'

In the fortnight following Ahithophel's second visit we received news of more flagrant miscarriages of justice, and more vile atrocities than we'd ever heard of happening in Israel before. It was no accident that we were told about them, I'm sure. But I did wonder whether the worthy Ahithophel might somehow have been involved in their perpetration, not merely in the reporting of them.

By way of example, in the land of Dan—the most northerly tribe—a riot broke out in which twenty people died. It started when a gang of dispossessed farmers overran the estates of the entrepreneur who had seized their ancestral plots. Gaining access to the house itself by conspiring with his slaves, they set upon the man and his wife and children with knives and clubs, hacking and bludgeoning them to death before themselves being brutally attacked by some of the landgrabber's hired men.

Elsewhere, a sanctuary was looted by a mob of peasants, who claimed they were taking the sacred vessels to sell for food; but they butchered five unarmed priests in the process.

The fact of the matter was that although the three years of famine had almost been forgotten by many of us, there were those who at the time had had to sell their land and in some cases their children, and eat all of their livestock, even their donkeys. For these families there was no prospect of recovery and the hardship went on, exacerbated by the corruption of the legal system.

Some of the tales we heard came across as too outrageous to be true, but I myself saw a well-dressed merchant assaulted and fatally wounded by robbers in Jerusalem itself, barely a stone's throw from the palace, and no one made any attempt to go to his aid. I don't pretend to be any less guilty than all the others who simply stood by and watched; I was just too stunned to react at all.

The very next day after this incident, Ahithophel came again, and this time he was blunt.

'The current state of affairs must not be allowed to persist any longer, Absalom,' he said. 'Our present government lacks the power to act because its overlord is hopelessly ineffectual, and hinders the work of his own ministers. For his own good and for the good of his people he must be—removed.'

'For his *own* good?' repeated Absalom. 'What nonsense is this? You're intending to kill him!'

'Not necessarily; such extreme measures may yet be avoided. No one is in any hurry to slay the Lord's Anointed.'

'And since when have religion or superstition meant anything to you?'

'Whenever they have the force of arms on their side, Absalom. There are many men in Israel who would happily see David deposed, but never murdered. We can be careful; we *must* be careful. But we must also act. At once.'

'So just what are you proposing?'

'I'm proposing that we talk candidly; man to man, face to face, with no more fudging of the issues. That way we can thrash out some proposals together.'

'And who is the one who's been responsible for this—fudging? Don't you start blaming me.'

'Absalom, this is no time for adolescent squabbling. We have to start work before it's too late.'

'And if I refuse? If I won't help you?'

'Then I look for someone who will. But should that be your decision, you needn't bother to make any elaborate arrangements for your own old age.'

Absalom's throat tightened visibly. 'God damn you, Ahithophel. That's blackmail.'

'It runs in my family, you'll find. So! What are you saying to me?'

'I'm saying . . . oh, I don't know what I'm saying! I need more time. You can't just walk in here and expect me to decide on the spot whether to pit myself against my own father and risk my neck into the bargain. How can I take a thing like this so lightly?'

'Do you imagine that *I* take it lightly? Do you imagine that I relish the prospect of betraying a man I have served since before you were born? If there were any other way, I would have taken it. I've tried, believe me. I've tried everything I could think of to get your father to wake up to the perils he's casting himself and his people into. But it won't work; nothing works. I've come to the end of my patience.'

I think this was the moment when Absalom accepted that Ahithophel was being thoroughly sincere. The elder statesman's mask of deadpan efficiency had slipped only slightly. But we both glimpsed the genuine fear that lay behind it. The revelation did nothing to ease Absalom's agony, however. I watched it consuming him, while Ahithophel composed his features once more and folded his manicured hands in his lap, aware that his message had gone home. He was content now to await the response he regarded as inevitable.

But he'd underestimated the violence of the young Prince's torment; if there was one thing beyond the powers of Ahithophel's comprehension it was a man allowing his emotions to cloud his reason.

After an eternity had passed, Absalom looked at him, hollow-eyed, and said, 'Come back tomorrow morning, sir, I beg you. Please give me till then. One more day can't make so much difference after all this time.'

Ahithophel surveyed him levelly. Then he said, 'Very well. If you insist. Until dawn tomorrow. Don't get up, Zoheleth. I can show myself out.'

I knew it was no consideration for me which had prompted him to say this. He didn't want me following him. Outside he would have men hidden, to watch Absalom lest he go straight to the palace and reveal all.

Absalom threw himself face down on his couch and said, 'Help me, Zohel.'

I poured him a goblet of wine and squatted beside him, but that wasn't what he wanted. He moaned into the cushions, 'Tell me who I am. I don't know any more. For sixteen years I was a Hebrew prince: circumcised, civilized, a son of the Torah. I had the best father anyone could have wished for. He loved me, my mother loved me, everyone loved me, I was happy. How can it all have gone wrong?'

'I don't know, Absalom. Everything went wrong for me the moment I was born. But I did learn one lesson from my childhood which is worth passing on: you're best off forgetting about your past. It's usually painful and you can't do a thing to change it. But you can change your future.'

'What future have I got? And how can I change it, if I don't even know what I want? I spent three years in Geshur flagrantly disregarding God's commandments, eating pork till it came out of my ears, breaking the Sabbath—even losing track of when it was! I worshipped the Baals and poured libations to Astarte, and made fertility magic with profligate priestesses under the stars! I thought I'd found paradise, Zohel, but even that turned sour. I missed my home and my people and the ways I'd been brought up with—I even missed the endless festivals, the confounded fasts, the sickly sanctimonious music of the Tabernacle! Do you know, I couldn't get the melodies of my father's psalms out of my head? Even the words too sometimes. And yet I never used to think all that mattered. I never thought Adonai mattered . . .

'So I agree to come home, I allow myself to believe everything will be all right again once I'm back in Jerusalem. And now look at the predicament I'm in. I try to pray to Adonai, but he doesn't listen any more than the deaf-mute idols of Syria listen. Perhaps there *are* no gods, Zohel. They are just the products of our own imaginings, the fancies of our dreams.'

Part of me so desperately wanted him to be right. This same part had been trying to persuade the rest of me, ever since the first time I'd fled from the weeping King, that what his own son was now saying was true.

Yet to hear such thoughts expressed aloud appalled me for some reason, just as it had appalled me to listen to David bewailing his own spiritual malaise. All of a sudden the universe we were living in felt so big, so empty, so utterly without meaning . . . I sat there on the floor with my head tipped back against the seat of Absalom's couch, imagining the crushing weight of the sky up above, aware that at any moment the elements themselves might break their bonds and devour me if there truly were no guiding hand to restrain them.

Eventually Absalom's voice, dismal and dreary, stirred me.

'Why don't you just say it, Zohel? Ahithophel's right; we *have* to do it his way. There isn't any choice.'

'Absalom, it will be so dangerous. I'm scared.'

'It was you who told me I couldn't give up the throne without a fight.'

'No, Absalom—'

'You did. Remember.' Still lying prone beside me, he thrust out his arm, shaking back the wristband so that I couldn't fail to see the crusted brown scab which marred his smooth skin.

'Be fair, Absalom. I couldn't let you kill yourself. I'd have said anything.'

'But I need to be able to trust you. I don't *want* you to say just anything. I want you to tell me what you really think.'

'It's not my place to tell you what to do.'

'But now we're back where we started! Whose place *is* it? Who *will* tell me what to do?'

I was still holding the goblet which I'd offered to him, but I'd forgotten all about it, and jolted by the rush of bitterness in his voice I spilled it over my tunic and onto the floor. Before I could get up to look for a cloth, Miriam was by my side cleaning up. Neither of us had noticed her come in; I'd no idea how much of our conversation she might have overheard. Though my heart was thudding at her closeness, at the tumbling of her sleek hair over her shoulder when she leaned down to wipe up the wine and the veil slid from her head, Absalom didn't sense her presence until she spoke to him.

'My lord, the door you walked through once before is still open.'

He didn't even look at her. His face was buried in the cushions, the heels of his hands pressed against his eyelids, and his own hair, mussed from lying, tangled over his back like the coiling fronds of a rampant black fern. In a cracked, muffled whisper he said, 'I don't know what you're talking about, woman. This is no business of yours.'

'My lord . . .'

I could see the love and pity brimming in her eyes, overriding her fear and her awe of him.

' . . . my lord, Nathan could speak to Adonai for you. Maybe he could even show you how to find him for yourself and receive his answer in your own spirit.'

Absalom sat bolt upright. He dashed the goblet from her grasp and flung it at the wall with all his strength. There was sweat on his brow and he said, 'Get out, before you make me do something I'll be sorry for.'

'My lord.' She curtseyed hurriedly and withdrew. As she went out of the room I could have sworn I heard a door closing, yet there was no door the way she'd gone, only a curtain.

Absalom was shaking all over. I'd seen him angry so many times, but not like this, not even against Amnon. He was like a rising whirlwind, sucking energy from the very air round about him, teetering on the brink of wreaking mindless destruction on whatever chanced to be within range of his fists or feet if nothing stopped him. Still, I was wiser than to speak and risk him venting that fury upon me.

It wasn't Miriam he was angry with. It was Nathan he hated, with a white-hot intensity which he must have been holding in the flame of his own anguish for some time; quite possibly ever since their fateful encounter over seven years previously. But I think the flame had flared up much hotter of late; probably because he'd already thought of going back to consult the elusive holy man long before Miriam had made the suggestion, yet he knew he could never bring himself to do it.

For Nathan was so obviously the man who would be able to see a way out of Absalom's plight. I couldn't imagine why I hadn't thought of this before. Witnessing the gradual disintegration of Israel and her king must have been more painful for the prophet than for almost anyone. He'd lived through the heady days when David, the plucky and godly shepherd boy from Bethlehem, had risen to power and proceeded to exalt Adonai's people above all other nations, thus demonstrating the omnipotence of the one true God for the world to see and to wonder at.

Now Nathan's heart must be breaking as he watched the whole edifice crumbling, the empire decaying from within, law and order breaking down. Soon life would be like it had been under the Judges before the time of Saul, when, as the saying goes, each man did that which was right in his own eyes.

For years Nathan must have been crying out to God for change, with every fibre of his being; but not the kind of change which Ahithophel had in mind. There had to be a third way, and perhaps Nathan already knew what it was.

If only Absalom hadn't been so wilful, so wanton as to defile himself with Bathsheba! And not merely the first time, but all over again so much more recently. He'd always been so easily led, despite his protestations that he'd been the only one with initiative among

167

David's sons. From what I'd seen, just about anything could tempt him—a dare, an insult, a chance to show off or to challenge authority. Bathsheba had led him into soiling his own flesh and trampling his innocence into the dirt. Now Ahithophel was leading him to risk his very life.

Yet when it came to apportioning judgment, Absalom would carry the blame. His own sin had cut him off, not only from Nathan but from Adonai also, and there was no way he would lower himself to repent. For when he had claimed he'd prayed to Adonai and been left without guidance, it had been a lie. He knew perfectly well what Adonai was asking him to do; and he wouldn't do it. He would sooner have slit Nathan's throat than looked him in the face.

Not that I was in any position to condemn Absalom. I'd cut myself off from Adonai just as surely as he had. *Why?* I asked myself honestly for the first time in years. *Is it truly because of David, and what you've seen him become, that you have torn yourself away from the love of a father infinitely more powerful and compassionate than the one whose loss Absalom is still mourning?*

Then it came to me that I didn't want Adonai to shine his light into the dark places of my life any more than Absalom did. When I'd sung the Song of the Bow to David, I'd seen how the intensity of that light could break a man. And though something was telling me deep in my soul that Adonai only ever breaks what is already cracked and useless, in order to build something strong and lovely in its place, I was too terrified to let him do that to me. My dark places existed because of what had been done to me by others, unlike Absalom's, but the guilt I'd wrapped them up in was as real and as crippling as his. The scars in my soul were ugly, but at least they weren't bleeding, and I dreaded having them reopened.

Also, I knew that if I opened myself to Adonai, if I let him wash all the filth out of me, there was something else which would have to go with it. I would have to relinquish my hatred for Ziba, my resolve to get even with him when the opportunity presented itself. Hadn't David said, *Vengeance is mine, says Adonai*? Yet from what I'd observed, his God seemed singularly reluctant to take it. I didn't think about Ziba very often, but when I did, I was more determined than I'd ever been that he shouldn't go unpunished.

I was so wrapped up in my own ruminations, I hadn't noticed Absalom get up to retrieve his goblet from the far corner of the room where he'd thrown it. There was a crinkled dent in one side, but he filled it to the brim with wine and downed the whole contents in one gulp. He was no longer shaking.

'Zohel,' he announced with resignation. 'I've made up my mind.'

I already knew what he was going to say, but that didn't stop my heart sinking. I studied the handsome, haggard face, the dark rings beneath his beautiful eyes, and thought: Absalom, the hero of men, the darling of women, the champion of the oppressed, who can manipulate each and every individual who crosses his path and make them all love him, is going to give himself up to be manipulated by the craftiest, most devious schemer I've ever had the misfortune to meet.

I knew he'd made the wrong decision, and so did he, and neither of us had the will or the humility to change it.

'Go and find Ahithophel now,' he said. 'There's no point in waiting till morning. Let's get it over with. Tell him I'm ready to talk.'

14

I took no part in the discussion which ensued. Ahithophel flatly refused to sanction my presence in spite of all Absalom's protests. Already I wondered grimly what kind of kingship the seasoned statesman intended for his protégé. Clearly he reckoned the young Prince woefully lacking in relevant experience, and didn't doubt for a moment that he himself was the person most qualified to instruct him.

So whilst the pair of them sat in intimate conclave, hatching conspiracy, I amused myself by exercising Gatis. I walked her round and round the courtyard; from now on she wasn't to be seen outside the confines of our house. She padded obediently beside me, her eyes soulful and her tail between her legs. I knew it wasn't merely her own freedom she was pining for. I reached out and stroked her spontaneously; it was the first time I'd ever done that with affection.

But when Ahithophel had gone, Absalom insisted on burdening me with the gist of their conversation—and not only once, but until my head was pounding with it. We talked in his bedroom while he got changed, for it seemed that in the short space of time since he'd dressed that morning, Syrian clothing had somehow become abhorrent to him. Another bad sign in its way, I thought, as I packed up his skimpy tunic, and the cloak of Tyrian purple; Ahithophel could have persuaded a starving wolf to guard a sheepfold. The last thing Absalom took off was the sun and crescent moon, which he dandled wistfully between his fingers, then carefully buried in the bottom of a chest.

'Come off it, Absalom,' I teased him, helping him into a modest linen robe. 'Those don't mean anything to you, not really. Why don't you throw them out?'

But he didn't answer me directly; only sat on the end of his high Egyptian bed and began pinning up his hair ready to cover it. He'd never done that, even before going to Geshur. He said, 'I have to be seen at the Tabernacle at least once a day, from today, Zohel. You will have to remind me to go.'

I smiled wryly, securing one of his ringlets which had already

170

slithered loose. 'An intriguing piece of advice for you to be given by a man who's in Talmai's pay.'

He touched my hand lightly. 'Don't mock me. Please. This is hard enough already. When I'm King I'll have to *lead* half the rituals, never mind *be* there. I'll be the guardian of Adonai's cult whether I like it or not. I'll be responsible for ensuring he's rightly honoured.'

'At least for a while.' I couldn't resist a final gibe; I was imagining his minions in a few years' time replacing the Ark of the Covenant with an Asherah pole. But he took me the wrong way.

'What do you mean, at least for a while? If we succeed, it's for good. There's no going back. Once I've been crowned . . . anointed . . . we daren't even *think* what might happen if things go wrong after that.' Then he grinned apologetically. 'I'm sorry. I'm as scared as you must be, I guess. But you mustn't goad me. It's more important than ever now for me to know I can trust you. That's what Ahithophel says we must do first.'

'What? And who's "we"?'

'Ahithophel and I! We must gather around ourselves a nucleus of men we can depend upon entirely, and incorporate them into our planning. That way we can delegate some of the workload; and they'll be handsomely rewarded once we're in control. I need you to be the first.'

I sat down heavily on the bed beside him. It hadn't really occurred to me that I faced a pivotal decision as surely as he had done. But of course he was right. Agreeing to act as his squire-cum-butler and being party to a conspiracy were two different things. Yet if I expected him to continue confiding in me when things got tough (and I was forced to admit that made me feel good) I should have to belong to his inner circle.

I said, 'I just wish I felt a bit happier about all this. It gives me a bad feeling in my stomach.'

'Zohel.' Absalom put his arm around me, making me ashamed of my reticence. 'If you say no, it'll be more than a bad feeling in your stomach you'll have to contend with. Think how much you know already. You're as vulnerable to blackmail as I am.'

I held my head. 'Would I be on the run just from Ahithophel? Or from you too?'

'From now on that will make no difference. Ahithophel and I must think as one. I'm very fond of you, Zohel, I always have been.

But there's no way I could save you if you tried to get out now. Perhaps if you hadn't learnt to speak or write you'd have stood a chance.'

I searched his face, for some reason suddenly recalling what Tamar had said all those years ago, that any love you gave to Absalom was wasted, and that he was nothing but trouble. Perhaps he never *had* cared about me; perhaps he had only taken me under his wing as a way of getting back indirectly at Amnon. But I knew that Tamar had loved him as much as anyone, underneath.

I also knew that for the first time in his life, he really did need me. He needed someone he could lean on, someone who would be straight with him, and always be there, come what may. So I said, 'Very well, Absalom. You can trust me.'

'And you mean that of your own free will?'

'Oh, Absalom, now who's making things difficult? Ahithophel has put pressure on you; now you're putting pressure on me. What's the difference? I've given you my word. Isn't that good enough?'

He squeezed my shoulders reassuringly, but then let go. 'It's good enough for me. I just hope it's good enough for Ahithophel.'

Not half as much as I do, I thought, but I didn't want to talk about that any more. I picked up the cloth he'd got out to make a turban and began winding it around his head, though I didn't make a very good job of it and had to start again. I wasn't used to doing it; the most substantial head-covering he'd ever worn before was a rakish kerchief thrown haphazardly over his loose curls. He sat in silence while I struggled, so I asked, 'Who else will you approach?'

'Shimei and Sheba to start with, or they'll find out anyway.'

'Your mother has little more time for them than she has for Ahithophel,' I cautioned him. 'Are you sure a thing like this won't prove too much for them to handle?'

He heaved a resigned sigh. 'Ahithophel has little time for them either. He says he "doubts they are the stuff of which conspirators are made". But they've never let me down yet.' He chuckled sheepishly. 'And they've kept a fair few guilty secrets for me in their time.'

'But they haven't had to suffer any hardship for you, have they? You can hardly compare boyhood confidences with premeditated treason. Suppose they get caught and tortured for what they know?'

'Aren't you letting your imagination run away with you, Zohel? How do I know *I* can stand up to torture? How do I know *you* can?'

One look into my eyes told him that.

'All right, so you've suffered, though how you expect me to take account of that when you won't talk to me about it, I can't think. But I hope to God this nightmare isn't going to go on long enough to involve things like torture. I'm hoping we can just take the King by surprise and get the whole business sewn up overnight.'

It didn't escape my notice that he'd said 'the King' and not 'my father'. I said, 'I hope your wish is granted. But surely you have to be prepared? I mean—I'm not sure that Shimei and Sheba could care less about affairs of state. So long as they have access to a plentiful supply of wine, they're happy. Don't you think it's important that they should fully support what you're doing?'

'What *we're* doing, Zohel.'

I looked at the floor. 'Yes. What *we're* doing.'

'Quite frankly I don't think their views are important, so long as they love me and I can bank on their loyalty. They'll do what's required of them. But as it happens, I think they *will* believe in our venture. They are both Benjamites, remember, and of Saul's clan Aphiah; they carry Saulide blood. The Saulides still think of David as an upstart. Besides, you've heard Shimei curse him yourself.'

It was true. But as I proceeded to point out to Absalom, by the Saulide argument, being David's son he'd no more right to the throne than his father had.

'Maybe not,' said Absalom. 'But Shimei and Sheba are my friends.'

He seemed to have forgotten what Ahithophel had said about the place of personal affection in politics; but I wasn't inclined to press the point further. So I said, 'All right. And who else?'

'No one else of my choosing. But Ahithophel has allies of his own. He will bring men with him the next time we meet, to launch the first phase of our campaign.'

'And what will that consist of?'

'Mobilizing support for me among the people who matter.'

I pursed my lips. 'And who are they? The rich few, or the poor majority? I don't see how you can champion both.'

'I shall champion *all* those who have suffered under the present administration.' Unexpectedly he broadened his shoulders, and his hand balled into a fist. 'Every man who's been wrongfully accused or discredited, every man who has come up against discrimination; in fact everyone who's discontented, for any one of a thousand reasons ... I'll fight for them all! Many of them may be poor, but

173

there will be plenty more affluent ones too.'

Still wishing I felt as confident as he now sounded, I made a final adjustment to his turban and busied myself collecting up spare pins, lest I be tempted to say something negative again. But Absalom and I had known each other a long time, and he'd learnt to read my undisguised thoughts just as I could often read his. He took the box of pins from me, and seized hold of both my hands. 'Zohel, will you stop worrying? The decision is made now; the worst is over.'

He meant it, too. Until that morning, his mind had been in ferment; the conflict of loyalties and emotions had all but pulled him apart. But now he'd resolved upon the direction he would travel, now he could see a clear path to walk down, now he had my solemn promise of fidelity, he was almost his old buoyant self once more.

The next meeting of the conspirators—the first at which the newly co-opted committee members were present—took place two days later, after dark, at our house. We were well on into summer, and the night was oppressively hot, but Ahithophel wouldn't let us talk in the courtyard. Absalom objected that it wasn't overlooked from outside, but Ahithophel was adamant: it was overlooked from our own rooftops, and one of our own slaves might hear us. Sooner or later their ranks would be infiltrated, for sooner or later one of Ahithophel's unexplained absences would be questioned at the palace.

He brought with him two other men, and I was shocked when I found out who they were. One was none other than Seraiah, the official court secretary; the second a certain Amasa, one of the highest ranking officers in David's standing army. Seraiah was an elderly, unworldly-looking character, with watery eyes and a scholarly frown. Amasa was young, in his late twenties at most; he had strong, noble features and a firm square jaw. I learned later that he, like Joab, was a nephew of David's, but they were children of different parents and had never had any time for one another. Besides, although the two crack soldiers were presumably first cousins, Joab was older than Amasa's father.

We crowded into a disused storeroom, which was windowless and couldn't be reached except through the kitchens; so late in the evening these were deserted. A less promising launching-party for a junta it was difficult to imagine, I thought. We sat on the floor, for there was nowhere else to sit, and the only light came from a couple of puny oil lamps which Absalom had me set at the centre of our circle. Illumined from below, each face was half sunk in shadow, and its defects were magnified: Shimei and Sheba looked dissipated, Amasa fanatical, Seraiah coldly withdrawn, Ahithophel himself sly and supercilious. Only Absalom inspired any sort of optimism within me, for he now appeared oddly exhilarated, almost radiant. I wondered what the rest of them thought of me.

But though Absalom was being groomed to take David's place, control of the campaign rested with Ahithophel; that much was made plain from the beginning. It was he who outlined the strategy, he who dealt with all the questions, fielded the objections and smoothed out the differences of opinion. And somehow he melded this motley assortment of dissidents into a close-knit brotherhood, who by the end of that very first session knew they might have to die for one another, and believed themselves capable of doing it.

Ahithophel scarcely raised his voice above a whisper, but his strength of will and clarity of thought couldn't have been more forcefully communicated. There was no longer any need for him to paint sordid pictures of Israel's degeneracy. What was called for now was something positive, something dynamic; we needed to hear a voice of authority girding us for action. All this Ahithophel was well aware of, and he'd come primed to deliver the goods.

'David is frail and failing,' he said, 'But just look at his son! In Absalom we have everything we could wish for in a monarch. He's young, he's handsome, the people love him. He fought like a hero in the war against the Ammonites; he displayed the conviction and courage necessary to slay even his own brother, because he is one of that rare breed of men who can see that righteousness counts for more than sentimentality. What better evidence could we ask for, as proof that he will be able to stand firm against his father?'

I thought, this is the first I've heard of Absalom's distinguished military record, to say nothing of his high standards of personal integrity; but I could see everyone else nodding in approval, and Absalom himself smiling, high on his own renown.

Ahithophel continued, 'And look at the good reputation he's already earned among the population at large. He's charmed droves of men from every social class by his innate sense of justice, and his willingness to show mercy and compassion. You only need look around this room to see the truth of that: we have within our circle representatives of every stratum of society! A professional soldier, frustrated because he longs to do his job but is given no room to manoeuvre. Two kinsmen of His late Majesty King Saul, rest his soul—even *his* adherents are uniting behind Absalom! Two members of the King's own privy council, myself and Seraiah. And Zoheleth here, risen from the ranks of the commoners. I tell you, the hardest task is already done: the winning of support for Absalom's cause. All that is required now is the tidying up of details. If we keep our heads and act as a body, we cannot lose.'

Again I was forced to swallow my scepticism; as far as I could see, the conspiracy as yet had no real existence outside Ahithophel's mind, and here he was talking as though there were nothing left to do but apply the finishing touches. But the others were still nodding; and I soon decided I had seriously underestimated the amount of work Ahithophel had already done. So far as he was concerned, the involvement of Absalom himself hadn't been the first step along the way, but one of the last.

'So what do we *do*?' demanded Shimei, fired with youthful enthusiasm. 'When do we start?'

'Two most pertinent questions, Shimei ben Gera, and I shall deal with the second one first because the answer is easy. As I believed I'd made clear, we have already begun. I have agents up and down the land who have been researching for some time into the views of the tribe leaders, the clan chiefs, and the elders of the cities. I think it is fair to say that at least three-quarters of them are in sympathy with our ideas. Amasa has been carrying out a similar programme of research among the officers of the army, with similar results. What we must do next is build on their work. Each of us will assume a specific responsibility and concentrate our efforts upon the kinds of people with whom we have the most contact, and whose views we can assess most accurately. Those who can be relied upon will be informed, when the time comes for us to—go public, as it were.'

'And how do we do that?' enquired Sheba. 'Do we take half the army and march on Jerusalem?'

Ahithophel shook his head indulgently. 'Certainly not; we don't wish to wind up soiling our shoes in a bloodbath. Most untidy. We merely proclaim Absalom king. If anyone wishes to challenge us . . . well, he may try it if he so desires, but then the blood which flows will be on his own head and not on ours. And I don't think such a man would get very far.'

Absalom's eyes glittered, with mingled excitement and horror. 'You mean to anoint me, and crown me, right in the middle of Jerusalem? How? Where? In the Tabernacle? In full sight of the palace? How do we oust David, and drive him out?'

'What is all this talk of "ousting" and "driving"? We *avoid* confrontation. We simply—relocate the capital, Absalom. We have you invested somewhere else, somewhere more conducive to the establishing of our powerbase. Perhaps we shall choose some place to the north, a city like Shechem or Samaria. That's where most of your support appears to be concentrated. The northern tribes are heartily sick of being treated like second-class citizens and are ready to espouse any cause which will lead to David's downfall. David can be left in possession of his precious palace at first. We merely sweep the political ground from under his feet. We leave him to find out by and by that the people are bringing you gifts, and swearing allegiance to you, and looking to you for leadership.'

'But what about Joab and Abishai?' Sheba asked. 'Won't they bring a great host against us wherever we base ourselves?'

'And precisely whose great host would you be referring to?' responded Ahithophel sweetly. 'Your esteemed Joab and Abishai will find themselves in much the same position as David. Their army will simply no longer be available for their use; Amasa will see to that. But we must not be tempted to rush things, my friends. As I said, there remain a few rough corners to be polished off before we are ready to risk coming out into the open. Seraiah has to finish canvassing the opinions of David's council; you will of course appreciate the need for particularly exquisite discretion in that area. Shimei and Sheba, you must rally any who remain of Saul's own family, along with your fellow clansmen. Absalom himself will assess which of his half-brothers can safely be included in our calculations. We don't want to risk them all pitching in together against him, from sheer jealousy. Divide and conquer, that must be our policy.'

Absalom said, 'I wouldn't cooperate with Adonijah if he were the last man on earth, the little yellow-belly. Over twenty years old and he still can't let go his mother's skirts.'

Ahithophel cringed a little. 'Very well, my lord. You must be permitted to indulge your personal tastes every so often, I grant, if you are to be king. But David has other sons.'

'None who count for anything.'

Shimei sneered, 'You mean, none whom you ever speak to.'

'That will be enough, thank you, Shimei,' warned Ahithophel. 'It may be that Prince Absalom is right on this occasion. Adonijah is too feckless to become a serious opponent, and would probably be more trouble than he was worth as a comrade. And the other royal sons are indeed very young. No; Absalom may have enough to do as it is, administering the public handouts.'

'Public handouts?' Absalom barely mouthed the words; he was gaping at Ahithophel now as though at some idol shedding miraculous tears.

'But of course,' replied Ahithophel, feigning surprise that the notion should have provoked such a strong reaction. For not even Seraiah or Amasa seemed prepared for this latest departure, and they were conferring in hoarse whispers behind Absalom's back. Ahithophel went on, 'The people are suffering hardship *now*, after all, and especially the population of Jerusalem itself, many of whom are only here in the city because they have lost their land and have nowhere else to go. We must not allow them to be in want any longer. Absalom will provide them with corn at his own expense; out of the goodness of his heart, you understand, not for any political motive . . .'

I couldn't bite my lip any longer. I ventured, 'But sir, that sounds incredibly dangerous to me. Is it really necessary? Won't it just arouse people's suspicions?'

'A commendably cautious attitude,' Ahithophel conceded. 'You may perhaps prove yourself a useful companion for Absalom to have around after all. But I don't think you quite appreciate my thinking on this point. *People's* suspicions have been aroused already; that's what we want. Absalom's public profile must be gradually but relentlessly raised, so that when folk hear he's been made king, it will seem to them the most natural thing in the world. We don't want to fuel *David's* suspicions, that's true, nor the suspicions of those remaining loyal to him—my venerable assistant Hushai for one.

'But the fact is, they are suspicious already. They've been on their guard ever since they learned of the spectacular failure of David and Absalom's attempt at reconciliation. It's Absalom's silence that's worrying them more than anything else; the way he seems to have accepted this blow to his pride without a murmur.

'You mustn't forget, my friends: I am even now the one who stands at the right hand of the King in council. I know his thoughts

178

and those of his courtiers almost as soon as they think them. With all due respect,'—and he nodded deferentially to Absalom—'With all due respect, many of those in positions of importance regard our noble Prince here as a harmless posturer, only to be accorded any kind of circumspection when his high opinion of himself has taken a battering. A little flamboyant beneficence on his part will serve to put their minds at rest, curious as that may seem. They will assume he is merely indulging his vanity as of old, and seeking to recover the prestige he must consider he's lost as a result of being rejected by his father. They will conclude that if they allow him a little fame and adulation he'll be content, as he generally used to be. And I shall ensure that David interprets his son's philanthropy in the appropriate light.'

Absalom asked in a small voice, 'And how am I to get the wherewithal to lavish this—this banquet upon the people?'

Ahithophel accorded him a slight smile. 'Ah! You need not fear for the proceeds of your charming little estate at Baal Hazor, let us put it that way. You have a wealthy grandfather, Absalom. And Seraiah just so happens to be a close friend of the keeper of his vaults . . . However, the source of your munificence must remain a closely guarded secret. Let the people think you've gained access to your father's treasury, and that you're releasing resources he's been hoarding. As for David himself—it will do him no harm to speculate.'

Throughout this explanation, Amasa and Seraiah had continued with their whispered altercation; now Ahithophel raised an enquiring eyebrow at each in turn. Amasa coughed, running a hand through his neatly cropped hair, and said, 'I don't know, my lord Ahithophel. I'm not sure about this. I think the boy—Zoheleth, did you say it was?—may just be right. The public handout business is too risky. Suppose a riot breaks out?'

'Then Joab and Abishai will crush it, with faultless efficiency, no doubt,' Ahithophel assured him. 'It needn't involve us at all. We shall simply ensure that the crushing is regarded as further evidence of the callousness of David's regime.'

'But suppose Absalom himself is arrested?'

'For distributing food? I hardly think that likely, unless he says something inordinately stupid while he's doing it. And even if he *is* locked up for a while, Amasa, every cause benefits by having its martyrs.' It occurred to me that Ahithophel might feel happier if

Absalom *did* get thrown into prison: that way he'd have less scope for acting irresponsibly.

Then Sheba piped up, 'Why don't we invite Joab and Abishai to join us? Joab must be just as dissatisfied with his lot as Amasa here.'

Amasa bristled visibly; Ahithophel put him at his ease by saying, 'Joab wouldn't desert David if you paid him his own weight in gold, though he's one of the few who dare to speak their minds to him.'

Absalom said, 'Don't fret yourself, Amasa. I wouldn't have Joab in my camp if he came on bended knee and fastened my sandals with his tongue.' He slapped Amasa affectionately on the leg; I saw the soldier stiffen again, then relax. Plainly he hadn't yet made up his mind what to think of Absalom the man, as opposed to the cause.

And indeed, who could have blamed him?

15

The public distribution of corn was scheduled to coincide with the festival of Tabernacles when Jerusalem was sure to be packed with pilgrims. All of these we could count upon to report what they had witnessed, once they returned home. In the meantime Absalom continued to apportion justice where he was able, and to listen sympathetically even when there was nothing he could do.

But he no longer did this at home. He sat on a makeshift tribunal by the city gates, greeting all who came to him, making a great show of embracing and kissing mangy beggars as though they truly mattered to him, and gathering scabby peasant children into his arms. I was astounded that he should be allowed to get away with acting so ostentatiously, but presumably Ahithophel was right: David would take comfort from his son's arrogant conduct, rather than viewing it as a cause for concern. After all, attention-seeking behaviour had always been characteristic of him. And the only serious crime Absalom had committed to date had followed upon a period of atypical withdrawal, not one of posturing, as Ahithophel liked to call it. In addition, since muggings and murders were now taking place in broad daylight and nothing was being done about that, I guess I should hardly have been surprised at what Absalom was being permitted to carry off.

My chief duty during this time was to stand behind Absalom's chair on the tribunal, shading him from the sun with a branch of palm, and exercising passive supervision over the slaves who fetched and carried for us and organized petitioners into something resembling an orderly queue.

I suppose I enjoyed those months, basking in Absalom's reflected glory. It was still important for me to feel that I *was* somebody; that I counted for something in a world which had always been against me.

Whilst we were out and about in Jerusalem being seen as much as possible, our fellow conspirators were working away in secret. Shimei and Sheba surprised and impressed me by their efforts among the Saulides; on several occasions Absalom received clandestine tokens of allegiance from members of the clan of Aphiah. But it also surprised me that neither they nor the people they canvassed objected to Absalom's lack of Saulide blood.

Ahithophel and Amasa continued their intrigues among gentry and soldiery respectively. Seraiah journeyed in person to Geshur to secure the financial backing which we were shortly to have need of. I don't know how he explained his absence at court, but so far as we knew, no one suspected anything. Throughout that period of preparation, no one betrayed us, no one gave us away through carelessness; not even Maacah had any clear idea of what was going on. Nor did Miriam. I know, because I was spending any spare time I had with her, when she would let me. She grew more beautiful to me by the day; Maacah was just growing old.

At last the torrid heat of summer began to abate. The feast of Tabernacles was fast approaching, and all across the city on rooftops and in courtyards the traditional shelters were appearing: little wooden huts festooned with greenery, fruit and flowers. Every year at this time each household would build one as a mark of gratitude for Adonai's provision—both during the exodus (when such shelters were all that the fugitives had to protect them from the extremes of the desert climate) and since the resettlement of Canaan.

Every year the pilgrims came in their thousands, to make their offerings and receive God's blessing. Every year the same prayers were chanted, the same songs of thanksgiving for God's bounty were sung, even by folk who had no bread and whose children had been sold into slavery. I don't know if this was a testimony to Israel's unshakeable faith, or to her blind stupidity. But the irony of the whole scenario seemed lost on everyone until Absalom set out to exploit it.

I rode by his side through the crowded streets, both of us revelling in the shouts of acclamation which broke out spontaneously for him from the multitude, just as they had done on the day of his triumphal return from Geshur. There the similarity ended, however. This time he drove a respectable four-wheeled carriage, the horses were harnessed with plain leather straps, and Gatis was nowhere to be seen. Absalom himself was dressed like a distinguished diplomat, there were no rings in his ears, and his face was unpainted. It scarcely needed to be; he was flushed with anticipation, and his eyes glittered bright as any jewel.

In front of us marched a formidable escort of Talmai's body-guards, but they too wore unassuming woollen tunics and simple sword belts rather than the showy bronze and studded leather they had favoured previously.

A second company of slaves followed on behind, carrying huge storage jars full of corn. These had been brought up from Egypt, where they had been procured in exchange for Syrian gold—indeed, you might have said that one kind of gold had been exchanged for another, as the little beggar-children scrabbled and squabbled over the bright yellow grains which spilled out along the way.

Our procession halted square outside the Tabernacle of Adonai, where pilgrims were passing in and out, to and fro, continually; we'd already drawn a sizeable audience by the time the jars had been lined up on the ground and I had got down from the carriage. Absalom remained in it, making use of the extra height it gave him, and began addressing his swelling congregation.

'Citizens of Israel!' he called out, spreading his arms wide as if in welcome. 'Men and women of the Chosen Race, sons and daughters of the Living God! Is it right that the heathen should witness you, of all people, going without the basic necessities of life? Is it right that pagans should mock you and the Lord whom you serve? Is it right that I, the son of your King, should allow you to suffer deprivation when it lies within my power to help you? Isn't this the Promised Land, the land flowing with milk and honey, the land to which your forefather Moses brought you, sacrificing his own life for you in the process? Brothers and sisters, you have endured long enough! How fitting it is, that at this special time of year we should be furnished with fresh evidence of our Creator's love towards us!'

Despite my own valiant efforts and those of Absalom's slaves, there was no hope of maintaining any kind of order. As soon as the distribution commenced, the crowd surged forward, kicking and shoving; it took the Syrian guards all their time to prevent Absalom himself from being suffocated in the crush. People were yelling and screaming and crying, thrusting forward baskets and water-jugs and looped-up garments—anything which could be filled and carried away. 'There is no need to panic!' Absalom was shouting. 'There is plenty for everyone!'

His face was redder than ever, though I'm not sure whether it was from excitement or raw terror, and the more crazed the mob became, the more he was caught up in its frenzy. 'Behold the manna from heaven!' he was bawling, punching the air with his fist. 'Your God will supply all your needs; he will prepare tables before you, anoint your heads with oil, make your cups overflow! For too long you have been sickly and starving, for too long you have watched your inheritance being wrested from your grasp, your ancestral lands being plundered and your wives and children dying like rats in the gutter! Did your God make you so that you could eke out your lives in grinding poverty? By no means! Adonai has the resources to provide for you, and the will to do so! No longer shall his bounty be withheld!'

I doubt there were many who even heard him, but I recall his every word, for I was standing there desperately trying to keep track of how much grain had been given away and how much we still had left to go, all the while thinking: for God's sake be careful, Absalom; don't let your heart run away with your head now, of all times. Yet he sounded so convincing, I was almost persuaded that he believed all this pious propaganda himself. Perhaps he really did care about the plight of the poor and needy; after all, once upon a time so many years before, as a half-slewed youth of sixteen, he'd rescued me. And even if his concern for me *had* been bound up with his hatred of Amnon, it had been real kindness I'd seen in his eyes.

I shall never know how we didn't provoke a riot that day. But by some miracle no one was trampled to death, no one was smothered, and no street-fighting broke out, because there really was enough corn for everyone who wasn't too proud to clamour for it. Somehow Absalom avoided disparaging David directly, so no one incited the mob to violence or looting.

And incredibly, there were no repercussions later either. For days afterwards I woke up each morning convinced that today would be the day when Absalom would be arrested and imprisoned, or worse. But nothing happened; I'd forgotten that Bathsheba was ill, and that Ahithophel was still in charge of David's intelligence service.

However, when I'd all but stopped worrying, a summons to appear at the palace was brought to our house. But it wasn't for Absalom; it was for me.

'What can I do?' I begged of Absalom, feeling a white chill sear through my body like the edge of an ice-bladed sword.

'You must go,' he said, and he was gripping my shoulders. 'Just be careful what you say. And keep your ears open—there's no knowing what you may overhear.'

'But why now? Why does he want to see me now, after all this time? Do you think he suspects something? What if he interrogates me? Tortures me?'

'He won't. You're Zohar, remember. One of the Shining Ones. Play your harp to him.'

I thought he was taunting me, and grew angry—angrier almost than if he'd chosen to remind me of my claim that my childhood had prepared me for anything. I slapped his face, but he didn't lose his temper; he was always more tolerant when he was sober. Not a drop of wine had passed his lips since the first meeting of our Circle, nor had a woman shared his bed. Such things made you weak, Ahithophel said. A man must be totally in control of himself if he aims to control others.

So, shivering with fright, I went to the palace in the company of the runner who'd brought the message. I was taken to the King's private chambers and left alone with him. David looked as bad as I'd ever seen him. He lay on a couch swathed in blankets, his eyes and cheeks cavernous as an unwrapped mummy's. I followed Absalom's advice to the letter, taking up the harp which stood in one corner and sitting cross-legged on the floor to tune it. It wasn't mine, nor was it the one he used to play; it was too small, as though crafted for a young child. Fleetingly I wondered if some other boy played for him these days, and if this poor creature too had been exposed to the burning touch of Adonai.

As soon as I began playing—though my fingers were stiff and awkward from fear and lack of practice—the King's lips started moving. But this time he wasn't praying. He sounded delirious. Anxious not to miss anything of import which he might chance to give away, I strained to listen. However it was all a jumble of disconnected words and phrases: *Bathsheba is dying—it's all been my fault—Absalom, my son, I love you, where are you?—Zohar, is that you?—Solomon will be king—Nathan, all that you prophesied is coming to pass—Adonai, I've had enough, why won't you take me?— Zohar* ... Then all at once his eyes found my face, and focussed, and he said quite clearly, 'Zohar, you came! Now come closer, and kiss me.'

He stretched out one wasted arm and took my hand; I forced myself not to pull away.

'She's dying, Zohar,' he said. 'Or so they tell me. I haven't seen her for so long ... But Nathan says Solomon must still be king after me. He says it's right. Even when she's gone I shall have no choice . . . Zohar, I'm so unhappy. How can I have turned Absalom out of my house? I don't care what he said to me, I don't even care what he believes any more. I'd give anything to hold him in my arms again.'

'Anything?' I said. 'Even the promise of the throne?'

'You know I would if it were mine to give. For a while I even allowed myself to believe it might be, with her out of the way. I thought I could win over Nathan, perhaps even Adonai. He has changed his mind before now. He spared a whole town once for Lot when he asked him. But is that all Absalom cares about these days, being king? Has he no love left for me at all?' I shrugged helplessly, but then he added, 'Hushai says I'm too trusting. He says Absalom's plotting against my life. But I can't believe that, can you? That's why I asked you here, Zohar. You're closer to Absalom than anyone else is these days; do you think he wants me dead?'

'No,' I answered, honestly. 'He doesn't want you dead.'

David smiled and squeezed my hand. 'You don't know how much solace that brings to me. I knew Hushai had to be wrong. No matter how close a man is to Adonai, he can be wrong on occasions—and I should know. Absalom does love me, I'm sure of it. One day he'll see there is more to life than ambition. Then things will work out between us.'

I walked home in a daze. I hadn't lied, but I had deceived. David still wanted to believe the best of his beloved Absalom, despite everything. But ought I to repeat to Absalom all that David had said? Wouldn't I simply confuse him? Or would I be selling him short if I didn't convey to him the love his father still bore him?

In the end I told him; it was getting so that I could no longer hide things from him even if I wanted to. But Ahithophel was there too. He said, 'Keep things in perspective, Absalom. Nothing has changed. Your father has always claimed to love you; he tells me so practically every day, and has been doing so since before we started making our plans. But he does no more to prove it than he's ever done. Still, at least we now know that not even Hushai's suspicions about us are likely to make him take action; because Hushai must have a pretty good idea that you're up to something, mark my word, or he wouldn't have dared to come out with that scandalous accusation against you.'

I asked in alarm, 'How can Hushai know? Who can have told him?'

Ahithophel tugged at his neatly trimmed beard, the hint of a frown linking his eyebrows. 'He's like Nathan, Zoheleth. Their kind have a way of divining these things.'

I groaned. 'Then sooner or later Hushai will get through to him! Surely he won't let David go on believing his position is secure, if he knows all about the conspiracy!'

'Oh, I'm not sure he knows anything so specific as yet. But I fear you're right, in that he certainly *will* learn of it. That's why we must be ready to push ahead with the next phase of our operation before he ruins everything.'

'The next phase?' Absalom repeated. 'You mean the proclamation? We haven't even decided yet where to do it . . .'

But I wasn't listening. I was studying Ahithophel's face, reading the emotions behind the mask. He was apprehensive, I decided, and he was bitter. He resented the presence of his erstwhile underling at court as much as he claimed to resent Bathsheba's. If Hushai knew Adonai, then his influence at court would grow and grow, until it put Ahithophel's own position as David's chief adviser under threat. This must surely be the real reason why Ahithophel had mooted this conspiracy. He was old enough to be my great-grandfather, he was one of the most highly respected men in Israel, yet he was subject to base human jealousy like anyone else.

'Anyhow,' Absalom was saying, 'I thought you and Adonai were on good terms, Ahithophel. You were keen enough to encourage *me* in my devotions.'

'I've told you before,' said the grandfather of Bathsheba, 'What is expedient and what one believes are not necessarily the same thing. In fact, they seldom are.'

As soon as the festal month was over, the members of the Circle met again. It was early morning; the kitchen slaves weren't even up, and Ahithophel was resolved on taking care of our business before they appeared. He came straight to the point, announcing that the time was now ripe to crown Absalom king.

'We can't afford to wait any longer,' he said. 'And there is absolutely no reason to. The elders of every city in the north are with us, and all know exactly what we mean to do. All of them have men they can trust to deal with any local opposition which may arise, and in addition can mobilize forces to march on Jerusalem, should that prove necessary. We can count on the support of almost every officer in David's army of the rank of captain or above—with the exception of Joab and Abishai, of course, and their immediate associates and subordinates. Only the situation to the south gives cause for concern. Support for David is still strong there; most of the authorities I didn't consider it worth the risk of approaching.'

'But the southerners are in a minority, as you've often been at pains to point out to us,' observed Amasa. 'We can deal with them once our base in the north is solidly established. So where is it to be?'

Ahithophel paused delicately before answering. Then he said simply, 'Hebron.'

Momentarily we were all too stunned to speak. Then Absalom seized the old counsellor's wrist. 'Hebron? Are you mad? That's not in the north! It's the deep south . . . more than that, it's the very place my father had himself invested as king!'

'All the more reason to choose it, don't you think? After all, David had much less entitlement to the throne than you have. Ishbosheth was Saul's rightful successor. In Hebron we have a most fitting precedent.'

'But my father had Adonai's anointing! Ishbosheth was the impostor.'

'The King's legitimate offspring, an impostor? He was the eldest surviving son of the lawful ruler of Israel, Absalom, just as you are.'

'But Hebron is the very cradle of my father's dominion! He made his capital there for seven years! He knows half the population by name.'

'He doesn't know the present elders,' said Ahithophel. 'It's a good ten years since he even went there. But *I* know them. And the more junior members of their council are some of our staunchest admirers.'

'With respect, sir, so they may be,' Amasa interjected, clearly struggling to remain calm. 'But it's my firm opinion that we would be exposing ourselves to extreme and totally unnecessary peril by heading way off down there! You're virtually talking about invading enemy territory. I thought we wanted to avoid a bloodbath?'

'Indeed we do,' replied Ahithophel. 'And that's precisely why I'm advocating Hebron. Suppose we choose Shechem, or Beth Shan, or somewhere further north still? We merely give the southerners an opportunity to unite behind David and rise up against us, and all of a sudden we have a barbaric civil war on our hands which may go on for years, with who knows what outcome! No, if we have

188

the courage of our convictions and go for Hebron now, our success is assured. For one thing we'll be right there on hand when our opponents try to muster against us, so we can nip any trouble in the bud. And for another, once it becomes public knowledge that even *Hebron* has welcomed us with open arms, the city councils we don't yet control will follow. Last but not least, it will be devastating for David himself, because he'll know he can't raise troops there, or flee there for refuge when Jerusalem becomes too hot for him.'

Amasa was shaking his head, his brow deeply furrowed, but he couldn't marshal any more cogent arguments.

Shimei suddenly punched one fist against the other. 'I can't see what all the fuss is about. Why does it matter *where* we crown Absalom? It's only a ceremony. And haven't you spoken to Zoheleth here since he last went to see the King? David is almost at his last gasp. How can a bedridden geriatric coordinate any credible opposition to us at all? Let's stop wasting time talking and get on with it!'

'Never underestimate your adversary,' said Ahithophel icily. 'That's the first rule of combat, is it not, Amasa? So. Does anyone else have any points to raise?'

Thus chastened, Shimei glared sullenly. Sheba gave a noncommittal shrug and looked at the floor. Seraiah merely sat deep in thought as he always did. I waited to see how Absalom would react now. He hunched up his knees and leaned his head on them, and said meekly, 'Whatever you think best, sir.'

'Good.' Ahithophel ran his eyes around the room, ensuring he had the full attention of each of us. 'Now listen. We can't just go strolling into Hebron as a handful of defenceless individuals and expect the elders of the city to risk planting a chaplet on our noble Prince's head in the middle of the market place surrounded by his father's partisans. Nor can we expect assistance from the regular army—not until the whole thing is out in the open and Amasa's allies can declare for us publicly. What we must do is take a large number of civilian supporters—which doesn't mean that some of them can't be armed, of course—to Hebron with us. If we have a whole host of men on the spot to—swell the chorus, as it were, when the proclamation is made, the locals will think twice about crossing us; at least to begin with. And once word gets out and the rest of our cities ratify Absalom's investiture, it will be too late for anyone to take action against us anyway. Well, Absalom? Does this seem good to you?'

Absalom was apparently too overwhelmed to think or speak for himself, so I asked, 'And how are we going to transport a vast horde of peasants to Hebron without anyone noticing?'

'Without anyone noticing, it would be impossible, I agree. But whether our entourage is noticed or not is largely irrelevant if we have a plausible pretext for its travelling south with us. And it wasn't chiefly peasants that I had in mind. Considerably more impact will be made if we are accompanied by Jerusalem's nobility.'

With this preposterous proposal Ahithophel at last succeeded in provoking a visible response from Seraiah; though the grave scholar merely raised one eyebrow. But his old colleague knew very well what strength of feeling this must denote.

'I'm quite aware that most of the metropolitan aristocracy know nothing of our plot, and would deplore it if they *did* know. But again, everything hangs on *why* they think they are being invited to Hebron.' Ahithophel couldn't resist a sly, sideways smile. 'Now, Absalom, I'm *sure* I remember you once telling me that if Adonai allowed you to return here from Geshur without having to stand trial for Amnon's murder, you would offer a magnificent sacrifice to him, and worship him in Hebron, in the presence of all the people—'

'What?' said Absalom.

'Come now, my dreamy Prince, surely you remember? There wasn't a day went by while you were in exile that you didn't pray for an embassy to turn up and recall you . . . isn't that what you told me? Or did I hear it from Zoheleth?'

Absalom at last raised his head, and he no longer looked so dazed. 'I think I did once vow that if Adonai brought me home, I would worship him. Full stop.'

'Well, the time has come for you to—fulfil your religious obligation, I feel. And naturally, you *would* have been more specific about *where* this act of worship was to take place, if you hadn't been so distracted by your homesickness at the time . . .'

Absalom was starting to snigger. 'I seem to remember once making the same vow to Baal Geshur,' he rejoined. 'Which god do you suppose answered me?'

But Ahithophel was in no mood for levity. It was only the ingenuity of his own plan which had been causing him to smile. Now he looked daggers at Absalom, who averted his gaze and cleared his throat.

'I'm sorry. But God knows how long it is since I got back home. Why should I have waited all this time before discharging my duty?'

'Everyone knows that you have a mind like a butterfly, Absalom.'

Ahithophel's tone was icier than ever. 'You have simply just remembered, and that's all there is to it. So, we send Zoheleth to His Majesty to ask his permission for you to hold the ceremony. I think the lad is more likely than anyone else to be admitted to David's presence without a lot of tiresome bureaucracy; I could make the request myself, but I think it would be most unwise to allow your father and Hushai to start speculating about how much I have been seeing of you.

'Then we invite two hundred or so unsuspecting (and unintelligent) worthies from the capital to go with us—we shall ensure they are significantly outnumbered by their secretly armed counterparts from other parts of the country who *are* in the know—and we set out for Hebron as soon as possible.

'Meanwhile we send word to the elders of our cities and the leaders of the northern tribes to await our signal and then to publicize immediately their allegiance to the new king. We shall have chains of beacons lit upon hills up and down Israel, *and* chains of trumpeters, so the signal will be clearly and quickly transmitted from one town to the next. At the same time Amasa—who must remain with the garrison in Jerusalem throughout—will announce the defection of the major part of the army. That ought to cause enough consternation at the palace for us to be able to carry the day.'

'And if riots *do* break out?' asked Amasa brusquely.

'Riots where, exactly? In Jerusalem? I can't see that being beyond your ability to handle.'

'No, not in Jerusalem. In "our" cities, as you call them. What if the elders can't carry their own citizens with them?'

'As I told you before, Amasa, I simply don't see rioting being a problem. Though since you have brought the subject up again, perhaps we could incite a few riots ourselves, then have them quashed at once as an exhibition of our efficiency ... ? Bear in mind that once you've come clean about where the sympathies of most of the troops lie, you'll be able to call on the provincial units which you'll have at your disposal to assist in the—how shall I put it?— "restoration of law and order". As a matter of fact we could then proceed to demonstrate our clemency also, by publicly pardoning the ringleaders—hardly a sacrifice, if they are our men anyway.'

Amasa raked his short hair with his fingers and nodded cautious approval; as a soldier his respect for Ahithophel's strategic thinking was growing.

In a thin, sick voice I enquired, 'When do you want me to go to see the King?'

Ahithophel pondered the question briefly. Then he answered, 'First thing tomorrow, if he will receive you then. If not, then the morning after. I shall see Jehoshaphat about it today. The sacrifice will be held the third day from whenever I manage to get you an audience. Today we make final arrangements: we draw up invitations for the great spectacle and we despatch bulletins to all our supporters so that they may ready themselves for what lies ahead. We also work out exactly what you will say to David when you see him, Zoheleth, and how you are to respond if he starts to ask difficult questions. Then the day after tomorrow, if you've seen him by then, we leave.'

The moment the meeting finished, I began packing my things for the journey. There was so much to do, and Absalom was in no fit state to do any of it. He drifted around the house as though drunk, at one moment euphoric, the next in despair.

'I'm going to be king after all!' he was saying to me with one breath. 'A week from now I shall have everything I ever dreamed of!' Then with the breath following he would be sighing, or pounding on the wall with his fist, crying, 'What's going to become of my father, Zohel? What if they kill him? He never wanted Ishbosheth to die, but the wretch was beheaded just the same.'

So it was left to me to sort out his belongings, to organize the slaves according to which were to come with us and which were to stay to guard our property, and to move Maacah and Miriam out of the house again, for safety—at long last we had to explain to them exactly what was going on. There was no point in sending them to Shimei's kinsman this time, nor indeed anywhere else in Jerusalem. So they departed, with an escort, for Baal Hazor. Absalom knew everyone who mattered there—it was likely to be the safest place in Israel for a while.

That evening Shimei and Sheba invited themselves to dine with Absalom and myself, and they arrived laden with enough wine for a dozen Nephilim as their contribution to the meal.

'Oh no, not for me,' chuckled Absalom, covering his goblet with one hand when Sheba tried to fill it. 'I've got far too much on my mind.'

'All the better reason for diluting it a little,' Sheba exhorted him. 'Come on, man. Relax for once. You're getting so serious in your old age! Not at all like the Absalom we used to know and love. We don't leave for Hebron until the day after tomorrow at the earliest. Who cares if you don't get out of bed again until then?'

'Sheba, I haven't had a drink for months. It will go straight to my head.'

'Lucky you. We have to drink six jugfuls each before we feel any benefit these days, eh, Shimei?' Sheba took hold of Absalom's wrist, moved his hand aside and filled the goblet. 'Just one, for old times' sake? Before long you won't be lowering your royal self to share a table with the likes of us.'

'Oh, very well. If you insist. Just one.' Absalom took a conciliatory sip, then grinned broadly. 'Ah, that's good. From your father's own vineyards, I'll warrant, Shimei? I'd forgotten how fruity it tasted.'

'A toast to His Majesty King Absalom!' boomed the flattered Shimei with mock dignity, rising to his feet. 'Don't just sit there, Absalom. It's not unlucky to toast yourself. Don't you want to be successful? And why are you looking so dubious, young Zoheleth? You never used to be averse to indulging in a little liquid refreshment.'

'I—don't feel too well,' I apologized lamely; the sight of Absalom draining his cup in one gulp and smirking inanely when Sheba refilled it was making me queasy. But how could I deny him the right to enjoy himself one last time before the coming ordeal? Ahithophel would have stopped him, I know, but Ahithophel was elsewhere, and in any case I disapproved of the way he browbeat Absalom. So I picked at my food and played with my cup, while my three companions gorged themselves and guzzled wine as though it were water, told bawdy jokes and threw nuts and figs at one another, yowling with laughter. Absalom stripped off his turban and most of his clothes, and was drenched in olive oil from a mock anointing when one of our Akhaian eunuchs tugged at my sleeve and told me we had a visitor from the palace.

It was a slave of Ahithophel's, bearing a sealed tablet addressed to Absalom. I asked what it was about, but the courier either couldn't or wouldn't speak, only gawped at me with terrified fish-eyes, then fled. When eventually I succeeded in getting any sense out of Absalom, he just wrapped his greasy arms around my neck and slurred, 'Zohel, my precious, what would I do without you? Open it yourself, and tell me all about it in the morning.'

'Morning? What's that? I'm not expecting to see any morning, are you, Shimei?' slobbered Sheba. Grinding my teeth, I thrust Absalom away, broke the seal and read the letter.

Ahithophel of Giloh, senior adviser to His Majesty King David— may he reign for ever and ever!—to my lord the Prince Absalom ben David, greetings.

An unforeseen difficulty has arisen. My only brother, in Giloh, has been involved in a serious hunting accident and is at the point of death. He has been asking to see me; I must go to him, or tongues will wag. Tonight I shall remain here at the palace and prepare myself to travel at dawn. I intend to return on the third day whatever happens. Hold everything until then. However, I have made the necessary arrangements for Zoheleth, for tomorrow; it will be best for him to keep the appointment, for we may not easily be able to reschedule it. He need not be specific about dates and times. S. and A. have been informed of the development. No need to contact anyone else; they will wait until they receive communication from us before acting in any case. The peace of Adonai to you.

I tried everything to make Absalom understand. I began reading Ahithophel's words aloud to him, but he simply chanted the grandiloquent phrases after me, imitating the counsellor's dispassionate but deliberately ambiguous use of language, to the uproarious delight of Shimei and Sheba. I held the tablet under his nose so he could read it for himself and check the seal was genuine, but he crossed his eyes on purpose and then pretended to pass out on the floor, exploding into laughter when Sheba grew concerned and patted his face to bring him round. 'Absalom, you crazy fool!' I shouted. 'This could ruin everything! We're going to be without Ahithophel for two whole days! Suppose I say the wrong thing to David, or Hushai works out that the sacrifice is just a front? We shan't be able to go to Hebron now until— God knows when!'

'Hallelujah!' crooned Absalom. 'More wine, Sheba! I shall have all the time in the world now to sleep off my hangover.'

Speechless with fury, I flung the tablet at the wall and stormed out into the courtyard. A delicious rush of cool air took the sting out of my cheeks and made me feel a little calmer, so I went up onto the roof to get myself together. I lay on my back with my arms behind my head, gazing up at the star-strewn sky, listening to my heart hammering, and willing it to quieten down. There's no need to get hysterical, I was telling myself, this isn't the end of the world. Why should two days matter, after all these months of scheming and dreaming?

But it didn't work. The more I thought about it, the more desperate I felt. The conspiracy was doomed; it had been doomed before it began. Absalom was an irresponsible rake with a mess of pottage where his brains should be; he hadn't acquired a shekel's weight of maturity in all the time I'd known him. Nor could Ahithophel be as clever as he liked to think he was, or he wouldn't have cast his lot in with Absalom in the first place. And what was the shifty old slyboots up to now? Why couldn't he have sent word to his kinsfolk that he was laid up too, and unable to make the journey? Family ties as a rule meant no more to him than wheat-chaff. Suppose this was a trick? Suppose Ahithophel *was* working with Bathsheba after all, and this whole plot had been the most elaborate set-up Israel had ever seen? Or perhaps the aged states-man had simply had enough and decided to abandon the cause, and we would never set eyes on him again? Oh, God . . . *Adonai, why didn't you warn me? Why did you let me get mixed up in all this? I knew you once; before I learnt to speak to anyone else, you used to listen to me . . .*

I was still lying there half trying to pray when I heard doors banging below, and somewhere a hailstorm of shattering pottery. Curled up with my hands plastered to my ears I could still hear Shimei yelling and cursing, accusing Absalom of treating his life-long friends like dirt already, giving himself airs and graces and looking down his nose at men who had pledged their lives for his cause.

'You're not fit to sit on Saul's throne! You don't even have his backbone, let alone his blood! We should be looking for a *worthy* successor for our ancestor. It would serve you right if we went straight out of here to the palace!' he screamed, and now I could hear his lurching footsteps down in the courtyard. 'It would serve you right if we went to the King himself and told him—'

Then there was a muffled cry and a scuffling, and Sheba was saying, 'Keep your voice down, you drunken saphead! What does it matter if he won't come with us? Leave him be, he's too far gone to get his money's worth out of a woman tonight anyway. We'll find some girls without him.'

Their footsteps receded, and I heard the gate bang shut behind them. Absalom clearly hadn't been with them; I imagined him flaked out somewhere snoring, and had no desire to see him that way in the flesh.

So I stayed where I was, and I must have fallen asleep myself, because it was much later when a eunuch whispered in my ear, 'Master Zoheleth, get up! Someone else is here. I think it is the lady Bathsheba.'

16

'Bathsheba?' I sat up, scraping crust from the corners of my eyes. 'Where? At the gate?'

'No, master. With Lord Absalom.'

'What!' I scrambled to my feet, ran to the parapet and looked down into the yard. But it was dark and deserted, plunged in shadow.

'Inside, master. In his room. Another slave let her in; she bribed him with silver. She was dressed as a man, though; he didn't know who she was. She told him she was a messenger come from Ahithophel.'

'Ye gods.' I was all but paralyzed with dread. 'And how did *you* know?'

The lad dropped his gaze; the pale lashes curled over his downless cheeks like a girl's. 'I watched, master. Please forgive me.'

'You watched? Where from?'

He quailed still more. 'The roof, master. There is a place . . . you can see through a little window high above my lord's bed . . .'

I ordered, 'Take me there.'

He found his way across the unlit rooftops as easily as he might have walked along a road at midday. Ahithophel had been right at least to convene our Circle in that airless old storeroom, but quite apart from official meetings, I fell to wondering for the first time what incriminating words we must have let slip elsewhere. Our Syrians and Akhaians had had plenty of time now to learn Hebrew.

Presently I found myself huddled in hiding, two men's height above the courtyard, squashed for security between the cowering eunuch and a length of crumbling parapet, and squinting down into Absalom's bedroom.

'My dear Absalom,' Bathsheba was cajoling, 'There really is no need for you to be so cagey with me. We used to tell each other everything! You see, I know what's on your mind already, so it would do you no harm to talk to me about it. I could share the burden with you. You'd feel so much better.'

Absalom said, 'I felt fine until you came here.' His face was still flushed but in the soft yellow lamplight I decided that his eyes looked clear; Bathsheba's sudden appearance on the scene must have sobered him up pretty quickly.

'Nonsense, my poor harassed hero.' Her voice was smooth and sickly-sweet as honey. 'I know very well that you were already upset before I put one foot across your threshold. You'd been quarrelling with Shimei.'

'That was nothing,' Absalom growled. 'He was drunk. He wanted me to go out on the town with him and Sheba because . . . How did *you* know we'd quarrelled?'

Bathsheba shed her heavy masculine coat and shook out her hair, which had been pinned up beneath her turban. She answered nonchalantly, 'I met him on my way here, and Sheba too.'

'My God. What did they say to you?'

'Absalom, calm down, I implore you! You're tense as a bowstring and trembling all over. You'll make yourself ill.' She extended one slender hand to touch his; they were both sitting on his bed, but he was hunched against the head of it as far from her as he could get, clutching a blanket around his shoulders. She said, 'There was nothing they could have told me which I didn't know already. I have relatives in high places, don't forget.'

'Ahithophel hates you! He wouldn't trust you to tie up his sandals!'

'Yes, you have become rather friendly with my illustrious grandfather of late, haven't you?'

'I—'

'You don't want to take every glazed syllable that drops from his lips as a pearl of God's truth, you know. He told you that we didn't get on, did he? Well, I suppose he had his reasons. He must have come to the conclusion that you wouldn't agree to work with him if you learnt I was in league with him too.'

'I don't know what you're talking about! And I thought *you* were supposed to be ill? They were building your tomb!'

'Oh I *was* ill, my dear, I was. He told you the truth about that at least. But it is amazing how rapidly one can recover when one has to. And I knew that if I wanted to help you, I should have to do it very rapidly indeed.'

'You can't help me. There's nothing in the world you could do which would be of the slightest use to me.'

'No?' She sidled closer, and this time succeeded in placing her hand over his. 'The night is young, Absalom. There is plenty of time for talk later. Let us share a cup of wine and—renew our old acquaintance.'

'Bathsheba... I don't know what you want with me, but I'm tired, and I wish you'd go. I've drunk too much as it is. I'm all—'

'All confused? Then how do you think I feel? I take the risk of coming here to assist you, to offer you friendship and advice... gold, jewels even, everything I have, so that you can realize your ambitions; and all I receive in return is a callous rejection, and a lecture from you saying you don't know what I want with you! Isn't it obvious? Or are you blind? I love you, God damn you, you're the most beautiful creature I ever saw.'

I couldn't believe what I was hearing. I certainly didn't believe *her*; and nor did Absalom, at least at first. But he *was* beautiful, and he knew it, and as she gazed without faltering straight into his eyes, I watched his will crumple. Heaven preserve us, I thought, he isn't sober at all. He's out of his senses! Being careful not to make a move until she was sure he was ready, Bathsheba continued drowning him in an ocean of lascivious glances; then she wound her arms around him and cradled his head against her breast.

'There, isn't that better? I can feel the tension leaving you already.' She stroked the wild blue-black hair from his face, prized his fingers from the blanket, and kissed him softly on the bridge of the nose. He closed his eyes, then opened them again and looked back into hers. The blanket dropped away.

'Bathsheba... what did you mean? What you were saying before—'

'About how much I love you? Do you want to hear it again?'

'No. Not that. About helping me. I don't understand. Solomon—'

'You think I want to see Solomon on the throne? How credulous you are sometimes, Absalom. Perhaps that's why I can't resist you. You're so innocent.' She kissed him once more, smoothing away the perplexity from his brow. 'Don't frown like that. It mars your beauty. I fear you've been listening to your father's black lies as well as to Ahithophel's white ones.

'*I* haven't been the one blowing Solomon's trumpet all this time. He's been your father's choice of heir all along; or ever since Nathan the holy man got to him. But David pins the blame on me because that's what he wants you to think. Don't you see? He just wants to get round you, so you'll love him despite how despicably he's used you. But you know him far too well to fall for such a crude ploy, I'm sure. Solomon is just a little child. I wouldn't want him weighed down with royal responsibilities at his tender age!

'*You're* the man Israel needs now, Absalom. David is no longer fit to govern. Solomon won't be ready for years. And you *know* all this is true, or you wouldn't have been spending so much time with my grandfather ... of *course* I'm aware of what the pair of you have been up to. All you need to tell me is what I can do to—be of assistance.'

Even if I'd jumped off the roof and run straight round to his bedroom door, I would have been too late to gag him. And if I'd shouted down from where I was and thus owned up to eavesdropping, I reckon it quite likely he would have had me torn limb from limb before he was sober enough to stop and think what he was doing. So all I could do was crouch there and listen as Absalom disgorged everything, convinced by Bathsheba's sympathetic murmurs and caresses and complete suppression of any sense of shock, that she knew most of it already. She made no comment, nor sought to rush him when he digressed into arrogance or self-pity, until he said, 'Before Sabbath next, we travel to Hebron.'

'We?'

'Your grandfather and I, with all the other members of the Circle except for Amasa ...'

'Ah, your young friend Zoheleth of course, and Shimei and Sheba—'

'And Seraiah. Zoheleth has an appointment with my father tomorrow to ask his permission for us to hold a public sacrifice there. It's most important that he should believe this to be the true purpose of our journey. Perhaps you could be there, and use your influence ...'

' ... Whereas in fact, you mean to have yourself crowned king?'

Momentarily he pulled away from her, frowning again; just for that instant the alcoholic fog in his head must have cleared enough for him to grasp what he'd done. Then she folded him once more in her bosom, and I was too sickened to remain hidden any longer. I was also too panic-stricken. Jabbing my companion in the ribs to have him guide me downstairs, I realized too late that I should have dismissed him as soon as he'd shown me the hiding-place. I'd been too distracted to think. So once we'd crept silently down the steps into the courtyard I dragged him into a doorway and got my hands around his throat.

I said, 'One word of this to a soul, and you won't need to mourn your lost manhood any more. Do you understand me?'

He nodded, his moonlit eyes wide and bright with horror. I let him go, and he stumbled away into the shadows. I didn't know if it was my sudden use of violence which had appalled him, or the fact that he'd heard my name mentioned in connection with conspiracy. After all, I'd been overseer of the eunuchs ever since they'd arrived, and because of my own past I'd always tried to treat them fairly. They'd grown to trust me.

For a dozen racing heartbeats I stayed where I was, hanging onto the doorframe and wrestling with my conscience. Then I made straight for Absalom's room, urgently calling his name as though some emergency had arisen, thereby giving myself an excuse to burst in on the lovers without knocking. I stood open-mouthed at the foot of the bed, feigning stupefaction. Absalom snatched up the bedclothes to cover himself, but neither of them could find words to tell me to leave.

I gasped, 'Absalom, are you mad? What in God's name are you doing?'

Bathsheba recovered herself before he did. She said with passion-less venom, 'Get out of here, Zoheleth. You have been half your life in service to the son of a king and you have learnt no respect.'

'Your pardon, my lady, but I am no man's servant. I attend to the needs of Prince Absalom of my own free will! And precisely because I *do* respect him. Or I did until now.'

I looked him directly in the eyes; he wilted visibly in the heat of my contempt. Bathsheba bristled with exasperation and said, 'Absalom, tell this ignorant slave to leave, since it seems he is too ill-trained to obey anyone else, even his Queen.' She was seeing a side of me which she can't have imagined existed.

Absalom whispered, 'Zohel, please. We've done nothing to be ashamed of.'

'You think not? I beg to disagree.'

'Absalom, this is intolerable!' Bathsheba's every pore was bleed-ing poison now. 'Have this creature removed at once. Have him stoned! I cannot credit such insolence.'

I was still holding Absalom helpless with my eyes; he must have been able to read the despair in them without my needing to put on any more of an act. I half expected him to strike me, for he still wasn't master of his mind, and I saw the truth was dawning for him that in my vehement accusations I wasn't referring primarily to his sexual promiscuity. But instead of venting itself in anger, the realization was for the moment swamping him in guilt and misery. He hung his head, seizing clumps of his hair with white-knuckled fingers.

'Bathsheba is going to help us, Zohel. And she knew everything before I told her, anyway.'

'She didn't, Absalom. She tricked you. Just like she tricked everyone into believing she was dying, so she could see whether David and Nathan would go back on their promise to Solomon if they thought they could get away with it. Of course she wants her mewling brat upon the throne; it wouldn't bother her if he had to be installed on it this very day! *She* would rule through him!'

'Then why did she come here? How did she know I was lonely and anxious? She loves me.' Impulsively he drew her towards him with a certain forlorn defiance; she closed her eyes as if in blissful confirmation of his assertion. But it was painfully clear to me that she was biding her time now to see how this bizarre altercation would turn out.

'Absalom, how can you be so pathetic?' I demanded. 'She doesn't love you; she never has. And you *weren't* lonely and anxious—you were dead drunk! Anything she *did* know, her spies will have told her.'

'Why should she need spies when she has Ahithophel?'

'Do you really believe that? Do you honestly think Ahithophel would breathe a word about anything, to her? Why didn't she come here *with* him if that's the case? Why did she wait until she knew he wouldn't be around? Oh, don't try to tell me she couldn't have known. This dying brother in Giloh is her kinsman too; the news will have been carried to her as surely as it was to her grandfather. She came here to make you confess to everything with your own lips; now she'll take it straight back to David!'

Absalom pulled Bathsheba closer; she rocked him in her arms like a mother protecting a naughty child from his irate father. 'Don't let this spiteful slave upset you,' she soothed him. 'He's only jealous. I'm not in any hurry to go back to the palace.' She nibbled his ear gently with her perfect white teeth. 'I shall even stay here as your hostage, my darling. I won't make the slightest attempt to leave unless you want me to.'

'You see,' said Absalom. 'She loves me. She'll even come to Hebron with me if I ask her to.'

Bathsheba seemed fleetingly disconcerted. Then she cooed at him, 'My angel, people might talk! It might jeopardize your cause if too many folk knew that the favourite wife of the tyrant was your mistress. Besides, I have the needs of a new baby to consider. I like to feed him myself, you know.' But when Absalom stiffened she blew softly on his cheek and said, 'Still, I would come if you couldn't bear to be apart from me.'

I felt more desperate now than I had when I'd come in; I couldn't believe that though I'd confronted him he wouldn't admit what a fool he'd been. Perhaps he'd been right that time when he'd said that Bathsheba enjoyed the means of gaining power over men, as much as the end; but the end was what really mattered to her. If simple seduction could get her what she wanted, why waste her intelligence on anything more complex?

I said, 'For God's sake wake up, Absalom! Perhaps she *will* agree to come to Hebron—but only if she can find a way of incorporating the journey into her own plans! Perhaps she *will* provide gold to finance your coup—but only so she can get you even more inextricably entangled in her web! She wants you *dead*, Absalom, can't you see that? What better way to go about it than to have you kill *yourself*? She'll goad you on until there's no going back, then undermine everything! Everything you've built will come crashing down, and you'll fall with it.'

'How?' Absalom retorted, and now he was struggling with the arousal Bathsheba's caressing was kindling within him, as well as with the wine. 'How do you think she's going to do that? Once I've been crowned in Hebron it will be too late for *anyone* to bring me down.'

'How should I know?' I wrung my hands in frustration. 'I don't know how her mind works! But that's what she wants, you mark my words.' For a second my eyes met hers, and that one look convinced me I was right.

'Anyhow,' I blurted, all at once remembering I had another arrow in my quiver of arguments, 'Anyhow, she isn't the only one whose discretion we need to worry about. Someone else overheard you spewing out secrets.'

'What? Who?'

I let my eyes roll upwards to the little skylight above the bed.

'One of our eunuchs.'

Absalom made a strangulated sound in his throat and gaped at me, cornered. But not so Bathsheba. She loosed her hold on the stricken Prince who slumped wretchedly into the pillows, while she leaned back with sleek satisfaction against the ornate Egyptian headrest. 'So it is you who are the fool after all, little serpent. Hardly as cunning as your name, are you?' I didn't say anything, only felt something congealing inside me. She went on, 'I shall repeat nothing of what Prince Absalom shared with me in confidence, outside of these walls. But as for your pretty little friend from Akhaia, now... that is quite another matter. I don't suppose you have received the same assurance from him.'

Of course there was no reply I could give. For all I knew, he'd come to me simply because he felt more loyalty towards David than the majority of native Israelites seemed to do. It wouldn't have been the first time in history that such an ironic thing had happened. I cursed myself in silence, and Absalom said, 'Have him killed, Zoheleth.'

I mumbled, 'It's too late. He could have told all the rest of them.'

'Kill them all.'

'Kill them *all*? How can I? The stench of the bodies would stifle all Jerusalem! We might as well run out in the streets and tell the whole world what we're plotting.'

'What a pity you didn't think of all that earlier,' remarked Bathsheba.

I'd had enough. A blind red rage rose up inside my head, and I screamed, 'How dare you blame me, either of you! I'm not the one who gave everything away! I'm not the one who can't control his tongue... or any other part of his anatomy, Absalom ben David!'

A moment later I was fighting for my life. Absalom, stark naked, had me pinned to the ground with his knees on my shoulders and one hand around my neck; with the other he struck my face until my nose bled and I could barely see through one eye. I was coughing and choking, heaving for breath, but instead of air I got a mouthful of his hair, and I could only taste blood. All I could do to retaliate was writhe and twist and bring my knees up into his back; I finally succeeded in putting him off balance, and as he fell forward on top of me I did something I hadn't done to anyone in a long time. I sank my teeth into his flesh.

He cried out and let me go, clutching at his shoulder. I'd bitten him right over the collarbone, so hard I'd drawn blood. He opened his mouth again to curse me, then saw the mess he'd made of my own looks and flung himself on the ground, beating it with his fist.

I'd been on the point of running out; now I was overwhelmed by a wave of abject but fierce indignation as I took in what life had done to him, how it had changed him. I stammered, 'Oh, Absalom, I'm sorry,' and hauled him up onto his knees. Temporarily Bathsheba was forgotten, as we dabbed at each other's wounds and our fury subsided into thin contrite laughter. Then that subsided too, and Absalom pleaded, 'Zohel, what shall we do?'

I sank onto my haunches, trying hopelessly to think. I was still out of breath from fighting him off, and my mind was racing to match. It was some time before I could compose myself enough to order my thoughts, and still longer before I could voice them. Then I answered, 'I—I think we should station a guard at the gate; one we're pretty sure we can trust, but we'd best threaten him as well, to be on the safe side. He can make sure none of the other slaves get out, and no one else gets in. That way we'll give ourselves longer to decide on our next step.'

'Always assuming you aren't closing the door of the stable when the horse has already bolted,' rejoined Bathsheba drily. She lay at full stretch on the bed, swathed in her voluminous coat and watching us disdainfully down the length of her nose.

'That's a chance we'll have to take,' said Absalom, and pulled on his undertunic. Then he stepped outside and began calling for the chief of his bodyguards; I stared at the floor, willing him to return quickly as I couldn't bear being left alone with Bathsheba. Almost at once he reappeared, and I exhaled my relief. He dropped onto the bed and moaned, 'Now what?'

I knelt a while longer in thought, then said, 'I reckon we should go to Hebron as soon as possible. The longer we leave it, the more likely it is that our plans will leak out. One of the slaves will manage to give us the slip; or Sheba won't be able to stop Shimei squealing, just to get back at you. Or you'll blink your eyes for a second and this witch will be gone.'

Bathsheba didn't condescend to rise to my bait; Absalom muttered, 'Shimei won't squeal. He'll be back here to apologize once his headache has worn off, if I know him.' Then something fell into place in his mind; his lower lip quivered slightly and he whispered, 'You mean, we shouldn't wait for Ahithophel? You seriously think we should move ahead without him?'

'Why not? He's already organized my audience with your father. Seraiah as court secretary is better placed than anyone to issue the invitations to the sacrifice. Amasa's officers have their orders and are only waiting to hear that you've been crowned. We can't *afford* to wait for Ahithophel. Suppose he can't get away by the third day?' I didn't say, 'Suppose he never comes at all?' but I did think it. I couldn't help fearing he might have got cold feet.

Absalom said, 'He'll still be at the palace; he doesn't leave until dawn. We could send someone to see him and persuade him not to go to Giloh after all.'

'Send whom? I thought we were keeping everyone here.'

'You or I will have to go; and I can't be the one. I'd never get past the gates. It will have to be you.'

'There is a third possibility,' drawled Bathsheba, smiling.

Absalom's eyes lit up, but I rasped, 'No way. *She's* staying *here*, until we leave for Hebron, new baby or no. Anyhow, why draw attention to ourselves by contacting Ahithophel at all? He'll hear that we've left Jerusalem soon enough. He can join us directly from Giloh later on. I'll see David in the morning, Seraiah can do the rounds of the aristocracy in the afternoon, and we can be on the road the day after.'

Absalom laughed bitterly. 'You think the most important men in Jerusalem can be persuaded by anyone but Ahithophel to drop everything and hike off into the desert at a day's notice? What if they won't come?'

'I'm sure they *will* come. The sacrifice will be taking place under His Majesty's auspices. No self-respecting nobleman with a concern for his own status in society is going to ignore a royal request. It would be an insult to the King. Besides, we can tell them that Adonai has instructed you to fulfil your vow immediately, as a sign of your obedience to him.'

I didn't specify who I meant by the title 'king'. Absalom managed a smile; it seemed that my studied ambiguity wasn't lost on him. Unless of course he was amused to hear someone who had once claimed to know and love Adonai weaving a web of lies about him apparently without a second thought. But then Absalom's frown returned and he said, 'I still think we should gain Ahithophel's approval. He ought to be informed of our intentions.'

'Very well,' I agreed finally, and with some reluctance. 'I'll do my best to see him. I'll tell him that we travel the day after tomorrow and that he must meet us at our destination.'

'Only if he won't change his mind about his brother and come with us.'

I grimaced. 'That goes without saying.'

I'm not sure what I *would* have said to Ahithophel if the opportunity had been granted to me, except that I couldn't have resisted asking him if he could tell me where his granddaughter was at that precise moment in time. But the watchmen at the palace gates were no keener to admit me than they would have been to do the same for Absalom. It was the middle of the night, I was reminded; His Majesty's august privy counsellor would long since have retired to bed and would not take kindly to being disturbed by a worthless slave who had clearly been roundly beaten by somebody already. My protestations that I was a free man fell upon deaf ears, and my claim that I was known personally to the King as well as to his adviser was simply disbelieved.

Rankled, I returned home. Something heavy had been dragged up behind Absalom's door and I couldn't get in there either; plainly I wasn't expected back so soon, and social calls weren't exactly being encouraged. 'Absalom? Absalom!' I persisted frantically. 'Absalom, you confounded Canaanite, let me in!' For my failure to gain access to the palace had somehow brought about another change of heart within me: all at once I was no longer convinced it was such a good idea to proceed without Ahithophel after all. But there was no response whatever to my plaintive cries, so that I began to fear Bathsheba might have taken the obvious short cut already, and murdered Absalom personally.

Eventually I heard the heavy object being moved and Absalom appeared, rumpled and bleary. I told him what had happened and he swore under his breath, but then said, 'Just go to bed, Zohel. I hate to think how late it must be. I'm shattered. We'll talk in the morning.'

I couldn't get enough peace even to doze. My brain went on grinding round like some great stone quern whilst my heart beat loud as a hammer on a blacksmith's anvil. Soon I decided it would be better now if I tried to stay awake, for dawn was on its way and I realized I still had a chance of intercepting Ahithophel before he left, if I was up early enough. Predictably, that was the point at which I fell asleep—but it was a troubled, dream-infested sleep which left me more exhausted than I'd been before it came to me. When I surfaced, it was light; and there was no denying that my mattress was damp.

Sick with self-loathing, I tore the blankets from it and hurled them into the far corner of the room. I found some clean clothes and set off for the palace without breakfast. The sentries' watch had changed, but the roughnecks who constituted the morning shift were no more disposed to let me pass than their colleagues of the previous night. There was no point in my going to Ahithophel's quarters in any case, I was told; he had walked out through this self-same gate just before daybreak.

I sat in the dust by the palace wall, scolding myself for not having had the sense to wait there all night for Ahithophel to come out. I wanted nothing more now than to break my bad news to Absalom and get my head down again, yet I knew I must not go back. I had no idea how he would see things in the cold light of day; he might even be tempted to give up on his bid for the crown altogether, once the gravity of the crisis he'd caused penetrated his wine-softened skull. And there was no way I could let him do that. Now that Bathsheba knew as much as she did, I had no doubt but that the details of the conspiracy would become public knowledge before the week was out, and the members of the Circle would wind up as dead as if they'd forged ahead with their plans; and probably much sooner.

So after a while I got up and wandered aimlessly through the streets. I could rarely do that and remain anonymous any more, but my face was barely recognizable: one of my eyes was still puffed up, my cheeks were swollen, and my nose and lips were crusted with seeping scabs.

Once the sun had climbed high enough to be seen above the rooftops, I returned once again to the palace. Thankfully there had been another shift change; I said I had an appointment to see His Majesty, and when I gave my name the guard summoned a slave who went off to investigate the truth of my claim.

I was duly admitted to David's apartment. He was lying motionless on his couch as usual, hovering somewhere between consciousness and oblivion, and he didn't know who I was until I spoke. Then the wrinkles around his eyes creased into laughter lines and his drooping mouth spread into a smile, and I was racked with guilt. I tried not to look at him as I relayed the Prince's request, and thankfully he was too drowsy to notice, so I needn't have worried about his remarking on the state of my face. I don't think he really understood what I was saying, and I was thankful for that too, because he asked no awkward questions. It didn't seem to strike him as at all strange that his rebellious son was wanting to offer a sacrifice to Adonai, nor did it even seem to please him. He just nodded vaguely and said, 'Absalom... a sacrifice... go in peace, my son,' so that I wondered if he'd forgotten already who I was and imagined he was talking to Absalom in person.

I got out as soon as I could, and informed Jehoshaphat that a large party would be leaving Jerusalem for Hebron the next day, by order of the King, for the purpose of performing a public act of worship during which Prince Absalom would fulfil a vow made to Adonai whilst he'd been in Geshur.

'And of whom is this—large party to consist, Master Zoheleth?'

I answered, 'The Prince will be inviting two hundred of Jerusalem's worthiest citizens. Of course it is very sad that His Majesty himself won't be well enough to attend.'

Jehoshaphat pursed his lips, and momentarily I glimpsed the anxiety he was harbouring on his King's behalf. But all he said was, 'I shall have you shown out, Master Zoheleth.'

'No,' I said, smiling gently so that he'd be touched by my understanding and let me have my own way. 'I need to see Lord Seraiah concerning the matter of the invitations. If you would just be so good as to give me directions to his chambers.'

Jehoshaphat hesitated, but only for a moment. I was still smiling ingenuously, a wing of heavy fringe hiding the ugliest of my disfigurements, and he said, 'Very well. No doubt you remember how to find Absalom's old rooms. Seraiah's apartment is that way and a little further; ask again when you're nearer.'

I thanked him effusively and pushed on with my quest, working out what I would say to Seraiah as I went. He spoke so little as a rule that I found him somewhat intimidating. I all but ran along the once familiar corridors, simultaneously piecing together the details of my speech.

I must first of all ensure that Seraiah put Amasa on the alert, so that the army would be ready to muscle in and stand up for us once the proclamation had been made; and if any detachments could actually be sent to Hebron along with us as protection, this would of course be of enormous benefit. Personally I couldn't see why this should pose a problem; it would be viewed as perfectly natural for a party of civilians as distinguished and wealthy as the ones we proposed taking along to be accompanied by a military escort. We must merely ensure that the squadron was chosen by Amasa and not by Joab.

Secondly I must draw his attention to the distribution of invitations; although time was horrendously short, care would have to be taken that no man of consequence was inadvertently passed over. Seraiah would know more about that than I did, and would doubtless have ready access to the relevant lists of names and addresses. Beyond this, I couldn't think of anything else which demanded immediate action—so far as I knew, Ahithophel had already got everything in hand. The bonfire of conspiracy had been carefully built, the wood and the kindling were in place. All that was needful now was a spark to set it alight.

I found Absalom's former apartment without any conscious effort, and chanced upon a house-slave who gave me further directions to Seraiah's. But once I started following them, I discovered that either the slave hadn't been sure of the way himself, or else he'd lacked the clarity of thought or speech to communicate it effectively to me. Then again, in my agitation perhaps I hadn't been concentrating. For I found myself wandering unknown passageways which seemed to lead nowhere but round in circles, or to end in narrow winding staircases delving down cheerlessly to the lower levels of the citadel. Quite by chance I emerged onto an open sunlit terrace and tried in vain to regain my bearings. Balconies and buttresses, tiered apparently haphazardly one atop the other, fell away steeply down into the blue-misted valley, and late-flowering creepers cascaded over the criss-crossed walls like laughing green waterfalls.

Then an unexpected movement in a tiny garden immediately below me attracted my attention. Guiltily I shrank back, hoping that whoever was there hadn't noticed me, and waited to check that no one was preparing to come after me. Only then did my mind register what my eyes had seen, and I could have been felled with a feather.

I was standing on a balcony with a parapet made from individual stone columns, waist high, joined only by a rail along the top. Dropping to my knees and then to my belly, I wormed forward until I could get my head between the columns and look down whilst remaining virtually invisible from below. But I still couldn't credit what my eyes were telling me.

In a low-slung chair, set among a glorious jumble of flower-filled pots, with butterflies dipping and flitting about his head, his ushabtis lined up like a troop of soldiers around his ankles, sat my father. He wasn't twitching, or humming, or snivelling; there wasn't so much as a fleck of spittle on his lips. His hair and beard were combed and shining, and on his lap lay a heap of carefully plucked blossoms. He was making a garland.

He wasn't alone. Across the garden from him, seated in a matching chair, was an old woman, fast asleep over her sewing. As I watched, spellbound, my father twisted together the two flowers at either end of the chain he was making, and got up out of his chair. He was still limping badly, but he walked unaided to where his aged companion slept. Tenderly he looped the garland about her neck, then limped his way back to his chair, and sat down, exhausted and elated.

I couldn't contain myself any longer. I scrambled to my feet, my hands shaking, my bladder aching, and my mouth dry as desert dust. All thought of Absalom, Ahithophel and the conspiracy was wiped clean from my mind, as all at once my past rose up to meet me, and broke through the cloak of normality in which I could usually manage to wrap myself.

I clambered clumsily over the parapet, and hanging momentarily from two of the column bases, my legs water-treading the void, I let myself drop into the enchanted garden, half believing I was dreaming. I heard a voice croaking, 'Father? Father!' but it sounded far too hoarse and far away to be my own. He got up again and came towards me, but I could hardly see him for the film across my eyes. Then I was locked in a fierce embrace, and I listened to a voice I'd never in my life before heard say anything coherent, repeating, 'Micha! Micha! My little Micha, where have you been? Oh, Adonai be praised, it is really you . . .'

I don't know how long we stayed like that, clinging to one another until we could barely breathe. It felt like a lifetime and like the blink of an eye, both together. But after a while he took my head from his neck, and held me at arm's length, looking me up and down, mentally devouring me. It seemed that he didn't even notice my blotches and bruises. All he saw was the son who had been lost to him for so, so long. And once I could blink away my tears, I looked at him: his eyes were still the eyes of an infant, but they were steady and bright and blissfully happy. I said, 'Father, I can't believe it. You look so well,' but he just beamed, 'Micha! Micha!' over again. Then he placed one finger against his lips, and with the arm he couldn't bear to unwind from my shoulders he pointed at the old woman, still sleeping, utterly unaware of the drama unfolding around her.

My father said, 'She is beautiful, yes? That's my aunt Michal. She has always been so kind to me. So very kind.' He smiled at me blithely, and blew her a childlike kiss. 'So has the King. Do you know, when he was well, he used to come here to see me twice a day? He used to send me presents, and let me have my supper at his very own table. I still could if I wanted to, every night. But it isn't so nice now he isn't there.' He lowered himself once more into his chair; I sat at his feet and he drew my head onto his lap. He whispered, 'I would have been so happy, but I thought you were dead.'

'I thought *you* must be dead.' My voice came out all hoarse and broken again, and I hardly felt able to string more than three words together. 'But I didn't know ... I mean, I never saw ... I couldn't even tell that you cared about me! All this time ... and back in Lodebar you never once spoke my name, you were ... Micha?' I raised my head. 'Did you say my name was Micha?'

'Micha. Micha.' He nodded, beaming more broadly than ever. 'Yes, of course.'

'I never knew.'

My eyes were locked on his, but I couldn't see a thing. Next he was shaking me, and in consternation asking me, 'Micha, why are you crying? Micha! Please; don't cry. Everything's all right now. It's all right. We're together after all. You can stay here. We won't be sad ever again.'

Paradoxically, hearing him speak about the future like that brought me painfully back to the realities of the present. 'No,' I mumbled into his clothing, the fragrance of the flower garland bitter-sweet in my nostrils. 'I can't stay now. Not yet. There's someone I have to find. An important man at the palace.' But even as I spoke, I could barely recollect who the man was, or why it mattered so much that I should find him.

For a moment I feared that my father might resort to whimpering, the way he would have done so long ago. He pleaded, 'Don't go away, Micha. Don't go off and leave me. Don't get lost again. Please say you'll stay.'

'I'll come back,' I assured him. 'I promise. When I've found the man, I'll come back.'

He didn't say more, so I deemed it best to go while I still had the willpower. I said again, 'Don't worry. I'll come back,' and with one sideways glance at Michal, who was by now snoring audibly, I sprang up and hoisted myself back up onto the balcony, considering that in this mode of departure lay my best chance of getting away quickly, before I changed my mind.

But the full implications of what I'd seen and heard in that little garden still hadn't come home to me. I had to wander up and down the corridors of the palace for a harrowing eternity while the real significance of my encounter with my father and Michal sank in. I can only be grateful that I didn't happen to be at the head of one of those bottomless flights of steps when the revelation dawned, or I would doubtlessly have fallen and broken my neck.

Half my lifetime ago, on the first, and until today the last, occasion on which I'd laid eyes on Michal, she'd been requesting permission to care for Mephibosheth. I hadn't had the remotest idea who she might be referring to—the name had just been so many syllables to me. All I knew was that Michal was the daughter of Saul, and the sister of Jonathan, and then from what she said to David I found out that this man known as Mephibosheth was Jonathan's son.

Now at last I understood. My father Merib—for that was the only name by which I'd known him—and the so-called Mephibosheth were one and the same. Like me, he'd never heard his true name used, for his identity, like mine, had to be kept secret. But he was none other than the grandson of the great Saul himself, which meant that I, Zoheleth the serpent, alias Mamzer the mongrel, Parhosh the flea, Abattiah the pumpkin, was . . .

. . . incapable of coping any longer. Giddy and nauseous, already weak with lack of food and sleep, I passed out; right on the threshold of Seraiah's apartment.

17

I came round ferociously angry.

I know they say you're supposed to see pinpricks of black before your eyes when you're fainting, but that hadn't been so with me. I'd seen a host of identical images of Ziba's obnoxious face, and once I'd regained consciousness I could see or think of nothing else. Any remaining interest which I had in the conspiracy had been obliterated—even though it was Seraiah himself who revived me.

I'm sure he would have been a good deal taken aback at finding me on his doorstep at all, let alone in a crumpled heap. But I don't know to this day whether I said a single word to him. As soon as I could stand, I fled; no doubt he went hot foot to Absalom regardless, rightly supposing that something was badly wrong.

But I didn't care any more. Everything now was turned on its head; I felt like a little boy again, and my abused body and bruised heart were what ruled me. Politics belonged to another world, populated by a different sort of people. Let those people go to Hebron without me.

I had only one notion in my mind, and that was to find Ziba and make him face me. I was angrier than I'd ever been at what he'd done to me, because now I knew he hadn't been abusing just anyone. I *wasn't* a worthless nobody. My blood was every bit as royal as Absalom's, for I was the great-grandson of Saul; little wonder I'd been so intrigued by what Tamar had told me of him long ago, and by the Song of the Bow.

Possessed now of this one precious pearl of knowledge, I wanted all the rest which went with it. I wanted to know how a degenerate slave had got away with treating the kinsman of a king like offal, and I wanted to know why I'd never been told who I was. I wanted to know why my father and I had been brought to the palace, and how this self-same slave had managed to get rich in the process. So I would search for Ziba until I found him, for I'd seen him in Jerusalem before, and would have been willing to lay a bet that he was living in the city. Then when I found him, I would make him tell me everything.

Later on, as soon as I got the chance, I would make him pay.

I had no idea how I was going to do either of these things. I was far less prepared for this potentially hazardous confrontation than I'd been for briefing Seraiah. But my sense of purpose was twice as strong.

Upon leaving the palace, the first thing I did was go to the market and exchange a silver bangle I was wearing for a knife. I don't think I had any clear notion of how I might use it; it merely crossed my mind that such a thing might come in handy. I concealed it in the folds of my clothing, and then began asking anyone I met, where I might find a man called Ziba.

'Don't you know the name of his father?' enquired the first person I accosted, the keeper of a fabric stall who I knew was there often, and likely as anyone to know where any man in Jerusalem might be found.

I shook my head. 'No. I don't really know him. I've been told to deliver something to his house.'

The stallholder looked suspicious. 'He's a free man, then? He owns his own place?'

But I couldn't swear to that either; I've met several slaves in my time who were wealthier than men who call themselves free.

So the merchant couldn't help me, and I approached someone else: a farmer come to town to sell off some young goats. He was no more help, and neither were the elders at the city gates, though I must have looked so manic by this stage that I doubt they'd have told me if they knew—which they probably did. Eventually I gleaned some vague directions from a blind, one-legged beggar, in return for the only coin I had on me, and having nothing else to go on, I followed them up.

It turned out that the fellow hadn't cheated me, for once I was in the right part of town, everyone I asked had heard of Ziba. 'He's a favourite of the King,' I was proudly informed by a neighbour of his. 'He has fifteen sons and twenty servants, and the finest house this side of the palace. Carry on to the end of the street—you'll not miss it.'

A favourite of the King, I muttered to myself, grinding my teeth as though the words were a curse, and my estimation of David sank still lower.

You certainly couldn't have missed Ziba's house, once you knew what you were looking for. Two stone lions flanked the threshold, Assyrian style, with flat lotus-crowned pilasters built into the wall behind them in the fashion favoured by the Egyptians. Clearly Ziba's rise in status since our ways had parted hadn't been accompanied by a refining of his taste. The guard standing to attention at the door was got up more brashly than any of Absalom's had ever been, but he let me through into the courtyard without a murmur because I flattered him by calling him 'sir' and by referring to Ziba as 'my lord'.

Everything about the courtyard too was showy and garish. Egyptian sphinxes rubbed shoulders uncomfortably with Cretan snake goddesses, Akhaian amphorae, Canaanite lampstands, and deities from the east with slanted eyes and six or eight hands. Everywhere there were slaves standing on ceremony, or cleaning, or carting things about.

After a while a once-attractive youth in a gaudy striped tunic came and asked me my name, and I said without thinking 'Zoheleth'; realizing at once that I should have said 'Micha'. That way, Ziba would have been warned even before he set eyes on me that I knew my true identity, and that he wouldn't be able to hide anything.

I cursed myself, determined to come up with some other method of putting Ziba at an immediate disadvantage, but the longer I was left standing there, the less able I was to think. I was as angry as ever, but I still hadn't eaten and was suddenly aware of being painfully hungry. The gnawing in my belly became a throbbing ache, and that was when I realized that I was terrified too. I sat down quickly on a wall, pricked by a nagging suspicion that when Ziba appeared I would be struck as dumb as he must remember me.

I needn't have worried. As he came mincing into the courtyard, pampered and scented and dressed to kill, it was clear from the grossly ingratiating expression on his suety face that he'd certainly heard of Zoheleth, personal attendant to Prince Absalom himself, and was eager to make a favourable impression on him. For I hadn't acquired the nickname until after he'd dumped me in the palace kitchens, and he was hardly likely to have recognized me on Absalom's tribunal robed and turbaned and smiling.

But he recognized me now well enough. He would have known that shock of unruly black hair anywhere; and that bruised, scabby face hardened in sullen but cowed defiance. And as he looked at it, a wash of white spread across his own.

I wasn't granted space to savour his revelation, however, because at once he began yelping at his slaves to have me thrown out. But I was too quick for them. Before they could get within a spearlength of me, I had Ziba round the neck, with my new knife at his throat. There was no need for me to threaten him aloud. The slaves remained at bay, needing only to glimpse the madness in my eyes.

'What do you want from me?' he husked, half choking, and wriggling ineffectually; I was acutely conscious of how feeble he'd become, for all his muscle had run to fat whilst I was coming into the very pride of my manhood. My fear was all gone, and in its place a delicious surge of pure aggression coursed through me. I held the knife closer, watching the puckered flesh turn white around the point, where a tiny gob of thick red blood glistened in the midday sun.

I said, 'Send the slaves away,' and smiled to myself as I reflected that these were the first words he would ever have heard me speak. I couldn't conceive of any more fitting circumstances in which he could have learnt how I'd risen above what he'd done to me. But at the same time I was incensed, because there was nothing I would have enjoyed more at that moment than pushing my knife right through his gullet and watching his worthless life spill out at my feet—and it was he who had put that poison in me too.

'No, no,' he gibbered, when he could find breath to reply. 'That really isn't necessary. They won't do anything to hurt you.'

But *I* might do something to hurt *you*, I thought, and didn't need to say, because my knifepoint was still more eloquent than I was. So he waved his podgy, gem-encrusted hands at his minions, and they backed off warily. Then he began wriggling again, pleading with me to let him go, and he sounded so pathetic that I almost finished him after all. The temptation to make him suffer the way he'd made *me* suffer was all but overwhelming, and I hadn't allowed for how strongly it might affect me. Swallowing hard, I reminded myself that I'd come here for truth, not vengeance; the latter would have to wait for a time when I could exact it without forfeiting my own life into the bargain.

'I'll let you go when I can't see one slave anywhere,' I told him, so he waved again, and the ring of glowering eyes and scowling mouths surrounding us retreated still further before melting away between the pillars of the colonnade. At that I released him, for I knew that if I didn't, I might fall prey to temptation in spite of myself. He stood massaging his throat and glaring at me. I don't think he'd ever been so humiliated in all his life.

I still held the knife in my hand, and there was no longer the remotest possibility of any of his slaves getting to me before I got to him. I was vulnerable from behind, but I had good ears, and Ziba's eyes too would alert me soon enough if someone should creep up on me. He stammered, 'You still haven't told me what you want.'

I wiped my blade clean between two fingers, then licked his blood from the tips of them. '*You* still haven't invited me to sit down.'

'What?'

'For a man of such substance you seem oddly unenlightened about how to treat a guest; let alone a royal one.' I'd been learning from Ahithophel; but I wished I felt as cool as I sounded. The aggression had gone to my head like wine.

Turning whiter, he motioned me to take a seat, on the wall where I'd been sitting earlier. He sat opposite me, and his fingers were quivering in his lap. I could see him wondering whether I meant any more than that I was a member of the Prince's household, but when I said, 'What do you *think* I want, Ziba? I want the truth,' of course he knew. He opened his mouth then closed it again, having no idea where to begin.

I said, 'I know my real name, so there's no need to tell me that. I know my father's name too, *and* where he is. I just want to know why you never told me.'

I was startled to hear my own voice wavering, for I'd reckoned my fear mastered, if not my aggression. Then I decided it wasn't quite fear that I was experiencing, but some seething amalgam of feelings I couldn't put one name to. Dread, horror, guilt and despair, everything I'd felt in Ziba's presence as a child . . . and the whole molten mixture was bubbling up inside me, threatening to pierce my cool veneer at any moment. Ziba's eyes flicked rapidly down to the hand that held my knife, but curiously enough that was steady as a rock, and the taut white knuckles said: if you don't tell me I *will* kill you. He cleared his throat, and simpered, 'It was for your own good. Truly, it was only ever for your own good.'

The veneer was pierced.

'My own good? Don't you *dare* add insult to injury! I've had more than enough of your—'

'I'm not lying. I'm not lying to you, I swear it!' He must have seen the knife start jerking in my grasp. 'You—were very young. It wasn't safe to tell you. You might have told others.'

'What others? I never saw a soul apart from my father and you. And how *could* I have told, anyway? I couldn't even speak!'

He cringed at the spite in my tone as surely as he'd done at the bite of my blade. 'You—don't understand.'

'Oh, I see. You think I'm stupid. You always thought I was stupid, didn't you? *That's* why you never told me the truth!'

'No. No!' He took to gesturing weakly with his hands, as though he thought he might soothe me. He was only too aware that in my present condition I was capable of anything. 'It was after King Saul and his sons died on Gilboa ... if the Philistines had suspected that any of Saul's heirs still lived, they would have hunted them out and butchered them, and had their bodies nailed to the walls of Beth Shan along with their kinsmen's.'

I retorted, 'Ishbosheth survived too, and he was Saul's son. *He* didn't go into hiding.'

'No? So why do you think his lackeys made him king way over the Jordan in the backwoods of Mahanaim? And he was a full-grown man, for heaven's sake. Your father was barely five years old, and there was no one left in Gibeah able to protect him. Do you really think anyone wanted to see a five-year-old's head hacked off and hawked around the cities of Philistia?'

'I can't think why you should have cared,' I snorted. 'I'd have thought you'd have counted it the best thing that could've happened to him.'

He clammed up then, his mouth a tight line between his flaccid cheeks. I seized my knife in both hands and brought it back up towards his chin, but now I *was* trembling, and Ziba's eyes, fixed on the point, told me I'd better listen and stop lashing out if I wanted the facts. Reluctantly I lowered the knife once more.

He said, 'When the news of Saul's defeat reached Gibeah, there was panic. The Philistines were expected to rampage south and turn up outside Saul's stronghold at any moment, intent on raping, murdering and looting. Your grandmother Sarah, Jonathan's wife, was at her wits' end. Her husband was dead, herself and her children in peril. So she took her own life—but not before she'd killed Mebunnai your father's twin brother, and had a go at your father himself.

'His nurse managed to save him, and they fled the fortress. But in her haste she lost her grip on him. He fell down a flight of steps, knocked himself out and broke both ankles and one hip. He still hadn't come round when she brought him to my master in Lodebar a week later, and by then his bones had set crooked. We knew he'd be crippled in his legs as soon as we saw him. It didn't take much longer for us to realize he'd be crippled in his mind as well.'

He paused, but I said nothing. Somehow I'd always assumed my father had been born with his disabilities. I brushed one hand across my face, then mumbled, 'Why you? Why did the nurse bring him to you?'

'My master Machir was a distant kinsman of his, and the girl knew of no one else. She stayed with us a while and looked after the boy. When we found out that the Philistines hadn't exploited their victory we didn't know what to do. It seemed like this half-alive cripple would have to be awarded the crown, for who else was entitled to rule us? But the next we heard, Ishbosheth too was alive, and had been proclaimed king in Mahanaim.'

There was grief mixed up with everything else inside me now, and I couldn't keep it hidden, from Ziba or from myself. He was growing calmer all the time, whilst I was going to pieces, but it was too late for me to back out. Ensuring he could see how alarmingly the knife was twitching, I whispered, 'But you still kept my father's survival a secret?'

'Yes. There was more reason to than ever, lest civil war break out. There were those who would have said your father had more right to the throne than Ishbosheth, being as he was the first son of the king's first son. War among our own people was the last thing anyone wanted. It would have been playing right into the Philistines' hands. But that was exactly what happened—between Ishbosheth and David.'

'David wasn't even related to Saul.'

'No, but he'd been anointed by Samuel, which made him "Adonai's choice". The way things worked out it was the northern tribes who backed Ishbosheth, and the southerners, David. Until Ishbosheth was murdered, that is. Then David held undisputed claim to the kingship.'

'Except—there was still my father.'

'Quite. But he was a child, and a backward and deformed one at that. David was the finest warrior and cleverest statesman Israel had ever produced. There was no way Mephibosheth could stand against him, whatever support he got from the Saulides. And there was a real danger that David would do what so many kings among the nations have done: root out and destroy all rivals. So you see,'—Ziba folded his arms across his chest and smiled at me unpleasantly—'Machir had good reason for keeping your father's identity a secret, wouldn't you agree? We told the wretch that he'd been found as an infant exposed on a hillside, and that no one knew what had become of his parents. And we gave him a false name.'

'Merib.'

'That was the shortened form, which his nurse took to using. In full it was Meribbaal, on the grounds that a name like that would never in a thousand years have been given to a prospective ruler of Adonai's people.'

Momentarily I pictured my father as he might have been, sound in body and mind and seated on the throne of Israel, with myself as heir at his right hand. Then misery washed it away, but Ziba was still smiling. Despite everything, he was starting to relish my discomfort. I murmured, 'But why didn't you tell him the truth when he got older? He could have kept the secret for himself.'

'Oh yes? He couldn't hold his own water, let alone keep a secret.' A wave of shame threatened to engulf me; I held my eyes on Ziba's and somehow rose above it. 'No,' he said, 'We all had to face the facts sooner or later: your father was a dolt, as wet between the ears as he was behind them, and between his legs. He never learned to speak properly, did nothing but snivel and dribble,'—I saw Ziba shudder even as he reminded himself—'and his own dear nurse could see he had no future. He was a wreck, physically and mentally, would never get better, and she saw it was all her fault. She ran away from the house in the end, and I got the job of taking care of him myself.'

'Care,' I said bitterly. 'So that's what you called it.'

'You think I volunteered for the task? You think I welcomed the prospect of being saddled with an incontinent cripple for the rest of my life? I was angry. Very angry. But I was a slave with no rights and no choice in the matter—or in any *other* matter. Machir even had the documents altered so that I was registered as Meribbaal's property.' He lowered his voice and said without remorse, 'I took my pleasure where I could.'

'And me?' I demanded, my own anger rising again, along with the tide of grief I was finding it harder and harder to fight down.

'You?' said Ziba vaguely, being deliberately obtuse. 'What about you?'

'What do you think? Who *am* I? I must have had a mother, for God's sake. Who was she?'

Ziba shrugged his shoulders, and I realized that he was now actually enjoying telling me all this; somehow in the course of our conversation our roles had changed. He was now the aggressor, and I the victim, as of old. Something crumbled inside me—another of my defences against the grief.

'Your father was so backward in every way, it scarcely seemed worth explaining the facts of life to him . . . There was a prostitute in Lodebar—well, there were a good few, but one was more brazen than the rest. I suppose her friends egged her on, for a dare most likely. She wouldn't have done it for any other reason, I'm sure, and he certainly wasn't trusted with any gold of his own which he could have given her. Nine months later, she deposited you on our doorstep.'

The tide of grief was rising higher and higher; I blinked hard several times but couldn't clear the fog from my eyes. Ziba was smiling again, or rather leering; nor was he through with belittling me.

'If it had been up to me, I'd have taken you and left you where we claimed we'd found your father. But Machir insisted you were sprung of royal seed, however filthy the womb you'd been sown in, and we must bring you up accordingly. He even squandered a good Saulide name on you; I'm told there have been a number of Michas and Michals among your forebears. Not that your father could ever have guessed that you were his. As far as he was concerned, babies might grow on trees.'

If only you could know how wrong you are, I thought furiously. But I didn't trust myself to speak. What had passed between my father and myself that morning had been so special, so sacred, I wasn't prepared to soil it by dragging it through the dust of this man's scorn.

'And pretty soon,' Ziba continued almost casually, 'It became quite apparent that you were as feckless as your father was. You never understood one word that was spoken to you, or said anything in return. So it was back to the dreary old business of false names and secret identities. I think even Machir, sentimental stooge that he is, began to wonder if we'd done the wisest thing. You see, Mamzer—I do beg your pardon, *Micha*—so much needless hassle could have been avoided if poor Meribbaal had

222

simply—shall we say—disappeared, when his unfortunate nurse did.'

I couldn't control myself any longer. The tears boiled over all down my swollen cheeks, but somehow I kept my eyes locked on his, and my fingers hard around the knife-hilt, and blurted, 'So why did you bring us to the palace then? That was hardly in keeping with—concealing our identity, was it?'

Ziba's hideous smile broadened, for in my despair I'd granted him the opportunity to boast of what he plainly regarded as his master-stroke. He said, 'I'd a brother who was already in service at David's court, and well respected there. The King asked one day if any of Saul's descendants were by any chance still living, so that he might show them a kindness for Jonathan's sake. Naturally Machir took pains to ensure that the request was genuine. Even after all that time, it could still have been a trick.'

'Better for you if it had been,' I choked.

'I beg your pardon?'

'You could have danced on our graves every night and gone into the Tabernacle to pray every morning, with your head held high and without so much as a whiff of blood on your soft white hands.' I scraped the hot tears from my face and sobbed, 'You'd have had every accursed thing you ever wanted.'

'Hardly,' he corrected me, so calmly, so sweetly. 'A few hours of exquisite happiness, I confess, and a sense of relief that might have lasted a few hours more. But it came to me at once, that should your father be brought to *live* at the palace rather than *die* there . . . well, he would be in need of long-term specialist attention. And as my brother pointed out to the King, I was the only person qualified to give it.'

'You used us!' I leapt to my feet, and would have gone for him with the knife after all, except that I couldn't see a thing for tears. 'It wasn't enough to lie to us, and beat us, and torture us, and worse. On top of all that you had to use us to win your place at court. And to get all this!' I waved my free hand around the cluttered courtyard, then made another futile attempt at drying my eyes.

'Not quite,' said Ziba. 'I used your father. I didn't use you.'

'What?'

'I never told the King a thing about you.' Ziba shrugged again in the renewed intensity of my staring. 'After all, my brother didn't even know of your existence. And I was going to have enough on my plate seeing to the whims of the Cripple.'

I said, 'But you *didn't* have to look after him, did you? Michal offered to care for him. She loved him even if you didn't. You should've been sent back to Lodebar.'

'Michal could attend to the Cripple himself, but not to his estates. *They* still had to be administered. There was no need for me to stay at the palace so I was given this house, my freedom, and an acceptable salary for my services. A fair deal, or so I decided at the time. Though on reflection I think I could have asked for more.'

'Estates?' I repeated, and unexpectedly I found that the tears had dried up of their own accord. Only when he saw my jaw drop did Ziba realize he'd made a mistake. 'What estates?' I demanded, and as his face swam back into focus I held the knife beneath his nostrils.

He tried everything to avoid telling me. He feigned a fit of coughing, then a griping of the stomach; the exhibition might have made me laugh had I been in any better a mood. But in the end no amount of time he could gain for himself enabled him to come up with any means to get out of telling me the truth. David had restored to my father all that had once belonged to Saul: his herds, his fields, his vineyards, even the dilapidated fortress at Gibeah. Every acre and every stone which had once been Saul's, and all the income accruing from them, were now Mephibosheth's; and presumably they ought one day to be mine.

'Except that the King still doesn't know of your existence,' rasped Ziba when I pointed this out. 'Your father's will has already been sealed. Upon his death, all his wealth passes to me, in gratitude for what I have done for him. If he should outlive me, it goes to my sons.'

I yelled, 'My father would never have signed such a document! He wouldn't leave a shekel's weight in sheep droppings to you!'

'Come, come now—Micha. Since when has your father been able to *read* anything, let alone sign it? And who but me could act on his behalf?'

'You thief! You lying, cheating thief! The King *will* know of my identity. I shall tell him!'

'And you expect him to believe you? No doubt a hundred half-starved youths show up at the palace every day claiming to be great-grandsons of Saul.'

'He *will* believe me! And if he doesn't, he'll believe my father.'

'If your father can stop dribbling and piddling long enough to get a look at you.'

I could take no more. I bolted out into the street, bawling obscenities, vowing I would die before I let him get his hands on what was mine. And no doubt he was already working on how to sweep me out of his way.

18

I arrived back at Absalom's towards sunset, as limp as a withered vine. I've no idea where the rest of the day had gone, except that I know I didn't go back to my father's garden as I'd promised. I was in far too crazed a state. I don't even know how I found my way home; I certainly have no recollection of the journey. Vengeful and hopeless by turns, I still needed to be alone for a while, to get my weeping done and my next steps planned.

And I'd somehow assumed I *would* be alone; in my mind I'd let Absalom and my fellow conspirators move on without me, so as far as I was concerned, there was no longer a place for them in Jerusalem. For so long I had prided myself on not needing anyone; now for the first time perhaps it was true. I existed in my own right, with reference to no man alive. The city had become nothing to me but a combat zone in which the final battle of my war against Ziba and all that he stood for would be fought out.

Thus I was both bewildered and distressed to find them all still there, with the exception of Amasa; waiting, as it transpired, for me to return before they did anything. They would never have waited if Ahithophel had been around—he'd have seen to that. He'd have known I could have been arrested or murdered, or might simply have deserted, and that everything must go ahead without me.

But with neither Ahithophel nor me to hold his hand, it appeared that Absalom was lost. He'd been at the wine again, and was pacing about like a prisoner in a condemned cell. Shimei and Sheba were there, conversing brow to brow in hushed tones; in his gentle, scholarly way Seraiah was futilely trying to talk sense into the irresolute Prince's head; and Bathsheba reclined on a couch hennaing her nails. The moment I put my nose around the door, Absalom clapped his hands and made to drag me inside. Then he saw that I was in shock.

'By all the gods, Zohel. What's happened? Did he refuse permission?'

'Who? Permission for what?' I sagged onto a couch not an arm's reach from Bathsheba's; that in itself should have spoken volumes to him.

'Zohel!' cried Absalom in incredulous despair. 'Have you been—?'

'Drinking? No. But you have.' I raised my head to look at him, and that little effort all but finished me. 'Don't worry, Absalom. David has approved the sacrifice. Go ahead; go to Hebron.'

'You see, my darling?' Bathsheba interposed, blowing on the nail she'd just left off colouring, 'I told you he wouldn't think twice about it. He's much too far gone to think about *anything* these days. You must move at once, before you lose the initiative entirely.'

Seraiah said, 'My lord, will you at least let me issue the invitations now? We could still go tomorrow. We daren't risk changing Amasa's orders again.'

But Absalom wasn't listening. He was kneeling by my couch, holding me up by the arms and peering right into my bleary eyes; just then he could have been sixteen again, and I could have been the tongue-tied eight- or ten-year-old with the mark of Amnon's belt across my legs. 'Zohel,' he repeated, 'For the love of God, what's happened to you? Is this all because I . . . ? I thought we'd made it up.'

'Absalom,' I sighed, 'Just leave me alone. This isn't to do with you. Please—get ready and go to Hebron. I'll be all right here.'

'Here? What the hell are you talking about?'

'I can't come, that's all. It won't make any difference. I don't matter to you any more. I was your contact with David. I've played my part . . .' I was dozing off with my eyes open.

'You think I'd leave you here on your own? You'd be lynched the moment the proclamation was made! And why in heaven should you want to stay? Are you ill? How many times do I have to ask you: what's happened?'

'You wouldn't want to know.'

'I certainly would.'

'No, you wouldn't. Believe me, you wouldn't.'

He let me go, and I flopped back exhausted among the cushions; I'd had nothing you could rightly call sleep in two days. I lay there listening while they argued over me as though I were somewhere else. Bathsheba was maintaining that I'd always been moody and wholly unreliable; Shimei and Sheba were convinced I was sickening for something and would only get in the way later on if I came.

'Just leave him here,' said Sheba casually. 'It might even look better if he stayed.'

'That could well be true,' agreed Seraiah. 'No one will suspect that Prince Absalom intends remaining for any length of time in Hebron if he's known to have gone there without Zoheleth. Everyone is used to seeing them in each other's company.'

Shimei said, 'Ahithophel wouldn't like it. He'd say it was too dangerous. Who knows what the lad is up to? Can any of *you* ever tell what he's thinking? Because I can't. He's always been strange. We shouldn't leave him here unless it's with a knife in his back.'

I sat bolt upright and said to Absalom, 'I'm the great-grandson of Saul.'

Absalom laughed tensely. 'Yes, and I'm Pharaoh Tutankhamun.'

'No, I mean it. I'm Micha, son of Mephibosheth, son of Jonathan, son of Saul.'

Absalom took in the whole room at one nervous glance; every one of his companions was gaping at me. He said in a taut voice, 'This is no time for acting the goat, Zohel.'

'I'm not acting the goat.'

'Then you really *are* sick.'

'You see. I told you you wouldn't want to know. But my father— Merib the Cripple—he's Mephibosheth, the kinsman of Saul who has eaten for nearly ten years at the King's own table.'

'You never even let on that you *had* a father. You said you were an orphan.'

'I said nothing of the kind. *You* said that.'

Absalom pressed his hands to his cheeks as though afraid that even they might no longer be real. I saw his world in smoking ruins around him; in the background the others had begun mumbling, and no longer wanting to hear what they said, I launched into a garbled explanation. The whole lot came out, though by no means in its logical order: how I'd spent my early years at Lodebar with Ziba and Machir, and my idiot father; how the pair of us had been brought to the palace but separated; how Ziba had exploited Mephibosheth for all he was worth, having lied to us both about who we were; and finally how I'd come across my estranged father that morning in one of the palace gardens, and realized at last who he was.

The only thing I didn't disclose was how Ziba had treated me when I'd been too young to understand.

When I'd finished, you could have snapped the atmosphere like dried-out papyrus.

Absalom moaned, 'Why *now*, Zohel? Why do you have to come out with this now?'

'Because I only found the truth out now. Are you saying you don't believe me?'

He looked right at me, then answered, 'No.'

Bathsheba said, 'We no longer have a choice, Absalom. We must get rid of him.'

'Get rid of him?' screamed Shimei, leaping to his feet. 'This boy should be on the throne of Israel!'

'Huh! I never heard such a sudden change of heart in my life!' spluttered Sheba, though I can't imagine why he should have been so shocked; if there was one thing you could rely on about Shimei it was his unreliability; and after that, his temper. But then I caught Bathsheba's eye, and it was like realizing you've just been stabbed in the guts. I thought: my God, I'm as good as dead already, I'm another rival to Solomon.

'No, just think, man!' Shimei was blustering on. 'His father isn't fit to rule, we can all see that. But *he* is! Look at him! He's young, strong, good-looking. Everything Absalom is. And he's descended from the only lawful monarch Israel ever had, not a self-proclaimed upstart like David. David was a confounded outlaw before he came to power; he led a band of criminals in the desert, he ran protection rackets, he even collaborated with the Philistines! Saul was crowned openly, in a full assembly of the tribes, by Samuel himself. This boy is his rightful heir.'

For a moment he stood gazing at me, his shoulders heaving. Then he fell on his knees at my feet, kissing my sandal straps. Absalom held his head, and I was distraught.

Sheba blew out a sharp breath between his teeth and said, 'The expedition to Hebron will have to be shelved after all. Too much has gone wrong. We need to think about this, investigate the facts. Suppose Zoheleth *isn't* telling the truth? Or suppose someone isn't telling the truth to *him*?'

'It's the truth,' I whispered bleakly. 'My father isn't the idiot he was thought to be. You wouldn't believe what a little kindness has done for him.'

Shimei left off his kissing. 'Are you saying—my lord, are you saying that *he* should be king? Mephibosheth the Cripple?'

'No. I don't know what I'm saying.' Somehow Shimei's perfectly predictable reaction to the revelation of my identity had in fact thrown me completely; it just hadn't occurred to me that anyone would want to make *me* king. That had been the least of my worries. Now all at once it seemed to be the most pressing.

Seraiah said quietly, 'Sheba has a fair point. We must discuss this matter rationally—and to my mind, with Ahithophel and Amasa present. Things may look different to a large number of people once this new factor is brought to the public's attention.'

'There is absolutely no reason for it to be brought to *anyone's* attention,' rejoined Bathsheba, as though addressing a wayward child rather than an erudite scribe. 'No one outside of these four walls knows of it besides Mephibosheth, and I scarce think it likely *his* ravings will be listened to, without other evidence to corroborate them.'

I sniped, 'Ziba knows.'

Bathsheba let out a shrill laugh. 'From what you've said, he isn't going to shed many tears at your funeral. —Absalom? You've gone remarkably quiet all of a sudden.'

Absalom shook his head, the hair falling in his face so I couldn't read it. He said, 'I can't believe I'm hearing all this. An orphan, and one I myself snatched from my own brother's clutches, comes out with a half-baked story about his lineage and the next thing I know, my two best friends and one of the sanest intellectuals in Israel are ready to abandon me at a whim, whilst the woman I love wants me to commit cold-blooded murder. I trusted you, Bathsheba. And you, Shimei, and Sheba, and Seraiah. —And you, Zohel.'

Sheba fidgeted uncomfortably. 'I'm sorry, Absalom. But we were relatives of Saul before we were friends of yours. Nor have we ever made a secret of it. Don't you at least think that the facts ought to be established? Suppose we crown you and *then* the whole thing is leaked? We'd have another revolt breaking out hot on the tail of yours! Then it could be you we have to rescue from the lynch mob.'

'But this is Israel, confound you, Sheba!' Absalom turned on him; his hair flew round and I saw he was white-hot with wine-heightened fury. 'We don't *have* a hereditary monarchy in Israel.'

Shimei, ever quick to quarrel with Sheba, but quicker still to spring to his defence when someone else was the aggressor, seized hold of Absalom by the brooches at his shoulders. 'Too true,' he sneered. '*Adonai* chooses our king; that's the system, isn't it? So by what right do *you* stake your claim? You don't suppose for a moment he'd choose you, with *your* mother!'

Absalom was shaking. Both of them were still on their knees near my couch, but they both sprang up now simultaneously. Absalom roared, 'What are you calling me? A foreigner? A pagan? Do you see any evidence of that in this house? Do you? And my mother is the staunchest friend I have. The only friend I can rely on, by the sounds of things! She loves me! She'd *die* for me! You care for nobody, she was right. And Ahithophel was right. I should never have included you in my plans. You only ever wanted to be near me for what you could get out of me.'

As usual it fell to Sheba to drag his two friends apart before they floored each other. But even after they'd been separated, Shimei was still bawling and cursing, rounding off with: 'I've had enough of your high-handedness! I won't be patronized by you any longer! You think you're God Almighty and I'm nothing but a brainless wine-bibber. Well, ben David, I'm through with you and your pathetic little plot, do you hear me? This is the final straw. Until you see sense and recognize your true lord and master, you can count me out!'

He slammed the door and was gone before any of us could stop him.

'Go after him!' Bathsheba hissed at Absalom. 'What if *he* runs to David?'

'He won't,' said Sheba, dropping onto a chair, drained utterly. 'He hates David more than he hates anyone, since he handed over those seven kinsmen of ours to the Gibeonites.'

'We're better off without him anyhow,' snarled Absalom. 'With a temper like that, he's a liability more often than an asset. If he *does* change sides, he'll do our opponents more harm than good.'

I thought: and what about *your* temper, then? And your moods, if it comes to that?

Then he asked miserably, 'What about *you*, Sheba? You implied that I ought to defer to Zohel as well, if what he says is true.'

'I don't know *what* I think any more, if I ever did,' Sheba admitted, regarding me with a strange blend of disapproval and grudging admiration. 'I'm beginning to wish I hadn't got mixed up in this fiasco in the first place. Why did Ahithophel have to go off and leave us in the lurch? I wish he'd come back.'

'Don't we all,' murmured Absalom.

Having reddened the last of her nails, Bathsheba replaced the caps on her bottles and got up resignedly. She went to stand behind Absalom, wrapping her arms around his shoulders and leaning her head on his neck. He covered her hands with his own, squeezing them tightly, more to reassure himself than her, if he imagined she needed it. She spoke into his ear, but her words were directed towards the rest of us.

'It seems to me that you're all being cruel to yourselves as well as to Absalom. Just think of the months, years even, that you and he—and especially my poor grandfather—have devoted to boosting his image in the eyes of the people. The greater part of the nation stands poised to declare for him, to fight for him—yes, to die for him if necessary. But who would risk his neck for Zoheleth? He's little more than a bodyslave now, whatever his lineage. Would you all throw away the fruits of your labours just as the harvest is ripening? Give yourselves a chance! Go to Hebron, install Absalom as king the way you planned. Once any opposition has been crushed, he can contemplate abdicating in favour of Zoheleth at his leisure, should anyone still consider it desirable.' Absalom smiled a faint smile, and Bathsheba added poignantly, '*I* shan't desert you, my darling. But a woman's love is stronger than any political allegiance.'

Like hell it is, I thought, certainly where you're concerned. But Absalom basked in the warmth of her flattery, more desperate than ever to suck in affection wherever he believed it could be found. He was flirting with a spider whose design was the same as that of any other of her species: to lure her victim to destruction.

Seraiah said quietly, 'The argument is sound, Absalom. You must have the courage of your convictions. Permit me to issue the invitations while there is still enough time.'

Absalom replied weakly, 'Yes,' and with that single, simple word kicked away the last piece of scaffolding from the tottering edifice we'd built. Seraiah bowed swiftly and left. There was no going back now.

Bathsheba kissed Absalom tenderly on both cheeks. 'I must leave you too, for the present,' she said. 'I cannot come to Hebron straight away, you must accept that. Whatever do you suppose would happen, if my absence from the city were to be discovered before your coronation? For your own sake everything here must appear normal until then. I have dallied here too long already, yet I was loath to leave you. One night's absence from my chambers is unlikely to have rocked many boats; there are many friends I could have been visiting. But two? We must not push our luck, my darling.'

Absalom clung to her fiercely. He whined, 'You promised to come with me. You promised.'

'And so I shall, if you insist. But don't make things hard for yourself! If I stay behind in Jerusalem for a few days now, after that we can be together for ever. Why add an unnecessary risk to necessary ones? If you love me, you'll admit that I'm right.'

'At least stay tonight. My bed is so cold without you. I—'

But she brushed her finger against his lips to silence him. 'Don't be a slave to your feelings. The longer I stay, the worse will be the parting. You're your own worst enemy, Absalom.'

Those are possibly the only true words you've ever spoken, I thought, as she belted her huge coat, pulled swathes of it over her head, and slipped away. I was no longer remotely interested in keeping her under surveillance. Sheba then announced, 'I'm going to get my things together. I'll be back at first light,' and Absalom and I were alone.

He'd no idea what to say to me, though it was clear he wanted to say something. He stood with his arms crossed over his chest, his hands on his shoulders where Bathsheba's had rested, his eyes misty with distance. I'd no more idea how to break the ice than he had. Eventually he wandered away to his bedroom and opened the door. Gatis padded out, eyeing him reproachfully. She was always locked in there when the conspirators came; Seraiah as well as Ahithophel took especial exception to her.

Absalom crouched down and buried his face in her fur.

I went to bed, but again I couldn't sleep. I relived that morning's confrontation with Ziba over and over, and each of these recapitulations was more painful for me than the last. Then I was caught in a repeating cycle of violent separations from my father, and tearful reunions.

But when I succeeded in banishing these disconcerting images from my head, something worse took their place. Perhaps I *was* asleep by this time, and dreaming—I could no longer tell. For next I saw myself ensconced upon David's throne. I say David's throne, because that's what it most resembled: it was ornately carved and flanked by white stone lions. But it was enormous. The lions were

233

larger than life-size, and the seat could have accommodated four men quite comfortably. I was huddled in one corner of it, woefully naked except for a crown and a plush purple robe with gold trimmings. The crown was so heavy I could scarcely raise my head, and my bare feet wouldn't touch the ground.

Then as I peered from beneath the crown down the long lofty throneroom, echoing footfalls rang out suddenly from far off, and came closer, and there was Absalom running and stumbling towards me, with his sword drawn. Unable to move, I waited for him to run me through, but with a great cry he threw the weapon aside. Next I thought he was going to embrace me, but he didn't do that either. He simply looked at me, and walked away.

After that, I lay on my back, I lay on my front, I lay on my side with my head wrapped in blankets, but Absalom's face wouldn't go away. Micha, you stupid fool, I rebuked myself, get a grip on reality, remember who you are. Zohel, Absalom's lackey, is dead; you are Micha, grandson of Jonathan, great-grandson of Saul, and any debt you owed to Absalom is long since paid. He cares nothing for *you*, or *your* claims and rights, and his fists are every bit as brutal as Ziba's ever were. Look after yourself, Micha, the way you've always done, because no one else is going to do it for you.

But none of my arguments convinced me, and when finally I tore away my blankets and got out of bed in disgust, Absalom really was looking at me.

He was hanging in the doorway of my room, his hair loose and dishevelled, his eyes hollow as a corpse's when the vultures have picked it. Low lamplight left patches of shadow across his face, and they looked like drifts of black snow, between which the fine lines of his bones stood proud like wind-stripped rocks. He said, 'Come with me tomorrow, Zohel.'

'Micha.'

'Micha, then. Please.'

'Why? You can trust me to stay here. I won't make any trouble for you. Not yet.'

'But Micha, I—'

'Don't concern yourself. I'm not going to fight you for the throne. Not for a while, put it that way. I'm not ready. I've got a lot of thinking to do.'

'Do you think that's what I'm worried about? Do you think that's why I'm here?'

234

'Maybe. I can't see your hands. Maybe you have a knife in one of them.'

He made a strangulated sound halfway between sobbing and swearing. 'If I had, I'd as likely use it on myself as on you.'

'Whatever for? All your dreams are about to come true. Pull yourself together, Absalom. You've suffered a few setbacks, I'll grant, but nothing has gone wrong yet which is too bad to be put right. Go to Hebron, send for Ahithophel. Arrest him, if he won't come straight away. When he's back with you, you can reward him richly enough from the royal treasuries to enable him to overlook a spot of humiliation. Once you've been crowned, Bathsheba will be powerless against you—especially when she realizes how wide-spread your support is ...'

He asked again, 'Do you honestly think that's what I came here to talk about? Do you honestly think I'm not sick to the teeth of weighing up whether it's worth going ahead with everything or not? Of course I shall go ahead. I've no alternative, I've gone too far already.'

'Then what *do* you want? I'm tired, and I'm all mixed up inside. I don't want to lose my temper with you.'

'I want to hear you say you don't hate me.'

'What?'

'Heavens above, Zohel—I mean, Micha—I've known you for nearly ten years; for nearly ten years you've been the only person I could rely on to tell me the truth without wanting to flatter or degrade me! My whole life I've been surrounded by servile sycophants who are only interested in my looks, or the power they think I have, or soon will have, and which they think they can get me to share with them! I thought you were interested in *me*! I thought you *cared*!'

I closed my eyes. This was *all* I needed. 'Of course I don't hate you, Absalom. Why on earth should I?'

He shrugged helplessly, presumably considering the reason too obvious to put into words.

I said, 'I've told you. I'm not interested in staking a claim to the throne. And do I *look* like I hate you? Do I *sound* like I hate you?'

'I only know you haven't spoken a word to me since you told me about your father.'

'You were too busy talking to Bathsheba. I thought *she* cared about you?'

Smashing both fists against the wall, he wheeled about and left. I remained gazing at the doorway, somehow still seeing his vanished silhouette against the emptiness beyond, and it was encircled by dancing ghosts—his flurry of temper had shaken the lamp on its hook and it swung dizzily, causing the shadows to leap and sway like drunken demons.

I went back to bed, but sat up, leaning on the wall and watching a wan full moon rise into my window until it all but filled it. *Did* I care about Absalom, after all this time? Did I want to? Did I even know what caring was? Perhaps he and I were two of a kind: we could each cope with loving ourselves, but that took up all the capacity for love which we possessed.

Or perhaps we didn't even love ourselves. Perhaps that was the root problem for each of us; but for wholly different reasons.

In the end I went to Hebron in spite of myself. But I wasn't persuaded by Absalom. I went because Sheba said that he wouldn't go either, unless I did, and that unlike Shimei, he *would* betray Absalom to David if he didn't get his way.

Both Absalom and I were equally shocked at the change in his attitude since the previous night. He'd left us troubled and indecisive, now he was ruthlessly resolute, and there was no way Absalom could risk losing yet another member of the Circle. I was angry as well as confused, but too tired and drained to want to create difficulties, or make far-reaching decisions; I simply let events take their course.

I'd no idea why Sheba should consider my presence so vital all of a sudden, yet I conceded that I did at least care enough for Absalom not to want to see his head on a stake through my own doing. Ziba would still be in Jerusalem when I got back, no doubt. By then I might well be chief steward of a king, and thus in a much stronger position from which to set about wreaking my revenge.

19

Our procession left Jerusalem shortly before midday, with more or less its full complement of eminent guests: heads of ancient families and representatives of the nouveaux riches, civil servants and veteran war-heroes, scribes sacred and secular, those in the know and those blissfully ignorant of what they were already embroiled in. A division of priests accompanied us, carrying ram's horn shofars and psalteries. Ostensibly they came to assist with the pledged sacrifice, but most of them were up to their necks in the conspiracy. Hemmed in among the priests walked a placid, perfectly snow-white bull fetched from Absalom's estate at Baal Hazor, the halter around its neck ribboned with flowers. Amasa had succeeded after all in providing us with a military escort—no doubt Bathsheba's gold had lined a few pockets and silenced a few wagging tongues. In addition there were dancers and drummers and cymbal players and flute girls; no one seemed to have invited them, but they could be relied upon to appear spontaneously whenever the gorgeous Prince Absalom so much as showed his face in public with more than a handful of servants.

At first I rode with Absalom, in his respectable four-wheeled carriage, about halfway down the column. We had twenty-five of his Geshurite bodyguards immediately in front of us and twenty-five behind, all got up quite as respectably as the carriage. Even our Akhaian eunuchs had their heads covered.

Ahithophel would certainly have been impressed with the image we presented—indeed, he would have been impressed with every-thing, except the presence of one large Syrian hunting hound, who could scarcely be left behind in Jerusalem with no one to take care of her. But with regard to Gatis too, Absalom demonstrated exemplary if uncharacteristic discretion: she travelled in a covered baggage-wagon in the charge of a slave who was used to her, and after a while I wound up there also, for I simply couldn't keep awake enough to stay with Absalom. The rocking motion of the carriage and the rolling mono-tony of the stony landscape brought the sleep which had eluded me for so long, and when he had to stop me falling for the third time, Absalom packed me off to get some rest. I obeyed with profound gratitude, for it relieved me of the pressure of trying to make conversation with him. The gulf between us now was as wide as the dry ground made when Moses raised his rod and the Red Sea parted.

A fit young man, unencumbered by baggage and hangers-on, might run from Jerusalem to Hebron in an afternoon quite comfortably. By the time our company arrived, it was almost dark. It could have seemed suspicious, to anyone who cared to think about it, that accommodation for such a large number of important people was subsequently organized so swiftly, when the travellers themselves hadn't known they would be requiring it until the night before. But Ahithophel's administrative capabilities knew no bounds; his contacts in Hebron had been half expecting us for several days and had compiled an extensive list of those able and willing to offer hospitality to the élite of the capital at short notice. Nor was Seraiah to be despised as an administrator. He'd sent runners in advance of us to give warning of our imminent arrival; two more to Giloh to summon Ahithophel himself; and others to our supporters up and down the nation who must be ready to supply troops and to swell the chorus hailing Absalom the moment the signal was received.

Not that the majority of our hosts in Hebron knew anything whatever about the conspiracy. They didn't need to.

Absalom and I were lodged, along with the rest of our household, at the home of the most venerable among the city elders. Unlike his junior colleagues, he was as innocent of our true designs as our sacrificial victim was of its impending doom, and treated Absalom with the same deference he would have shown to the Prince's father.

He was offered a fine curtained bed in a private room, and from the window, as I helped him shed his dusty outer garments, I could just about discern against the twilight the silhouette of an elevated citadel rising above the jumbled roofs of the hilltop town. Absalom was gazing at it too, with an abstracted and oddly wistful expression on his face, and I realized we were looking at what had once been David's palace, and Absalom's home. I could see the memories which the sight of it had brought back to him, drifting like wisps of cloud behind his eyes.

No one but slaves lived there now, I knew: the place was maintained by half a dozen royal retainers who kept it in good order in case His Majesty should have business to attend to in the south.

Perhaps in days gone by, David had indeed made such visits; but by now his faithful housekeepers must have grown grey over their work, and probably forgotten what their own master looked like. By this time tomorrow, they might be serving his son.

When I'd folded Absalom's clothes and turned back the coverings on his bed, he dismissed me with a vague gesture of one hand, and no words. I hovered in the doorway a while, watching him, but he made no move to lie down. He'd had less sleep than I in the past few days, but the fuel of anticipation was keeping him going. He went and stood by the window with his chin on his upturned palms, and for a fleeting moment reminded me painfully of his father, the first time I'd seen him from close by.

Along with dawn the next morning came a rush of frenzied activity. I dressed Absalom in plain white linen, and veiled his glossy curls beneath a flowing kerchief over which the golden circlet could later be placed. This latter was an exact copy of David's, and had been fashioned by the same craftsman—who'd been under no illusions about the purpose behind his latest commission. It was now in the care of the priests, together with the obligatory gold-trimmed cloak (the rest of it dyed with Tyrian purple) and the jar of oil which would be emptied over Absalom's brow.

Even as I made the final adjustments to the folds of his robe and stood back to appraise my handiwork, Ahithophel walked in, having hastened from Giloh overnight. He appeared weary; not just with the journey, but older somehow. There were neat little mourning rents in his gown—he would never have permitted himself anything more ostentatious. But I concluded I'd been unfairly cynical when I'd read his letter—he had cared about his dying brother.

Momentarily the two of them stood and looked at one another; Absalom had caught his breath, and Ahithophel seemed about to reprimand him. Then Absalom sprang forward and embraced him, undoing all my efforts with his attire, repeating effusively how happy he was to see the old schemer, and above all how relieved. Ahithophel coughed in delicate embarrassment, and held his protégé at arm's length.

'Well, my son,' he said, 'Perhaps you have acted prudently, as things have turned out. On balance it may have been wise of you to lose no time on my account. Everything seems to be in order here. It's possible you have the makings of a king after all.' Never before had I heard him call Absalom 'my son'. Presumably no one had deemed it politic to tell him what had caused the Prince to proceed so rapidly with the final phase of our plans.

After a hurried breakfast of which I ate little and Absalom nothing, the procession formed up once again and set off for a high place just beyond the town, where the sacrifice was due to be carried out. Hebron's population lined the streets, cheering and waving and throwing flowers, honoured because the son of the man they themselves had made king was now come among them to pay his dues to Adonai.

The high place had once been a sanctuary of the Earth Folk, the Canaanites whom the Children of Israel had displaced when Joshua led them back into their Promised Land. But there was no trace of the old religion left there any more. The images of abominable deities were long gone, the hole from which the Asherah pole had been torn was grown over with thorns and weeds. Absalom, walking barefoot up the hill, surrounded by the chanting priests, was pale and tight-lipped. I wondered whether in truth he wouldn't have been more comfortable with Asherah and the Baals presiding than with the plain horned altar, on top of which the fire was already burning, and with the suspicion that as the first clouds of autumn began to gather overhead there might indeed be a God in heaven who was watching, and disliking what he saw.

But for a clearing about the altar, ringed by priests, and a priest-lined aisle down which the victim would be led, the hillside was thronged with people. The guests we'd brought with us had been granted pride of place and an unobstructed view of proceedings but they were comprehensively surrounded by Amasa's men. Further away milled the locals, who so far as we knew might be friends or foes, but I surmised that we should find out soon enough. With everyone so intent upon securing a place from which he might see the smoke of the fire, or smell the simmering blood, or catch a glimpse of Absalom himself, no one paid any attention to the ranks of rebel forces who were steadily massing on every side.

At first the act of worship proceeded like any other. Psalms were sung and prayers offered, by the priests and then by Absalom. I couldn't believe that the unsuspecting multitudes weren't immediately put on their guard by the tremor in his voice, and by the way it kept breaking like a boy's as he prayed, but perhaps they dismissed all this as mere nervousness. Even the spotless white bull remained placid to the end.

While its blood was being poured out over the altar and its flesh cast sizzling into the blaze, a veritable herd of additional victims came lowing and bleating forward: cattle, rams, goats, lambs, all freely contributed by the generous citizens of Hebron as fellowship-offerings whose meat would be used to feed the worshippers, after the designated parts had been reserved for Adonai. Absalom's bull was consumed in its entirety by the flames: it was a burnt-offering, a symbol of Absalom's complete dedication to the Lord—as Ahithophel asserted when he stood up to speak.

It was at this point that something began squirming deep down inside me, something that threatened to expel the total contents of my bowels onto the ground as I listened to him. For I knew that every word he uttered was a lie; and not only a lie, but a blasphemy. It was so long since I'd given any thought to the things of God. But what was happening was so blatantly a perversion of everything Israel held sacred, that I simply couldn't bear it. I looked round fearfully for reassurance from the other members of the Circle: surely they must be squirming too? Yet here was Sheba, flaccid arms folded, jaw locked impassively; there was Seraiah, nodding serenely.

After an interval I held my hands to my ears, not only to shut out Ahithophel's rhetoric, but because in the background the priests had begun intoning one of David's own psalms, one which I'd sat and practised on my harp, in its composer's presence. I felt I should be wrenched in two.

When once again I dared to listen, Ahithophel was subtly twisting the meanings of his own words, artfully shifting the direction of his speech, veering away from extolling the Prince's dedication towards his God, towards praising his commitment to his country, to social justice, and to the restoration of law and order throughout the land. He reminded the Hebronites that they had once before been brave and responsible enough to crown as king a man who, whilst not conforming in terms of his dynastic credentials to every person's preconceptions of what a monarch should be, was nevertheless proven to have been the right man for the job. Now, that same man's job was done, his period of ascendancy was over, and again the people of Hebron must be the ones to show the nation the way forward by acclaiming his peerless successor.

There was silence when he stopped speaking. It was a pregnant, awesome silence, spiced for Absalom and his backers with pungent expectancy, and for outsiders with disbelief. Then the priests who were in the know raised their shofars and blew on them until the very air trembled, and at their signal, the cry went up.

'Absalom is king!' bellowed Ahithophel.

'Absalom is king!' echoed Seraiah; it was the first and last time I ever heard him raise his voice.

'Absalom is king!' chorused Amasa's men, and the rebel troops, and then a multitude of anonymous voices, and all at once it seemed that the very gates of hell had burst open and all its chaos had broken loose. Men were shouting and jostling, clapping their hands, stamping their feet, or else hurling obscenities; here and there scuffles began and blows were exchanged. Our two hundred worthies from Jerusalem huddled wide-eyed as infants, not knowing what had hit them, as the ring of guards surrounding them shouldered in closer and squashed them together like sheep awaiting their shearers.

All the while, the shofars went on blaring, and when finally they ceased, the air seemed to carry on ringing with their strident tones. It took me some few moments to grasp that this was no echo, but the passing on of the signal. From village to village, from hilltop to hilltop, spreading out across the nation like ripples from a pebble cast into a pool, the trumpets would blast and the people would shout, until there was no man, woman or child between the Great Sea in the west and the eastern hills across the Jordan, between Egypt in the south and the northerly cities of the Syrians, who could claim not to have heard that the Chosen People had a newly chosen king.

As for me, I can't say whether I was shouting or not. I was too overawed by the whole scenario, half convinced that at any second the sky might fall on our heads because of what we'd done. At first I think Absalom was struck the same way. He knelt in the dust before the still-smouldering altar, both hands on the rogue royal circlet as though he feared it might vanish, his eyes drawn irresistibly upward to the thickening clouds above him.

Then in the blinking of an eye, everything changed. A giant of a man, wielding the biggest sword I've ever seen in my life, succeeded in breaking through all the cordons Amasa had set up, and made a direct lunge for Absalom. Fortunately the latter was too stunned to panic, though he had every reason to do so. He was unarmed, off guard, and hadn't had to defend himself in combat for going on ten years—if indeed he'd actually done so then. He ducked to one side in the nick of time and clung to the nearest horn of the altar in a singularly unkingly fashion, calling for sanctuary. The giant hesitated just long enough for one of Amasa's men to plunge a knife in his back. A respect for what was holy must have run deeper in the would-be regicide than it did in his intended victim—deeply enough to cost him his life.

The atmosphere had soured irrevocably. There were more than scuffles going on now. Despite the fact that most folk present were no better equipped for battle than their neophyte king was, full-scale fighting appeared to have broken out in every quarter. Men wrestled and grappled and punched one another, calling their neighbours spineless cowards or shameless traitors. Where Amasa's forces were stationed, defenceless civilians were set upon by remorseless warriors kitted out in full panoply and operating with rigidly coordinated discipline, and these worked their way steadily through the scratch battle lines of those who ventured to come against them.

Meanwhile the rebel squadrons who'd turned up from various towns in the vicinity did more damage than those under Amasa's direct control. But brandishing a motley selection of weapons, both bronze and iron, and lacking in any training or drill, they were just as likely to kill one another as they were to cut down the reactionaries. Their captains bawled out orders and had their heralds sounding trumpets, but they could barely be heard, and in any case each of the officers acted on his own initiative and so their soldiers blundered in each other's way.

Acutely aware of my own pitiful lack of experience in combat, I could think of nothing better to do than get away as quickly as possible. Just then I knew I didn't care a jot if they tore Absalom limb from limb, or Ahithophel, or Seraiah, or Sheba, or all the lot of them. (Where *was* Sheba? I was pretty sure I hadn't heard *his* voice shouting for Absalom.)

I didn't get very far. My sandal slipped on something slimy and my legs went from under me; I found myself grovelling on hands and knees through a moving forest of dusty leather and sweaty flesh. Then I saw that I was crawling through a pool of entrails, whose erstwhile owner lay across my path still half alive and groaning. But he'd owned a sword too, and his fingers were on their way to stiffening around its hilt. I prized them free and wobbled to my feet, the proud possessor of a ready-blooded blade.

I didn't get the chance to use it. As I stood there blinking the dirt from my eyes, I realized the riot was already over. The only horns blaring now were our priests' shofars, the only raised voices were hailing Absalom. Dissenters had been rounded up or silenced permanently; if any remained at large they were wise enough to keep quiet of their own accord. Absalom was enthroned upon the shoulders of two army officers, the purple cloak streaming from his shoulders and the circlet bright as fire against his white headdress and tumbling blue-black mane. He was laughing manically like some wine-sotted reveller returning from a party, delightedly grasping the hands outstretched towards him eager for the blessing of his touch. He was in his element, the centre of attention in a way he'd never known before.

The next few hours were spent feasting and toasting; the gates of David's old fortress were battered down and his retainers sent scurrying away like rats. Absalom was carried to the throne and set upon it, well-wishers bowed before him, and messengers came to announce the good news that sundry rebel factions had seized power on his behalf in centres all across the land. Then the halls and courtyards were invaded by multitudes singing and dancing and praising Adonai.

It was only when Absalom retired to spend the night in the King's private chambers that he began to stagger beneath the burden of what he'd taken on. The mere act of lying on the bed where his father had once lain with his mother, and watching me hang up his clothes in a cupboard which still contained a couple of David's ceremonial mantles, seemed to disturb him more than a little. He got up and went to the window, scanning the fading skyline with clouded eyes.

I said, 'You should get some sleep, Absalom.'

'Your Majesty.'

I stiffened; I'd been minded to try to narrow the gulf between us. He cursed under his breath and consented to lie down again, but after a few moments' deliberate tossing and turning he pummelled the pillows with his fists and sat up. I was disinclined now to ask him what was amiss, but he told me anyway.

'How can I sleep in this place? All this stuff of my father's, still here . . . do you know, this confounded bed still smells of him?'

'It can't do. He hasn't been within spitting distance of Hebron in all the years I've known him.'

'But it does, I tell you.' He rolled over angrily, and then slid right onto the floor. 'Take these covers away. Get them out of the room before their stench makes me puke.'

'Please.'

I shouldn't have said that. I hadn't planned to; no doubt it was the wine I'd knocked back, to settle my stomach, speaking through me. He sprang like a stone from a catapult and came for me, but I ducked beneath his arm, just as he'd avoided his own assailant earlier, and began furiously hauling the blankets from his bed. He picked up a water jar and smashed it against the wall, then swept all the paraphernalia from David's old dressing table onto the ground: scent pots, oil flasks, combs and ring-boxes, everything, until he stood in a spreading mess of sticky wreckage. Before he could get around to wrecking me too, misery devoured his wrath and he muffled his face in the curtains which still graced the head of the otherwise denuded bed. He was mumbling incoherently; still bristling with indignation I set to clearing up around him, obtrusively.

Although I couldn't make out more than one in four of his words, it was perfectly clear what he was talking about. He was harping on his childhood, stressing over and over how happy he'd been here, how strong had been the ties of love binding together his own little family within a family. David and Maacah had been tender as two doves with one another, and passionate as raw adolescents; he himself and Tamar had been carefree and innocent as lambs in springtime. Then he started moaning that everything had been ruined, but that nothing which had gone wrong had been his fault.

I growled, 'Then whose fault *was* it, Absalom? You used to blame Bathsheba. Now it seems she's your ally. And your consolation.'

Of course, I was just being peevish; I considered I'd good reason to be. He started wailing all the louder, complaining that he'd never had anyone he could trust, and especially not me, since he hadn't even known who I was. He cursed his good looks, he cursed his royal birth, and everything else which he held to blame for the fact that he'd never had any real friends. Naturally I dismissed every word of it as drivel. There was no way that Absalom could ever have been happy, to my mind, out of the public eye. He was like a drowning man thrashing out at the water which threatens to engulf him, and trying to drag any would-be rescuer down with him. But I had the sense to stay out of his reach. I went on scraping up the potsherds and wiping up the mess, until he got a grip on himself and began to speak lucidly.

'You won't get the better of me, you know, Micha ben Mephibosheth. You won't deflect me from my chosen course now. Men gave their lives for me today, have you considered that? I'm king of Israel, emperor of every land your confounded great-grandfather struggled to win, and more besides. I'll crush everyone who gets in my way, including you if need be.'

I wasn't going to wait around to hear any more. I stormed out of the royal apartment into the adjoining passageway, and ran at once into Sheba, lurking in the shadows by Absalom's door.

'Sheba! What the hell—' I blurted out, before he seized me by the wrist and clamped his hand over my mouth. I writhed in his grasp and would certainly have bitten him, had he not realized I was about to do so, and let me go. He held a finger to his own lips, and I submitted to him in so far as I dropped my voice to a breathy whisper.

'What the hell are you doing?'

'Listening.'

'To what? Sheba, that isn't a knife you have in your belt, is it? In God's name—'

'My lord Micha, I have to speak with you. Please come with me. It's most important.' Before I could protest any further he was striding away down the passageway, and I was too intrigued not to follow. ('My lord Micha'?) Echoing afar off were the anthems and refrains of Absalom's triumphant admirers, still revelling. We were heading the opposite way.

Only when we could no longer hear any human sound, and had gone beyond the range of the lamps that had been kindled along the walls, did Sheba stop walking and turn to face me. It was too dark to see anything save the glint of his eyes, but I could feel his stale breath hot around my mouth, and his hands gripped my tensed biceps.

'My lord Micha, this cannot go on. Absalom sitting on the throne of Saul, when he's already getting to be as moody and morose as his father is—and worse, when a hale young descendant of Saul is still alive, against all the odds! Micha, you *have* to stake a claim to what is yours, before it's too late. The situation is still confused everywhere. Make the most of it; take advantage of it! Everyone will back you.'

'Everyone? Amasa? Seraiah? Ahithophel?'

'Perhaps not them. But Shimei will, and I will. Every man of the tribe of Benjamin will.'

'What good is one tribe against eleven? Think, Sheba! You're courting disaster. Once there is schism within the Circle, every member of it will be finished.' I could hear myself arguing so logically, so rationally, whilst all the time I was falling apart inside. 'I don't *want* to be king, Sheba. Can't you understand that?'

'With respect, my lord, I'm not sure that what you *want* is of any relevance. What about your duty? What about the good of Israel?'

'Sheba, I'm not *interested* in what I ought to do. Look what the kingship did to Saul! The pressure of it shattered his sanity! Look what it's done to David! And maybe it *is* ruining Absalom already. Do you think I want that for myself too? I tell you, I'd gone through more than enough torture for one lifetime before I got my second teeth!'

'So, you know Adonai and still think you can't be king? You're one of the Few, you've met with God Almighty, you're a Shining One like Moses whose face was radiant for days afterwards, like Joshua who prayed and the sun stood still, and you still think righteousness is of no account?'

'Who told you I knew Adonai? I know him no better than you do! Why don't *you* fight Absalom for the throne? You have blood of Saul's in your veins too—as you're always so keen to remind us. *You* put your head in the noose!'

'Do *you* think that's what *I* want? Do you seriously think all this is an excuse for me to find a way of seizing power for *myself*?'

'I've no idea *what* you want. I never have had. Personally I always assumed you wanted nothing more than an excuse to spend your life in a drunken stupor, just like Shimei. I wasn't aware that right-eousness came high on *your* list of priorities, either.'

If I'd been in his shoes, I'd like as not have struck a man who spoke to me like that. But he merely snorted in frustration; after all, I guess you don't strike someone you're trying to set up as your king. With forced civility he said, 'Be reasonable, Micha. Do you think I'd want to sit on a throne which I knew I was keeping warm for someone else? I'd be looking over one shoulder at you all the time, to see if you'd decided you fancied sitting on it after all. And I'd be looking over my other shoulder at Absalom.'

'That *is* a knife, that lump in your tunic. You meant to kill us both.'

'Micha, for heaven's sake see sense, will you? I don't want to kill anybody. I just want to help Absalom. I don't think he's doing the right thing any more.'

'It's too late. He can't go back now. He's either King of Israel or a dead man. He's a self-confessed traitor.'

'You could pardon him.'

For some reason, it was only when he said this that I realized he was in deadly earnest. He really did think I should be king, and he really did consider it feasible for us to set about bringing this to pass. Sheba's change of heart might not have been quite so sudden as Shimei's, but it was every bit as complete.

I tore free and ran.

I had no idea where I was going. I couldn't go back to Absalom tonight, that was for certain. And I couldn't face losing myself among the rowdy revellers. So I blundered off into the warren of blind corridors, wanting nothing more than to be on my own. For pounding away inside my brain was the appalling question: what if Sheba is right? David once said that Adonai had a job for me, that he would never have poured out his spirit upon me if I hadn't been destined for something special. Supposing this was it?

Oh yes, I knew perfectly well how Saul had been destroyed, and I'd watched with my own eyes the inexorable decline of David. But this didn't stop the fever of ambition flaring within my breast, and that frightened me more than anything else. From early childhood I had seen myself as worthless, a nobody who could only survive by scavenging and biting, and only find meaning as someone's page or butler or squire. Now I was a man in my own right, a man of royal blood. And I feared lest that knowledge might go to my head like unwatered wine, so that I should no longer be able to control my actions any more than my thoughts, and was terrified I might end up doing something I'd regret for the rest of my days.

If only there were someone who could tell me what to do. If only Tamar were still alive; without warning I found myself pining hopelessly for her gentle smile, her warm embrace, her astute sense of humour. If she were here, she would have teased both Absalom and me, made us patch up our quarrel, made us both laugh, then everything would have been all right.

Or if only I could speak to the intimate friend I had carried in my heart as a child... if only I had never come to identify him with Adonai. Because there was no way under the stars in which I was going to risk consulting *him* in my present circumstances, pride or no pride. He would only direct me to face up to reality, and to my responsibilities. And the more I fretted, the more convinced I became that he must want me on the throne of Israel. I could conceive of no other reason for his choosing me. It had been so long since I'd let him get near me; I'd somehow forgotten that God's ways are not necessarily man's ways.

So I squatted in a bleak, cold corner with my head in my hands, and made my own decision. In the morning I would run away. As soon as it came light, I would return to Jerusalem and forget Absalom for ever. I no longer needed to serve him to give my life meaning. I would find my father, and we'd go back to Lodebar together. Without Ziba there, the place would hold no fear for us. We would live out the rest of our lives in glorious obscurity, making up for lost time by nurturing the love we'd been cheated of, and I would watch my father grow old as a happy man. Then when I had laid him to rest with his illustrious ancestors, I would go in search of Ziba again, and I would make him pay.

With my mind made up, I sank back against the wall and slept the sleep of the dead.

20

I arrived back in Jerusalem to find the city in uproar. News of the revolt had of course got there before me, and the streets were rife with contradictory rumours. I heard that the palace guards had risen up behind us and that David and all his household were dead; I heard that Absalom had been assassinated by his fellow conspirators; I heard that Bathsheba and Solomon had fled the country and gone to Egypt to raise their own army. Each and all of these things might have been true, and I'd no idea what to make of any of them. Then I heard that Saul's line was to be restored.

I nearly fainted on the spot. Where had *that* story come from? Had Shimei been going round shouting his mouth off? Had Bathsheba deliberately been scaremongering? So far as I was aware, these were the only two people in Jerusalem who could possibly have been responsible for spreading stories of my ancestry; I couldn't imagine that either my father or Ziba would have done so. Or had Sheba gone ahead and murdered Absalom, and made himself king in his place?

I didn't know which of these alternatives was worst. If the truth about my birth *had* somehow leaked out, I was undoubtedly in acute danger. Yet no one was paying the slightest attention to me. Distracted individuals scuttled back and forth in all directions, many of them carrying huge packs on their backs, but as far as they were concerned, I might have been an ant or a dead fly. Finally I succeeded in ascertaining what appeared to be the facts: David was still alive, and was preparing to leave Jerusalem along with any who cared to accompany him.

I sat down in the nearest shop doorway to get my breath back and my thoughts straightened out. I wasn't in the way—like all the rest, the shop was closed, and there was no sign of the owners. I undid my turban and wound it around my face and shoulders, desert-style, so that no one should recognize me. Certainly I couldn't risk going near the palace now. But where else could I go? I should have given myself time to think out my strategy before running out on Absalom—now I was every man's enemy.

Yet I'd been in no fit state to think clearly about anything since encountering my father. And now it was too late. I watched the refugees running by; they all looked so bewildered. I wondered if *anyone* rightly knew who controlled Jerusalem any more. Surely Absalom wouldn't be assuming that *he* did, and yet it seemed that David was poised to abandon his capital city without a fight. Nothing made sense to me.

After a while I began to feel conspicuous again, since it appeared I was the only person in Jerusalem not in a hurry. I conceived a half-baked notion of seeking asylum in Absalom's old place, but when I got there it was all cordoned off and under guard by palace staff; I'd as good as forgotten that Maacah and Miriam had been sent away to the north. As for the slaves we'd left behind to keep an eye on the place, there was no sign of them, and to this day I've never found out what became of them.

Next I drifted to the home of Shimei's kinsman, whose hospitality we'd been glad of once before, but this establishment too was virtually under siege. I was vaguely curious as to whether Shimei was inside.

But whether he was or not, the policing of his house must mean that he or one of his close relatives was known to be—or at least suspected of being—implicated in the conspiracy. I fell to speculating about just how much David's intelligence men had discovered. He no longer had Ahithophel to rely on, but there was Hushai. And of course there was Nathan. I shuddered. Like as not he knew everything.

It was then that I began to ask myself whether my father too might be in danger. David was so gullible sometimes—supposing he'd come to believe that even Mephibosheth could pose a threat to him now? The more I pondered this question, the more convinced I became that I would have to chance going to the palace after all.

I started heading that way, trying as I walked to make up my mind how best to go about gaining admission this time. However, the gates were undefended and I walked right in. Apparently David's security forces were being stretched beyond their limits, and all palace personnel not required for duty elsewhere in the city had been pulled back to guard the throneroom itself, since even within the old King's own household no one quite knew who could be trusted. There was little point in keeping outsiders at bay, if those already on the inside might turn around and knife their displaced sovereign at any moment.

When eventually I located my father, confined in that same obscure little garden with Michal, I decided that for once in my short and mixed-up life I had made the right decision. Mephibosheth was in a state of utter panic, babbling and whimpering, and the aged Michal was helpless to control or console him. I couldn't get near him either; like many of those who are weak in mind, he was remarkably strong in body and unaware of his own strength. He was also much too distraught to recognize me.

Not so Michal. Somehow she knew who I was straight away, for she kept saying my name over and over in her distress. At length I got her sitting down—she was almost as agitated as my father was—and I asked her as gently as I could manage, 'What's the matter with him? What's going on?'

At first she could tell me nothing clearly. But as I stroked her thin white hair and murmured words of reassurance she grew calmer, until she could explain: 'What you've heard is true. The King *is* leaving the city. He's taking most of the royal household with him—well, I mean most of its members whose loyalty he can still count on. Any other Jerusalem folk who are determined to stand by him, or any who are just plain terrified of Absalom, are welcome to go too, and your father was so desperate to be among them. He thinks the world of David, you know. We sent word to his steward Ziba to fetch a mule for him to ride, one from the estate. Ziba refused.'

'Refused? What right had he to refuse? Why does he think David employs him?'

'Oh Micha, it's not for me to say! Perhaps he thinks your father isn't fit to travel; and he's probably right. Who would take care of him? I'm too old to go trailing off who knows where. He'd be a liability without me.'

'I should've thought David himself was way past that sort of thing, my lady. He's been as good as bedridden for half my lifetime.'

'I know, I know, I thought so too.' Michal began shaking her head again forlornly, then glanced up suddenly as Mephibosheth's whining grew louder. He was beating his head against the wall, a habit of his which I remembered from Lodebar. I began to despair. Michal went on, 'David's had nothing but slippers on his feet since the day he got up to welcome Absalom home. But today he has boots on; Abigail has seen him. She came here to tell me how things were going with him. She said he'd had no choice but to get well—his physicians have never found anything wrong with him anyway except in his head.'

'It's amazing how rapidly you can recover when you have to,' I quoted, under my breath—Bathsheba's words. Then aloud I asked, 'But where will he go?'

'David has friends in many places,' Michal answered, and unexpectedly gave a watery smile. 'Probably more than Absalom suspects, Abigail says.'

'Then why is he giving up Jerusalem without a murmur?' I demanded. 'Absalom will come marching straight up here when he finds out. He'll be invincible once he holds the capital.'

'Please, don't. Don't talk like that.' She dissolved into despondency once more, and I cursed my impatience. 'What will become of us, Micha? Absalom will kill us all. He was such a lovely child. I can't believe this is happening.'

I held her as she wept; the sound of her sobbing seemed to wound my father almost physically. At each of her cries he let out a sharp anguished howl like someone being stoned, so that I began to be frightened of him the way I'd been as a little boy. Please calm him down, please don't let him hurt me, I caught myself saying inside my head before I realized what I was doing. Then I was more miserable than ever.

Michal wiped her eyes and whispered, 'Abigail reckons David doesn't want to see his beloved Jerusalem reduced to rubble by fighting his son for every square inch of it. Nor does he want to wind up besieged here, walled up like a ram in a pen, forced to stand by and watch while the "wolf of starvation devours the wretched remnant of his flock" as Hushai puts it. So he's all set to flee eastwards, beyond the Jordan, probably to Mahanaim, and play for time there.'

'Mahanaim, eh?' That was an irony, if ever there was one. When David had had himself crowned in Hebron, Mahanaim had been Ishbosheth's base. 'And what good is time going to be to him? The longer he leaves Absalom to dig himself in, the less chance he has of ever shifting him.'

'Hushai doesn't think so, from what Abigail tells me. He thinks the people will slowly see sense and drift back to David once it becomes clear that his son's not fit to govern.'

It's *David* who's not fit to govern, I thought fiercely. I crouched there, still holding Michal, and still watching my father shambling pathetically about the garden, every now and then pausing to claw at the soil or pull a helpless plant up by the roots. Michal said, 'Micha, *you* could go with him. With you to look after him, perhaps he *could* go with David.'

I tugged at my lip. 'I don't think that would be very wise, my lady. I've been too close to Absalom for too long; Father would hardly be safer as a result of being seen with me! And don't you know they're saying that Saul's line is to be restored? What on earth can *that* mean? But it would be so easy for someone to use it as an excuse to get rid of him. And me.'

Before she could reply, I sensed movement behind me. Half expecting an armed posse already, I spun around. But it was Abigail, dressed for travel, white-faced and earnest. Wringing her hands she exclaimed, 'Heaven preserve us, Michal, are you and Mephibosheth still here? You have to get ready at once, I mean it. You can't hang back any longer. The royal party's about to leave! David's already been out to the Mount of Olives to offer sacrifices for the journey, and returned. When he goes out of the city this time it'll be for good. It's all over for us here.'

'How often must I tell you, Abigail? I'm not coming. This is my home. I'm too old to leave it.'

'By tomorrow it will be *Absalom's* home! Do you want his unprincipled rabble to find you?'

At this Michal began weeping again, silently, the tears pouring down her once proud cheeks like autumn rain. Abigail cast me an exasperated glance, appealing for me to back her up. Devoid of suggestions, I just stared. More vexed than ever, Abigail virtually elbowed me aside, and seized her sister-wife's hands. 'Michal, if you won't think of yourself, at least think of Mephibosheth. You can't let Absalom get hold of *him*.'

'I *have* thought of Mephibosheth! I sent to Ziba for a mule for him to ride. I had to send twice before he even troubled himself to say no! How can Mephi walk to Mahanaim on those crippled feet? How can he carry his belongings?'

Hearing his name, my father shuffled closer, gaping at Michal and Abigail by turns, understanding just enough to be terrified.

'*If* Micha will help him,' said Abigail pointedly, 'He might at least make it as far as the city gates before David walks out through them.'

'What would be the use? Do you think *David* is going to have time to find transport for him in a crisis like this?'

'At least it will stop him believing what Ziba's been saying.'

'What? What are you talking about? Have *you* seen Ziba?'

'Oh, Michal, if only you'd stop crying for long enough to listen to me! It's hardly surprising Ziba wouldn't provide you with a mule. He'd sent *all* Mephibosheth's mules to the palace already, so laden with provisions that they could scarcely stand, along with his good wishes for the King's health and prosperity. They say he met David on his way back from the Mount of Olives, and told him that Mephibosheth was staying in Jerusalem by choice, waiting for the rebels to make him king.'

So this was the explanation of the rumour. And it was all my fault.

Michal crumpled in our arms. 'Why, Abigail? Why would he do that?'

'Isn't it obvious? He wants all Mephibosheth's inheritance and privileges for himself; immediately! He's no longer content to wait for him to die—no doubt he's afraid that David will discover who Mephi's true heir is. And it seems to have worked. David has given orders for all of Saul's land, and all his wealth, to be made over to Ziba. As from today.'

I was beside myself. David must be more credulous even than I'd taken him for. How could he believe such a thing of a man who had sat at his own table for years, and who was so simple, so childlike in his thinking that he barely knew what a king was? Bathsheba *must* have been involved in this heartless decision, I was sure, and it wasn't Mephibosheth she wanted to destroy. She'd been content to suffer his presence all the time he'd been at court, for she at least knew he was no threat to her precious Solomon. It was *me* she was out to disinherit, before David even found out who I was.

Though I hadn't moved or spoken, Abigail must have smelt my anger, as if my very flesh were smouldering. She rebuked me, 'Don't you think *David* isn't despairing? His heart is broken! The son he loved more than anyone or anything in the world has risen in revolt against him. He could believe *any* man capable of treason after that. This will be the death of him, Micha, can't you see? How can he go back to living as an outlaw now, in his condition? I tell you, he would have given in and let Absalom *keep* the blessed throne if it weren't for Hushai goading him, and Nathan harping on the will of Adonai.'

By now I had my head in my hands. Somewhere above me, Michal was quavering, 'Then we'll have to get Mephi to David after all. He *must* be told the truth.' I heard her struggling to her feet, then from the cracks between my fingers I watched her distractedly starting to gather together my father's ushabtis which were lined up as usual on a wall. She was too worked up to think clearly; normally she wouldn't have done such an insensitive thing without taking time to reassure him. He went back to wailing alarmingly, and tried to prize the brittle figures from her hands. One of them fell, and smashed on the pavement; Mephibosheth grovelled on all fours for the pieces, yowling, tears and snot running into his mouth. In spite of his distress, he must once again have understood more than he was given credit for, because he began screaming that David hated him, David thought he was wicked, David would never be his friend again.

It was painfully evident that we would never get him to walk ten paces in that state. I said, 'Michal, Abigail, you stay here with him for now. I'll go to David on my own and tell him the truth. Then I'll come back for you and we'll find somewhere safe to go when my father's—more himself.'

From Abigail's face I discerned that her opinion of me had risen a little, but Michal put down the ushabtis and clung to me. 'Don't leave us now, Micha! It's so dangerous out there. You'll be killed! Then where shall we be?'

'Why should I be killed? I don't think many people know who I am. Not really. Not yet.'

'But they'll recognize you as Absalom's attendant. You said so yourself.'

'Not with this scarf up round my nose. David *must* be told the truth.'

'But where *can* we go that will be safe? There's nowhere. In a civil war you can trust no one. I should know.'

For an interval none of us spoke, for it seemed there was nothing constructive to be said. Then Abigail made a suggestion. 'David is leaving ten concubines behind to take care of the palace. I know which of *those* I can trust. They may be able to hide you somewhere in the cellars or the slaves' quarters. Perhaps Absalom won't think to look for you inside what will be his own stronghold.'

I pointed out dubiously, 'You came here saying we had to leave at once.'

'Leave this apartment, yes. And so you must. But outside of the palace, who *can* we trust? Do *you* know of anyone, Micha? Because I don't. I can't recall the last time I walked in the city or the fields.

Don't forget: I'm the wife of a king. I have less freedom than the meanest of his slaves.'

From the fleeting wistfulness in her eyes and voice, I wondered if she didn't rue the day she'd married him. For since the arrival of Bathsheba, those who'd been supplanted would scarcely have been worse off if their lord had divorced them.

I said, 'Ten concubines to garrison the holy citadel! David must finally have flipped over the edge.'

'To take care of it, Micha, not to garrison it. I told you. He'd rather Absalom strutted right in here and strewed the walls with his standards than razed them to the ground. He knows Absalom isn't going to butcher ten buxom young beauties.'

I ground my teeth. Abigail had known Absalom even longer than I had. Then something Abigail had said fell into place in Michal's beleaguered mind and she implored her, 'Aren't *you* going to stay with us?'

'Until Micha gets back from seeing David I will. Beyond that, how can I? My place is with my husband.'

Michal didn't argue. It was as though she'd forgotten that David was her husband, too.

I announced, 'I'd better get going.' Then I patted Michal's hands and added, 'I'll come back. I promise.'

As things turned out, I'd no trouble catching up with the royal entourage. Even with the full complement of the Thirty, David's personal bodyguard, marching in its van armed to the teeth, it could scarce make headway through the crowds. By now well-nigh every man, woman and child in Jerusalem must have taken to the streets, and even in the time I'd spent conferring with Michal and Abigail, the atmosphere had noticeably soured. In among the terrified masses—who probably cared little whose subjects they were, so long as they and their loved ones could live quiet lives—prowled menacing bands of aggressive-looking youths brandishing clubs and bawling slogans for Absalom.

It soon became inescapably obvious that I wasn't going to get within a stone's throw of David himself. I did at least manage to get where I could see him—which was more than most folk could have claimed—by climbing on a wall and up into a tree whose branches hung out from someone's yard. And he was indeed walking on his own two feet, unassisted. But he was so thin that his clothing drooped, and it was so long since his flesh had seen the sun that it was sallower than beeswax. He wore none of the regal accoutrements, just a drab woollen robe which he had torn in token of grief. Exactly what he grieved for, I couldn't be sure, but the added lines on his face showed that he was deeply troubled.

To his left and to his right walked Joab and Abishai, neither of them so much younger than their uncle, yet both of them still in the vigour of their manhood. It was true, though, that not all of their bulk was made of muscle any more. Perhaps they would welcome even a civil war, if things came to it; provided that their bodies weren't so far out of condition as to be past redemption.

While I was contemplating Joab's enlarged midriff and the way it pushed his breastplate out like a tilted shutter, David stumbled. Joab sprang to his aid by instinct, but David repulsed him brusquely. It wasn't for want of a mount that *he* wasn't riding, I concluded; he had something to prove.

It dawned on me then that not one of the ousted King's noble companions was riding. He had some of the grandest personages in Jerusalem with him (and would have had more, had his son not kidnapped them): Zadok and Abiathar the chief priests, Jehoshaphat the court recorder and herald, Hushai, Ahithophel's assistant—and now presumably successor—not to mention the eldest of Absalom's half-brothers, Adonijah, with several of the younger ones too, and their mothers. All of them were walking, as though this were some pilgrimage or funeral cortège; and perhaps indeed it was both.

When I realized that nearly all of David's wives were with him, and most of his concubines, and any of their respective children who were old enough not to need carrying, I found myself looking for Bathsheba. It took me a while to place her, because as ever, she wasn't with the other women. She was walking alongside a white-bearded patriarch wearing a plain homespun brown cloak—the mark of the sons of the prophets. Nathan, the most revered seer since Samuel, Nathan, the mouthpiece of Adonai no less, consorting with *her*! I wished he were close enough to spit on.

For all of a sudden I felt sure that I *did* know how Bathsheba's mind worked. I knew exactly why she had come to Absalom the very night that Ahithophel had gone away. She might not have known all that much about the conspiracy, but she'd known that it existed. And she was utterly convinced that once Absalom rose in open revolt against David, he was finished. Since this was precisely what she wanted, she dared not run the risk of him abandoning his plans now that Ahithophel wasn't there for him to lean on.

No doubt Absalom would be expecting Bathsheba to remain in Jerusalem so that he could lean on her instead. He was going to be very disappointed.

But there was no sign of her precious Solomon. Perhaps he walked with the other children, to escape recognition; I scanned the faces of those I could see, but none looked more arrogant than the rest, or more evil. Perhaps she'd sent him away elsewhere for his protection.

Just then a rise in the noise level behind me drew my attention away. Twisting around in my tree I saw that a second cavalcade was approaching to join the first. It proceeded from the direction of the Tabernacle, and at the head of it marched a company of priests, four of them bearing what could only be the Ark of the Covenant hung from poles across their shoulders.

Of course I'd never seen it. Normally only the High Priest ever did so, and even he was only granted the privilege once a year, on the Day of Atonement. But I'd had it described to me by Tamar, when she'd told me the stories a boy's father ought to teach him. It was smaller than I'd imagined; it might have fitted inside any one of the storage chests Absalom had brought from Geshur. But the lid, and the feet, and the poles, and the rings from which it hung were leafed in pure gold, and the two winged creatures, which sat facing one another across the top, I knew were made of gold all through. The very sight of this object, as holy as it was priceless, caused the crowds to shrink back.

But then I saw how many soldiers followed on behind it. There were thousands of them, all chanting for David, all fully equipped with the latest iron weaponry. Something knotted up in my belly. Amasa must have been significantly over-optimistic in assessing the percentage of the armed forces which he and Absalom would be able to call upon. Just *how* significantly remained to be seen.

When the two columns converged, a halt was called while brief discussions took place. I was far too far away to have a hope of hearing what was said, but I could see David himself deep in conversation with Zadok and Abiathar and one of the priests who'd been carrying the ark. The latter was gesticulating with mounting urgency; David was shaking his head; Zadok and Abiathar were manifestly intervening on the side of their colleague. At length the priests and the ark were integrated among David's household, and the troops who had accompanied them joined onto the end of the original procession. The priests appeared satisfied, David more deeply troubled than before, his shrunken shoulders hunched and stooping.

I found it curious, though, that the presence of the ark amongst his followers should give David fresh cause for concern. Wasn't the thing a symbol of the protection of Adonai? What more could any fugitive ask for? Certainly it would ensure he experienced no further problems with the crowds. No doubt many of them were old enough to have borne witness to the chilling fate of Uzzah, the only Israelite since Moses who had ever dared touch it directly.

David's way should have been clear now to pass out of the city, but before he could do so his expanded company was once again brought to a standstill. For a reason which wasn't at first at all clear, pandemonium had broken out among Ziba's pack-animals. They were snorting and kicking and bucking and would not be driven forward for anything. Then a stone hit one of their handlers on the temple and felled him, and the mules' bizarre behaviour was explained.

It might be thought incredible that a solitary meddler could cause such consternation, but positioned as he was behind a parapet on one of the few buildings in Jerusalem more than one storey high, there was little that anyone could do against his barrage. He must have collected a goodly supply of pebbles in advance, for they came one after another like the harbingers of a hailstorm, striking indiscriminately amongst women and children as well as amongst mules and muleteers; few were directed at the palace menfolk, for most wore helmets and breastplates and small stones would have done them little damage.

But David himself was horribly vulnerable, hence the hold-up while someone fetched him his armour from the baggage train; in the meantime Joab stood over him with an upturned shield. Abishai barked at one of his subordinates to have the sniper caught and summarily disposed of, but the issuing of this command brought down a hail of curses along with the missiles, and when I heard the wine-emboldened voice I knew at once who it belonged to.

'You may silence me, but you'll never silence the cry of Justice, David ben Jesse! How many murders have you sanctioned already? Criminal! Butcher! What about Ishbosheth? What about Abner? Saul's kinsmen, both of them! And what about the seven you betrayed to the Gibeonites? Innocent men, devout worshippers of

260

God, every one! You stole Saul's kingdom and you did your level best to wipe out his family—but you'll never succeed, you'll never be rid of him! If only you knew what I know, ben Jesse! But it wouldn't do you any good. You took what belonged to Adonai's anointed, so now it will be taken from you, are you listening? Your wanton, wastrel son will get everything you own. Yes, the throne of Israel will be desecrated, it will pass to the son you got upon a witch-woman, a pagan, because you are a dog, and worse than a dog!'

Half a dozen soldiers were hammering on the door at ground level below where Shimei stood—quite visible now, swinging precariously out over the street—but it was locked and barred and they couldn't get it open. When finally they succeeded in kicking it to pieces, Shimei ran from his rooftop onto a neighbour's, across a plank which he then threw down the drop behind him.

'I'll follow you right across the Jordan, do you hear me? I'll curse you till I unhinge your mind! You'll never be free of me! Cut out my tongue, and my lips will still curse you! Seal my lips, and I'll still throw these stones! Cut off my hands, cut off my head, and my spirit will haunt you, and drag you down to Sheol to be with me! And you needn't think they'll bring your tainted bones back to Jerusalem for burial. You'll be left for the vultures in a foreign land. You'll never see Zion again!'

Joab and Abishai were indescribably enraged. They set archers to taking pot shots at the roof, but Shimei was out of sight once more and all they had to aim for was a disembodied voice. David himself stood calm, even impassive. I couldn't tell if it was faith or fatalism that braced him. Perhaps he could even feel pity for Shimei, the poor pugnacious youth who had once been his son's friend and who now ranted like a prophet and fought alone, drunken and mad. But all around the silent David, riot was breaking out worse than in Hebron, so that I began to fear I would never get down from the tree with my life. Then I saw Ziba.

I don't know how I hadn't seen him before. He was standing not a spearlength from David, rubbing shoulders with courtiers and aristocrats, men who'd been comrades of the King when Ziba himself had been nothing but a slave. And as I gazed in disgust upon his sneering face and corpulent figure, swathed voluminously in tawdry gold-flecked robes, he saw me too. I was partially hidden by criss-crossing branches, and still had my kerchief round my nose, but from the way he stiffened, and from the loathing that fogged up his eyes, I knew he'd recognized me.

As ever, the sight of him drove all reason from my head. My mind went into spasms, and I wound up convinced he was going to have me dragged down from my vantage point and denounced, for some fictitious crime, to the gullible old King. I know now that he wouldn't have done it. The last thing he wanted was to provide me with an opportunity to get near David and tell him my story; as Abigail had said, it was of paramount importance to him that David should never find out that Mephibosheth had a son. Ziba must already be thanking his lucky stars that Shimei hadn't been more specific in his references to the survival of Saul's line, and praying that he wouldn't choose to be, further on. But at the time I could see none of this. All I could see was that Ziba's hatred of me was even stronger than his greed. I had humiliated him in his own house and before his own servants, and I knew he would try to pay me back for that, regardless of what it cost him.

So with one reckless leap, I was on the ground and running, vowing as I ran that David *would* learn the truth, that I *would* get back what was mine, swearing afresh that I *would* have vengeance on Ziba before *he* got vengeance on *me*. For I was adamant now that the debt which he owed me could be paid for with nothing less than his life, since that was what he'd first stolen from me: my very self, and my self-respect, long before he stole my property. And there was no way I could exact that penalty in public, and at a time like this.

21

Michal, my father and I were installed by Abigail in a wing of the palace I hadn't even known about. You reached it by means of a hundred stone steps winding round and down from a room in the harem which hadn't been occupied since the days of the Jebusites. Abigail locked the door behind us as she left, promising to give the key to the youngest of the ten concubines, a simple, warm-hearted girl she'd befriended when David had introduced them on the newcomer's arrival some months earlier. I'd never met this girl myself, but Abigail assured us that she was too warm-hearted to forget us, and too simple to want to betray us.

Our dismal new apartment wasn't quite a cellar; since the palace was built on terraces, we had windows and fresh air despite being so far below the main residential levels. But we hadn't a courtyard, or even a door to the world outside, and the windows were high up and barred and in any case too small to climb out of. I wondered what such quarters could ever have been used for.

Whatever the apartment's original purpose had been, it felt like a prison to me, and reminded me much too keenly of the small dark places which had scared me as a child. I would wander disconsolate from room to room, gazing out at the greying autumn sky, stretching my hands between the window bars to feel the heavy spots of the season's first rains. We were well provided for: food and water were left for us—though we never saw who brought this—our pails were emptied, and clean clothes fetched along every other day. So we'd no complaints about Abigail's arrangements on our behalf.

But I'd never been so morbidly depressed since leaving Lodebar. Immured in semi-darkness with a frightened old woman and a drooling cripple, I feared I must go mad; for there could be no doubt but that Mephibosheth's condition was deteriorating. He whimpered for most of each day and a good half of each night, his moans echoing through the sparsely furnished chambers as though some subterranean monster had been incarcerated with us. So much for my coming back to Jerusalem to whisk my father away to freedom.

In fact while Michal grew more and more fearful of what might happen when Absalom turned up, I found myself secretly looking forward to his arrival. Not only was I missing my freedom; in spite of myself, I was also missing him. There was a curious sense of loss deep inside me, and it took me some time to accept what it was, because it was something I had least expected. But now I no longer needed Absalom for status, I found I missed him as a friend. I missed his bright smile, his light-hearted banter, his boundless optimism... it was all too easy for me to forget I hadn't seen him like that for years, and that so much now stood between us.

But days went by, and he didn't come. Perhaps he'd decided he preferred to rule from Hebron; or perhaps he'd already been defeated, and David was eating and sleeping and walking about above our heads as though nothing had ever happened to change things.

We never received any news, but perhaps our gentle jailer expected us to be there a while. For after the first few days we began to discover, placed beside the tray with our regular rations on it, scrolls for me to read, gaming boards and counters for my father, and one time there was a hand-loom with yarn for Michal to amuse herself weaving.

She didn't use it. She just sat in a high-backed chair staring vacantly out of the window, and barely ate, while Mephibosheth played with his new games and his ushabtis and tried vainly to involve her. I think she had decided that whoever won the war, the three of us would be the losers; as for me, I'd almost lost sight of who we were hiding from. I was sure now that if I could get David on his own, or even Absalom, for long enough, we could iron out our misunderstandings. I didn't want to be king; it was just a matter of convincing whichever of the two of them came out on top that I'd be no threat politically so long as I got my material inheritance back. It might take a little longer to convince Sheba of the modest extent of my ambitions, but after less than a week spent mouldering in our man-made Sheol I was inclined to consider that even this might not be impossible.

For food we were normally given bread and dried fruit, and sometimes cured meat or stewed vegetables; there was plenty to stave off hunger, but little of it was fresh, because the concubines would scarcely be any freer to go to market than we were.

Then on what must have been about the fifth day of our confinement I went upstairs at the usual hour, to find three bowls of soup waiting there for us—steaming, spiced, and brimming with cucumbers. Perhaps it was Shabbat, I reflected, carrying the tray carefully down the narrow twisting staircase, and this explained the reason for our unexpected treat? It was so easy to lose track of time down here, I couldn't be sure if it was the Sabbath day or not.

We tasted nothing strange about the soup as we tucked into it. This too was no doubt because it felt like forty years since we'd had anything so highly seasoned. Its rich, tart flavour and heartening warmth tempted even Michal; she didn't have much, but rather more than she'd been having of other things lately. Then we heard someone shouting from very close by.

I rushed to the window and swung up onto the sill, hooking one elbow round the bars and straining hopelessly to see down the other side. But just as I did so, the someone jumped up, and it was a boy perhaps eight or nine years old, yelling frantically, 'Don't eat any more of that! It's poisoned, you must make yourselves sick! I'll get the key and come round to help you.' Then he was gone.

Even as I got down I could feel my stomach cramping, though at that stage it might well have been suggestion. But the lad had seemed so earnest, it never occurred to me not to take him at his word. Knowing I could help none of us if I saw to myself last, I rammed my fingers down my throat till I was retching, and coughing my guts up onto the floor; soon there was a presence beside me and a voice saying, 'Here. Drink this. It'll make it easier,' and I turned to see the boy crouched unflinching in the mess I'd made. Feeling too ill now to do anything but obey, I drained the flask he was holding to my lips; it was worse than drinking blood, and the rest of my soup came up all over his hands. He barely winced.

I managed to stay on my feet long enough to help him with my father. The boy had brought two more flasks of whatever vile concoction he'd given me, and somehow he coaxed Mephibosheth into drinking one. For someone so young, our rescuer was remarkably patient, and for someone not used to my father, remarkably sensitive. Soon the poor man was spluttering and spewing, clutching at his belly and whining with pain. Thankfully after that he passed out—his constitution wasn't as hardy as mine, and the poison had been in him longer—and we laid him on his bed to recover. The boy touched my hand lightly, and said,

265

'Don't worry. He'll be all right.' I gulped and nodded, and sat down before I fell down.

But neither one of us could induce Michal to drink. She insisted that she'd hardly had any of the soup, and that if we made her sick like that, it would be the death of her anyway. But she said she was tired, and would go to bed. Thus relieved of the presence of both my cell-mates, I was free to devote my attention to the newcomer.

He was an odd-looking boy, very slim, with fine pointed features and hair unstyled and straight, and slick as black oil poured over his head. His eyes were too large, liquid and solemn and heavy-lidded, but he smiled very slightly when he caught me watching him.

'Don't *you* want to lie down?' he asked, getting on with clearing up as though he did it every day. 'The stuff I made you drink can hurt more than the poison. I can do this alone. I don't mind.'

I did feel rough, but the last thing I wanted was to lie down. I said, 'What I want is to know who tried to kill us. And how you came to find out.'

He said, 'It doesn't matter now. They didn't succeed.'

'It matters to me,' I persisted, then my head cleared and I blurted, 'Bathsheba! It was Bathsheba who did this, wasn't it? Or at least, she arranged it.'

He didn't reply, just went on mopping up, with the pall of smooth hair falling over his face. Somewhat ungraciously, considering what he'd done for us, I crawled forward, grabbed him by the shoulders and swung him round to face me, demanding that he answer me, and truthfully.

But he wasn't in the least perturbed by my bullying. He said simply, 'These are pieces of wild gourd, not cucumber; and I wouldn't like to guess at what else might be in there. But I reckon if you hadn't coughed it up you'd have been dead by morning. You'll be ill enough as it is; some of the badness will still be inside you. Please. Go to bed. I'll see that the others are looked after.'

I might well have had another go at him, but for the fact that all at once I was seized by a desperate desire to relieve myself. It was the same after that for half the night. It was the same with my father too, except that he wasn't quick enough, and we had to pile his soiled garments and bedclothes in a corner out of sight and wrap him in spare blankets. I went to sleep exhausted once he was settled. When I woke it was light, the soiled things had been replaced, and the boy had vanished.

I lay for a while on my pallet without so much as trying to sit up; partly because I felt too fragile to move, and partly because I needed to think. I was in no two minds about the fact that Bathsheba had been behind this attempt on our lives. The fact that she'd left the city with David was presumably an integral part of her plan; her alibi, no less. There were ten concubines and their children still in the palace, and only one of the women had been willing to help Abigail, whilst any or all of the others might actually be in Bathsheba's pay. And it was quite conceivable that Abigail's friend was so simple, she'd given us away. Yet despite all this, and despite what I'd seen for myself of Bathsheba's enmity towards me, I was still finding it hard to credit that she would dare or indeed bother to eliminate me literally. Perhaps I should have been flattered that she must consider me so dangerous; perhaps I was even giving her and Solomon sleepless nights. The thought of this was gratifying, but of no help in explaining who our young visitor had been, nor how he'd come to learn of Bathsheba's intentions.

Just as I was reluctantly reaching the conclusion that I would have to try to get up and see how my companions were, our little friend reappeared. I didn't hear him come in, but as if he'd materialized in answer to my thoughts, he was there kneeling beside me with one hand on my brow, and a bowl in the other.

I groaned, 'Not more food. I couldn't face it.'

'It's not food,' he said. 'Well, not exactly. It's water, with salt and honey in it. You must drink all you can, to get back the strength you've lost.'

He made me sit up and take the bowl between my fingers; I was shocked at how giddy I felt when no longer lying flat. Uncomfortable at being made such a fuss of by a boy half my age, I asked him, 'What about the others? Shouldn't you be seeing to them too?'

'What makes you think I haven't? Your father will be all right, as I told you before. I've given him something to make him sleep again. It'll be best for him to get over the worst of it without knowing anything about it.'

I leaned back against the wall, to slow the room's spinning. 'How come you didn't do the same for me?'

'You said last night that you wanted to talk.'

'So I did. Well yes—I do.' Now my head was supported, things looked more stable again, and I focussed on his thin, indoor face. I said, 'Aren't you rather young to be practising witchcraft?'

He shrugged. 'There's nothing magical in the use of herbs and flowers and things. And so long as you know what you're doing there's no risk in it.'

'And how do you know what you're doing? How come you're so well versed in such matters?'

'What else is there to do when you're walled up all the time in a pit like this?' He waved one slender arm vaguely, but he meant the whole palace, not our dingy rooms. 'I read, I help the women in the herb gardens, I grow things from seeds when I can get them, I collect things when people don't want them, I—make studies.'

I must have failed to look suitably impressed, for he clammed up then, and took to playing with his hair. After an awkward pause I asked, 'What about—my great-aunt?' I caught myself before giving too much away; whatever else he knew, it was still possible he didn't know who we were.

'Michal?' he returned without hesitation, sweeping away my doubts on that score. 'I'm afraid things aren't so good. I think she's decided to die.'

Of course, I'd thought the same, but to hear him put it so bluntly offended me somehow, and brought back piquant memories of Tamar. My dismay came out in indignation. 'What a thing to say! As if anyone could "decide to die"! Anyway, she can't. Who would look after my father? I can't do it.'

The boy shrugged again. 'Naomi who looks after all three of you now might be persuaded.'

'The girl who brings our food, and the games and the scrolls? We haven't even seen her yet.'

'She brings your food, but not the other things. I brought those.' He finally shook the hair from his brow and looked me in the eyes; his own evinced a curious blend of confidence and shyness, wisdom and innocence, shrewdness and naïvety.

I demanded, 'Who are you?'

'I'm sorry. I should have said.' He seized my hands as if we'd only now met. 'In full my name is Jedidiah. But you can call me Jed.'

'Jed ben . . .?'

'Ben David, of course. We're all ben Davids in the harem. Or our mothers have to pretend we are.'

'And who is your mother? Not—what did you call her?—Naomi? No, I thought not. So how did you know we were even here?'

'Oh, everyone mothers everyone else in the harem,' he returned blithely. 'No one can keep a secret for very long. Especially those who aren't very clever.' He grinned, then turned grave again at once. 'Don't tell Naomi I said that. But I know who you are. I'm glad to have met you.'

He offered me his hand again in solemn mock-formality, then scrambled to his feet. 'I have to go now; I'll be missed.'

I said, 'That's not why you're going. You don't want me asking you any more questions.'

'Maybe.' He shook his head, and the hair slid back across his eyes. 'But I know how long I can disappear for, safely. I'll see you later.' And again he was gone.

Next I tried standing up, but it was a mistake. So I lay back on my pallet sifting through the new pile of scrolls which I saw Jedidiah had left me, and I made myself drink more of the honeyed salt water as he'd prescribed. Most of the scrolls comprised sacred texts, which didn't really interest me; or rather, they threatened to raise ghosts in my head which I preferred to leave undisturbed. The others were covered in rounded, uneven letters which I soon realized were Jedidiah's own. But they told no childish stories, nor were they exercises such as tutors set for copying. He'd composed dozens of descriptions of the different kinds of plants you might find growing on the hills around Jerusalem, the kind of thing most folk would simply refer to as grass. Here and there were dried pressed flowers glued onto the papyrus with resin. After the list of plants came a similar catalogue of butterflies, but there were no specimens to look at here. Either he'd not had the heart to capture any, or else he'd had no opportunity.

In the afternoon he came back, and this time he stayed longer. He was still disinclined to talk much about himself, but happy to lecture me endlessly about the things he'd written on his scrolls. Now and again he slipped away to check on Michal and Mephibosheth; both slept on, which in Michal's case was ominous because he hadn't given her any medicine.

'I think it would be better if we had her moved upstairs,' he said. 'She's not going to get well, Micha, but she might wake up. There ought to be a woman with her all the time.'

I didn't know how we could move her; normally I would have lifted her quite easily, but not the way I felt just then. I still hadn't taken any solid food, and still couldn't face any.

So he had me let Naomi come downstairs, and I saw her for the first time: a plain, bulky, lustreless creature with slightly cast eyes and a vacuous but genuine smile. I wondered how David had come to acquire her, but she certainly came in useful now. I think she'd have been big enough to carry me, let alone Michal, who was as light and shrivelled as a fallen sparrow. I knew I would never see the old lady again.

But I saw more and more of Jed. In the days that followed, he spent whole mornings or afternoons with me: we talked, we read, we played senet, we worked out tunes on his flute or his child-sized harp. And still Absalom didn't come, but at least Jed would bring news now. It seemed that our rebel king was showing no signs of wanting to leave Hebron; the novelty of his exalted status hadn't yet worn off, prolonged as it had been by lively celebrations and a surfeit of alcohol.

Meanwhile David had arrived in Mahanaim, where he was gradually amassing supplies and support, though apparently not all of his army had yet crossed over the Jordan. No doubt Ahithophel would be reaching his wits' end with Absalom, for he ought to have occupied his father's capital long before now.

Jed also told me that the Ark had been returned to the Tabernacle. I'd seen for myself that David hadn't been happy about taking it with him, and apparently had insisted after all on its being brought back even before they'd got it outside the city. I asked Jed why he thought this might be.

'Everyone calls Jerusalem the City of David,' he replied. 'But my tutor says it's the City of Adonai, so that is where the symbol of his presence must remain.'

'And if Absalom takes it?'

Jed smiled darkly. 'My tutor says Adonai is capable of looking after himself. And he says it's for Adonai to decide who—"reigns as regent for the Divine".'

'Who *is* your tutor, Jed?'

'His name's Nathan. He's a prophet.'

'Yes, I know who he is . . . Did he make the harp for you too, and tutor you in that?'

Jed's lips went taut, and he squirmed a little, as my questions were again becoming too personal for his liking. Eventually he answered stiffly, 'Nathan gave the harp to me, but he didn't make it. It was a present from my father; he'd heard I wanted one. I think he wanted to teach me himself.' Then his smile was back and he said, 'Nathan can play almost as well as my father, or so everyone says. And he's probably a better teacher.'

'You're very lucky,' I enthused cautiously. 'There can't be many boys who are so privileged as to be getting their education from the holiest man in Israel. Or does Nathan tutor *all* the boys in the harem these days?'

'He doesn't teach *anyone* here at the moment. He's with my father. We're all on holiday.' He stretched luxuriously, but I was sure it wasn't study he was glad to be free of, just the prescriptive nature of schoolwork, maybe.

I said, 'You haven't answered what I asked you, you know,' but he slipped out once more, alleging that he must see to Mephibosheth.

My father mended slowly, the more so I think because he missed Michal. Sometimes he would shuffle round calling her name, but I didn't know what to tell him. Then one day I caught Jed sitting with him, holding his hands, explaining so slowly and so gently that she was at peace now, young and beautiful again, reunited with her beloved brother Jonathan, his father. Mephibosheth was listening, entranced; I crept away, too shamed to disturb them.

But afterwards I made Jed sit with *me*, and I asked him, 'Was all that true? Is that what happens to us all when we die? Did Nathan tell you that, or someone else?'

'I'm not sure if it happens to everyone. You have to worship Adonai, I think. But Nathan knows no more than the next man. He says it hasn't been revealed to us yet—the whole truth about God, and about life and death, I mean. I just study the scriptures and get my own ideas. And I learn my father's psalms, and think about the words.'

Now it was my turn to clam up. Jed was nursing his harp, brushing his fingers idly across the strings; I flattened my palm against them to deaden the sound.

'What's the matter, Micha? I thought you liked my playing.'

'I do. I mean, I did.'

'You're shaking! What is it?'

'It's nothing,' I lied, but then I couldn't even endure the sight of him holding the thing, and I snatched it from his hands, telling him to go away and leave me alone. But he wouldn't; he feared I was ill again and kept pestering to be told what was the matter, so that in the end I had to admit to the memories he'd stirred within me. Little by

271

little the whole lot came out: my wretched childhood in Lodebar, when my identity and indeed my very name had been stolen from me; the love I'd learned from Tamar, and shared with Absalom and with Maacah; the hours I'd spent with David, until the fateful day when I'd sung him his own Song of the Bow.

But I still kept two things back: what I'd suffered from Ziba, and what I'd experienced of Adonai. Thankfully Jed was too unsullied to stand any chance of guessing at the former, but as for the latter, he put two and two together straight away from the clues he'd gleaned. He stared at me astounded, and whispered, 'You know Adonai? You? You're—a Shining One?'

I sniggered bitterly. 'It's faded so much?'

'You don't understand, Micha. It's what I've always wanted. You had what I only dream of, and—you're telling me you just threw it away?'

'Well, you go on and find it,' I retorted. 'And you keep it. I don't want it back.'

'Why ever not? If what Nathan says is true, you had a friend who would never let you down, who you could always talk to when you were lonely, who would guide you, who had a special job for you to do, if only you'd bothered to find out what it was—'

'So this is something else you claim to know all about, is it? You know nothing, Jed! I'm sorry, but I mean it. Saul knew Adonai— and Saul was my own great-grandfather, let me remind you—and look where it got him. Nathan knows Adonai, so they say, and so you say, yet he's in league with the wickedest woman in Israel and means to set her brat on the throne once she's disposed of Absalom and me. And there's David himself . . . can you believe your father was once a hero? Because if I were your age, I couldn't! Adonai has brought him nothing but misery. You're too young to have witnessed his decline—but *I've* seen it. And I saw what it did to Amnon, and Tamar, and Maacah . . . and Absalom. It broke my heart.'

Jed didn't answer. He went on staring at me, and I couldn't tell if he was loving me or hating me; all at once I felt like a worm. How could I not have realized how much my friendship already meant to him; how could I have trampled all his dreams beneath my feet? He looked so hurt, so lost, and I didn't know what to say. Would there never be anyone I could risk growing close to without the whole thing turning sour? I opened my mouth, hoping something positive might come out, but he hushed me.

'You're the one who doesn't understand, Micha. It wasn't Adonai who brought Saul down. And I don't know what you're thinking about Nathan and—and Solomon's mother, because it certainly isn't true, and it doesn't explain why he says that Solomon must be king. And what right have you to speak of my father's—decline? What right has anyone? He's out there beyond the Jordan raising an army, Micha, and he'll lead it himself, if General Joab will let him.' Then he saw my remorse, and reached out to take my hand. 'I'm sorry too. You'll understand one day, I'm sure you will. But tell me how to do it; tell me how to contact Adonai.'

'Oh Jed, I don't know any more! I've spent half my life trying to get away from him.'

'I'll wager you've not managed.'

'How dare you! How dare you suggest I . . .' Then I saw the hurt in his eyes again, and again I cursed my hard heart and loose tongue. I muttered, 'Perhaps no one can escape the hand of the Lord once he's been touched. But the knowledge of God isn't for everyone. Not yet. He has to choose you, he has to call you for a special purpose, like you said.'

'He has done, Micha. Nathan is convinced of it. Yet he says he can't release the power in me, and I'm not sure why. Perhaps the right person has to pray for me. I think it's you.'

I began to protest, but he was still staring at me, pleading, as though he was the one locked in a cell, and it was I who held the key. I knew he'd got it all wrong; that if Adonai truly wanted him, there was no need for me or anyone else to do anything. Jed himself was the right person to release the spirit within him. But he said, 'My father helped *you* to be reborn, I know he did. Nathan told me about the boy Zohar who made such beautiful music and radiated light like the sun. That was you, wasn't it?'

'Jed, if David told Nathan all about me, he'll have said that *he* didn't do *anything*. Because he didn't, not really.'

'Then will you do that same nothing for me?'

'You're spouting nonsense. It wouldn't work. Nothing would happen.'

'Well if nothing happens, it can't do any harm, can it? And I'm not spouting nonsense. It's been coming clearer to me all the time we've been talking. Now I've never been more sure of anything in my life. Come on. Put your hands on my head. Just say one prayer for me.'

He'd closed his eyes already; he knelt by my mattress with his face and his palms upturned, waiting. Grinding my aversion between my teeth, I laid my hands on his sleek head—what else could I have done?—but I did nothing else. I didn't pray, either aloud or in silence; I didn't even pretend to.

But it happened none the less, so I knew I'd been right. The heat, the tears, the laughter, the ecstasy, the radiance on his face so intense I could scarcely look . . . in short, everything which had happened to me, and more besides. For soon he was praying aloud for himself, in a heavenly tongue that made no sense to me, just as David had once done in my presence years ago. Before long the joy was too great for him to bear, and he fell back on the floor, abandoned, oblivious. I sat and watched him, but for myself felt nothing. There was nothing I would have allowed myself to feel.

When at last he came back, there was no need for him to ask me what had happened. Still convinced he had me to thank for it, he flung his arms around me and lay with his head in my lap as though I were his father, not his friend; if his father had had anything about him, I thought grimly, he would have been the one to act the part of midwife at Jed's rebirth. Resigning myself to enduring his misplaced gratitude until he could bring himself to leave, I leant against the wall and closed my eyes; I still wasn't well. So I was half asleep when his voice said, 'Micha? Micha, wake up. There's something I must tell you.'

I mumbled, 'You don't have to explain. I know how you're feeling.'

'Of course you do; that's not what I mean.'

Grudgingly I opened my eyes. 'Well, go on then.'

'I've never said this to a living soul before; I was always told not to. But—well, I know I can trust you.'

He paused, and took a great deep breath; I wished he'd get whatever it was over with, and let me have some rest. He must have known what I was thinking, because when he began again his words came in a gushing torrent.

'You see, Micha, I'm just like you were. I've always been hidden away in secret in case something happened to me; kept all on my own, away from other boys, never let out to play with them, not even allowed to eat the same food they ate. My mother paid Ruth to look after me all this time, even before she left with my father—Ruth's another of his concubines, you know, but cleverer than Naomi,

274

worse luck for me—and she hadn't to let me out of her sight. She didn't always manage, and these days she lets me have my own way when Mother's not breathing down her neck, because I know how to get round her. But if Mother knew I was here with you, if she knew how many times I'd given Ruth the slip, when she thought this was the safest place to hide me . . . Micha, you mustn't tell this to *anyone*, but you must have guessed by now. My name *is* Jedidiah—that's what Nathan told my father he must call me, because it means "Beloved of the Lord". But my mother calls me Solomon.'

22

That very afternoon we got word that Absalom was on the move. He was reported to be heading straight for Jerusalem, with roughly half of what had once been his father's standing army in tow. In addition he had a sizeable but ill-disciplined auxiliary force consisting of whoever wished to belong to it, and equipped with whatever weapons and armour its troops had found to hand.

Jed and I spent the remaining daylight hours up on the roof, looking out for his coming; as Jed was at pains to point out now that we'd nothing more to hide from each other, why should we need to hide from anyone? We were friends, so he would see to it that Bathsheba didn't harm me or Mephibosheth, and I would ensure that Absalom didn't find out that he and Solomon were one and the same.

It was true that Bathsheba could do little more mischief to us now, because even if Ruth tried to contact her regarding the failure of her poison plot, Absalom would be at the palace gates long before the message got through. Then *he* would be the one calling the tune, at least for a while. So far as Absalom himself was concerned, Jed had suddenly conceived a wild notion that he might well choose to butcher *all* of David's remaining sons indiscriminately, so it would hardly matter if he *did* find out which one was Solomon. But I *did* warn him that we'd best keep the pretence up for now, and stick with the official story: that he was Ruth's son, and that no one knew the whereabouts of Solomon. And I must keep calling him Jed, to be on the safe side.

'I'd rather you did anyhow,' he informed me, flicking the wind-whipped hair from his eyes. 'It's what Father used to call me, before Mother stopped me seeing him. It was a long time ago, and I was very small, but I remember.'

'So you don't get on with your mother at all?'

'I wouldn't say that. She has her uses.' He smiled sardonically, and for a moment I could see her in him, and Ahithophel too.

But most of the time I had no difficulty in remembering not to call him Solomon. For I still found it hard to believe that such a fine son could have been born to Bathsheba. It felt so strange to be standing arm in arm with someone I'd hated since he was a baby although I'd never even seen him. And it was stranger still to think that this person would one day sit upon the throne of Zion which Absalom was about to occupy, and which in other circumstances might even have been mine.

'Why *did* you save my father and me?' I asked him more than once as we leaned over the parapet drinking in the view—bare, neatly swept rooftops, empty streets, lonely blue hills hazed by distance. The fresh air had made me feel stronger already. 'Why didn't you just let us die? Or don't you want to be king of Israel any more than I do?'

He hunched his narrow shoulders. 'I knew you were in trouble. It was my duty. Why did you come back here to save your father when it was the most dangerous place for you to be? It's just the same.'

'Saving your own father is one thing, but saving your political rivals is something quite different, Jed. What *do* you want for your future?'

He scuffed one sandalled toe against the parapet. 'It's not my place to want anything. I have to—"realize my destiny"; Nathan says that's what matters, not chasing my own rainbows. I'm the one who will build the Temple which my father has always dreamed of; that has been prophesied, so that's what will happen, one way or another. Adonai will cause it. He doesn't need the sort of stratagems my mother thinks are called for.'

Now it was my turn to smile. The childlike nature of his faith and his quaintly grown-up way of speaking seemed incongruous. Yet the hours he'd spent in solitary study, or in conversing with his distinguished tutor, had taught him words and phrases most boys his age would never use. And he'd needed no books to tell him that all the scholarship in the world was as nothing when compared with the personal knowledge of God. Now he had that too, he was at peace.

In the event, Absalom didn't reach us until the next morning. He stayed overnight as a guest of the elders in Bethlehem, his father's birthplace—it seemed he wanted to press home the point that everything which had once been identified with the old King was now subject to the new one. Or perhaps he was merely seeking to avoid landing up in Jerusalem after dusk, when people might be reticent about taking to the streets to welcome him.

So he timed his arrival to coincide with sunrise, but if he expected a dazzling reception he was disappointed. On this occasion there were no crowds hailing him or waving palm branches or strewing his path with flowers when he passed through the city gates. Half the population had fled with David, and most of the rest cowered in their homes waiting to see how things would turn out. Here and there handfuls of the mean-looking youths who'd been in evidence at David's departure gathered on street corners and shouted their slogans, but their appearance and attitude only served to scare off timider folk who might otherwise have ventured outside.

Naturally, the pretender's procession was impressive. As well as soldiers and dignitaries and assorted groups of civilians who'd promoted his cause, there were musicians, dancers, tumblers and acrobats, even workers of magic and eaters of fire. But the music sounded hollow somehow, and the pounding of marching feet on stone resounded unnervingly down the deserted alleys and between the cringing houses. It was as though a passing troupe of entertainers had struck up with a wedding song at a funeral; everything was out of place and ill-timed.

And it was all so pagan! Either Ahithophel had conceded that this no longer mattered because of the manifest lack of opposition, or else he no longer held the sway over Absalom which he'd held before their short period of separation. For borne aloft on a great garish float came the gilded statue of some loathsome war god, awesomely attired for doing battle in heavenly places. It was daunting enough in itself, and yet it was dwarfed by its helmet, which was crested and horned the way that Syrian soldiers wear them. Then the god raised his head to look at the palace, and I realized that this was no statue at all, but Absalom himself; and that aside from the helmet, the metal-studded kilt, the gem-encrusted baldric and extravagance of garlands, he was as good as naked. The glossy gilt sheen on his skin owed its effect to gold powder in the body-oil they'd daubed him with—what on earth that had cost, I wouldn't like to imagine. I couldn't see his sun and crescent moon for all the greenery around his neck, but I didn't doubt he'd be wearing them.

'God help us,' said Jed quietly, and I knew he felt as I did.

Never before had I been so sure that the revolt was doomed to failure. Absalom had entered Jerusalem unopposed by any man, but it wasn't primarily earthly forces he'd have to fear from this point on.

I groaned, 'Jed, I have to see him. I have to warn him to give all this up at once, before it's too late.' I was no longer asking myself whether I should care. I knew that I did.

'It's too late already,' Jed responded bluntly, and unquestionably he was right; I'd already said the same to Sheba. But even if David could have found some way to pardon a flagrant traitor, there was no way that Absalom would listen to me, not when he held David's City in the palm of his hand.

I said, 'Your mother knows he's finished, too, doesn't she? That's why she's been pretending to support him, all this time urging him on so he'll kill himself, and she won't have to do it.'

'Of course.'

'I can't stand this. I can't abide seeing him like that, all painted and perverted. He was my friend. He protected me from Amnon. He loved me.'

'Not as much as he loves himself, I think.'

'That's a spiteful thing to say! How would you feel if it was me down there? No, I *have* to make him listen; or at least I have to try. Surely you can understand that?' Jed made no response and wouldn't meet my gaze.

Then all at once he rounded on me. 'Micha, no! Stay here! Look how he's swaying; he's drunk as well as deranged. He'll have you killed sooner than look at you.' Jed was tugging on my arm as though he had the strength to restrain me physically; I must admit I was moved by the fervour of his concern.

'You're the one who was harping on duty just now,' I reminded him, and there was no more he could say, except that he promised me he'd pray for me, and that he wouldn't let up until he saw me back safe.

I marched into the palace unchallenged. Anyone could have done so any time they liked, since David's departure, and scavengers probably had. When I got to the throneroom, an armed guard had been posted on the threshold in advance of Absalom's arrival; however the swollen-headed sentries were hardly less inebriated than Absalom had appeared to be. When I requested an urgent audience with the King they simply laughed—being Amasa's creatures they'd no idea who I was, which was possibly just as well. I repeated my entreaty and they finally condescended to reply, telling me I'd have to wait my turn when His Majesty arrived. I glanced about me and saw for the first time that there was another suppliant present besides myself, and that it was Hushai.

Hushai! I must have gasped audibly, for he acknowledged my surprise with the raising of one eyebrow. Then he deliberately composed his features again, into a mask of impenetrability. Ahithophel had trained him well.

Presently we heard Absalom approaching. There was laughter echoing along the passageway, and long-broken voices, slurred at the edges... memories were fanned in me and I could have sworn that I once more felt Amnon's belt marks singing on the backs of my legs. I turned away into the wall, unable to look Absalom in the face when he walked by, though I smelt his perfume and the wine on his breath. When I dared to look again, it was to see Ahithophel and Seraiah's backs as they entered the throneroom behind him, and Sheba and Amasa reaching up to draw the curtain further to one side so that the flock of hangers-on which they'd brought with them could pass through. So Sheba was still playing Absalom's game; but he too must have been drinking, for his feet caught in the curtain's hem, and it plunged to the ground, pole and all. Thus I was able to watch Absalom take up his position on David's seat; but he didn't sit on it. He stood on it, with his bangled arms punching the air, then he tossed the great helmet to Amasa and a deluge of ringlets fell free— they were thick with gold dust and hung almost to his hips.

At this juncture someone must have told him that there were men waiting to see him, for he started crowing that business could wait: now was the time for celebration, since he was invincible—David had turned tail and run like a rat from a house fire. But when he heard that one of the men was Hushai, he laughed out loud and flung himself supine across the throne's arms, his hair spilling out over one of the lions' heads so that the beast seemed to have acquired a living blue-black mane. 'Hushai too!' he guffawed. 'What do you think of that, then, Ahithophel? It appears that your former underling once again recognizes the superior wisdom of his old master and wants to be with him on the winning side! Where are you, Hushai? Come in, kneel down where I can see you! What has become of your touching loyalty to my father?'

'May the King live for ever,' said Hushai smoothly, stepping towards him and bowing low. 'I side with the King who has been chosen by Adonai and acclaimed by the people of Israel. His I shall be, and with him I shall remain.' His serenity was disquieting.

'Do you hear that, men?' Absalom gloated, tilting his head further back so as to harangue Hushai from upside down. He was evidently oblivious to the ambivalence of Hushai's statement. 'So much for David's charisma! He can't even count on his closest personal friends when they have to make a choice between him and me. Now I possess the two shrewdest counsellors in all the world! What say you, Ahithophel, sir? Won't you welcome our latest recruit?'

Ahithophel's expression was blacker than a storm cloud. He would have floored Hushai on the spot if looks could do the work of fists, but Hushai merely touched his own forehead in acknowledgement of the other's seniority then turned to Absalom once more, and said, 'As I was zealous in service to your father, so now I shall wait upon you. For whom else should I serve but your father's son?'

Who else indeed, I thought sourly, but then suddenly found myself being propelled unceremoniously in Absalom's direction. I almost tripped; his minions had much to learn about courtly manners.

But Absalom's manner changed abruptly when he saw me. The drunken leer disappeared; he twisted about until he sat upright on the throne, hands clasped around the lions' heads, with the knuckles showing. The language his body was speaking belied the offhand tone of his voice.

'So; the spineless little traitor seeks to return to the fold, now that the day is safely won.'

I averted my eyes. 'With respect, Your Majesty, at no time did I betray you. It upsets me profoundly that I should have permitted you to draw that conclusion. I left because it was becoming impossible for me to remain loyal without—absenting myself for a while.'

'I have better things to do than sit listening to riddles, Zoheleth.' He used the name deliberately, and uttered it with some venom. 'Make your point clearly or get out.' The apple in his throat was working up and down fit to choke him. Sheba went rigid.

'Your Majesty . . . my lord, I think I should speak with you alone about this.'

'Today I meet with no one behind closed doors, little serpent. I've had my fill of secrecy. Now I'm King in the open, and henceforth all conversations will be conducted in the open, as is fitting. Speak here, and now, or not at all, as you will.'

'Very well.' I didn't dare look directly at Sheba, but I could still see him from the corner of my eye, and now he was trembling. 'My lord, after I—I mean, after we quarrelled, the last time I saw you, in Hebron ... well, my lord, I came upon Sheba here, lurking outside your room with a knife in his belt. He was minded to make me king, and I believe he'd still do it, given the chance. I was afraid he would force me; so I ran. You see ... it's not just that I'm scared of assuming the burden. It's rather that—I know it isn't God's will.'

I could tell he believed me; we hadn't been close all those years for nothing. He said, 'So even you can see who has the divine right to be king.'

'Yes, my lord.' That was true too, but not in the way he would be thinking; still, I hardly cared what he thought for the time being, until I could get him alone.

'Come and stand before me, Sheba.'

The accused came forward at once, but he didn't stand. He prostrated himself full length on the ground as though Absalom were God incarnate, and began babbling, mostly incoherently, but everyone heard him admit that my allegation was true; and everyone heard him say that I was the great-grandson of Saul.

The atmosphere thickened then, like coagulated milk. Sheba must have sensed it too, for he ventured to lift his head a little, searching for sympathy from those who stood by. He might have won some, and so might I, if I'd decided in that moment to change my mind and claim what Sheba saw as my birthright. For up until now, very few of those present would have known whose seed I carried. But I said, 'My lord Absalom; gentlemen; this is Israel and we are God's people. Who my ancestors were counts for nothing. Adonai chooses whom he chooses.' And the moment passed.

I guess the matter might have ended there, had Absalom had sense to let it rest. But he leaned forward until his nose was almost touching Sheba's and demanded, 'What about the knife then, Sheba ben Bikri? Did you merely intend to threaten Zoheleth, or use it on me?'

At that, Sheba fell to babbling again. Plainly it was my mention of the knife which had terrified him more than anything else—after all, his Saulide sympathies he'd at no point kept secret. As for that knife, I don't think he even knew himself why he'd been carrying it; it was just instinct, because the political climate was so volatile. But by the time he'd finished inventing excuses, and Absalom had finished pelting him with ever wilder and more ludicrous accusations, both of them were screaming like demoniacs. I couldn't think what to do;

previously Sheba had always been the one to keep the peace, while Shimei did the raving. The more they argued, the more confident Sheba became. The puffed-up Prince might now in theory be a king, but he couldn't be at all sure as yet that his fellow conspirators would stand by and watch while he acted like a despot and treated one of their number like an insubordinate slave.

Indeed Ahithophel, Seraiah and even Amasa tried, each in turn, to intervene, but it was soon blatantly obvious that the altercation could end in nothing but an irrevocable rift. So I wasn't surprised when Sheba leapt up and announced that enough was enough; he'd had more than he could take of this shambles and should have had the courage to leave when Shimei had. Absalom did sober up a little then, and even went some way towards apologizing, but it was much too late. Sheba stormed out, saying yes, Absalom had been his friend since childhood, but he'd changed, and there were limits.

'Have him arrested,' snapped Ahithophel. 'Have the guards bring him back; stone him for treason.' But Absalom only shook his head weakly, incapacitated by remorse.

Hushai said gently, 'My lord Absalom, Ahithophel is right. If you let Sheba leave now, he will only cause trouble later.'

Too true, I thought, but trouble for David as much as for Absalom, and it's David you're worried for. Ahithophel's countenance waxed blacker still; hearing Hushai agree with him, for whatever reason, seemed to aggravate him more than the possibility of being contradicted. Taking advantage of the awkward pause to put in a word of my own, I ventured to ask Absalom if I might resume my duties as his personal attendant, now that he'd had proof of my fidelity and of my complete disinclination to vie with him for power. Because his defences were down and he was feeling the loneliness of leadership acutely just then, he said yes. I sighed with relief. I would wait for him in his chambers that evening, and thus get him on his own as I'd intended.

Some of the toadies present then took to praising vociferously their new King's clemency, oozing sycophancy about how it was the mark of a great monarch to show mercy to those who had wronged him and to restore a weak and wretched sinner to his former place of honour upon his heartfelt repentance, and so on and so forth. It was all so much hot air, but it buoyed Absalom's battered spirit enough for him to salvage his dignity and ask his two advisers what they considered his next move should be now that Sheba was gone.

Hushai replied promptly, 'I hardly think it matters, my lord. You have taken Jerusalem; what need is there for contriving further operations? There is no virtue in labour for its own sake. You are tired, the people are tired—tired of conflict and hardship and austerity. If you must do something, inaugurate a week of carnival. Use some of the wealth David has been hoarding, to give your subjects a good time. Then they will be loyal to you for life.'

This proposal cheered Absalom considerably; it was hard to imagine what else Hushai could have suggested which would have appealed to him more. Clapping his hands, he turned to Ahithophel to elicit the elder counsellor's approval, but it wasn't forthcoming. Ahithophel said, 'My noble colleague's recommendation is well conceived, but ought not to be brought to birth prematurely. The people of Israel are easily bought, and I have myself advised buying them in similar fashion on previous occasions. But securing the favour of the masses should hardly be our prime concern at present. We can turn our attention back to them later, when the enemy is destroyed.'

'My father?' blurted Absalom, with a brittle laugh. 'I told you, he has run away like a mangy cur with its tail between its legs. Let him end his days in the desert; we merely flatter him by continuing to pay him heed.'

'I fear you are wrong, my lord,' persisted Ahithophel. 'Remember, only a fool underestimates his adversary. Every day that we leave David to his own devices is a day for him to accumulate more support and more supplies. It might have been better for us if he'd remained in Jerusalem and fought us for it.'

'How can he coordinate any credible opposition from a cave? That's all there is east of the Jordan and south of Syria—a wilderness of crags and cliffs and holes in the ground.'

'With respect, my lord, if you had listened more to your tutors when you were a boy you would know this is not the case. And what *I* happen to know is that David is staying with a certain Barzillai whose estates rival your own in size and value and in the wealth that they furnish.'

'Then let him remain there! Let him rule a kingdom of ploughmen and shepherds. What do I care?'

'You will care a great deal when you find that the people are looking to the east for guidance and for justice and for everything else that matters, whilst you possess a pretentious palace, and nothing else but delusions of grandeur.'

'Too much womanly weeping for your beloved brother must have moistened your brains, Ahithophel! Why should they start looking to the old relic now? They've done nothing but groan under the weight of his incompetent tyranny for years!'

When Ahithophel replied, his tone was cool and cutting as before; but I can't have been alone in hearing the sharp breath he took in before speaking. Absalom's gibe, even crueller perhaps than he'd meant it to be, had stung the phlegmatic old bureaucrat deep deep down, and there was no denying it. He said, 'Why should they look to David now? I shall tell you why—Your Majesty. Because they watched him flee barefoot and *weeping* into exile, so now he is a victim of oppression just as many of *them* have been. They will come to identify with him. They will forget his faults and remember only his triumphs. And they will feel guilty for allowing the architect of their empire to be driven from his home like a leper.'

'Then what do you say we should do? Ride out there and finish him? Weren't you the one who didn't want a bloodbath?'

'Slaughter was not exactly what I had in mind, Absalom. Surrender fits into my picture more neatly. And if we ride out against David at the right time, we shall *have* his surrender, complete and unconditional, with the minimum of casualties. I am sure that he and his generals will appreciate the wisdom of sacrificing the life of one tired old man in order to ensure the survival of his doughty followers. The right time is fast approaching; indeed, it would have been here already had we not dallied so long in Hebron. But first you have to show him that there is absolutely no chance of your being persuaded either to accept peace terms which involve *his* survival, or to leave him alone to stew, over in Gilead. He has to know that you mean business, and that between the two of you, this is a fight to the death.'

'He must know that already. I'm sitting on his throne, aren't I? How can there ever be peace between us now? If I fell into his hands, he would have no choice but to slit my throat.'

'You really think so? When he hadn't even the courage to kill Amnon, whom he never truly loved, despite the fact that the lout had raped Tamar, whom he loved as his own flesh? No, Absalom. You have to *prove* to him that it's all over. You have to do it in such a way that all his henchmen are convinced too, so that there is positively no way that your intentions could be misconstrued by anyone. You have to show David and the world that you regard him as a dead man, and that you will stop at nothing until you have made that inner vision a reality.'

Absalom made as if to protest further, then checked himself. Briefly he passed one hand across his brow; he appeared confused, and I could well understand it. Hadn't Ahithophel maintained that there would be no need to deprive David of his life? Hadn't he argued against confrontation all along? Had he changed his mind, or had David's personal annihilation been a hidden item on his agenda since the beginning—hidden, because he'd known that Absalom hadn't until now been ready to espouse it?

But aloud Absalom asked none of these questions. I think he knew he hadn't the acumen to think through the answers he might get; or else he couldn't face them, or he couldn't be bothered, not now. He just asked meekly, 'How?'

'By lying with his concubines.'

For a moment Absalom was rendered speechless. Then he seemed to cast off his confusion and his remorse and his petulance and his horror all at once, the way a man rids himself of a heavy coat when the sun comes out. He'd had enough of all things weighty; he slapped his thighs, and both the lions' heads, threw himself exult-antly against the back of the throne, and gave himself up to a helpless and most unmajestic fit of guffawing.

Eventually, with his eyes streaming and his cheeks red as grape-skins, he said, 'Why, Ahithophel, that's an even more splendid idea than Hushai's! How many did the feckless cuckold leave here? Ten, was it? Do you think I can manage ten in one night? What a challenge! I've never had such fun in my entire life. You're a genius, Ahithophel. An utter genius.'

Ahithophel coughed drily. 'Perhaps so, my lord, but this ap-proach can hardly be called original. I have often heard tell of its employment among the nations. When a king dies, his successor takes over his harem along with all else that was his. To do so while there is yet breath in the previous incumbent's body conveys a most eloquent message.'

'Then I'll do it tonight. I'll have them come to my father's old chambers, one by one.'

Ahithophel pursed his lips. 'You are right to want to act as soon as possible,' he said. 'But the deed must be accomplished in public, my lord, and it must be done, or at least begun, in full daylight, so there can be no doubt as to whether or not it has taken place. A wedding canopy must be erected on the palace roof, and you must perform the ritual there.'

'Ritual!' Absalom hooted, doubled up with laughter once more. 'Well, I never heard it called that before. At any rate, not by a Hebrew.'

Ahithophel wasn't even smiling. He said, 'In this instance it *will* be a ritual, Absalom. It must be perceived in that light by everyone.'

'Yes,' acknowledged Absalom, wiping his eyes and calming down a little. 'Yes of course.' Then he was laughing all over again; and I cringed, for to me his laughter sounded as hollow as the music which had accompanied his procession.

So the canopy was duly set up, Ahithophel having designated a place on the roof which was plainly visible from beyond the palace walls, and the bizarre ceremony began. There was feasting and merrymaking to put folk in festive mood, though Absalom himself took care to get no drunker than he was already, lest he be unable to perform. Then the concubines and their children were rounded up by Amasa's men, but Jed wasn't with them; as he'd assured me, he knew very well how and when to make himself scarce.

The prisoners were terror-stricken, convinced that Absalom meant to kill them all. When they awoke to his true intentions, the women were scarcely comforted. In fact, I think some of them would sooner have died than be ravished under the eyes of the world and of their own little ones. To watch simple Naomi taken by force, and to hear her screams, and to wonder which of the other despairing and degraded young girls was Jed's guardian Ruth, was more than I could bear. So far as I know, Absalom serviced them all, but I didn't wait around to count.

I went first to find Jed, to make sure he was all right, and to show him that I was. He was where I should have expected him to be: in the hidden apartment with Mephibosheth. He'd gone there to see to my father as much as to hide from Absalom; the two of them pored over a senet board as though nothing else mattered in the world. Once again I was amazed; I wouldn't have imagined my father capable of sitting still long enough to hear the rules, let alone comprehend them. Jed was extraordinary, and I told him so.

He smiled, all innocence and humility. 'Don't worry about us,' he said. 'We're getting along very well.'

I half shrugged. 'So I see. I'm fine too.'

'I knew you would be, as soon as I thought about it. Adonai has brought you through too much to let you go under now. But I'm glad you came back to prove it.'

'I—can't stay. I still haven't seen Absalom properly, on his own. I have to go to his chambers tonight.'

'That's all right. I'll stay here with Mephibosheth until Naomi . . .'

'Jed, do you know what he did to her? To all of them?'

'Yes. I know.' He stole an anxious glance at my father, meaning: don't say too much in front of him. It was as though Mephibosheth were the impressionable child and Jed the adult. 'I saw the women being assembled. I heard what the soldiers said.'

'Poor Naomi. We should have done more to protect her. If only she'd been down here when it happened.'

'Perhaps it's as well she wasn't. Everyone knows that ten concubines were left here. They'd have searched till they found her—and us.' Then he noticed alarm growing in my father's eyes, and laid a comforting hand on his wrist. 'I'll stay here all night, Micha. You'll be back in the morning?'

'I . . .'

I couldn't find the words to break the truth to him, but he discerned it somehow. Those who are close to Adonai have a sight and understanding all their own. He whispered, 'You mean to become his servant again? After what he's put you through? Micha, in God's name—'

'Jed.' I knelt before him, and cupped his thin face between my palms. There was liquid desolation in his over-large eyes. 'You're so wise in everything else; be wise in this too. I know that what he's doing is wrong, and he won't change my mind. But even if he won't listen to me, even if he marches against David, I can't just desert him.'

'You'll be killed, just like he will. I'll never see you again.'

'I thought you said Adonai would protect me?' I hugged him impulsively—he was so slight in build that there seemed to be nothing of him, yet the whole future of Israel was vested in that fragile frame. He clung to me momentarily when I tried to let him go; the poor child had never had another friend in his life, and I knew all too acutely what that was like. He kept repeating over and over that I must be mad, that I must *want* to destroy myself; and in a strange way I suppose he might have been right. Alongside loyalty and friendship perhaps there was something inside me which was trying to punish me for my past.

But Jed could see he would never win me over. As soon as he heard Mephibosheth starting to whine he forgot himself and pulled away from me. He placed my father's hand over the best counter for him to move next, and I slipped away before I made things any worse.

I was admitted to the royal apartment without question; a couple of our Syrians were standing guard. It felt so strange to be once again in David's quarters, but to be waiting for his son and not for him.

As I hung there looking about me, thinking that *this* place *did* smell of David, and that the very walls and curtains were imbued with the aura of his personality, something launched itself at my legs. I looked down and there was Gatis, her tail lashing the air and her tongue lolling as she set about licking me all over. I couldn't help but grin, and reach out to stroke her; at that she grew more enthusiastic than ever, leaping up to lick my face so that I wound up tussling with her on the floor, laughing and sneezing as she tickled me with her fur and covered my nose in saliva. I could no longer even recollect why I'd once shunned her offers of unconditional friendship.

The dog and I were curled up together asleep by the time our master returned, so I didn't hear him come in. It was only when he threw himself on the bed with an exaggerated groan that I stirred; and he said, as though I'd never been away, 'Good morning, Zohel. Do you know it's nearly dawn? Don't ever let anyone tell you that taking ten women in one night is good recreation! The first five, maybe. After that... ye gods, what a chore! Still, it's an achievement, don't you agree? If Amnon could see me now!'

Deciding there was no reply I could give which wouldn't provoke another argument, I said nothing. I helped him shed his soiled clothes, then sent for hot water and bathed him; he was slick with sweat and semen and not a little blood, and the stale gold body-oil; and his ringlets had gone to rats' tails. All the while I kept my silence, whilst he prattled on, boasting and teasing me mercilessly, eventually demanding to know if I'd had my tongue cut out.

'Come on!' he urged me. 'Speak! Say something, scion of Saul! You're as shy as the day I met you, but you had plenty to say for yourself yesterday. So you can't kid me that you've regressed in my absence.'

I gritted my teeth, convinced that if I spoke I would shout, and got on with washing his hair; it was so thick, it tangled as soon as you looked at it. But he wouldn't let me off the hook. He kept goading me for a response, then at long last realizing that something was bothering me, he tempered his tone and asked me more kindly what I was thinking. I burst into tears.

I don't know what had brought everything so suddenly to the surface, but I hung over the side of the bath tub sobbing my heart out. He got up out of the water and threw a towel round his shoulders, bending beside me and asking, 'What *is* this? What *is* all this nonsense, Zohel?' But although he called it nonsense, he spoke gently now; perhaps he still had a heart of his own, somewhere underneath all that arrogance.

I'd tried to work out beforehand what I would say to him, how I'd attempt to reason with him and to explain to him calmly the error of his ways. Now the whole lot poured out of me in a barely comprehensible jumble: how he was doomed, he was condemned, he was going to die and lead thousands of misguided Israelites to their deaths alongside him, at the hands of their own former king.

He said exactly what I expected him to say. He'd won already; everyone who mattered was on his side: Ahithophel, Seraiah, Amasa, Hushai, Bathsheba. David had only Joab and Abishai who were worth reckoning with, and their muscle had run to fat many moons ago.

'You haven't got Hushai,' I wailed. 'He's working for David, he's out to delude you. And you haven't got Bathsheba. She's gone away with David—or didn't you know that? Why do you think she wasn't here to fall into your arms when you arrived? She's counting off the days until your funeral.'

'I knew very well that she would have to go with him for now. She sent me word to say so! What excuse could she have given him to avoid it, for heaven's sake? But she's supplying me with gold from David's own treasury, Zohel. I could hardly have more solid support than that.'

'It's a trap, can't you see that? The gold is bait, she's just luring you on!'

'She loves me, Zohel.' He assumed his pertest pout. 'She just can't resist me.'

'Absalom, you blind fool! She wants your annihilation, she doesn't want *you*! How often must I tell you? That's why she seduced you! Lying with Bathsheba is as good as lying with death itself!'

'Zohel, you'd better shut up. I'm warning you. Or I shall decide you *are* a traitor after all. You want me to give up my cause so *you* can be king.'

'That's the very last thing I want.'

'Then how come you say I'm fated to lose everything? How can you know? How can Bathsheba know?'

'Bathsheba knows because Nathan has told her. Nathan is God's prophet. He knows everything.'

'I thought you'd shut the door on God? I thought Adonai meant nothing to you any more? Because he means nothing to *me*, Zohel. He has no power to rival Baal's.'

'What?'

'It's Baal I make my offerings to these days, so you'd better get that straight. It took Adonai three years to bring me back from Geshur—if indeed it was he who answered my prayers. It's taken Baal fewer *weeks* to have me installed in Jerusalem since I made my sacrifice in Hebron.'

'You didn't sacrifice to Baal in Hebron! You sacrificed to Adonai.'

'Not in my spirit. If your precious Adonai can see inside us, then he knows that even if you don't.'

I was wasting my time. Drained and depressed, I fell to crying again, but Absalom wasn't to be softened by my tears any further. He was exhausted, and little wonder, and went to sleep on David's bed with the damp towel wrapped around him and his loose wet hair, still half clogged with gold, staining the bedclothes.

Hushai's week of carnival went ahead, but Absalom got little peace to enjoy it. Ahithophel nagged at him continuously, insisting that he face up to responsibility and accept that something decisive must be done about David.

Eventually, when seven days had passed and no one could so much as look at a winejar without throwing up, Absalom was persuaded to sit down and apply himself to the matter seriously. His Majesty insisted on posing upon the throne for the occasion, adorned with all the trappings of royalty, surrounded by fawning courtiers and waited on by his handsome personal servant wafting a palm branch ceaselessly above his even more handsome master's head—a service which was wholly unnecessary because we were well into autumn. But he wanted everyone to witness that Saul's great-grandson was prepared to perform such a humble task for him even now that the secret of his noble birth was out.

Absalom announced that anyone present who wished to put forward a plan for his appraisal should do so. Then when all had been heard and considered, a decision would be made.

Ahithophel went first. He proposed that he himself and Amasa be authorized to select twelve thousand fighting men the moment the meeting was adjourned; they would then set out immediately in pursuit of the exile and his horde. Having marched non-stop they would launch their attack without pitching a camp or even building cooking fires, thereby catching the enemy completely off guard, and hopefully while some of them were still en route crossing the Jordan. Their primary aim would be the capturing and killing of David personally; in that way civil war would be averted, since with the old King dead his men would have no reason to fight on. Ahithophel and Amasa would then lead this army home (along with their own) rejoicing like a repentant adulteress returning to her husband, and Absalom would be able to pardon all the conquered with impunity, thus winning universal praise and respect. For what ruler would want to slaughter his own subjects, when instead he could have them indebted to him for ever?

'You mean to set out *today*?' Absalom queried in astonishment. 'Wouldn't it be better to take time to prepare properly? I thought I was supposed to be the reckless one?'

'Today may already be too late, my lord.' Ahithophel was struggling to remain patient, but the effort was fast becoming too much for him. 'David is no longer languishing in Barzillai's bedchamber. He has transformed his motley entourage into a formidable fighting force, and his jumble of tents and wagons into a military encampment. In the past week his army has practically doubled in size, whereas ours may in point of fact be shrinking... but I don't suppose you've been sober for long enough to learn any of that.' He paused deliberately, so that Absalom could easily have reprimanded him had he chosen to; but it was still more natural for him to accept chastisement from Ahithophel than to chastise him in return. Ahithophel went on, 'And growth promotes growth, my lord, whilst once a thing goes into decline, that trend is hard to reverse. Seven more days from now, we may be significantly weaker, and his power may have increased tenfold.'

Judging from the audible murmurings around the room, most of those present acknowledged the wisdom of these words. Absalom, however, was less than impressed. He seemed reluctant to allow Ahithophel and Amasa to dispose of David with so little ceremony—I thought perhaps he'd had a fresh twinge of conscience, but more likely now he wanted the pleasure reserved for himself. He proceeded to call on Hushai to give his advice, if indeed he had any that differed from Ahithophel's.

'Most assuredly I do, my lord,' he answered levelly. 'If I may say so, Your Majesty was most prudent in demonstrating the need for thorough preparation before a campaign of this nature is undertaken—*if* you are firmly convinced of its necessity. David himself is a seasoned warrior and his recent experiences will have hardened him. Joab and Abishai too will have been training hard already, and will be as fierce now as a couple of mother bears robbed of their cubs. They aren't going to risk losing their revered uncle by allowing him to sleep rough among his troops at night; Ahithophel and Amasa will never find him by assaulting his camp in the dark. No; we must give ourselves time to assemble and drill an army drawn from every corner of our empire—an enormous army, many as the grains of sand on a seashore, to outnumber David overwhelmingly. That way, even if he takes refuge in some walled city we'll be strong enough to demolish it brick by brick. And, Your Majesty—I feel it would be best if you led this host yourself; that would be a great inspiration to officers and men alike.'

If I'd needed any further evidence to convince me that Hushai was a double agent, I had it now. To put Absalom in charge of any kind of military operation was sheer insanity. But it was of paramount importance to Hushai that Absalom himself be cut down, just as it was to Ahithophel that David should perish. And Hushai knew exactly how to play on the pretender's vanity. It didn't appear to worry Absalom in the least that he'd only fought one battle in his life, and that had been as a private soldier—if indeed he'd fought at all and not simply stood gawping, with his father's bodyguards protecting him.

Since no third option was propounded, Absalom declared that he would now give careful consideration to the alternatives he'd been offered, and he invited anyone who so desired to speak in favour of either one. Amasa and Seraiah both spoke up for Ahithophel; the rest muttered platitudes, wanting only to be seen to agree with their King once they'd deduced his preference. Certain that Absalom would pay me no heed whatsoever, I said nothing, but carried on waving my palm branch, though my arms ached like a Phoenician galley slave's. Presently, with flagrant disregard for what the surviving members of his original Circle had advised, he decided for Hushai.

Then everyone began clamouring at once, with about as much understanding of one another's words as the builders of Babel had had after God confused them. The toadies praised Absalom's prudence, claiming that anyone could see Hushai's plan was the best one; Ahithophel, Amasa and Seraiah were almost tearing their hair out in frustration. I'd never before seen Ahithophel lose his cool completely, but I saw it now. He flung every argument he could think of at his protégé, but they ran off him like water from an oiled blade.

I knew it wasn't only Absalom's stubbornness that was infuriating the old counsellor; he was angry with himself as well. He was angry at the energy he'd invested in this wastrel; he was angry that for all his reputation for shrewdness, he was going to wind up the loser, while his own granddaughter got everything she wanted. I recalled how he'd once said that he and Bathsheba were too alike to get on with one another, but in the end it had been she who'd outwitted him. If they *had* worked together, they *might* one day have ruled the world—Maacah had said this was Ahithophel's desire. But he had let jealousy destroy him; though cleverer than most, he was shown to be no wiser.

And Absalom, taken aback at his adviser's aberrant behaviour, concluded he'd gone mad and had him forcibly removed from the throneroom.

That same afternoon I was on an errand for Absalom, when I saw Hushai whispering to a slave girl in the corner of a courtyard. Setting down the burden I was carrying, I stole closer to listen, concealing myself round the back of a sturdy column, but I couldn't hear what was said.

So when the slave girl went her way, I followed her. Bribing the guards on the gates, she left the palace, and I continued to tail her, away through the streets and out of the city. By the spring at Enrogel on the outskirts of Jerusalem, I watched her meet up with two boys; she was making eyes at them and playing with her veil, but I knew that this was no lovers' tryst. I knew who the boys were: Jonathan and Ahimaaz, the sons of Abiathar and Zadok, David's chief priests. I still didn't hear what was said, but I didn't need to. David would know by tomorrow that Hushai's plan was succeeding.

I hadn't made up my mind whether to pass on what I'd seen to Absalom or not; but as soon as I got back to the palace, Ahithophel intercepted me. He'd watched the slave girl leaving, and he'd watched me leave after her. Now in a last desperate bid to make Absalom see sense, he dragged me before him and made me spill the beans.

But Absalom didn't want to know. He was still convinced that Ahithophel was mad—and one look into the counsellor's eyes just then might have convinced anyone. Absalom did agree to send a search party to fetch the two boys back, but only to silence Ahithophel's nagging, and the half-hearted hunters never found their quarry.

'Why should we care if my father knows of our strategy?' the new King sneered. 'We don't need to rely on surprise if we follow Hushai's plan. We'll crush David with sheer weight of numbers. Let him know what's coming to him! I shall enjoy the thought of him living his last days on earth in dread of me.'

Ahithophel said, 'I should have realized you weren't going to grow up. You'll die a greater fool than you were born. But I never thought you'd make a fool of me.'

He bowed stiffly and left before Absalom could stop him, and we never saw him again. Two days later we learned that he'd gone back home to Giloh, put his affairs in order, and hanged himself.

23

I'm not sure how many days passed after that before we marched east. I lost all track of time, just as I'd done in that dreary dungeon; for though I was free now to wander where I willed, I was still in prison. Ahithophel's suicide had condemned me to despair.

Of course, many other men in his predicament might have taken the same way out, though I should never have been one of them. No matter how bad things got, no matter how worthless I'd once felt, I'd always had a ferocious will to survive. But doubtless it had turned Ahithophel's stomach to think of being dragged in chains before David whom he'd forsaken. He'd finally been forced to face the fact that he was never going to mould Absalom into the kind of monarch Israel needed. And he'd been eclipsed for a second time by Hushai, a man he despised. I guess he recognized, too late, that he'd underestimated his junior colleague—and Adonai also.

But Ahithophel had always been so steady, so rational, and I'd always seen suicide as a crime of passion or of lunacy; I couldn't imagine any sane man taking his own life in cold blood. Perhaps the old counsellor *had* gone mad, at the end. Then again, he'd dealt meticulously with every document requiring his attention before fastening the noose about his neck.

Without him we were finished, and I said so to Absalom. But he ignored me, for Hushai had announced that now was the time to crush David.

And so we started out, leaving Seraiah behind in Jerusalem to take charge of affairs of state in our absence. We had with us horses and chariots and a great many Syrian auxiliaries to supplement our native Hebrew infantry and our baggage train, for His Majesty King Talmai of Geshur had left no stone unturned in assisting his grandson to carry out the policy he'd attempted to press upon him years before. But from the very beginning these additional troops gave rise to more trouble than they were worth. Many of those who'd supported Absalom all along resented the sudden appearance of foreigners in such large numbers, and started at long last to feel uncomfortable about Absalom's affinity with them. A chill wind of unease blew through our ranks along with the rain-laden autumn squalls, and caused officers and men alike to shiver. Amasa had problems maintaining discipline.

Meanwhile, we learned that all of David's army was now on the far side of the Jordan; unsurprising, for Hushai would have gone on playing for time had this not been the case. Still Absalom seemed happy to trust him—probably because Hushai was just about the only person he came into contact with who wasn't complaining or squabbling, and little wonder. As for me, I decided that whichever way things went next I was bound to finish up as dead meat, and sooner rather than later. So I might as well die beside Absalom, who at least had cared for me once. He'd promised long ago to make me his armour bearer, and so I should be, though I'd never witnessed a pitched battle in all my born days, let alone fought in one.

Our own fording of the Jordan was a nightmare. The place we chose is lucky to see rain one day in a hundred, and that had to be the day we were there. Nor did it merely rain; it was as though we were somehow mixed up in a re-enactment of the Great Flood, and I began to have serious doubts about God's covenant with Noah. I don't know how many horses and mules we must have lost, and some of our chariots and wagons had to be left behind because we hadn't got enough timber to make rafts for all of them; most of the rafts were only good for one trip before they broke up. Yet there was no evidence left of any casualties from David's crossing. Perhaps the waters had parted for him as they had for Joshua.

But once on the other side, there could be no turning back—of that at least I was in no doubt. Wet past my waist from wading, and scarcely any drier beyond there because of the deluge, I thought I should never see the Jerusalem sun again.

The rain wasn't the only weapon which nature threw at us. Soon the ground began rising, and instead of sparse desert bushes there was woodland, then forest. Although we were following a road, not threshing through sodden undergrowth, the wheels of our vehicles cut deep ruts in the surface and we found ourselves trudging through mud up to our knees; at one point my left sandal came off and got embedded, and I had to dig it out with my sword, for I hadn't a spare pair with me. Putting it back on was like strapping rotting pondweed to my foot. After that the forest grew thicker still, and darker, and danker, and I began to imagine a spy of David's concealed behind every moss-fingered trunk.

In those conditions there was no way we could have made it to Mahanaim in a day even if we'd set out before dawn. We camped in the middle of nowhere, in a clearing made among the trees for growing crops. There was a village there, but it was deserted; the senior officers slept in the houses rather than put their tents up and get them soggy. Absalom and I had the largest house, which meant that it was the coldest, too. So I got a fire going, for the makings of one had been left in the hearth. The occupants hadn't been gone long; most likely they'd fled on being warned of our approach. Absalom huddled in his cloak and fretted, then when he started taking out his misery on me, I walked out and went to share a jar of wine or two with the sentries sitting in the rain. I couldn't make up my mind which was the worse place to be.

For I only had to listen to them reminiscing about the wars of their youth to feel my own callowness like a dead weight in my stomach. While we'd been kicking our heels in Jerusalem, Amasa had had Absalom and me undergo some haphazard weapons training, but even then I'd felt ridiculous. My grandfather Jonathan had been a tried and tested commander before he was eighteen, and I didn't even know how to hold a sword or spear properly. I had David's Golden Age to thank for that, and I began to resent the years of peace which had left my hands as soft as a scribe's and my flesh unscarred. If I'd been older and more mature, I might rather have resented the fact that wars must happen at all.

Early next morning we pushed on, and though the weather was little better we made Mahanaim by evening. We halted within sight of the city walls, but with the heavy cloud-cover dusk came early so we couldn't see David's tents. Scouts were sent out to reconnoitre while we got unpacked, pitched camp and set about cooking an evening meal. Even Absalom and I had to make do with goatskin above our heads that night; the rain was showing signs of letting up, but he was in a blacker mood than ever, and a second time I sought refuge among the guards outside.

When I was sure he'd turned in, I went back to him. But I must have drunk more than was wise because I couldn't get to sleep and had to go out again to relieve myself. It was pitch dark; there was no moon, and even the stars were masked by cloud. While I was picking my way about, suddenly a brawny arm wound itself around my neck, a hand clamped over my mouth, and then my head was completely smothered in a swathe of damp scarf. I couldn't cry out, and all my writing and struggling was to no avail, for I was hoisted effortlessly into the air and put over someone's shoulder like a dead sheep.

Even as they carted me away, I couldn't believe what was happening to me. It appeared that I was being blatantly kidnapped from the inner sanctum of a closely guarded military establishment, when I'd been minding my own business within spitting distance of Absalom's security men, and within sniffing distance of Gatis. Yet my captor, or captors, strode along unchallenged, as though our entire army had been ensorcelled. It was uncanny.

Once outside the camp, my scarf was removed and I was given a mule to ride on. It was too dark to see my captors' faces, but there were two of them; then one said, 'His Majesty King David apologizes for the unorthodox nature of his invitation, my lord. But he requests the pleasure of your company at his table,' and the voice was Abishai's.

How he found his way back to the city without a torch I shall never know. Perhaps a lifetime of soldiering gives you cat's eyes as well as lion's muscles. But we got there as quickly as we could have done by day, and I was taken to Barzillai's house, where David was apparently still staying. There were bronze lamps burning on brackets, richly upholstered couches, and everything was dry ... except for the sorry little puddles that my clothes dribbled onto the floor.

When David made his appearance I was more amazed than ever, and became convinced I must be dreaming. He walked in unaccompanied and unaided, with no ceremony and yet with all the poise and bearing appropriate to a great warlord and emperor such as he had once been. There was almost a bounce in his step, his grey hair and beard were oiled and combed, and the lines on his face no longer made his skin sag, but had tautened like drawn bowstrings. He seemed taller than I remembered; and perhaps it was just the effect of the lamplight or of wine, but his sallowness had gone and there was colour in his cheeks. All in all he looked like a new man, except that his eyes were full of sadness and a bleak kind of tension.

I was lost for words, and he couldn't resist smiling at my discomfiture. He had a dimple in his chin which I'd never noticed before, perhaps because of his beard, but for a moment it gave him the look of a mischievous adolescent and for the first time enabled me to picture him running at Goliath with his shepherd boy's sling.

'Did Abishai pass on my apologies for your rough treatment?' he asked, and I nodded—the only response I felt capable of. 'Good,' he said. 'It may be that the sons of Zeruiah are becoming civilized at last. But you still look like a man who's seen a ghost. Perhaps it's my sprightly new image which has stunned you, and not your kidnapping at all?' He smiled again, and the dimple puckered. 'I must have told you that the years I spent as an outlaw on the run from Saul were really the happiest of my life. No tedious meetings to sit through, no dour ambassadors to entertain, instead getting up each morning to face who knows what new crisis, and growing tougher by the day. Never knowing where you'll sleep the next night, or where your next meal's coming from, or even whether you'll live to see the next sunrise ... it certainly makes you count your blessings, my tongue-tied young friend, and appreciate the simplest of pleasures. Speaking of which'—and he clapped his hands to summon a servant—'I should have offered you wine already (how remiss of me!) and something to eat ... and some dry clothes; just look at you!'

I stood bewildered while attendants came and went, bringing wine which had been warmed and mixed with honey, and hot soup and bread, and a fresh tunic and cloak; I let them dress me without protesting, and drained the wine in one gulp. More was brought to replace it, and I thought guiltily of Absalom mouldering in our tent with his teeth chattering.

'Yes, it's ironic, isn't it,' David remarked, watching me devouring the soup like someone starved. 'To think that I should find myself luxuriating here in accommodation lavish enough to rival my own home; and in the very city where Abner set up Ishbosheth in opposition to me all those years ago. Of course, Joab wants me to stay put here when he takes the field against Absalom tomorrow; they all think I'm made of glass, you know.'

Then a strange look passed across his incongruously sad, bleak eyes; he cleared his throat self-consciously and changed the subject.

'I really do apologize for abducting you, though; it was hardly very polite. In fact it was doubly discourteous for being the second time at least that I've had to compel you to come and see me. I must be a singularly tiresome companion.' His slight sideways grin was designed to elicit a response from me; I still didn't speak. So he said, 'But this time I wasn't being selfish. I was thinking of Absalom, and of your own good. I didn't want to risk your not coming, for his sake as much as yours, and I didn't want him stoning you for treachery.

300

To have you abducted seemed the easiest solution all round.' Then seeing my eyebrows go up, he feigned embarrassment and added, 'Ah well, you see, Abishai has plenty of experience at breaking into the camps of rival kings and stealing things which are precious to them. Saul was most put out at the mysterious loss of his spear and his water jar one night, many years ago . . . You must never assume that the Lord God has no sense of humour.' But it was the very mention of humour which seemed to wipe the smile from his own face; all at once the rest of him looked as sad as his eyes and he said softly, 'I'm sorry. I really am. Please forgive me. I suppose you want to know what you're doing here.'

Still loath to speak, I nodded once again. David was used to my silences from of old, so he continued undeterred.

'There's a whole host of reasons. For any one of them alone I might have resisted the temptation to send for you. But taken together, their force was too strong. First of all . . .' He sat down facing me across the table which had been brought in with my meal, and folded his hands upon it, deliberately adopting a businesslike tone to match his posture. 'First of all, in the unlikely event of my perishing in the forthcoming conflict—which I am almost sure I shall not, but Adonai has sprung surprises on me often enough in the past—there are some things I must say to you. And there is something I must give to you . . . Micha ben Saul.'

So he did know. I was more tongue-tied than ever, and sat staring helplessly at him, my heart thumping fit to burst. No longer able to maintain his detachment, he leaned forward impulsively, seized hold of my upper arms, and reading my mind said, 'Yes, I *do* know. I knew it had to be true the first time I saw you. Jonathan's face and hair, Saul's eyes . . .' He swallowed a visible lump in his throat, and made himself go on. 'I have permitted a monstrous injustice to be done to your father Mephibosheth. He didn't betray me, did he.'

It was a statement, not a question, and as such required no answer. I didn't even shake my head. David let out a long enervated sigh.

'Yes,' he said. 'I knew that too. I knew it as soon as I'd witnessed the will promising Ziba all his patrimony. I wasn't myself . . . But don't worry. It will be put right when—if—I get out of this alive. And you will inherit everything in your turn.'

Everything? I still couldn't find my voice, but my eyes must have done the asking for me.

'There are extensive estates; and there is the fortress built by Saul's father at Gibeah, if you can bear to go there. It's all closed up and half derelict, but the basic structure's mostly sound. And there's this.'

He felt inside the folds of his cloak, and drew from it a small sheathed dagger. The hilt and scabbard were tarnished and the design of them old-fashioned, but they were engraved exquisitely, and studded with gemstones.

'This was made for Saul's grandfather,' David said, a little wistfully, turning it over and over in his hands. 'Saul gave it to Eliphaz his Amalekite slave, when the pair of them were boys. Eliphaz used it to finish him when he was wounded by the Philistines on Mount Gilboa and couldn't manage to fall on his own sword. Here.' He leaned forward and pressed it into my hand, curling my fingers around it. 'I kept it after I had the Amalekite executed; he brought it to me stained with Saul's blood as proof of what he'd done. I'd no choice but to put him to death; he'd slain the Lord's Anointed, after all. But then I couldn't think what to do with this.'

Instinctively I drew the blade from its sheath, though of course the blood had been scoured off years before. I pricked my finger gently on the point, and a tiny bead of my own blood, rich and red, glistened bright against the bronze. Then in a rush of confusion, I replaced the sheath clumsily and thrust it back at David.

'What's the matter? Don't you want it?'

I held my head.

'It's yours by right, you know. Eliphaz left no family to whom it could go. Every one of his relatives was killed when Saul attacked Amalek. Micha...' Then something told him the reason for my perplexity, though I hadn't been able to analyze it myself. 'Micha, you can't run away from your identity, you know. None of us can escape the burden of our birth.' He placed the knife in my hands once again, and this time I kept hold of it. He said, 'There is only one thing of Saul's which I can't give you, because it's not in my power to give it.'

Of course, I knew what he meant, and must have shown it.

'I should have liked to, though, sometimes,' he went on fervently. 'God knows, I still would. You would make a finer king than *any* of my sons, I'm ashamed to say, and I must bear the blame for that. You see—you may have thought little about Adonai since you played the harp for me as a child, but you can't quench his spirit entirely once it has entered you and brought your own spirit to life. Adonai is still inside you. You can find him there again.'

I'd been staring down at the knife; now I jerked my head up and found myself looking right into David's eyes, and they were just like Jed's.

He said, 'I haven't exactly been an inspiring example for you, I know, and I'm sorry for that too. I'm sorry for so many things. That's another of the reasons I wanted to see you. To ask your forgiveness. To make you understand. When you were just a little boy I told you I'd explain everything to you one day. The day has come, I fear. It's going to be grievously painful for both of us.'

At that I found my voice. I started protesting all but unintelligibly, telling him it was of no importance whether I understood him or not; I didn't matter; it was Solomon who mattered, for *he* stood to inherit the one thing of Saul's which I would never have—and good riddance to it.

'Yes,' said David, from between clenched teeth. 'The ultimate irony, I suppose. *Her child.*' I was shocked at the venom in his tone. 'I have to admit, sometimes Adonai's ways aren't merely unfathomable. On occasions they seem indistinguishable from those of his adversaries. Bathsheba's son is the *last* person I would have chosen to succeed me. Perhaps Israel has become so wanton that Adonai means to use her next king to destroy her altogether. Nathan says that the covenant of Moses may not be irrevocable.'

He noted my confusion, but when he spoke again it was as much to himself as to me. '. . . Such a strange boy. He always was, even from birth. Eyes too old for a baby, always watching, watching . . . you know, he talked in full sentences from being eight months? It made your flesh crawl.' He shuddered even at the thought, and I wished there was some way I could reassure him, but I didn't know where to start. I'd taken it for granted that David had loved Bathsheba to distraction, else why would he have allowed her to displace Maacah and her family from their apartment, as well as from his affections? Now I was baffled, for he spoke as though he hated her—so much so that he couldn't even look at her son without feeling sick. He'd mistaken Jed's intelligence for something sinister because of his own ingrained prejudice. I so much wanted to tell David what Jed was really like, yet couldn't find the words to begin.

He cleared his throat once more. 'I have pleaded long and hard with Adonai to change his mind about Solomon, Micha, but since it appears that he doesn't intend to grant my request, there is something *you* must do for me instead. You must persuade Absalom to surrender.'

I started; David laid a hand on my wrist.

'Surely you understand this much at least? If Solomon is destined to succeed, it follows that Absalom must fail. Which almost certainly means that if he joins battle with us tomorrow, he won't leave the field alive. Surely you don't want that?'

I started mumbling that of course I didn't, but that I'd already tried to reason with Absalom till I was blue in the face; anyhow, it was partly my fault that he'd set out on this disastrous course in the first place, since I'd put it into his mind to fight rather than slit his own wrists.

But David whispered, 'Oh God,' when he realized that Absalom was living on borrowed time even now, and began rambling little more intelligibly than I'd been doing: Absalom was ruined, his army was a laughing-stock, Amasa hadn't the experience to co-ordinate it, Seraiah couldn't command the resources to provide adequately for its subsistence; whilst Joab and Abishai weren't merely superb leaders of men, but had access to boundless provisions. For the people of fertile Gilead regarded Absalom as a detestable Syrian, whilst David was revered as their saviour from Syrian incursions and protection rackets, since their territories shared borders with Talmai's. So much for the unanimous support for Absalom in the north. Apparently even Machir, my former guardian, was among the wealthy men who were supplying David with foodstuffs; and more significantly, so was Shobi, son of Nahash of Ammon, whom David had installed as king there after deposing his faithless brother. What was more, the men of Gilead who fought for David knew the local terrain like the backs of their own hands.

From the way he was talking, it was almost as though he wanted Absalom to win, and himself to be defeated; but he knew with grim certainty that this was not to be. 'You must try again, Micha,' he implored me, gripping my hand until it was almost crushed. 'Try harder; try *anything* to get him to give in. I can't bear to think of him dead. Not Absalom. He was everything to me.'

I said, 'But he's stolen your kingdom, your city, your palace.'

'I could forgive him all of that, to hear him once say he loved me.'

'He's slept with your concubines.'

I'd said that on purpose to pull him up sharp—and it did, but not the way I'd wanted. David's hand went limp around mine, and now it was he who couldn't speak. He stared at me, distraught, and mouthed: What?

I said, 'He raped every one of them. In public, on the palace roof. All ten of the women you left behind. And my lord... long before you went, he'd already slept with Bathsheba.'

David was devastated. But as he fell to rambling again, with his forehead pressed onto the table, I realized it was neither betrayal nor incest he was babbling about, but something to do with a prophecy. He kept repeating, 'Nathan's words... this is it, this is the fulfilment, it's all coming true...' and 'You *have* to understand, Zohel... Zohar... Micha... I so much wanted to tell you, to tell Absalom, and Maacah...' He could barely shape the syllables of her name without choking on them. '... All these years I've borne this burden, with no one to share its misery except Nathan, as if he could ever know what this feels like...'

Against my own will I whispered, 'Then tell me, if you need to tell it. I won't breathe a word of it to anyone, if you don't want me to. I'll be Zoheleth the silent serpent for you.'

'... I never thought it would matter. It was just one night; that was all the time we spent together as lovers, can you believe it? One exhilarating, disastrous night... I'd first seen her in the afternoon, when I got up from my siesta... I was walking on the rooftop, she was bathing by her window; and she was just so beautiful, so young, her flesh was so firm and smooth...

'Then all at once she looked up at me through the window while I stood there watching her, and I could have died of shame. But she smiled... Micha, she just smiled! It was my birthday, and I was feeling so old... and I knew there would be no party to lift my spirits—well, not one worthy of the name—because every man I would have wanted to be there was away besieging Rabbah: Joab, Abishai... Uriah.

'In my younger days I would have been there with them, but there was no need for it any more, and I'd let Ahithophel convince me that it was foolish to risk my life unnecessarily. I was master of a huge and stable empire, I had whole legions of crack warriors to do my fighting for me, and generals to plan my campaigns, and accountants to collect my taxes, and civil servants to govern my provinces . . . I was bored and I was middle-aged, Micha, and I was out of touch with God. I'd barely prayed for weeks—what need did I have any more of faith? My life had grown so easy, so secure . . . and then standing there right in front of my eyes was Bathsheba, young and beautiful; and smiling.

'So at nightfall I sent for her, and we lay together. She didn't resist me. She didn't even play hard to get. She enjoyed every kiss, every caress; and somehow she knew exactly how to excite me. She made me feel young—heroic, virile, the way I'd felt on the day I slew Goliath. We must have made love six times, maybe seven . . . and all the time I was thinking, how can something so wonderful be wrong? One night we had, and she'd shared Uriah's bed for two years and never conceived . . .

'So when she sent word that she was pregnant, I couldn't believe it. I was panic-stricken. The scandal it would have caused! I didn't know what to do, and there was no one I dared talk to. So I sent for Uriah; I made him leave the unit he commanded and come back to Jerusalem. I tried everything to get him to lie with his wife so I could pass the child off as his, but he wouldn't even go home. When he said, 'My men are away fighting, how can I go and take my pleasure with a woman?' I thought he must be sniping at me, I thought he must have twigged to what I'd done! Only afterwards, when it was too late, did I realize that never in a thousand years would Uriah have suspected anything so base of me. And if he *had* done, he'd have faced me with it straight out; he'd never have stooped to sarcasm.

'And I should've known he would refuse to sleep with her. He could recite army regulations by heart, and wouldn't have dreamt of infringing even the pettiest of them. He knew as well as any native Israelite that sexual relations are forbidden to soldiers in time of war. He would *never* have gone near Bathsheba when he was supposed to be on campaign, though he adored her with every fibre of his being.

'Oh, I've heard people say he must have neglected her, he must have treated her cruelly, for her not to have borne him a child in all that time, but it's not true. He was a fine man, Micha, one of the best. He treated Bathsheba like a princess—and all she could do was mock him for it.

'But the way I saw it then, there was only one thing left that I could do. I packed Uriah off back to Joab, with a sealed letter—that's how I know he didn't suspect me, or he'd have opened it—and Joab duly sent him and his unit out on what I have to admit was a suicide mission: an insanely exposed assault on the walls of Rabbah in broad daylight. It almost went wrong when some of the men refused to cooperate—you saw for yourself what happened to two of them—but I knew Joab was ruthless and professional enough to see it through without asking awkward questions. Not that it prevented him from putting two and two together for himself though, and eventually coercing Nathan to tell him everything. I knew he'd done *that* as soon as the Tekoan witch-woman he hired to talk me into recalling Absalom from Geshur tried to trap me with a parable—Nathan's style entirely.'

He paused, awaiting my reaction, but it was slow in coming because I simply couldn't credit the conclusion which was being forced upon me. At length I asked, but without any sound except a croak, 'You—had him killed? An officer in your own army, who'd done you no wrong?'

'Not just an officer.' David's voice was little steadier than mine. 'A friend; a real friend, one of my Thirty Companions, no less. In my Hebron days his dogged dependability had meant as much to me as Joab's or Abishai's. Oh, we hadn't really been close since his marriage, and I'd never once been inside his house in Jerusalem. But when we were younger . . . he'd abandoned his Hittite gods and undergone circumcision, and even consented to a change of name because through me he learned about the love of Adonai. Uriah, Uri-yah. "God is my light".'

I left the table and went to the window. I stood there with my eyes closed, letting the damp wind calm me. It was no longer raining. But David knew what I was thinking, almost before I thought it.

'I don't know *how* I could have done it!' he shouted. 'Except that I was just so *angry* when I thought that Uriah knew everything and had the audacity to be sarcastic with me. Not one of us is perfect, Micha.'

And the anger was still inside him; that much was clear. But anger I could cope with better than despair. I wheeled around and hissed, 'All right, then! Why did *God* let you do it? You'd been faithful to him from boyhood! Yet he let you go and ruin your own life and countless others because of one moment—well, one night!—of weakness! Why didn't he protect you? I want nothing to do with a God who is callous like that!'

'I hadn't been faithful from boyhood at all, Micha. I ran protection rackets as sordid as any of the Syrians' when I was hiding from

Saul. I resolved upon the murder of Nabal, Abigail's first husband, because he wouldn't pay up; and God *did* stop me before I went through with *that* abomination. Even before then I'd lied to the priest Ahimelech to get supplies; and what I'd persuaded myself was an eminently legitimate and supremely ingenious piece of deception later drove Saul to massacre the entire population of the priests' city. Later still I consorted with the Philistines, and would have fought on their side against Saul at Gilboa—if God had allowed it. God will only protect us from ourselves for so long. In the end he'll let us learn the hard way. And it *is* hard. It's desperately hard.'

I bit my tongue, for all at once my mouth felt dry as dust. I *was* beginning to understand, though God knows I didn't want to. After what David had confessed to me, I wanted to despise him more than I ever had, and yet I couldn't, for the torment in his face cried out to me. I'd always been special to him, because I was the only human being he'd ever met who'd experienced Adonai the way he had, and yet who'd suffered unspeakably; Nathan was so far removed from the kind of guilt we were stained with that David might as well have tried to confide in a tame dove. In running away from my King and from my God all these years, I'd only been running from myself and from my own ravaged childhood... though I'd never breathed a word about it to David I was sure he must somehow be able to see my scars. Yet I didn't *want* to speak of it, even now; especially now. I was absurdly afraid that by bringing it out into the open, its power over me would intensify. Weak at the knees, I sat down once more at the table, and lost in my own dismal thoughts I hardly noticed that David was speaking again.

'... I tried to forget what I'd done to Uriah, of course. I told myself that he'd probably have fallen in battle sooner or later anyway, without my intervention. And I tried to make up for using Bathsheba, by taking her as my wife. After all, she was carrying my child, so she was my responsibility. But I didn't love her; I never have. It was sheer lust that had made me bed her that night, and even my lust was dead long before we were married.

'Still, she knew how to be discreet. She said nothing about the affair to anyone; she's one woman who never lets her tongue wag independently of her brain, as I soon discovered to my cost.

'Seven months later she gave birth, and even then everyone assumed that the baby had come early. I wasn't responsible for putting the story about, but I was happy enough to let folk believe it, implausible though it was. The guilt was growing dull by then; and I was Israel's darling, capable of no wrong in the nation's eyes. My relationship with God was in ruins, of course, but I tried to forget about that too—it had been lukewarm for so long in any case.

'Then out of the blue one night, Nathan came and told me one of his confounded parables. I should've guessed what he was up to; the technique was already a favourite of his. But he started telling me this long-winded, sentimental story about a poor peasant who'd had his pathetic little pet lamb stolen from him by a rich and powerful neighbour... I wasn't really concentrating. I thought it was just another of his wearisome examples of the—what did he call it?—the "moral corruption" he claimed was "endemic in my kingdom", and I let it all wash over me. I was still high on our victory over Ammon, and my feet hadn't touched the ground since I'd marched in person into Rabbah itself and set the Ammonite crown on my own head; I'd barely been back in Jerusalem a week.

'When I finally grasped what he was saying, I was beside myself. I couldn't for the life of me think how I'd been found out. It was so long since Adonai had revealed anything to me, it simply hadn't occurred to me that he might still speak to Nathan.

'Oh, I repented, and I meant what I said, with as much of myself as I could at the time. Yet I can't deny I feared scandal more than I feared God. Nathan told me that Adonai had forgiven me, but the baby would die, and...' David had to take a deep, heavy breath before going on. '... And he said that my household would be shaken and ravaged by strife, and that one of my own sons would show his contempt for me by lying with my women.

'I was distraught at the prospect of Bathsheba's son dying. It was for this same child that I'd married a woman I didn't love, and murdered a man I *did*. So I forgot the rest of the prophecy entirely. In fact, it was only much later, when Nathan correctly predicted the three years of famine, that I fully accepted he was a true prophet and meant what he said.

'But I couldn't bear to think that the drastic lengths I'd gone to in order to cover up my sin had all been for nothing. I remember begging and imploring Nathan not to tell anyone what I'd done. I kept on and on at him until he agreed.'

'Why?' I demanded, vainly seeking to hide my growing sympathy behind a mask of belligerence. 'Why would a holy man like Nathan let himself be made party to a squalid cover-up like that?'

'Oh, there were sound reasons. The stability of Israel, for one—there was every chance that the people might rise up and depose me if their illusions about me were shattered. And the reputation of Adonai for another—I mean, what kind of God would choose an adulterer or a murderer as King? Not everyone understands that he is a God of forgiveness—or wants him to be. And for a third . . . Nathan was my friend as much as Uriah had been, Micha. It must have torn him apart to see me grovelling on the ground heaping dust on my head.

'So he gave me his word he'd tell no one; and he kept it, right up until the day when Joab held a knife at his daughter's throat and dragged the truth out of him. I was so afraid then—I knew I'd never manage to deal with Joab the way I'd dealt with Uriah. But I needn't have worried. Joab's devoted to me, and always has been. He was just so anxious for me, he had to know what was troubling me, and I wouldn't tell him myself. He swore too to let the matter go no further, and it didn't.

'But all that was much later too. When Nathan first swore his oath to me, my heart lightened. I thought that when Bathsheba's child died, that would be the end of it all. I began to feel better than I had in months. I even wrote psalms praising God for his mercy and for my restoration. Then Bathsheba started saying she wanted another son; and I must make sure this one lived to become King.

'I asked her to give me more time before I slept with her again; we hadn't even consummated our marriage, because for me the mere thought of touching her brought back such awful memories. And I told her it was Adonai who would choose my successor. But she said if I didn't give her a son and promise that he would one day rule Israel, she would tell the world what I had done to her, and that I'd brought her to the palace merely to keep her quiet.

'That's when I began to discover what she was really like. She'd known full well that my chambers overlooked her own. She timed her brazen bathing to coincide exactly with the most fertile part of her month. I don't doubt she found me attractive—power excites her as much as beauty does—but the real reason she wanted me was so that she could be the wife and mother of kings.

'I panicked more than ever, then. She kept reminding me that if I drove her to expose me as an adulterer I'd be finished, and Israel with me. I'm not sure she knew that I was a murderer as well; only Joab and Nathan knew that for certain, though I reckon she must

310

have been suspicious. Not that I think she would have let such a discovery upset her. She was much better off with her first husband dead, and she knew it, though she'd have been better off still if she'd possessed that extra piece of knowledge to blackmail me with.

'I didn't even stop to question whether I *would* be finished if the truth were to be leaked, because I was already torturing myself with that very fear.

'But I *should* have got the whole thing out in the open, Micha; and I should have done it myself, not waited for her to do it. However serious the consequences, they couldn't have been worse than what happened instead. Bathsheba has been blackmailing me since before Solomon was even conceived; I've lost everything that ever mattered to me because of her! I alienated the sons I already had, so that first of all the eldest of them raped my beloved daughter... yes, I know you loved her too, Micha, but don't you *ever* think I didn't, just because I allowed Amnon to live! How could I have done otherwise? How could I put my own firstborn to death for a crime no worse than the ones *I'd* committed? It all seemed like part of my punishment: I'd taken another man's pet lamb, now mine had been taken. So it was only when she was violated that I recalled the rest of Nathan's prophecy... and even then, I thought maybe this was it, that Amnon's lying with Tamar was its total fulfilment. But then there was Absalom... When things began to go wrong with him too, I understood what real hell is like. Because hell is where I've been for nearly ten years, Micha. In the days when I played my harp for Saul and felled giants, no man was my master, only God himself; and I learned to rule men by learning to let him rule me. Once I lost my intimacy with Adonai, I lost my authority over others. I grew weak. Since then I've been King in name, but in reality, little more than Bathsheba's slave.'

I said nothing. I was too broken inside now to be aggressive, but still too stubborn to reach out to him. I stared at my hands, folded on the table, and tried to stop them shaking. Then David asked faintly, 'How *is* Absalom? Is he—happy?'

I looked away. 'What do *you* think?'

'And... and Maacah? What about Maacah? I don't even know if she's still alive.'

'In body she is, so far as I know. Inside, she's been dead as long as Tamar.'

'I should have gone to see her, whatever Bathsheba said . . . I don't suppose she even believes that I love her any more. I miss her so much. Is she still in Jerusalem?'

'She's at Absalom's place in Baal Hazor, with Miriam, but we've heard nothing from them in ages . . .' My voice trailed off; I was thinking that I'd rather use Saul's knife on myself than be the one to break the news to them when Absalom was gone too. Instinctively I felt for its presence inside my tunic; David's eyes followed the movement of my fingers.

He said, 'You know, for so long I've lived in dread of going the way Saul did. Nathan kept assuring me that Adonai had pardoned my sin; that the anarchy in my house was merely a consequence of what I'd done, not a deliberate chastisement from God, and that there was no need for me to fear a decline into depression or worse. He was right in a way—I *had* repented, and slowly I *did* begin to feel Adonai's presence again when I prayed. But then I realized I couldn't forgive *myself*, Micha; and I could hardly bear to pray because I felt so filthy.'

He hung his head, and I couldn't deny him my comfort any longer. With my hands still trembling, and now flattened on the tabletop to lend me support, I moved round to stand beside him, then I knelt and took him in my arms. To my mind, it was he who was receiving the healing; it didn't occur to me that mine had begun too. I murmured, 'It's all over now. The prophecy *has* been fulfilled in its entirety. Adonai's curse is outworked.'

'No, Micha,' he said. 'You still don't see. Adonai didn't curse me. He hasn't brought about any of my suffering. He doesn't *need* to punish us the way you're thinking; disaster happens of itself, that is one of sin's properties. God *does* forgive us—totally, unconditionally, but sin can't be undone. God's grace can't cancel out the effects of the havoc we create. And my suffering *isn't* over. Absalom *will* die tomorrow, and I shall have killed him. Not just physically in the battle, but spiritually years ago when I allowed him to murder Amnon and run away to Geshur. When I neglected him and his mother, and let them turn back to the lifeless gods of Syria.' He grasped hold of my garments and buried his face in them so hard I could barely make out what he was saying. 'I shall be so alone without him. All this time I've kept myself going by believing that one day we might be reconciled.'

'But you *needn't* be alone,' I said gently; and even as I was speaking,

I couldn't believe that the words were coming from me. 'What about Adonai? You say he's forgiven you; all that is needed now is for you to forgive yourself. When I was a child, you told me I need never be alone again; and I knew that was true even before you said it. Even before I learned how to talk, I could pray.'

There was a long, long pause. David's head was still pressed into my clothing. I'd simply no idea what I ought to say or do next. So I just knelt there and waited.

It was only when he roused himself and looked at me that I realized he had been weeping, quite without sound, and that he'd been praying. His eyes were red and swollen, his cheeks blotched and awash with tears. But he was radiant. All the tension and the bleakness had vanished, and the black cloud which had kept the light of Adonai from his face for as long as I'd known him was gone. And I hadn't needed to do anything, except remind him of what he already knew.

'What a waste, Micha,' was all he said at first, and I just stared at him, because the joy in his eyes was so beautiful. Then he hugged me breathless, and his joy found its way into words too, pouring from him all mixed up with relief and fresh repentance. 'Nearly ten years I've wasted, holding Adonai at arm's length when he'd already shown me his mercy, just because I was too proud, too bull-headed to show mercy to myself, or to risk the world finding out what I was really like. You've brought the light back to me; you *are* Zohar still! Don't be a fool like I've been. Don't keep your own shutters closed, not now.'

But just then I couldn't even think about myself. I felt the last of my antagonism towards David melting away like snow in springtime. Far from having lost my respect for him through what I'd learnt, I was starting to admire him as I'd never admired anyone before. Yes, he'd sinned appallingly, tormented himself savagely, and had no one else he could blame for what he'd been through. But he'd found within himself the courage to admit all that to me, and he might have done it long before, if I'd been prepared to listen to him. Now he'd repented of his pride in addition to everything else, his repentance was complete and he could be free.

And he could also join battle with Absalom the next morning without fear of destroying his own sanity in the process. Because neither of us was in any doubt now but that this was the right thing for him to do; unless the rogue king surrendered.

Not until I'd come to understand David at this last hour had I appreciated what a deadly threat Absalom posed to Israel. For he was beautiful, and he was hungry for power on a national scale: a combination rare and lethal as Leviathan. For the beautiful people of this world are accustomed to get what they want by other means; it seems to be the ugly who find their way into politics and become tyrants. Perhaps David himself had made Absalom what he was, but it was too late to agonize over that now. The important thing was that Absalom had to be stopped, one way or another, before he wrecked Israel and all that she stood for, and David was the only man alive who could do it. For whatever else he lacked, once again God was with him.

I said, 'Will you tell the people what you've told me tonight, before the battle? Or will you wait until afterwards, when you have victory under your belt?'

'I shall tell them when God wants me to,' he said. 'That may not be for a while. Bathsheba is my wife after all, and I don't wish to appear to be trying to discredit her any more than I want her discrediting me. Perhaps God will be gracious enough to enable me to build something worthwhile with her now; perhaps we can put the past behind us and start afresh. My *fear* of exposure is gone, that's what really matters. And she'll see that as soon as she next sees me.' Yes, I thought, she will indeed, for you look ten years younger already. But then he added, 'You're changing the subject, though, Micha. Don't think you can distract me so easily.'

'What?'

'We were going to talk about *you*. *Your* relationship with Adonai. You once let me ruin it for you; the least I can do now is help you recover what you lost.'

Before I had time to respond one way or the other, he'd laid his hands on my head and begun praying for me; a moment later, and I couldn't have fought him if I'd wanted to. First I was crying; then laughing; next I was prophesying, and words I didn't know were pouring from my mouth; next I was lying on the ground, moaning and wailing while I told him between great juddering sobs every shameful thing that Ziba had ever done to me. David wasn't shocked; I don't think he was even surprised. He just sat smiling with his hand on my brow and let me cry all my guilt and my anguish into oblivion, and when I'd finished there was no pollution left in me. I didn't even hate Ziba any more; I didn't even care about revenge.

I don't know how long I lay there after that. I might even have fallen asleep, for I think that Adonai needed time to fill my cleaned-out soul with love so there would be no room for my past to come back. But presently David helped me sit up; I was dizzy and disoriented, so he gave me some more to eat and drink and said, 'You will try just one last time with Absalom? Now that you—understand.'

I was so elated, I might have promised him anything. I said, 'Yes of course; if you truly think it's worthwhile.'

'I know it is; whether or not he listens. If he dies tomorrow, I shall need to know that I've done everything in my power to prevent it. In fact . . . I think I want you to tell him all that I've told you.'

Growing surer of himself by the second, David implored me, 'Tell him everything, Micha. Don't leave anything out, or make excuses for me. Because I want *him* to understand too, to know I always loved him, and to know why I neglected him, and that I'm so, so sorry. Then—when the time is right, I feel it may be your task to tell everyone.'

He waited for me to ask him what he meant, but I'd barely heard what he said because I was already trying to work out how to put all this to Absalom. By the time his latest words fell into place in my mind, he was explaining them.

'I told you long ago that Adonai never reveals himself to just anyone. He only chooses those for whom a specific task has been prepared. I think this may be yours, Micha. You know me and you know Absalom, you've been a friend to both of us, you've seen the whole of this wretched conflict between us from both sides. You must record the truth . . . everything you've seen, everything you've heard. You must write an account which will survive my death—and your death—so that no one will be able to make me out to have been some kind of paragon.'

'Then you *aren't* going to tell the truth yourself?'

'I will, as I promised you, if Adonai directs me to. But suppose I do build something with Bathsheba which works? What would be the point in turning my household upside down all over again, and destabilizing Israel to no purpose?

'No, Micha. You must promise me something else before I let you go back. Promise me you won't let even one day slip past before starting your account, once you've returned to Jerusalem; and that you won't tell a soul what you're engaged upon until I'm laid to rest with my fathers and your work is complete. Then you must deposit it with Nathan—or with his school, if he dies before I do; that way it will be safe.'

'Safe? Why should it need to be specially kept safe?'

'Because there will be those who would like to suppress it; there may even be those who frankly disbelieve what you've written; or don't want to believe it. You only have to look at the past, Micha; men try to cope with sins too awful to contemplate by pretending they never happened. I'm the architect of Israel's Golden Age; and like Aaron's golden calf I was raised up on a pedestal by people who should have known better. When tomorrow's fiasco is over, and I ride home in triumph once more—and honestly, I can't see things turning out any other way—they'll raise me to that place all over again and make an angel of me. They may even convince themselves that my sons respected me, and loved one another as brothers should. The rape of Tamar, the murder of Amnon, even Absalom's rebellion may all be quietly forgotten. I don't want that. I want my successors to know of my mistakes, and to learn from them, and to avoid them.'

I said, 'I'm not sure, my lord. I don't know if I *can* promise this. The task may be too big for me.'

David hugged me again, stroking back the hair from my eyes; I thought I knew whose eyes he was reminded of, and I was right, for he said, 'Don't be like your forefather Saul. Don't make *his* mistake. Believe in God and believe in yourself. You *can* do it.'

'I shall have to pray about this for myself. I can promise that, but no more; not yet.'

'You're a wise man, Micha,' murmured David, and it was the first time anyone had ever called me a man, so far as I recalled, let alone wise. 'Perhaps you'll be remembered not as Zoheleth, but as Qoheleth: he who teaches wisdom.'

'No, my lord.' I drew away from him then, knowing that it was almost time for me to go, but that one more thing was needful before I did so. 'It won't be me to whom those to come will give that name. There is one who is already wiser than I am and he isn't yet ten years old. Your son, Solomon, my lord . . . you're wrong about him. He isn't like his mother. He saved my life, and my father's. From her.'

There was so much more I could have told him, but I was loath to scatter my pearls until I was sure he would gather them. For a while his eyes searched mine, lest they should detect there any uncertainty; and even when they couldn't he said, 'Micha, that's not possible . . . At least, he can't have known who you were.'

'He knew perfectly well who both of us were, and what threat we might pose to his succession. It didn't worry him, my lord. He knows he'll build the Temple you dreamed of, and that there's no need for him to eliminate his rivals the way that worldly kings do. He's generous, perceptive, selfless, it's no wonder that Nathan has upheld his right to the kingship all along. My lord—Solomon knows Adonai.'

At first David continued staring at me, dumbfounded. Then slowly he started to laugh: just a soundless, stifled chuckle to begin with, but before long it was a great, unbridled belly laugh that convulsed him and made him embrace me all over again. Between outbursts he was trying to talk; I don't think he cared if I understood him or not, but he was thanking me, praising me, telling me he loved me for bringing him the most marvellous news he'd ever received. Then he was laughing at himself for being so slow-witted, because it had never so much as crossed his mind that the son he didn't know might not be a monster at all. Bathsheba might have thought she controlled Solomon, just as she'd thought she controlled David, and through them the fate of Israel; and her grandfather Ahithophel too had suffered from similar delusions about himself and his own ability to manipulate people and events to suit his own plans. But in reality Adonai had been in control all along; no matter what chaos men and women caused, they would never succeed in frustrating his ultimate purpose. Solomon was a child after God's own heart, not only wise, but merciful . . .

. . . Which must also mean that there would be room in his heart and in his kingdom for Absalom.

Suddenly sober again, David rose to his feet and pulled me up after him. 'You must go now,' he said, and once more he was the sprightly, self-assured soldier to whom Abishai had delivered me; but he was so much more besides. 'Go back to Absalom and talk to him. Tell him I'm prepared to pardon him even now, and that he no longer need fear anything from Solomon. Abishai will guide you; then you must come and see me in Jerusalem when all this is over. If you *do* fail to win Absalom . . . then I can only pray that I don't meet either of you face to face tomorrow.'

24

I'd been smuggled out of Absalom's camp in thick, damp darkness; I returned on my own two feet in a wash of white light from a rising moon. The clouds had rolled back like the spindles of a great indigo scroll, and the papyrus of the sky was bespattered with stars. Abishai and his companion left me to confront the guards alone: a confrontation which I must confess to having enjoyed.

Except for these shivering, half-drowsy sentries and their colleagues posted at regular intervals around the perimeter of the encampment, Absalom's horde slumbered on in silence. For the night was barely half done. I was too excited to be tired; I felt the glow of Adonai bright as the moonlight about me, and from the expressions on the faces of the sentries as they waved me past, I deduced that this glow must be visible.

I don't know if Absalom himself had been asleep, but there was no way he could have slept through Gatis' greeting. She leapt at me, panting and yelping with delight, so that I was quite relieved when her master got up and dragged her away. He was in no mood for celebration.

'Where the hell have you been?' he demanded, dealing the over-enthusiastic hound a blow he might rather have bestowed on me. 'Amasa's had men scour every corner of this bog-riddled quagmire for you. You'll push your luck once too often, little serpent. I thought you really *had* gone over to David this time.'

'I had. In a manner of speaking.' I couldn't see the point of wasting time lying to him; I was far beyond caring now whether he was angry with me or not. But perhaps on reflection I should have stalled until he was calmer. He started ranting at me, shouting and swearing as manically as Shimei had ever done, and causing poor Gatis to bark all the louder. I couldn't get a word in, and simply had to wait for him to exhaust himself. In the meantime I forced myself to come back down to earth, for I had to find some level I could reach him from. Then I said, 'I didn't go visiting of my own free will, for heaven's sake! I was . . . translated, shall we say; and no, I *don't* know

318

how they did it. But I know why, Absalom. Your father can think of no one else but me who might get you to see reason. He still wants to settle things bloodlessly.'

To begin with, Absalom went on seething, and except for the hostile sideways glances he occasionally cast at me, he kept his eyes firmly on the floor. Finally he condescended to spare a little thought for what I was saying, and gave a bitter laugh.

'So he's afraid to fight me after all, now our conflict has come this far? The snivelling coward! I *knew* that as soon as he saw my legions in the flesh he'd be suing for peace.'

I said, 'I don't think suing for peace is what he has in mind, Absalom. It's more like absolute surrender: yours.'

'He expects *me* to bow the knee to *him*?'

'Oh, Absalom, he doesn't want you grovelling at his feet! He wants you in his *arms*, can't you see that? He always has. He doesn't want you to die.'

'And what makes him so sure I'm *going* to die?'

'Just *think*, you stubborn fool! He has everything on his side: superior numbers—don't interrupt me, it's true, whatever Hushai says!—access to limitless supplies, familiar terrain as far as a good part of his army's concerned, a fortified city to fall back on.'

'You mean, a fortified city to be burned alive in. That's what Hushai says we'll do. We'll surround it and storm it and fire blazing arrows over the walls and . . . He'd never take me back now, Micha. Even if I thought he loved me. I've violated his harem; written him off as dead. He must have been told that.'

'He hadn't until *I* told him. I don't suppose anyone else had dared to. I even told him about you and Bathsheba. But it made no difference.'

Predictably, that silenced him; though momentarily I thought he might strike me after all, for giving away his vilest secret. But I don't think he could have brought himself to look at me for long enough to take aim; something about my face must indeed have changed. He wheeled about and stood with his back to me.

'Absalom, please hear me out this one last time,' I implored him. 'Your father sent Abishai himself here to fetch me—his own nephew, one of his staunchest friends, the commander of his Thirty Companions and second only to Joab in rank and valour! You don't take a risk with a man like that unless you're desperate; and he *is* desperate. To reach you.'

'And what about the risks *I've* taken? I've risked my own life, and the flower of Israel's manhood, to come out here and vanquish him. Amasa is ready now; our entire army is ready. Tomorrow the two of us will lead our troops to victory.'

'Tomorrow the two of you will lead them and yourselves into a death trap! How blind can you be? You must have cinders for eyes and a stone for a heart, Absalom ben David! Aren't you human? Aren't you even frightened?'

He didn't answer me at once; then his head drooped forward and he said, 'Of course I'm frightened. I'm terrified. I'm scared witless. But courage isn't being unafraid, you know, Micha.' He spoke as though he imagined such a profound truth had never been thought of before. 'And it's not refusing to acknowledge your fear. It's facing it and beating it, that's what Amasa says. That's what I shall do.'

'Sometimes courage is admitting you're wrong,' I reminded him gently, then unable to hold myself in check any longer I sprang forward and grasped his arms from behind. 'And sometimes courage is thinking for *yourself*, Absalom! How long are you going to go on letting others use you? For years it was your mother, harping on your beauty and making you vain. Then it was Shimei and Sheba making you drunk so that you'd be no better than they were. Then Ahithophel made you ambitious and unscrupulous so that he could live out his fantasies through you because he hadn't the authority or the charisma, or a legitimate excuse, to seize power for himself. Then it was Bathsheba trying to lure you to your death; then Hushai deceiving you; and now it seems that Amasa must think all your thoughts for you! If you must be ruled by the desires of others, why not listen to me for a change, or to your father? Or . . . to God?'

He stood so long without responding that I wondered if he'd heard me at all. His head was bowed, with the tumbling curls veiling his face, but I could feel his whole body start to shake. With my heart thumping wildly I thought: this is it, I've won him, he's going to break down in repentance just like his father did, and everything will be perfect. I could almost hear him saying the words inside my head: all this time I've been a slave to my own vanity . . . why did no one ever make me face the truth?

And I'm sure that something akin to this was going through his mind too, as he stood there shaking and swallowing. Even when he turned round and raised his head to look at me I still clung to the hope, for there was a deep haunted sorrow in his dark eyes such as I'd never seen there before. But then for the first time since I'd walked in from being with David, he permitted himself to scrutinize my face without being distracted, and he could no longer deny what he saw. Moreover, when the last thing I'd said to him aloud filtered through to him, he knew what he was seeing. He said, 'So you too want to deceive me, little serpent.'

'... What?'

'Perhaps I'm not quite the fool you take me for. I've lost you again, and I know it. But not because you're a damned Saulide. I've lost you to my father and his accursed Adonai, just like I did when you were a boy.'

'No...' I began, 'No, you don't understand... I don't *want* to make a choice between you and your father. And there's no need for me to do so.'

'He's done something to you, though, hasn't he? He's bewitched you somehow, or drugged you, or changed you...'

'Something has changed me. But not the way you're thinking.'

'I want to know everything he said to you, Micha. Every single word, every syllable. And you'd better tell me, or I shall have you stoned for treachery after all.'

What choice did I have? David had insisted that he wanted Absalom told; now Absalom was insisting on it too. But I knew already that this wasn't the right time. The truth wouldn't make him understand, it would only make him dig his heels in further. Yet what other time would there be? Anything which wasn't said to him tonight would likely never be said to him at all.

So I told him. I told him the whole sordid saga just as David had told it to me; and Absalom went wild.

'Sorry? The swine has the audacity just to say—he's sorry? When he's ruined my life just like he ruined Tamar's and our mother's, and all because of his own despicable lechery and cowardice? My God, Micha... my own father, Adonai's anointed, is a common adulterer, a vulgar murderer... not that he even had the guts to do the killing himself! What right has he to pardon me? I don't *want* his pardon! And I don't want Solomon's either, he's nothing but the spawn of a harlot! I don't care if he *is* mutton-headed enough to spare my hide if he gets the throne; I shan't be so naive as to spare his! I've never been afraid of him anyway, do you hear me? It's *he* who fears *me* or he wouldn't have hidden himself away from me all this time . . .'

He broke off abruptly, because there was suddenly a scuffling at the entrance to the tent; and Amasa walked in. He'd just come from sleep, for his short hair was tousled and he wore only a tunic, but there was anxiety stamped all over him. Perhaps he'd merely heard Absalom shouting, and come thinking he was in trouble; or perhaps it was something more. But Absalom didn't wait to enquire. He yelled at him to get out, and when the young general hesitated, a volley of expletives rained down on him. So he left without saying whatever it was he'd come for, and Absalom began ranting again about his father being no better than Amnon: both of them had been like rutting animals, unable to control their base passions, thinking nothing of thrusting their tainted seed into other men's soil.

'And you think you're any better?' I retorted. 'You think that when *you* lay with Bathsheba it was somehow more honourable? At least David only took the wife of a friend; you took the wife of your own father.'

Of course that was the final straw. Beside his pallet there stood the figure of one of his hideous Syrian gods; the thing was barely two cubits high, but fashioned from solid stone, and he picked it up and hurled it at me. Thankfully he was too steamed up with fury to aim very straight, but in avoiding it I fell, twisting my arm and drawing blood. He didn't even apologize, just stood looking right through me as I clutched at the wound, and shouting, '*Why* do you think I took her? There was nothing else left I could do to make him notice me! He was my hero, Micha, I worshipped the very dust on his sandals, but I'd become invisible to him! What would *you* have done to make him see you, my little angel of light?'

Closing my eyes against the searing pain in my elbow I stammered, 'You broke the second commandment long before you brought abominations like that thing under your roof, Absalom. You shouldn't put *anything* in God's place, or anyone, even your father, even when he's Adonai's anointed. No one should be raised up so high; it's too far to fall.'

'There's no further he *can* fall now in my eyes. I could never respect him or love him after this. So you might as well lecture me on the fifth commandment too, though by this time tomorrow it will hardly matter. Here.' He threw me a scarf which had once been his turban. 'Get this wrapped round your arm, and stop moaning like that. You're not going to die.'

No, I thought, but you are; and it's not the pain I'm moaning about.

I'd barely got to sleep when the message came through that we were under attack.

It reached us in the barely intelligible words of a runner sent by Amasa. The poor lad was breathless and manifestly terror-stricken, and looked barely a day over fifteen. For Absalom and me, it was like suddenly being told that we were bereaved. We passed from vacant non-comprehension, through disbelief, to mind-numbing shock, before the panic set in.

For aside from the torchlight, it was still pitch dark. Nor at first was I conscious of any of the sounds which my inexpert mind associated with warfare. There were no voices shouting or scream-ing, no drums beating or horns blaring. Outside, for all I knew, the world was still sleeping, so silently and peacefully that conflict couldn't touch it.

Then all at once a single trumpet rang out in the distance, and something inside me answered it, twisting in my guts like the barbed point of a spear which someone was struggling to extract. While I stumbled about looking for my sandals I listened to Absalom assailing our visitor with questions. It was evident to me at once that he was only asking them to convince himself and the boy that he was in control; I don't think he even heard half the answers. But I succeeded in gleaning that David's army had marched under cover of darkness and swooped down upon our camp in three separate divisions; of these the largest body had taken up a position between us and the city, the other two were drawn up one on each side of us, and behind us lay trackless forest and swamp. We were to all intents and purposes surrounded.

We ought to have anticipated that the foe would move on us by night; or at least, Amasa ought to have. It had often been a favourite tactic with David, as it had with Saul, and Amasa's failure to take account of the possibility only served to illustrate his lamentable lack of experience as a warlord. Then my guts cramped up tighter as I thought, perhaps he *hadn't* been taken by surprise. There must have been some reason for his coming to our tent in the early hours, but we'd been arguing too hard to pay him attention.

'And why is it so damned quiet out there?' Absalom was demanding. 'Hasn't Amasa launched a counter-attack? What is the fool waiting for?'

'Please, my lord... Your Majesty... sir, I don't know what's going on. He just told me to fetch you; he said it was an emergency.'

Convinced that Absalom would linger irresolute for ever despite his superficial bravura if I didn't get him organized, I pulled on my clothes and set about sorting through his. I felt better once I had something to do, but Absalom had stripped off his night things and now stood naked in the middle of the floor, pale and still as a dead man upright. Fear had immobilized him totally; never having had to cope with a crisis the like of this before, I don't suppose he'd had any idea himself as to how his nerves would react to it.

So as patiently as I could, I helped him get dressed, but as soon as I touched him it was like a spell breaking. He began fretting, shivering and shuddering, hindering my work and knocking things out of my hands. He claimed that the bronze breastplate cut into the flesh under his arms and that the helmet chafed his chin; and no wonder, because he'd hardly ever worn them. His predicament might have been laughable had it not been so pathetic: a sweating, all but hysterical dandy whose only taste of combat in the recent past had been sparring for practice with Amasa, being equipped by an armour bearer even greener than he was, for a war he'd embarked upon of his own free will against an army whose commanders had been responsible for the annihilation of the hosts of Philistia, Moab, Edom and Syria... the inevitable outcome of their present operation didn't bear thinking about. Absalom was sick three times before I got him outside. Then a second runner arrived, maintaining that we weren't being attacked at all. We were indeed surrounded, but for some unfathomable reason no offensive had yet been launched. There was even talk of a truce.

Lest we waste any more time while Absalom subjected another ignorant messenger to a pointless interrogation, I resolved upon delivering him to Amasa immediately whether he fought me or not. As it happened he didn't—perhaps he smelt my determination—but he did insist that we take Gatis with us.

Going outside was like stepping over the threshold of a nightmare. There was now no cloud in the sky, and the whole camp was flooded in intense white moonlight illumining each detail of the scene bright as day, but draining the colour from everything so that men's faces were grey like shades in Sheol. Somehow panic and paralysis had invaded simultaneously and made their own uneasy truce amongst our men. Some had already begun running this way and that, seizing weapons, fumbling with armour, cursing one another's clumsiness, each man reliant on the next to tell him what to do because no clear orders were coming through the burgeoning mayhem. But for every man who was seeking refuge in activity, there were two standing stupefied. Because at last the truth was dawning that this nightmare was no figment of any dreamer's imagination. Nor was it a game.

For as with any war, there were those who had marched out with Absalom for no other reason than to be part of an adventure from which they might carry off some ghoulish souvenir. They had taken to the road whistling and joking; some had still been whistling and joking when we'd crossed the Jordan and swum through seas of Gileadite mud, and they'd sung raucous songs around last night's campfires which might still have been smouldering had the earth been less moist. When I close my eyes I can still see the dazed faces of those hapless dupes now, many of them scarcely more than children, white with fear as much as with moonglow, lined and haggard as starvelings' as grim reality took its toll. Squalid death or shameful surrender awaited them; I wondered if they cared which it would be.

We found Amasa pacing in his tent, with a handful of his captains around him. The moment we entered, he sprang forward and drew Absalom into their midst, rebuking him like a worried parent for taking so long in coming. Absalom's temper was on a short rein too. In a peevish growl he chided Amasa for sending him ill-informed minions who couldn't string together three words that made sense; were we under attack, or had a truce with David already been struck? Amasa was embarrassed to have to point out that he wasn't empowered either to join battle or to negotiate settlements without the authorization of Absalom himself; and in any case, David personally had been seen by no one. The three enemy divisions were apparently commanded by Joab, Abishai and a certain Ittai respectively. David was assumed still to be holed up in Mahanaim.

'Still in Mahanaim?' echoed Absalom, vacuously at first; but then he said it again, and this time he was crowing. 'So the worm *is* too yellow to fight me! And Ittai's a confounded Philistine, didn't you know that? A pirate, a mercenary from Gath, the very cesspit Goliath crawled out of, no less, and he's every bit as much a heathen as folk like to label *me*. Where are the yellowbellies' envoys? Tell them that we do no deals with Sea People.'

'With respect, my lord . . . they haven't sent any envoys.'

'I thought you said they were asking for a truce?'

'No, my lord. We don't know what they want. They have sent no communication at all. They are merely waiting.'

'Waiting for what?' Absalom scratched at the skin behind his helmet buckle, so that you could see how raw he was making it even by torchlight. 'Why don't they lay into us and get this thing over with, if they're so confident of victory?'

'I wish I knew, my lord. They could have wiped us from the face of the earth by now if they'd kept up their momentum after surrounding us.'

While Absalom and Amasa stared at one another nonplussed, and the captains shuffled their feet and tried to look nonchalant, something fell into place in my mind. Convinced that I was right in what I was about to say, but less convinced about my right to say it here in this conclave of military men, I coughed uncertainly and volunteered, 'Isn't it obvious, Absalom? Your father will have ordered them to use force only as a final resort. How often must I tell you? He's desperate to avoid shedding Israelite blood. Especially yours.'

Amasa growled, 'In that case they *would* have sent envoys.'

'Not if David isn't with them. Can you imagine that Joab and Abishai want peace? With Absalom? Joab hates you, Absalom, he's hated you for years, or had you forgotten? He's been biding his time, studying developments, counting off the days until he could mete out to you the punishment he believes you deserve. He must have watched your rise to prominence the way a hunter watches a beast walk into his trap. Now his day has come, and he isn't going to let his chance to exact retribution be lost through a last minute reconciliation; not if he can avoid it. He's waiting for *us* to provoke *him* so that he can go back afterwards and tell David that he only resorted to violence in self-defence. Don't play into his hands.'

There was silence. Amasa looked at me the way a lion might look at a mouse; yet the mouse had squeaked sense, and he knew it. Not that he was prepared to acknowledge as much; he turned back to Absalom and said as though he'd seen it all along, 'Attempting to parley with Joab or Abishai would be as futile as forming up to fight them. Either way they'd succeed in making out that we'd acted provocatively, and slice us to ribbons. Our best hope lies with Ittai.'

Absalom gaped at him. 'Hope of what?'

'Well . . .' Amasa cleared his throat and shifted his weight from one foot to the other. 'Either we offer him something to buy him off—as you said yourself, he's a mercenary, after all—or we bypass the sons of Zeruiah and seek to negotiate peace terms with David through him.'

If Amasa had suggested that we tear one another's guts out and save the enemy the trouble, Absalom couldn't have been more horrified. He retorted with mounting passion, 'So even *you* would sell me down the river? You'd renounce your cause *now* on the very brink of the final confrontation? I've told you, Amasa, I don't strike bargains with Sea People. I'll send Ittai and his pirates howling back to their ships, and I'll send you with them!'

'For God's sake, Absalom, what does it matter whether he's a Philistine or the Pharaoh himself? Since when have you been squeamish about treating with idolaters? He's our only hope of *survival*, damn you! We're trapped in this miserable swamp of a camp like so many fish in a net. If we try to make a fight of it now we'll be cut down before we can even get into battle formation.'

'You should have been better prepared, Amasa. That's why I employ you. You should have seen this coming.'

'*I* should have been better prepared? With *you* as my example? Perhaps you would care to give our colleagues here a demonstration of your superior skills as a general? Perhaps you would like to offer our charioteers advice on how to dig their wheels out of the bogs? Perhaps you would enjoy the challenge of getting our squadrons drawn up calmly under a barrage of enemy arrows and slingstones? Perhaps—'

But Amasa was never allowed to finish his tirade, because his voice was drowned by the blaring of a thousand trumpets and the yelling of ten thousand throats. The battle had begun without us.

We never found out quite what started it. There were about as many versions as there were so-called witnesses. Some said that one of our sentries had gone mad, unable any longer to bear the pressure of the enemy's statuesque procrastination, and rushed screaming at the nearest pair of eye-whites, thus offering Joab the excuse he'd been waiting for. Others claimed that some remorse-ravaged youth had seen his father's face among the ranks of the old King's host and bolted off seeking his forgiveness, only to be brought down by one of Joab's marksmen. I even heard it suggested that a crabbed old cuckold had espied his wife's lover standing at the right hand of Abishai, and had made a beeline for him, impaling him on the point of his spear. The only factor which the diverse stories had in common was that a single private soldier, acting on his own initiative, had lit the taper which ignited one of the most appalling conflagrations in Israel's history; and I use the word conflagration advisedly, because within moments of the fighting breaking out, daredevils of Joab's had put torches to our tents.

Most were too waterlogged to do more than smoulder. But some of the senior officers hadn't put theirs up until the rain stopped, and owing to their predilection for abandoned houses, they hadn't pitched them at all the previous night. These went up like tinder. We issued from Amasa's own tent to find chaos. Baggage animals bellowed and snorted, horses ran amok as their owners sought to harness them to mud-caked chariots. Flames leapt like pliant swords into the remorselessly rainless sky; for now when we might have welcomed a downpour the stars sparkled benignly and the moon beamed unctuously upon us, making no attempt to disguise her serene smile. Absalom clutched at my cloakpins with Gatis barking round his heels; he was insisting that I make his own chariot ready for combat, and when I protested that there was no time, he wanted the horse he'd broken for riding, or any horse at all. It seemed that I alone was relatively calm, for once again I knew I had a friend who was closer to me than a brother, upon whom I could confidently lay all my cares, and who was in ultimate control of everything, however chaotic it appeared. And in case I should fancy that my restoration to faith at David's hands had been a dream, I had Saul's jewelled knife tucked inside my tunic to remind me.

I don't remember much about the battle itself—not the early part of it, anyway. Confused images, jarring impressions ... there was noise, and filth, and blood, and I drew considerably more of it than I'd judged myself capable of. It's sobering to reflect on what you can bring yourself to do once you see that you must kill or be killed, and I can't even recall whether my elbow troubled me or not.

Still, I did see some things which I'll never forget. A smooth-cheeked boy lying supine with his eyes wide open and a muddy bootmark ground into his face ... an officer dying slowly with an arrow in his throat, his eyes wide open too, the lifeblood gurgling with every tortured breath and bubbling out between his teeth... a seasoned campaigner with one spear through both his calves, trying to crawl with his legs pinned together... a teenager howling like a wolf beside the body of a friend, pummelling the dead youth's chest as though with the force of his anger he could beat the life back into him.

But most of the corpses lay forgotten where they'd fallen, some bloated, some charred, all of them disfigured, a few looking so little like men that you couldn't even pity them; they had simply become part of the wreckage of war. I remember myself disembowelling some great hairy giant of a man who, if not twice as tall as me, was certainly twice as broad. I remember the expression on his face as he clutched at his spilling vitals—more one of surprise than of pain—and the smell of his breath as he fell against me. He was the first man I ever killed, and when I'd finished him there was vomit all down my chest, and my loincloth was sodden.

And all this time I had no idea where Absalom was. So much for my acting as his armour bearer... but in that pandemonium it was impossible to keep track of anyone. Our attempt at resistance was an unmitigated disaster—the three divisions of David's army advanced towards the centre of our camp inexorably, and gave us no time to coordinate anything. It was each man for himself, and we fought like wild things, but the end result was the same as if we'd simply stood there and waited to die. It was a massacre; long before dawn the edifice of Absalom's pride had crumbled, and nothing of his dominion remained for the new day's sun to shine upon but burning timber and goatskin, smashed chariots, ransacked wagons, and carrion. Those men who hadn't yet perished had run for their lives into the forest, with the enemy in pursuit; I could only assume that Absalom was with them, for I couldn't find him among the dead. And I had plenty of opportunity to search, for before the battle had become a rout I'd been left for dead myself. A toppling tent pole had knocked me out cold, and when I came round all the action had moved on. Or so I thought.

I lay where I'd awoken for some two score of my palpitating heartbeats, then managed to sit up, and struggled to get my bearings. Somewhere close by me, a lone bird was singing; the sweet sound was so incongruous that each time I blinked my eyes I saw orchards and vineyards and bright butterflies, and corn waving in the wind. After a while I staggered to my feet and began hunting randomly through the tangles of twisted bodies in search of Absalom, or Amasa, or anyone at all whom I recognized. Then gradually it came home to me that as well as the birdsong I could hear shouting; I looked around slowly, for my head was pounding fit to burst, and I saw that beside what had once been Amasa's tent, men were still fighting.

Absalom had after all commandeered a two-horsed chariot from somewhere, and stood high out of reach, with his feet planted one on each of its side panels and both his hands grasping the hilt of his sword, which he wielded like a scythe at any man who came near him. He hadn't been left to face the foe alone; half a dozen men stood shoulder to shoulder around the vehicle, and they too were bravely challenging all comers. But the last stand they were making was clearly futile; their opponents' numbers were growing all the time as the identity of the madman with the flailing blade leaked out. For you wouldn't have known who he was unless you were close to him; his mane of blue-black hair was bound up beneath his helmet, his face was covered in grime and gore, and his bronze armour was so filthy it could have passed for leather.

Then suddenly a trumpet began blasting nearby, and quite unexpectedly Absalom's assailants backed off. An officer ran up and set to haranguing them, but it took me some while to make sense of his blustering and gesticulating. The gist appeared to be that if this was Absalom he must not be harmed. David's orders were to bring him back alive; he must therefore be taken prisoner, and once this was accomplished, the pursuit of his misguided followers could be called off.

I shall never know how I got him away from them, though two factors undoubtedly contributed. One of these was that a second officer turned up and began arguing with the first; each of them seemed more interested in scoring points over the other than in seizing Absalom, and their men were content to stand about egging them on. The other thing that helped us was Gatis; she'd been standing beside her master in the chariot, from which she now sprang like a tiger and sank her teeth into the thigh of one of his attackers. In the fracas which ensued I managed to climb up beside him; he cracked a whip at the horses, Gatis bounded back to join us, and we were away.

Naturally we didn't get very far. We should have abandoned the chariot and fled on foot, but Absalom's pride wouldn't have allowed it. As it was, we got further than we would have done had anyone but him been driving. We wound and wove between the thickening trees with bare inches to spare on either side, and for a miraculously long time didn't get bogged down at all, partly because of the speed we were travelling at, and partly because the ground had dried out significantly with there having been no rain for several hours.

But the further we went, the denser the forest became; the trees were still dripping, the mud beneath them was still soft, and horrendously churned up by the feet of our retreating army and its pursuers. Even where there wasn't any mud, the ground was often knee-deep in rotting leaves. Presently the inevitable caught up with us; our wheels stuck fast and the chariot was rendered indisputably useless.

But even now Absalom wasn't prepared to make a run for it. We still had the horses, and he was convinced that we should be faster and less vulnerable to attack if we rode them. I did try to tell him that they'd be more of a hindrance than a help, that they might not ever have been ridden before, and that they would get us entangled in straggling branches, and so on. But I might as well have tried to reason with a mudbrick. He succeeded in getting the yoke detached, no simple task because it wasn't he who'd fixed it, but rigging up halters suitable for riding was quite another matter. While he was fumbling with buckles and cursing and swearing, we heard voices calling through the trees behind us, and the bunch of David's men whom we thought we had eluded fell upon us.

There were fewer of them now—for that at least we could be thankful—because their argument had ended in schism, but the officer they had with them was the one who had claimed to have no qualms about killing David's son. Fortunately for us, his men still seemed less than convinced; they hung back while he rushed at us, borne forward on a tide of ill-conceived heroism. Like too many others before him, he had eyes only for Absalom; and like the first man I'd brought down, he cried out with surprise as much as pain when I took him from behind. My sword severed his spine and he subsided like a sail when the wind has gone out of it. Absalom kicked him over on his broken back and finished him by severing his head to match. Emboldened by our success we took on his underlings with enthusiasm, and found them easy prey because they still weren't sure where their duty lay, and they were patently overawed at finding themselves face to face with the pretender himself. As a result they fought almost half-heartedly. I left Absalom to deal with a pair of them without thinking twice about it; somehow I managed to despatch the other three, for I was well excited now, high on my own rather unexpected valour.

So I was doubly dismayed to turn around when I'd completed my task and find him wounded. I hadn't heard him cry out—perhaps he'd been too shocked to—but he was hunched up on the ground staring white-lipped at his leg as though it belonged to someone else, with Gatis standing over him whining like a bereft infant. There was a sword slash in his thigh almost down to the bone, and the blood ran from it as wine runs from a shattered pitcher.

Hot and cold and nauseous all together with my own shock, I got myself together enough to rip the hem off my tunic and wrap it tightly round the wound; the gash was neat, but far too large for me to have any hope of staunching the blood flow entirely. The first bandage I used was soaked through in seconds, and by the time I'd got the flow under control my hands were slippery as a butcher's and the skirt of my tunic was all but gone. Absalom had fallen backwards and lain still while I laboured, so that I assumed he'd passed out. But when I checked, his eyes were open and I came close to passing out myself because I feared it might be all up with him already. Then he started trying to speak to me, and I saw there was blood mixed with the froth on his lips; and there was blood oozing out beneath his helmet.

I'd been so taken up with attending to his leg that it had never occurred to me to examine the rest of him. Now I simply couldn't credit it that I hadn't noticed the great dint in his helmet; someone must have brought a hefty sword down right on top of his head. Sorely shaken up now, I got the chin strap unfastened, and he howled and retched when I prized the helmet off, though I was as gentle as I knew how to be.

The cut, when I found it, didn't look too serious—though the finding of it took me quite some time because of all his hair. But the blow had made him giddy—either that, or the loss of blood from his leg had, or just the pain—and when he tried to sit up he collapsed against me, his vomit mingling with mine which by now was going hard on what remained of my clothing.

I couldn't think what to do; the horses had long since bolted, and there was no way I could get anywhere carrying him. There was no one in sight except the five unfortunates we'd taken care of—the fifth one must have felled Absalom whilst going into his own death throes—yet if we stayed where we were there was more chance we'd be found by the enemy than by our own. In the end, having no energy left and no other hope, I knelt there and prayed, still holding him against me to keep him warm, rocking back and forth in some futile attempt to soothe either him or myself, and all for far too long without doing anything more constructive... or so an unbeliever might have said. But by some impossible coincidence or miracle, call it what you will, I looked up presently to see a solitary soldier approaching; he was leading a mule, across the back of which was draped the body of its master's companion.

I don't know to this day whose side the pair of friends had fought on—indeed, it isn't unthinkable that one had fought on each. But as soon as I leapt up, the muleteer abandoned the animal and its sorry burden, and fled. I guess I must have looked pretty horrific with gore and sick all down me, my face caked in tear-streaked mud, my body naked below the waist save for a tattered and stinking loin-cloth. Unsure whether to start praising God for his mercy or pinch myself to see if I was dreaming, I staggered forward, disturbed to find how unsteady my legs had become all of a sudden, and proceeded to examine the corpse.

For a corpse it certainly was. The flesh was already cold and stiffening, and the right hand was gone entirely, the arm ending in a sort of brush of shattered bone and blood. With a half spoken and half meant promise to come back when all this was over and arrange a decent burial, I grasped the poor fellow's belt—rather a fine studded leather one, I noted, and under other circumstances I might have taken time to appropriate it—and deposited him on the ground.

Getting Absalom mounted in his place was a different matter. It might have been easier if he'd truly been unconscious, but he kept drifting under and then coming back again, and refusing to be loaded up like an inanimate piece of baggage. He was determined to sit astride the creature; despite the pitiful state he was in, his stubborn pride was indomitable.

To compound our problems, I'm not sure that the mule was any more used to being ridden than the horses we'd acquired earlier were likely to have been. It jerked its head this way and that, and at first wouldn't go forward whether I yanked it from in front or Absalom tried to urge it from above. There was blood dribbling down his leg again, and his eyes would roll and blink and close every time the beast moved under him; it galled me to reflect that he who had trained wild stallions and ridden them backwards, sideways and standing up, could no longer manage the mongrel offspring of a donkey.

Eventually we did succeed in making some forward progress. Absalom seemed to rally a little, telling me not to fret, he would be all right, we would both come out of this alive, we would escape to Geshur and live there happily ever after. But when he'd repeated these assurances for the twentieth time, I decided he was delirious, and only capable of remaining upright because he'd ridden so much in the past that his muscles could relax in a riding position as easily as they could lying down. Deciding it was best neither to look at him nor even to think, I concentrated on scanning the lie of the land ahead of me and picking the best route.

Not that I had any idea where we ought to be going. I was simply concerned to avoid swamps and precipices; for the further we went, the more hazardous the terrain became. It was almost as though the very earth was fighting on David's side, and as though he had trees in his army as well as men. I learned later that more of our troops had died in the forest than in the fighting—and more Israelites died that day than on any since the Battle of Gilboa. Some blundered into pits, some fell down escarpments of rock, some sank without trace in the bogs, some were torn apart by wild beasts. Absalom and I saw none of these monsters; but we barely saw any human beings either, certainly not living ones. I began to fear not so much being attacked as becoming lost for ever and spending eternity wandering as men and then as ghosts in this blind, rank jungle. I almost forgot that Gatis was with us, so subdued was she, plodding along with her tail scraping the ground. Would that Absalom's human followers had been half as loyal; never before had it struck me with such force how little those who'd fawned on Absalom had really cared about him as a person. Never before had I felt so bitter about it, either. He was too far gone to feel it for himself, however—which I suppose was another blessing in its way.

But I shouldn't have allowed myself to go back on my resolve and begin thinking instead of looking where I was going. All at once we emerged on the crest of a ridge; it was hardly a prominent one, and trees grew all over it and down the other side, but the ubiquitous mud made the modest slope lethal. The mule lost its footing, and went slithering downward towards a tangle of half-grown trees which were more densely packed than their taller neighbours, and whose waist-high branches intertwined and were infested with creepers... and there wasn't a thing I could do about it. Yelping frantically Gatis loped after her master's mount, but she couldn't control her gait either. In helpless consternation I watched both animals plunge into the thicket, and unbelievably, although this obstacle served to impede its momentum, the brainless mule kept on going. Or perhaps it wasn't as brainless as I supposed; perhaps it specifically intended to dislodge its debilitated rider. Whether it did or not, that was what happened. The mule made off into the depths of the forest, leaving Absalom entangled in a web of branches and what looked to me like wild vines.

Half crazed with urgency I set off down the hill, falling twice and ending up filthier and smellier even than before. When I reached him he was fainting, chiefly with exhaustion from trying to work himself free. His haphazard efforts had only made things worse: a thousand thorns had embedded themselves in his garments, and the briers to which they were attached embraced him as though they'd been created solely for that purpose and had now found a glorious fulfilment in carrying it out. His hair, which had strayed loose since I'd removed his helmet, was tangled up inextricably in a profusion of wet greenery, and his face, hitherto unscathed underneath the filth, was a mass of scratches and grazes. Gatis crouched a spearlength away, head on paws, tail dolefully beating on the ground.

Praying aloud as I worked, I pulled Saul's dagger out from where I'd stowed it and began hacking at the briers until my hands were as torn as Absalom's face. Once again I wished he would black out completely, for he was trammelling himself faster than I could free him. His injured leg hung useless now, but with the other he kicked out wildly, and his arms flailed and thrashed so that more than once he cut himself on my knife. At one point I came to the conclusion that I might just as well give up trying, and letting the knife drop out of my hand found myself bawling for help despite the risk it carried; but as soon as I raised my voice Absalom began moaning involuntarily, choking out gobs of blood as he did so, and the sound and the sight were so hideous that I stopped shouting and went back to hewing branches. He rambled some more about Geshur and how we could fly there on wings of eagles, or something, then mercifully at last lost consciousness.

Now I could hack away unhindered. Before long I'd disposed of most of the creepers which encumbered his body, and knew I should be able to lift him free of the more substantial branches once I'd dealt with the thorn withes and tendrils still caught in his hair. But it was so thick and heavy and clogged up with blood that they would never come away without tearing it. So the logical thing to do was to cut it off there and then and have done with worrying; with my heart in my mouth and my fingers trembling, I began to shear off the locks which had been the crown of Absalom's prodigious beauty since his boyhood.

And I nearly died for it. He revived instantaneously—you might have thought I'd been trying to saw off his leg—and got his hands around my throat. I can't imagine how he had the strength left in him, what with all the blood he'd lost and was still slowly losing, but he'd half strangled me before I succeeded in squirming round and biting him. And all the time he was screeching like a hunting-bird, 'Not my hair! Don't touch my hair! Leave my hair alone!' so that I wound up on all fours in the mud with my ears ringing. Then once again I heard voices, and footsteps threshing through the undergrowth.

I got up and stood beside Absalom, and Gatis stood with me, but there was nothing we could do now but wait and see who our racket had attracted. Absalom was still conscious but rapidly failing, and I knew that next time he closed his eyes he would never open them again. They were already glazing over as he looked at me, but the delirium was gone and he spoke my name quite lucidly, though he called me Zohel and not Micha. Then just as lucidly he said, 'Run for your life, little serpent. Run now. There's nothing you can do for me here.'

I muttered the usual platitudes, maintaining that it was impossible for me to leave him like this, that I'd rather die than desert him in his direst hour. But he reached out and turned my face to his, and said, 'You have to get away. There's something you must do for me in Jerusalem . . . Zohel, before we left I told Seraiah to set up a monument for me so my name would be remembered. You have to make sure it gets done. I'm serious, Zohel. It means everything to me. I've left no heirs . . . I don't want to be forgotten.'

So I promised him that I'd see to it, but still I didn't run, for I couldn't make my feet obey me. Nor did he say any more to force me, for his face had gone whiter than ever, and there was more blood on his lips. Somehow I knew that the men I'd heard coming would be

David's, long before I saw them; and as soon as I did see them I was sure of it, because they carried themselves with the strutting confidence of those who are assured of victory. They were bragging to one another of their own exploits; one had two shields and another a veritable armful of javelins—they'd been looting and stripping rebels' corpses already. But they soon stopped their idle boasting when they saw us, recognizing Absalom at once, for hair like that could belong to no one else.

Leering repulsively, the character with the two shields sauntered over and pushed me aside, warning me to stay out of the way if I knew what was good for me. He had his sword drawn and meant to finish Absalom with a single thrust. Then the one holding the javelins called out, 'Kill the youngster while you're at it. You know who he is, don't you? A snivelling Saulide.'

His leering comrade hesitated; I edged up closer, half protecting Absalom and blurted, 'King David won't thank you if you kill either of us.'

'Oh no?' The leerer curled his lip, but I knew I'd unsettled him because he didn't come any closer with the sword. 'I can't think of a more useful favour we could perform for him, when his son is a vile traitor and his son's lackey is a rival for the throne in his own right.'

'He's given specific orders,' I persisted, surprised at how level my voice sounded. 'I know he has. Absalom is not to be harmed.'

'And the Torah has given specific orders that a rebellious son is to be put to death,' retorted the leerer, but he still didn't move, and then another of his companions piped up with the observation that what I was saying was true; Joab himself was in the vicinity and must be informed that Absalom was here and still alive, then arrangements could be made for the Prince to be chained up and delivered to his father, in accordance with His Majesty's will and pleasure.

Quite what the point would have been in chaining Absalom then, I can't imagine; but it was plain that we were dealing here with private soldiers who possessed neither authority nor initiative; after all, in the time they'd already spent arguing they could have slit both our throats and no one need ever have found them out. Perhaps they couldn't trust one another not to spill the beans afterwards; from the way they behaved towards each other I deemed this very likely, for almost before I knew what was happening they'd moved on from arguing to brawling. There they were, swearing and cuffing and jostling amongst themselves while

Absalom hung there expiring, and in the end a couple of them broke away and went off in search of Joab.

He must indeed have been operating close by, for if the men hadn't returned with him almost immediately Absalom might have been dead before they did so. But it was clear, from the face of the fellow who'd suggested fetching Joab in the first place, that the general hadn't reacted in the way he'd expected or hoped. 'You saw him hanging in a tree?' I heard that familiar brusque voice demanding, before they came into view. 'Why didn't you kill him, you spineless coward? I'd have given you ten pieces of silver and my own baldric as a reward.' The so-called coward was reminding him of David's orders, claiming that he wouldn't have contravened them for a thousand pieces of silver and twenty suits of full armour. He was still carping when Joab himself stepped from between the trees. Complaining that enough time had been wasted already, he aimed his spear at Absalom's chest.

Even as I watched him prepare for the throw, it didn't occur to me that he could simply mean to cast the thing and despatch the son of his King and kinsman with no more ceremony than a common criminal might have deserved. But it occurred to Gatis. She bared her teeth and went for him, snarling and snapping, yet all to no avail. Joab hurled his javelin undeterred, with impeccable accuracy, while ten or so of his men who had emerged from the trees in his wake kept Gatis at bay with volleys of stones. Absalom was staring right at him, his limbs twitching and jerking, but I was sure he was dead already. Joab however was disposed to leave nothing to chance. He seized the spears of the two men nearest to him, and hurled those after the first.

When he threw the second spear I was angry; when he threw the third I was nearly sick. It was all so patently superfluous . . . but I think it was the raw hatred in his eyes that turned my stomach rather than the deed itself. Meanwhile the distraught Gatis, who seemed to me in that moment to be more human than most of the men I have known, was crying and licking at her wounds; finally Joab could stand the irksome noise no longer and made an end of her with his sword. The band of ten men who'd come with him moved closer to the stricken pretender, eager to get a proper look at him in his final hour, then as their commander stood by nodding his approval they took turns to plant spears into their enemy's lifeless body, almost as though they felt in need of a touch of target practice. Next, one of them sliced through what remained of Absalom's hair and dragged him to the ground; what they did to him after that I don't know. I couldn't look.

In fact the events which followed upon the end of the battle are as confused in my memory as those surrounding its beginning. I know I took it for granted that Joab would kill me too; I suppose I could have run off into the forest, but I was too overwhelmed to move, and in any case there was nowhere I wanted to run to. I remember kneeling there in the mud with my head down, wondering whether I would feel the cold metal against my neck before it was cut, or whether the whole thing would happen too quickly for me to know about it. And I wondered if it was true, that the dead see Adonai face to face; if so, I felt ready. Then I nearly jumped out of my skin, for instead of a sword across the top of my spine, one was tossed at my feet, along with a pile of jewellery, and most of the rest of Absalom's accoutrements. On top of the heap lay his sun and crescent moon.

'Take this lot back to David,' Joab rasped at me. 'And make sure he gets it, you little robber. There will be no one to save you from his wrath if you're caught stealing from him *this* time.'

Looking back now, I'm convinced that he'd planned everything. He'd insisted on David's remaining in Mahanaim not merely for reasons of security, nor even solely to ensure that the battle was actually fought. No; he'd engineered things so that he might have the satisfaction of dealing personally with the upstart Prince who had more than once got in his way and made a fool of him, and who more than anyone else was responsible in his eyes for turning the dauntless warrior David into a broken and unhappy old man.

At least the murderer had the sense not to send Absalom's mutilated carcass back to Mahanaim. I doubt that David would have recognized it without someone telling him whose it was. While Joab, bombastically and offensively victorious, had the signal given out that hostilities were ended, his ten thugs dug a pit, laughing and larking about as they worked, and when it was deep enough they kicked the Prince into it, and one of them flung his hound in after him. This made the others laugh all the louder; I guess they could conceive of nothing more ignominious for a man than to be buried in the same grave as a dog, though I know Absalom wouldn't have minded. Finally they covered the bodies with rocks; and from the vehemence with which they threw them, it was clear that they saw themselves as giving this rebellious son the stoning he'd asked for.

339

Epilogue

The sun is setting; from the window of my study I watch the light which bathes the walls of the courtyard soften to gold, then blush almost pink, while the shadows lengthen and the birds call softly, darting and diving between the vases and trellises. Indoors it's growing too dark to write, but just as I decide that I must stop and leave the closing part of my account until tomorrow, Miriam comes in with the baby asleep across her shoulder and lights the lamps, kissing me gently on the forehead as she brushes past. When she smiles these days there are lines around her eyes, and she has too many grey hairs for her to hide them with henna. But to me she is still as lovely as she was all those years ago when she served Tamar; and the baby—Ahaz, our fourth son—already has her perfect features and shy serene nature.

I follow her with my eyes as she slips out again and calls our three eldest sons to get ready for bed. Pithon the firstborn is twelve, Melech eleven and Tarea nine, and I hear their pounding footsteps as they come running. They are so self-assured, so boisterous, so full of energy, and so happy that they don't even understand what the word means. I'm just grateful that none of them are like I was as a child.

I still can't quite bring myself to believe that if things had gone differently with Saul, Pithon might one day have sat upon the throne of Israel, and I myself might be sitting there now. If Shimei and Sheba had had their way, I might have been doing so in any case. But I'm profoundly glad that I'm not. Saul's jewelled knife, his homestead and his estates are more than enough to render me content. By Adonai's grace I'm not the damaged and diffident person I once was, but I shall never be a leader of men. Solomon is a far finer king than I should ever have made.

It amazes me that this little place was once the seat of Saul's government; it seems like a cottage in comparison to David's palace, and that's to say nothing of the awe-inspiring (but hitherto unfinished) edifice which Solomon commissioned for himself upon his accession. Yet the Temple which he's had built for Adonai—though not as large as the palace—is more awesome still, far surpassing his father's most extravagant dreams. The work took seven whole years, but Solomon had all the time and wealth in the world. For Israel has been peaceful and prosperous throughout his reign to date, so much so that even the Golden Age of David pales into insignificance beside it, its light eclipsed as a candle's is when bright torches are lit. Our empire extends from the Euphrates to Philistia, and the tribute and taxes flow into the Jerusalem treasuries like great rivers pouring into the sea.

In addition to gold and silver and precious stones, Solomon has a wealth of women, both wives and concubines. He inherited all of David's harem, and since then he has taken to his bed daughters of most of the kings he's had dealings with. There are some folk who disapprove, and I myself am becoming more inclined to agree with them as time goes on. For by no means all of his women honour Adonai. But their fathers are kept happy and loyal by Solomon's policy.

It ought to have guaranteed him a wealth of sons also; yet for all his political power it may be that his seed lacks potency, because so far he has sired few. His eldest, Rehoboam, he has already named as his heir. But if I'm being honest, I have to admit that I see little of God in the lad. He is preoccupied with girls already; at the moment he's infatuated with one Maacah, a sly piece of work, every bit as haughty and domineering—and idolatrous—as her namesake was, but without the latter's warmth. The girl's mother was one of David's concubines; the father, so we are led to believe, was Absalom, and it wouldn't surprise me. Apart from his public performance beneath the canopy on the palace roof, he'd already visited the women's quarters often enough behind his father's back, and there used to be several little Absaloms and Maacahs running around in the harem—and even a Tamar, for he wanted her name remembered. They are now grown up.

I had my lord's monument completed as he'd requested (Seraiah fled to Geshur upon learning of our defeat) though it's ironic to think that if Rehoboam marries his Maacah, Absalom's blood may be passed down the royal line after all.

If I said that David took it badly when he was told of his favourite son's death, I'd be guilty of the grossest of understatements. Even though the barriers between the reinstated King and his God had been blasted away, he'd never been prepared to accept that Absalom's extinction was inevitable. Perhaps he cherished a secret hope that once his relationship with God was fully restored, a way would be found for things to work out the way he wanted them to. His unhealthily inflated but misdirected paternal affection must have blinded him so comprehensively as to cause him to forget that God never brings about what we want unless it is also for the best. On top of this, David's grief was all the more bitter because it seemed on the face of it that Absalom's death had been so unnecessary. For Joab had found him alive, and ought to have taken pains to ensure he stayed that way.

As events turned out, though, I wasn't the one to break the dire news to David. Ahimaaz (the son of the priest Zadok) insisted on being granted the privilege, which shows how little he understood of the workings of his King's mind. But Joab knew how he'd be received all right, so he sent a slave to beat him to it—a Cushite, for they are said to be the fastest runners on earth.

I didn't manage to overhear what story Joab gave the Cushite to tell, though I could make a pretty informed guess. But Ahimaaz knew the truth about Absalom's end; and against all odds he won the race.

I went after them, taking Absalom's personal effects along with me; I reckon Joab left me in possession of them so that unwittingly I might corroborate the Cushite's false account. But I was so shattered, by the time I dragged myself through the gates of Mahanaim the King had shut himself up in a guardroom over the portal and wouldn't see anyone. Eventually two of his attendants broke the door down because they were so anxious for him; I went in and took him in my arms as I had done the night before, but for once my presence couldn't console him, and especially when he caught sight of the sun and crescent moon and was forced to face up to the fact that his son had died in apostasy as well as in rebellion. He tore his clothes to tatters and kept repeating Absalom's name over and over again, and: oh, my God, not Absalom, not my son Absalom. He said he would sooner have died himself, if by some miracle it might cause his son to live again. I'm sure that Absalom would have searched out and killed only David, if he could have done, and spared all of his host, whilst David would have spared only Absalom.

Nor were there any sounds of rejoicing coming from outside the bleak gatehouse, either. David's whole army knew of his grief, and the atmosphere in the city was more like you get in the wake of a defeat, not a definitive victory. I soothed him and prayed for him and exhorted him to think of the future, to think of little Solomon, but for all my compassion it was Joab who ultimately penetrated the King's self-pity. He strode in, as angry as I'd ever seen him, and flung me aside. The sons of Zeruiah had as much sensitivity for the most part as stones have, but they knew how soldiers feel after battle.

'No sooner do we crush one uprising than you want to provoke another!' Joab thundered. 'Aren't you going to go out there and congratulate your troops on what they've achieved for you? Aren't you even going to give permission for them to celebrate? Absalom rejected you; he was nothing but a renegade wastrel! And in this city thousands of men who would sooner have perished than risk disappointing you are condemned to creep about like mourners with dust on their heads. Anyone would think that you'd wanted them to lose, that you'd rather they were dead and Absalom alive to strut around in all his arrogance! I'm warning you, David. You go out there and show some gratitude to your army, or you won't have one. We'll have mutiny on our hands before we've even cleared up the battlefield.'

Some kings I suppose would have summoned their guards and had Joab's head lopped off on the spot. But not David; for deep inside he knew that what Joab had said was right. He stood there in silence while Joab continued to rebuke him, but less virulently now. 'This is no time for weeping; at least, not for a traitor. Weep for the loyal and the brave who died to save you, if you must. But whatever you do, David, do it in front of your men. Speak to them. Promise them a holiday. They have served their God and their country well.'

'Get out,' said David, weakly, and Joab obeyed; but David in turn did as his nephew had bidden him; well, partially. He went before the army and the crisis was averted, even though he said nothing. He didn't need to. They saw the tangled emotions that racked his features, and understood.

And we must all give credit where it's due: Joab was no coward. Had I been in his shoes, I'd have kept out of David's way for as long as possible after killing Absalom. He didn't go entirely unpunished, though. Justice had to be seen to be done somehow, and Joab was officially relieved of supreme command over His Majesty's armed forces. Of all people, Amasa was appointed in his place; for despite his lack of experience he had potential. Presumably the appointment was made for political reasons also, for it was of paramount importance for national security that the rift between those who had followed Absalom and those who had stood firm beside his father should be healed as rapidly as possible.

If Joab hadn't been Joab, this diplomatic gamble might have paid off. But Zeruiah's son, true to form, went straight to Amasa and clasped him to his burly breast, assuring him with all fervency that he bore him not the slightest grudge. Too relieved to be suspicious, Amasa returned his embrace and Joab drove a knife deep into his young successor's flesh just beneath the ribcage. So Amasa died exactly as the great Abner had done before him, but in due course the deposed general was quietly reinstated. David had no choice; for even if another man could have been found who was capable of filling the vacancy, he would never have been fool enough to accept it. It was left for Solomon to dispose of Joab, when the time came.

For a while after the battle I did harbour real fears for David's sanity. But his repentance had been genuine, and total, and he surrendered himself utterly to Adonai.

And when the clouds of David's grief began to clear away, it was as though the sun came out upon all those who knew him. Absalom's death set so many people free; it freed Miriam to notice me for the first time, and it freed me from my struggle with divided loyalties. David and I remained close until his death, and both of us remained close to Adonai. Adonai's grace in turn freed me from the ravages of my past, for slowly I learned to love Miriam as she deserved, and to take her to my bed without remembering each time the touch of Ziba. The black memories didn't vanish overnight, but David soothed them away over months and years with his prayers, and Miriam herself slowly banished my shame with her patience, her kisses, and her gentle caresses. Many times in my life I'd been told that I was handsome, yet never before had I allowed myself to believe it, or even to ask myself whether it might be true.

The crushing of Absalom's revolt didn't mark the end of all David's troubles, of course; you simply can't have power without problems. Sheba wouldn't give up his ambition to put a Saulide back on the throne, and when I spurned his advances a second time, he staged a coup in his own right. It was put down with humiliating rapidity; he took refuge in some walled city but was betrayed, and the inhabitants reputedly threw his head over the wall right into Joab's arms.

David's last years were happy, and so utterly unlike his wretched father-in-law's; because in spite of the tragedies he'd suffered and the crimes he'd committed, he had the assurance of having been forgiven by his God. And equally importantly, he at last forgave himself. He no longer had anything to fear from Bathsheba's blackmail, though I wouldn't say their marriage was ever better than bearable—for either of them.

He died at a ripe old age, in the knowledge that his dynasty would continue; and that was something like fifteen years ago. Bathsheba outlived him, but not by very long. I think that one of her illnesses eventually claimed her.

So many people who have meant so much to me in different ways are gone now. Maacah died of unknown causes after we got back to Jerusalem and David sent for her (and Miriam) to take up residence at the palace once more. All her four children were dead—so much for her fertility rites and her dogged devotion to the Goddess—and they say she took poison, but she was too clever with her herbs and potions for any of the physicians to be able to prove it.

My father Mephibosheth's story ended more happily, though. I knew it would, as soon as I saw him waiting to welcome us on our return from Mahanaim. He was sitting by the roadside on a mule, dressed like the highborn courtier he was, but with his hair and beard and nails uncut, for he'd refused to let anyone near him to groom him since the day that David had left the palace. Now he was grinning like a crocodile at Machir, who stood beside him holding the mule's reins; our erstwhile guardian had come to Jerusalem ahead of us, among those who had brought the news of the old King's victory and made smooth the path for his return. I could hardly believe it when David ordered the entire triumphal procession to halt while he went over and clasped hands with both of them. Mephibosheth presented the King with his favourite ushabti, and after they had talked a while, David promised to restore to him forthwith all the property which had been made over unjustly to Ziba. My credulity was further stretched when I heard my father say, in words as clear as David's, 'Let Ziba keep everything, Your Majesty. It's enough for me to see you safely back.' I was so humbled then that any trace of desire for revenge on my childhood tormentor melted away.

Of course, this was one request of Mephibosheth's which David refused to listen to. Ziba wasn't dispossessed entirely, for it was always David's nature to be merciful, but my father was eventually prevailed upon to reclaim the greater part of what was rightfully his; if not for his own sake, then for his son's. Secure in the knowledge that he was back in favour with his benefactor the King, he died peacefully in his sleep only months afterwards. He wasn't old, but he'd had all he ever wanted from life. David spoke the prayers at his funeral, and Saul's property devolved onto me.

In addition to compiling this record as David bade me, I write songs to be used in the Temple, and I set down those of David's which he taught me, lest they be forgotten. Time has proved him right already in his prediction of men's reactions to the tale of his adultery with Bathsheba and the murder of Uriah. No one has yet read my version of the affair, but soon after her death rumours leaked out somehow, and unleashed a violent but short-lived storm. It was short-lived because when folk paused to think, they couldn't any longer believe what they'd been told, no matter how reliable the sources nor how plausibly the details meshed together. In the histories of David's reign which are already being drafted, the scandal receives no mention; and in some of them even the account of Absalom's revolt has been suppressed. David will be seen by posterity as a paragon of virtue, despite his own sincere desire to prohibit this from happening. In many ways he did deserve this unimpeachable reputation, for he was a gallant warrior, a great statesman, and a much-loved ruler and inspirer of men; and I would hate anyone to think that he was no better than the next man.

For I guess that there are those who, if they *did* believe the rumours, would conclude that Saul's successor got away with his sin, and that his God simply chose to overlook it because David was the apple of his eye. After all, Saul lost everything, when on the face of it his sins may seem to some to have been comparatively trivial, whilst David did finish up married to Bathsheba, the object of his base passions, and a son of their tainted union sits on Israel's throne.

But a cynic who drew such conclusions wouldn't understand the half of it. Adonai *has* brought good out of evil in the end; but at what a price.

HISTORICAL NOTE

We know nothing about Saul's great-grandson Micha except his name (2 Samuel 9:12; 1 Chronicles 8:34) and the names of his four sons (1 Chronicles 8:35). But we do know that 2 Samuel 9—1 Kings 2 (possibly excluding the last few chapters of 2 Samuel), often known as the Court History, was probably written by—or based upon the work of—someone who was an eyewitness of many of the events included and very closely involved with the characters concerned.

This account shows David 'warts and all'. Despite his remarkable military successes during the earlier part of his reign, despite the continuing prosperity of his empire, and despite his being described as 'a man after God's own heart', his latter years are shown to have been marred by indecision and ineptitude. He became a victim of his own jealous and quarrelsome family, and in particular of his sons, whom he seems for some reason to have been incapable of disciplining. They in turn became victims of one another. Readers of the account are apt to gloss over these negative aspects of David's personality, having perhaps been conditioned by the comprehensive whitewashing of Israel's most illustrious king undertaken by the author/editor of 1 Chronicles.

However, David's warts are plain enough for any discerning reader to see in the Court History. But how could this great man have proved unable to control his own household, when he had once felled a giant with slingshot, and was reputedly so close to God?

The biblical narrative provides few clues. Yet if David had fought shy of making public confession of a chain of sinful actions which, notwithstanding its appalling nature and consequences, God had fully forgiven, he would not have been the first to do so, and he certainly would not have been the last. And in seeking to cover up the truth, for whatever motives, he would have prevented himself from wholly facing up to the horror of what he had done, and thus coming to terms with it and forgiving himself in the depths of his own soul. He would also have condemned himself to years spent living in fear of being found out, thereby laying himself open to exploitation and blackmail.

When we allow ourselves to study David's character in this light, it becomes much easier for us to accept him as the composer of many of those songs in the Psalter which have traditionally been attributed to him, but which certain scholars have been reluctant to recognize as his. Indeed, we can make more or less informed guesses about which phases of his life individual psalms belong to, even when their subtitles give us no help. Although in his youth David was often in difficulties, and even in despair, and subject to powerful enemies (Saul in particular), in the psalms of this period he is always at pains to stress his own innocence. Later however he acknowledges his own sinfulness, his pride and his stubbornness, as well as his desperate weakness.

The following quotations are especially revealing:

'*I am drowning in the floodwaters of my sins; their burden is too heavy for me to bear . . . My whole body is diseased because of my wickedness; because I have been foolish . . . I am bowed down, I am crushed*' (Psalm 38).

348

'My sins have caught up with me ... they are more numerous than the hairs on my head, and I have lost my courage' (Psalm 40).

'I said, "I have sinned against you, Lord, show mercy and heal me ..." Those who come to visit me are not sincere; they sniff out bad news about me, then go out and spread it everywhere. All who hate me whisper to one another and imagine the worst about me. They say, "He is terminally ill; he will never leave his bed again." Even my closest companion, the man I trusted most, has turned against me' (Psalm 41).

'I am smitten with fear ... I see violence and riots in the city, afflicting it day and night, filling it with crime and tribulation. Everywhere there is destruction, the streets are rife with oppression and fraud ... If it were an enemy mocking me, I could endure it ... but it is you, my colleague and close friend. We used to talk intimately, and worship together ... Yes, my former companion broke his promises. His words were smoother than cream, but his heart was full of hate; his words were as soothing as oil, but they cut like swords' (Psalm 55).

'I once felt secure and said to myself, "I will never be defeated." But then you hid yourself from me, and I was afraid' (Psalm 30).

'Lord, I have cast away my pride and turned from my arrogance' (Psalm 131).

'When I did not confess my sins aloud, I was worn out with weeping all day long ... my strength was drained, as moisture is dried out by the heat of summer ... Then I confessed my sins to you, I did not conceal my evil. Happy are those whose sins are forgiven; happy is the man who is free from all deceit' (Psalm 32).

1 Chronicles tells us nothing of David's adultery with Bathsheba, nor of Absalom's revolt. Presumably the author deliberately suppresses the latter; but it is possible that he disbelieved the former. Perhaps the truth only came to light many years after the events, by which time the myth of David's virtual perfection would have been too well established to be seriously challenged.

RABSHAKEH

J. Francis Hudson

It is the twilight of the Bronze Age . . . the Sea People with their iron weapons threaten the tribes of Israel. Fearful that their God will not protect them, the Israelites demand a king.

The choice falls on Saul: young, bold, beautiful, with a burning desire for greatness and a deep hunger to know Adonai, the God of his people. But the enemy presses closer, the people cry out and Saul is afraid. Eliphaz Rabshakeh, Saul's slave and companion since boyhood, tells this moving story of a man torn apart by warring ambitions and the battle for his soul.

ISBN 0 7459 3497 8

SONG OF ALBION

Stephen Lawhead

A new cycle, mining the rich vein of Celtic mythology

Book 1: The Paradise War

Wolves prowling the streets of Oxford, a Green Man haunting the Highlands . . . Lewis Gillies is face to face with an ancient mystery. The road north leads to a mystical crossroads, and he finds himself in a place where two worlds meet, in the time-between-times. This world and the Otherworld are delicately interwoven, each dependent on the other. But a breach has opened between the worlds—and cosmic catastrophe threatens.

ISBN 0 7459 2242 2 ('C' format)
ISBN 0 7459 2466 2 ('A' format)

Book 2: The Silver Hand

The great king, Meldryn Mawr, is dead and his kingdom lies in ruins. Treachery and brutality stalk the Otherworld kingdom of Prydain. Prince Meldron, prompted by the cunning and grasping Siawn Hy, now claims the throne. But the bard Tegid Tathal chooses another—and the Day of Strife begins. Kingship and sovereignty, passion and power, heartbreak and hope lie at the heart of this story. The fate of Albion and the destiny of the long-awaited Champion, Silver Hand, are inextricably interwoven.

ISBN 0 7459 2245 7 ('C' format)
ISBN 0 7459 2510 3 ('A' format)

Book 3: The Endless Knot

Fire rages in Albion: a strange, hidden fire, dark-flamed, invisible to the eye. Seething and churning, it burns, gathering flames of darkness into its hot black heart. Unseen and unknown, it burns . . .

Llew Silver Hand is High King of Albion and the Brazen Man has defied his sovereignty. Llew must journey into the Foul Land to redeem his greatest treasure. The last battle begins.

ISBN 0 7459 2240 6 ('C' format)
ISBN 0 7459 2783 1 ('A' format)

All Lion paperbacks are available from your local bookshop, or can be ordered direct from Lion Publishing. For a free catalogue, showing the complete list of titles available, please contact:

Customer Services Department
Lion Publishing plc
Peter's Way
Sandy Lane West
Oxford OX4 5HG

Tel: (01865) 747550
Fax: (01865) 715152